Beverley Harper  Wales. She worked Sydney and, at o African Airways acc est in Africa. Intend one year, Beverley travelled to that continent and spent the next twenty years there. She met and married her Scottish husband, Robert, in South Africa and they have three sons, one of whom now lives in Botswana. Beverley returns to Africa once a year for research and to 'top up her soul'. She and Robert now call the Northern Tablelands of New South Wales home. *The Forgotten Sea* is Beverley's fifth novel. Her sixth novel, *Jackal's Dance*, will be available in October 2001.

Also by Beverley Harper

Storms Over Africa
Edge of the Rain
Echo of an Angry God
People of Heaven

THE FORGOTTEN SEA

BEVERLEY HARPER

PAN
Pan Macmillan Australia

First published 2000 in Macmillan by Pan Macmillan Australia Pty Limited
This Pan edition published 2001 by Pan Macmillan Australia Pty Limited
St Martins Tower, 31 Market Street, Sydney

National Library of Australia
cataloguing-in-publication data:

Harper, Beverley.
The forgotten sea.

ISBN 0 330 36272 0.

I. Title.

A823.3

Typeset in 11.5/13pt Bembo by Post Pre-Press Group, Brisbane
Printed in Australia by McPherson's Printing Group

My sincere thanks to Dr Satish Boolell in Mauritius
for taking time out of a very busy schedule
to enlighten me on the post-mortem process.
I wish I could say I enjoyed it!

Thanks also to Dr Arthur Beresford, Pathologist
(retired), for his editing of the post-mortem scenes
and for adding that little bit extra.

To Sayad Herro,
Mauritian taxidriver, tour guide, mine of
information and literary critic – thank you.

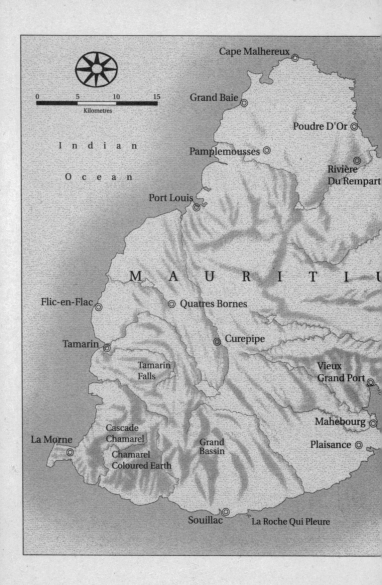

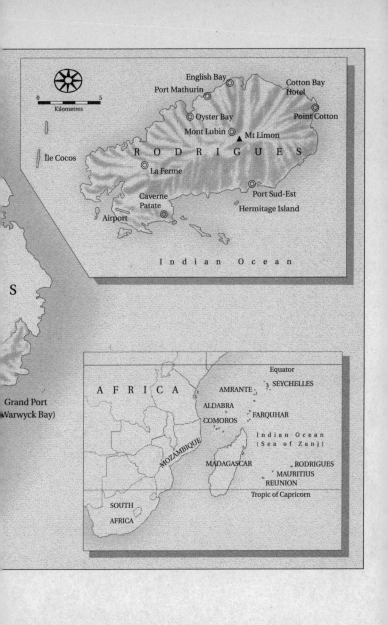

PROLOGUE

She had been beautiful once. Even now, her body bloated with intestinal gases and burnt to a crisp by a merciless sun, shrivelled and puckered from four days' immersion in the sea, hair matted and tangled, skin peeling, it was still possible to tell that this one had been a classic. One sightless eye stared down through the clear depths of the bay, down through aquamarine water to the sandy bed some four metres below, down to what had been her temporary resting place, until her body swelled and she floated back to the surface. That was yesterday, far out in the shipping lanes, out beyond the breakers' incessant pounding of the coral reef, out where the leisure cruisers and big yachts, the tankers and liners danced to the music of a restless ocean.

Watched with curiosity by the ever-hungry seabirds, her corpse rolled lazily with the tide and swell that bore the Indian Ocean from the west coast of Australia to the eastern seaboard of Africa. Sitting on the sodden head, one bird braver than the others had pecked and feasted on a single eye until the ocean's momentum caused the body to turn face down. The gull had hung around for a while, resting, but in the end took to the air in search of a more accessible meal. The lonely dead thing floated on, uncaring of the vastness, the impartiality and treachery of the sea around her. Darting fish nibbled at the water-soaked skin but, so far, the more serious carnivores had paid no attention to what amounted to a substantial meal.

At some stage during the night she had passed over the reef surrounding the island, slipping just above the jagged peaks of coral on the king tide of a full moon. In the calmer waters of the bay, with the rising tide behind her, she was eventually returned to the land where she had once lived and breathed. Face down in the fine white sand – a saturated bundle of lifelessness, a macabre reminder of the indifferent hand that fate deals to some and a clear caution against assuming that the here and now will last forever – dawn broke slowly to reveal her pathetic remains.

Not a pretty sight. Certainly not one that the authorities on Mauritius, that gem of a tourist destination in a trio of idyllic islands once known as the Mascarenes, would wish to become public knowledge. Their carefully nurtured image was of sparkling blue sea, emerald green palm fringes haphazardly angled along pure white beaches, gentle winds whispering through the casuarinas under an azure sky. This was ugly, messy. It ruined the illusion of peace and happiness, pleasure and beauty. This was something to be hidden away, a dreadful secret, shoved out of sight in a dark place to pretend it had never been.

But the inescapable fact was that it would need to be dealt with. And quickly. With a minimum of fuss. Then, and only then, could the image repair process begin. But before the pretence began to sweep reality under the carpet there were procedures to follow, which would guarantee a flow of rumours. Rumours that were unlikely to reach the laid-back ears of tourists tucked securely in their five-star hotels but stories that would, nonetheless, spread to every corner of the island.

Sayad Asgarally found her. It was a sight the young fisherman would never forget. He found her just as the sun edged its burning rim over the horizon on the other side of the island, as fingers of light washed the clouds, the sea, the land with the soft colours of another new day.

As he did every morning, Sayad had let himself out of the house quietly so he would not wake his parents. Like other cottages in the tiny hamlet – all five of them – his was built on a grassy incline that sloped from a tarred road down to the beach. Three cement steps were all that separated the narrow, noisy road from the front door. When trucks trundled past, crockery rattled in kitchen cupboards, furniture moved and dust billowed down from the roof as the small two-bedroomed cottage, built mainly from corrugated iron, trembled and threatened to fall over. A wooden verandah at the back squatted two metres or so above the ground, offering uninterrupted views of the beach, bay and the nearby town of Tamarin. Tropical paradise one side, an urban nightmare the other. Sayad had long since stopped noticing either.

His eyes strained in the half light of dawn to where he and his brother had dragged their pirogue – a couple of hundred metres away, beyond a scattered outcrop of black volcanic basalt – onto the beach. It was something he did automatically every morning, a quick check to make sure the boat was still there. Without it, his livelihood, and that of his married older brother, would be non-existent. Satisfied that all was as they had left it the night before, Sayad went down the wooden steps to the beach to light the family's cooking fire. A couple of small sticks was all he needed to boil the blackened kettle. Then he sat on the steps and drank the hot, milky and very sweet tea from a gaudy tin mug.

His thoughts were of nothing in particular. This was a day like all the others. Up early, out fishing until his stomach rumbled with hunger, back to the beach in Tamarin where the morning's catch would be sold, then home for a hot meal prepared by his mother. After that, a few hours working on the pirogue or fishing lines before returning to the reef to seek out whatever was on offer in the late afternoon. It was a monotonous life but Sayad knew none other and was well satisfied with his lot.

In the sweet stillness of early morning, sound seemed to be amplified. A baby bawled briefly next door before finding the soft breast of its mother. In

4

the house beyond that, old man Asgarally, Sayad's grandfather, was getting his early morning exercise. Sayad grinned, listening to the grunts, moans and squeaking bedsprings. The old man was a marvel, everyone said so. Eighty-two, having outlived two wives, the old boy still greeted each day, and his third wife, joyously and ready for action.

Sayad fantasised regularly about what took place between men and women – and if he had but known, his grandfather's ebullient ardour had him well wide of practical reality – but, so far, the closest Sayad had come was a hand on the voluminous breast of Bella from the markets in Tamarin.

Tea finished, Sayad picked up a pair of rubber sandals and made his way down the steps, across the soft sand to the harder surface where the tide, now turned, still licked and frothed. The day was rapidly getting lighter. In the east, the sun hovered just below the skyline. It would be another thirty minutes before it cleared the jagged, seven-hundred metre peaks of Trois Manelles to warm the western coast. But, as it did every morning, the instant the first fiery fingers appeared on the other side of the island, the shadowy western dawn seemed to burst into energetic life. Sayad noticed that a chunk of driftwood had come in on the tide, quite a large piece. He'd pull it further up the beach and take it home later. Once dried it would be good firewood.

Halfway between the house and the welcome flotsam Sayad's steps slowed. Driftwood did not flutter in the breeze. He narrowed his eyes against the sudden flare of sunrise. A bundle of discarded clothes perhaps? A tremor of dread ran through him. As he drew nearer, slowly now, not noticing how little ripples of warm sea water washed over his toes, Sayad was forced to acknowledge that clothes were not supposed to have legs. That old garments should have no curved female form. That long blonde hair, drying in the early morning breeze, would not, as a rule, hitch a ride.

Sayad was suddenly frightened. He was only seventeen and wanted nothing to do with what-ever, whoever it was on the beach. He'd pretend he hadn't seen it. Reason prevailed. There was nothing he could do about his footprints, which led directly from his house to the girl. The body would be found. The tide was going out. Soon other people would pass this way. Taking a steadying breath, he stopped five metres from the body, unwilling to go closer. Closing both eyes, he sent up a short prayer to his Hindu god, more to give him strength than for the departed soul of the thing on the beach. Turning away, he set off back the way he had come. His cousin, a policeman who worked in Tamarin, lived next door to Sayad. Let him deal with it.

Francois Prost was having a dream of the very best kind. The woman was young, beautiful and within reach. She did not seem to mind that Francois was overweight, balding and decidedly past his prime. Perfectly painted lips parted, eyes smouldering with passion as she leaned towards him, the message was clear. Francois knew – because it was his dream – that she loved him and was going to beg that he take her, that she was his to do with as he liked. And, oh God, the things he planned to do. Her voice was a musical whisper throbbing with desire but, instead of the words he was longing to hear, strange sounds tore at his eardrums causing him to snuffle and roll over. The dream evaporated and Francois was left with the inconvenience of an early morning erection with nowhere to go, and the unappetising truth that the telephone was ringing.

Cursing short and hard he reached out and snatched the instrument from its cradle. 'Prost.' His throat caught at the unexpected exercise of a voice still muffled by sleep.

He was unprepared for the hysterical babbling in Creole-accented French that offended his senses to the very core. A Parisian by birth and inclination, Francois rather wished that Mauritians would stick to English. Apparently a body had washed up in a remote bay on the west coast and the police would like it if he could come to the scene immediately.

Stumbling out of bed and into the bathroom, Francois relieved his painfully full bladder and rued the ensuing loss of his masculine display of virility. He was in a sour frame of mind. Yesterday his sleep had been rudely interrupted by the discovery of another body. A man found in scrub country who had departed the world two weeks earlier. Now this!

When his long-term friend Dr Satish Boolell, the police medical officer who normally handled all autopsies of suspicious deaths on Mauritius, contacted Francois and asked if he would like to do a six-week locum for him, Francois accepted with pleasure. Paris was wet and cold. He had just retired and was bored. His wife clearly found him a nuisance around the house, his mistress had shifted her affections to another benefactor, and a spell on a tropical island would do nicely. With law and medical degrees, not to mention twenty-five years' experience as a senior police surgeon in Paris to draw on, Francois was not only eminently qualified to fill in while his friend took some much-needed long service leave, he was also ready and willing to flex his fingers and mind over the clues inevitably left behind when a human spirit goes absent without leave.

Now, only two weeks into the job, it was clear to Francois that a holiday with an occasional foray into the morgue was not to be. Mauritius had only one police medical officer, and he was it. Yesterday was a case in point. As well as a post-mortem on the two-weeks dead body in the morning, he had dealt with a medical examination of a Creole woman and her thirteen-year-old daughter. The woman claimed that her husband had been consistently buggering both of them – her words. A false accusation as it turned out, the accuser finally admitting that all she wanted to do was get rid of the man and what better way than to enlist the aid of the police in a case she believed, in her ignorance, could not be proved one way or the other. Francois had set her straight with a none-too-gentle physical examination followed by a loud lecture about sphincteral muscles telling their own tale before sending her packing to face charges for wasting police time.

The daughter's story, once her mother had been removed from the room, collapsed under questioning. She admitted that she was seventeen, not thirteen, that although she'd been instructed to say certain things about her father, she did not have any understanding of what they actually meant. As the investigation proceeded, it became evident to Prost that the girl was also severely mentally retarded. He sent her home to her father who, he reflected sadly, would more than likely avail himself of her scrawny young body while his wife's scrawny old one was languishing in prison. Prost was never inclined to think well of the poor.

In the afternoon he'd spent three hours waiting for a man from Bombay to defecate. The Indian had been apprehended at Plaisance Airport on suspicion of carrying drugs. A physical examination of the man's luggage, clothing, and rectum had yielded nothing but the Customs officers had been adamant and an X-ray had been requested. Francois agreed with their suspicions. On the inside of the man's lower lip he'd found a tiny, crudely tattooed, cross – a means by which the body-carrier could identify himself to his contact in Mauritius. Francois wanted to let the man go so his contact could also be arrested. The Customs officers said no, that he had been detained for too long which would raise the alarm. It was their way of getting at the Frenchman for taking so long to reach the airport.

Francois bit back an angry explanation and tersely authorised that the Indian be admitted to hospital in Quatre Bornes for an X-ray. Sure enough, the man's stomach was shown to contain packets of an unidentified substance. Francois did some quick mental calculations. He knew condoms were often used to smuggle drugs in this manner. The packets looked to be around three centimetres long by two wide. Not easy to swallow. They would need to be inside the man before he checked in at Bombay Airport. It would take several hours to swallow so many. Check-in time in India was three hours before any international flight. The journey itself took seven hours. The man had been on the ground for three more. Figuring that the packets had been inside his stomach for anything up to sixteen hours and could, by now, be unstable, depending on the material from which they were made, it should not be long before his body tried to expel the undigestible foreign objects. Francois could not order the injection of a purgative drug to hasten the process because, even if through no fault of the medication one of the packets burst, then the unfortunate man's intestine would be flooded with three to four grams of what was probably heroin at somewhere between forty and fifty per cent purity. A lawsuit from the deceased man's family was the last thing he needed.

Cursing regulations that prevented honest men

like himself from using any means at their disposal to get a job done, Francois sat reading a medical journal while a nurse force-fed the reluctant Indian with bananas. The fibrous nature of the fruit worked just as well as any injection. By the end of the day fifty-seven condoms packed with heroin had been delivered into a bed pan. Another X-ray showed that the body-carrier had at last yielded his deadly load of contraband.

All in all, yesterday had been a day and a half, certainly the busiest since he'd arrived to fill in for Satish. By the law of averages today should be quiet, but no, some silly little bitch washes up dead. Francois was taking it personally. He scrubbed his teeth as though they were guilty, then spat water and frothy paste at the sink, slapped a handful of water into his mouth, swilled until his jaws ached then tossed his head back and gargled briefly, very briefly, stopping before he gagged. A quick sluice of water over his face and the wake-up process was complete.

Returning to the bedroom he checked the small travelling clock beside his bed. The police car would collect him in fifteen minutes. Shower or coffee? Not time for both. Opting for the latter he pulled on an old pair of shorts and a T-shirt, sliding his feet into well-worn canvas shoes before making his way heavily into the kitchen. Francois was twenty-two kilograms overweight. In moments of irritation, like this one, he took masochistic pleasure – or was it a self-pitying form of martyrdom, he didn't know – in plodding. It was too early for the woman who did his cleaning to be there so he had to make his own coffee. He coaxed a humming sound from the electric kettle which worked only sporadically and chased ants from atop the sugar – which they invaded nightly like a living black scum – by banging the container a few times on the counter, then heaped three full teaspoons of instant coffee, something he hated, into a mug, followed it with two of sugar and splashed a generous amount of milk on top. A forage in the refrigerator produced a small wedge of cheese and an apple. He ate both, taking alternate bites at each. The kettle finally wheezed to boiling point. There'd be ants in the water. Francois had learned to ignore their tiny black bodies but he detested the way his coffee always tasted the same as the smell of crushed ants.

His medical bag was at the hospital in Quatre Bornes. He could always send for it if needed. The patients of Francois Prost were never in a hurry. All he had to do at this stage was see if there was anything suspicious about the body – gunshot wounds, knife wounds, signs of a violent struggle. The police could do it just as well as he – any fool could. Francois had long ago given up complaining about being called to the scene where a body had been discovered. In a court of law, the judge and jury needed to know that a properly qualified officer had done his job. 'Yes, Your Honour. In my professional opinion, given all the expensive degrees I've achieved, the corpse was as dead as a dodo. I could ascertain this easily, Your Honour, by the fact that it had stopped breathing. What a truly magnificent legal and medical mind I possess! I may go? Thank you, Your Honour. It has been a pleasure to waste four hours of my precious day in the interests of justice.'

Francois cursed as the coffee scalded his mouth. He tipped some out and topped it up with cold water from the tap, remembering too late that he had been advised not to drink straight from the municipal supply. No time to change it now, a police car was turning into the driveway. He drank it down hastily, took a last bite of apple before throwing the core into the bin, grabbed a notebook and pencil off the dining room table and a white coat from the bedroom cupboard. He checked to see if his tape recorder was still in the pocket. It wasn't. Francois then spent some time tracking it down.

He'd left it on top of the refrigerator for some unremembered reason and, when he finally located it, was more than prepared to blame the cleaning woman. Ready at last, and thoroughly out of sorts, he let himself out of the house. Ignoring the disapproving look the sergeant gave his attire, he stomped towards the car.

'Good morn . . . ' The sergeant attempted a salute but it was too early in the morning for him too.

'Let's go,' Francois grumbled, getting into the back seat. A dog, one of the island's quarter of a million strays, ambled towards the car. 'Piss off,' Francois muttered in perfect Parisian French. The dog obliged, lifting its leg and squirting warm, yellow urine against the front tyre. Finished, it turned to sniff its own body waste then kicked back on stiff hind legs, sand flying out and settling on the sergeant's splendidly polished shoes.

A foot lashed out, sending the stray a clear message. The dog trotted away, showing no sign of fear or resentment.

The ride to the tiny bay on the west coast was undertaken in complete silence. Prost arrived one hour after sunrise and thirty minutes after the Tamarin police and entire local population – a surprising number considering there were only five cottages – had trampled away any evidence that might have existed. Francois surveyed the footprint-churned sand with a sardonic lift of an eyebrow before making his way to where the body lay, still uncovered, now well clear of the receding tide.

'Morning.' His greeting was directed towards one man – Detective Sham from police headquarters in the island's capital, Port Louis – the only one Prost acknowledged as having even a modicum of understanding of forensic medicine. He stopped beside the dead girl, pulled the white laboratory coat over his shorts and T-shirt and looked down at the body with no outward show of emotion. 'She been moved?'

'No, sir.' Detective Sham joined him next to the corpse.

'Where's the coastguard?' Francois couldn't have cared less where they were. He just wanted standard procedure to be observed.

'Coming, sir. They ran out of petrol.'

Francois' lip curled but he said nothing. He hunkered down, then wished he hadn't. His formidable stomach made such an exercise uncomfortable and he had to put his hands out to steady himself. 'Four days,' he guessed, going by the condition of her skin. He rose with difficulty, brushing sand off his hands. 'Three days to pop up, maybe a day floating. I think we'll find she surfaced the night before last.'

Sham nodded. 'That's what I thought, sir.'

'Had any reports of missing tourists?'

'None, sir.'

'Locals?'

'A few. No-one matches this description.'

Francois didn't ask how he knew her description, seeing as how she was face down and hadn't, according to Sham, been moved. He knew what the detective meant. Mauritius had a high incidence of suicide, mainly women, mainly Indian, mainly unrequited-love linked. This little blonde was Caucasian through and through. *Good*, Francois thought absently. *Makes my job easier.*

Police were combing the beach in the hope that some means of identification might have washed onto the sand nearby. Others were questioning local residents. No-one, it seemed, knew who the girl might be. None of the fishermen could remember seeing a blonde in any of the boats over the past four or five days, or any other day for that matter.

'Who found her?' Prost barked.

Sham propelled forward a frightened-looking teenager. 'Sayad Asgarally.'

'Did you touch anything?'

'No, sir.' The boy shook his head vehemently. He was in awe of the large, gruff pathologist.

Prost let his gaze rest on the boy's face for a long moment. Then he turned to Sham. 'You got a statement?'

'Yes, sir.'

'Okay. Let him go.' He looked back at the body. 'Flip her over.'

The girl was rolled onto her back. Two nearby policemen made audible noises when they saw the disfigured face. Detective Sham paled but was all professional interest. Prost's eyes flicked down the length of the inert body. 'Nothing obvious,' he grunted.

By the time the coastguard finally arrived, Francois had done about as much as he could at the scene. There were no obvious clues as to why the girl had died. She had not been reported missing, which was rather strange considering she'd been dead at least four days. All he knew as of now was that she was very dead and that the cause of death left his options wide open – accidental, suicide or murder.

'Get her to the morgue.' He turned to leave but stopped and looked back at Sham. 'And don't let anyone go through the pockets.'

'No, sir.' Sham hunched his shoulders, offended. He knew his job.

Prost made it to the morgue well before the body was delivered. On the way he'd stopped for some decent coffee and a croissant. Feeling marginally more cheerful, he entered the tiny post-mortem facility via the back entrance. As usual, a sign outside amused him. *Patients are advised that mortuary services are free of charge.* He'd questioned it with one of the staff when he first arrived.

'Don't you think that our clients are a little beyond caring by the time they reach us?'

'It's not for them, sir,' he'd been told seriously. 'Some staff members had a nice little sideline going. They were . . . ah . . . charging the relatives.'

Bloody hell! Prost had thought, vaguely entertained. *Never is humour blacker or are humans more base than in a morgue.*

The previous week, this fact had been graphically demonstrated. An Indian woman had been brought in to identify the body of her husband, the victim of a car crash. She had rushed to the cadaver, ranting and wailing, tearing at her clothes, tears streaming. She had struck at the dead man's chest, crying, 'Oh, my husband, my husband, why did you leave me?' She had been joined by her son who was similarly afflicted, crying, 'Oh, my father, I didn't get to say goodbye. Why did you leave us?'

Their grief had been impressive. An emotional outpouring of the utmost misery. Prost had been unmoved – he'd seen it all so many times before. All, that is, until the morgue attendant tiptoed to the woman and tapped her shoulder. 'Excuse me, Madame,' he'd said gently, pointing to a second corpse. 'That is your husband over there.'

Prost had left the room as quickly as he dared. The incongruity of the situation, and his reaction to it, an essential element in coping with his line of work. Most pathologists he'd met had developed a macabre sense of humour to help them deal with a fact they found impossible to escape – death had no dignity. The dead were at the mercy of the living. Pathologists were only human. Working with bodies required an escape valve, and humour, no matter how cruel, provided it. It relieved the certain knowledge that one day it would be their turn.

The morgue consisted of two rooms. A workroom where the actual autopsies took place and an adjacent room where bodies were stored until funeral arrangements could be made. This morning, the acrid smell of carbolic and formaldehyde was strong, a lingering legacy of yesterday's scrub-up to remove the stench of the last occupant's decaying body. The autopsy area was small and basic. The sign on the door said *Do Not Enter – Autopsy in Progress*, which was bullshit and everyone knew it. More often than not, the room was empty. Traffic in and out ignored the warning, a fact which had, on occasions, called up the stomach contents of unsuspecting young police officers. But this was a fairly rare event.

The slab was in the centre, a concrete monolith with a crude wooden block at one end, curved in the middle to accommodate a cadaver's head. Benches around all four sides held a variety of instruments. A sink stood in one corner. When he'd first arrived, Francois had been mildly appalled by the basic nature of the room. He was used to larger, cleaner and more pleasant surroundings. Still, it was only for six weeks and he knew the patients didn't mind.

Normally a corpse remained in a refrigerated state until identified. Once grieving and shocked relatives had viewed a body, the autopsy could proceed without the pathologist's work being hampered by a need to bear in mind that the sight of a loved one scalped, cut and cranked open, not to mention missing various bits, would prove distressing. However, refrigeration space in the room next door was limited. A bus accident three days ago had filled it to capacity – some of the victims were still not identified. Which left Prost no option but to carry out the autopsy and hope it wouldn't be too long before the dead girl's identity was known.

So, little one, what are you going to tell us? he thought, when the body was finally delivered. *What secrets do you hide and how well do you hide them?* This was the part of his job he enjoyed. An anonymous corpse was, if you knew where to look, a mine of information.

She lay face up. The puffy, peeling carcass of what had once been beauty. Blonde hair glued to her face. Tempted as he might have been to brush it back, Prost left it where it lay. The skin would come away with it, which might destroy a vital clue. Sand clung to her skin and clothing, fine white grains firmly fixed to the stickiness of sea water. For now, it would have to stay there. Prost would gently clean only those areas from which he needed a specimen. Later, when he'd finished, she could be washed down to remove the worst of it.

He assembled his instruments – scalpels, scissors, probes, forceps, a saw with an oscillating blade which cut hard tissue and bone, and a good old-fashioned dessertspoon. As in morgues the world over, the tools of his trade were largely discards from the operating theatre. Scalpels and scissors were blunt and the points of the forceps didn't quite meet. Frustrating as this undoubtedly was, Prost was so used to the inconvenience that he probably would not know what to do with new equipment. Satisfied he had everything ready, Prost stood flexing his fingers over the girl's body.

Her clothing was drying out, stiffening from immersion in salt water. Francois placed scissors around the band of her bleached khaki shorts and, using brute force rather than any cutting edge, hacked through, not stopping, but continuing down one leg, across the crotch and then up the other side so that the garment could be peeled aside. Lacy white panties followed and he allowed a moment to admire the good quality of them. *Not short of money*, he thought, removing her shoes. Nike runners. Also expensive. White ankle socks peeled off, taking a little skin with them. She wore a white tank top and over that a pale pink light-weight cardigan. He cut through the front of the tank top, rolled the girl on her side and removed it and the cardigan at the same time.

Each garment was carefully placed aside. 'Jeet!' he bellowed. The assistant appeared, a cigarette

20

dangling between his lips. 'Put that damned thing out and come here,' Francois snapped. He was not really irritated, simply in work mode.

Jeet knew this. Grinding the cigarette into the floor, he quietly went about his job. Each item of clothing went into a separate bag and was carefully labelled, but not before Francois noted the labels. The shorts were Wrangler, the knickers Christian Dior, Nike socks and shoes, the top bore a label he didn't recognise but it looked exclusive and the cardigan was by Pringle. Impressive, unless you knew, as Prost knew, that all these brands were made, under licence, in Mauritius. The girl did not necessarily have to be well travelled to buy them. She simply needed to belong to the top five per cent of Mauritian society to be able to afford them. The pockets of her shorts were empty, save for one boiled sweet of a pale blue colour wrapped in cellophane.

'I want that sweet analysed,' Francois ordered.

Jeet nodded and placed it in its own container, made some scribbles on a label and put it slightly apart from the clothing.

Francois picked up the girl's hands, one at a time. No rings. No ridge, paler skin or any other sign she had worn any. No necklace. Small gold stud earrings which he carefully removed and handed to Jeet. Knowing the current trend for placing decoration on the most obscure parts of the body, he checked nostrils, lips, belly button, nipples and the lips of her vulva for signs of piercing but found nothing. She had a tiny tattoo of a bear just below the bikini line. *Why bother?* he thought sourly, wondering at a mentality that desired defacement of the human body but, at the same time, opted to keep it hidden. A faint brown birthmark, shaped loosely like the map of Africa, was on her left arm, just below the elbow. Jeet wrote all this down as Francois dictated and then, at the impatient snapping of fingers from the pre-occupied pathologist, picked up a camera and photographed both the tattoo and the birthmark. The faded, jaded grey of the girl's one remaining eye had once been brilliant blue. Her obviously trimmed pubic hair was a golden colour so he assumed the blonde of her head was natural. Appendix scar – quite old.

Turning her on one side, Prost found marks, rather like those of a carpet burn, in the small of her back. Taking a scalpel, he scratched gently at the surface. The skin, sodden after so long immersed in the sea, came away easily. Faint bruising showed underneath. He frowned, studying the area, and bent nearer. Not carpet burn. He handed Jeet the small sample of skin to place in a formalin solution for later histological examination. It might bear a closer look.

His sharp eyes travelled over every inch of her body. The legs and feet were blemish free, save for what appeared to be a few mosquito bites. Francois was, by nature, a suspicious individual. He also had a tidy mind. He hated loose ends and detested mysteries. So he examined each bite closely until satisfied that they had been caused either by mosquitoes or sandflies. There was no evidence for it as yet but something made him suspect that this girl had been murdered.

Suicides generally meant hysterical enquiries from members of the family. Likewise accidental death. If she was a tourist, perhaps no-one had missed her. But tourists tended to come to Mauritius either with a group, or at the very least, with one other person. A romantic tropical island is not the place to be on your own. Someone would have reported her missing. The fact that they had not was odd, to say the least.

Murder – now that was different. A crime of passion is normally cut and dried but premeditated murder is often the result of preparation, cunning and intelligent smoke-screening. It was amazing how often a perfectly normal person, with friends, family and work colleagues, could go missing for days, even weeks, before it dawns on anyone that no-one has seen that person for a suspiciously long time. An intelligent, cold-blooded murderer relies on this fact, even makes use of such events as planned holidays to account for the victim's long absence.

Humming tunelessly, Francois' eyes ran up her torso. Small breasts, ribcage sticking out slightly. He'd seen that in other young girls. This one would have been around nineteen. Probably thought she was too fat! There was some bruising on both upper arms, fingerprints by the look of them. He picked up the scalpel again and patiently scratched away the outer layer of the skin. The bruises went deeper. Perfect imprints of a thumb and three fingers on both arms. Francois was glad the girl had been white. Bruises on a black skin can sometimes be missed.

The marks on their own may, or may not, be significant. Coupled with the abrasion on her lower spine, they could have been caused during intercourse. He needed something more. And then he found it. In the crook of her right arm, the main vein had been penetrated deeply and roughly. A search for other injection marks revealed nothing. That was good. A single puncture was an excellent indicator of foul play. Having cleared the area of sand, he dissected slowly around it, taking care to include some of the surrounding muscle, noting how the area was tinged with red, a sure sign that the injection had been administered ante-mortem. Jeet placed the sample in a jar which he labelled and then put into a small polystyrene box. All specimens taken from the body would travel to the police forensic laboratory in this airtight container. There, scientific officers would examine each and every one of them in minute detail.

'Okay, little one. Let's get serious here.'

Working quickly and efficiently, Francois took samples of hair from the girl's head, armpits, pubic area, eyelashes and eyebrows. He then scraped under each fingernail before taking clippings from several. Vaginal and rectal swabs were also taken. Finished with those, he set to work on the face and neck, checking for injuries. 'Frenulum intact, teeth in good order, no bruises. No-one punched you in the face, did they, my beauty?' Francois was talking mainly to himself. 'Lips a bit bruised. Hmmmm. Let's see.' He scraped at the skin on her lips and took some away from the jaw area. 'Heavy-duty kissing with a gentleman in need of a shave,' he observed.

Jeet looked at him politely.

'Signs of passionate kissing. Nothing wrong with that.' Prost went to move on with his work.

Jeet was still watching him, pen poised.

'Write it down, man.'

The assistant grinned behind his mask and scribbled furiously.

Francois examined the girl's teeth. 'All her own and well looked after.' Jeet faithfully wrote down his observations. Both men knew that if the girl was local then the exercise was probably a waste of time. Forensic dentistry was impossible since Mauritian dentists did not keep records. Besides, her clothing made Prost reasonably certain that she was a local. He shifted his attention to her neck. No bruises. He'd lay odds that the hyoid bone was still intact. Dissecting through skin and tissue, he examined it. Perfectly fine. No strangulation.

Prost moved on up to her scalp. First the skin. He cut from ear to ear, over the top of her head. With a fresh body, the business of pulling the front half of the scalp forwards over the face and the other half backwards is not too difficult. The skin is still firm enough to withstand considerable pressure. But, after four days in the sea, this girl's skin was fragile. It took a long time to expose the skull sufficiently to open it.

Once done, Francois picked up the electric saw. Cutting from just above one eyebrow, he only stopped when he reached the back of the head. The process was repeated on the other side. Putting down the saw, he inserted the dessert-spoon's handle into the cut and twisted off the skull. From long practice he made it look easy but it took skill to know exactly where to cut and how to expose the brain without destroying possible evidence. As expected, the brain was swollen and beginning to liquefy. No blood in either of the cerebral hemispheres, no sign of internal injuries. 'Ante-mortem injuries nil,' he barked at Jeet, checking the skull with fingers and eyes. 'And nothing post-mortem either.'

'Okay, little one. Let's take a look inside.'

Jeet adjusted his facemask. He did not mind the sight or sound of the deep incision which ripped the girl from abdomen to sternum so that the forensic surgeon could work unencumbered. Nor was he bothered by the breastbone being cut and cranked open. He was not, however, particularly fond of the smell. Even fresh bodies gave off a sickly odour as their inner workings were exposed.

Francois paid no attention to the smell. It was as much a part of his daily life as the aroma of rising bread is to a baker. Totally absorbed, he went straight to the girl's reproductive organs.

She was not pregnant, nor had she been recently. Francois checked this carefully. Backstreet abortions were a common enough occurrence and sometimes, when they went wrong, the evidence

26

of such an event was thrown into the sea to allow nature, and the ever-hungry sharks, to take care of.

Satisfied that an unwanted pregnancy had not caused the girl's demise, he started looking elsewhere. No water in the lungs. She'd died before entering the sea. Heart fine. Liver looked okay. No hepatitis-type symptoms. Not a habitual user of drugs in any case.

The stomach contents were next. Sometimes, if it was full, Prost favoured the method of tying off the top and bottom and putting the whole lot into a container. This girl's stomach was practically empty and the contents not immediately recognisable. The lab boys would have to analyse what little there was. Using his trusty dessertspoon, Prost scooped out the contents and slopped them into a jar. Then he turned his attention to the other organs. Pancreas, large and small bowels, kidneys, bladder, uterus and ovaries were all healthy. 'Clean living little thing,' he observed to no-one in particular.

Jeet just shook his head. As one of three mortuary assistants, he was used to pathologists. His regular boss, Dr Boolell, kept up a running commentary while working and it fell to Jeet to know what to write down and what to ignore. Dr Prost was more economical with his words but he worked the same way. Blood, bile and urine samples would be next, so he stood ready to receive them.

Nearly completed, Francois straightened and stretched. He'd been bending over the body for nearly two hours and his back hurt. At that moment the door opened and Detective Sham entered the room, his eyes studiously avoiding the cadaver. 'Finished?'

'Not quite.'

'I'll wait outside.'

'If you like.' Francois grinned sadistically. 'Though you might spot something I've missed.'

Sham didn't know Prost well enough to be sure he was joking. And he wasn't about to hang around long enough to find out. 'I'll just be outside.' With that, the decidedly pale detective left the room.

Francois bent to his task again. Liver, brain and kidney samples to check for oedema or renal failure, and a specimen of bile from the gall bladder which would be specifically examined for drug abuse.

'That's it.' He snapped off his gloves. 'Let's see what stories that lot tells us.' Opening the door, he went in search of the detective who had disappeared outside for a cigarette. Francois found him leaning, with studied nonchalance, against the wall of the building.

Sham looked up when he saw Prost walking towards him, dropped the cigarette, ground it out beneath his shoe and nudged himself away from the wall.

'All done,' Francois called cheerfully.

'Got anything for me?'

'Bit early to tell.'

Sham rolled his eyes. Dr Boolell was usually prepared to take a flyer on such things.

'But I can tell you that she was probably a local girl, she was not a habitual druggie, she wasn't pregnant, she was dead when she hit the water and she has an interesting puncture mark on her arm. Will that do?'

Sham nodded once. 'Thanks.'

'My pleasure,' Francois said pleasantly. 'Got to sew her up. See you around.' He returned to the morgue to perform the one part of his job he didn't enjoy. It was no problem cutting bodies open, that was exciting, but the need to make them pretty again for the sake of their relatives was onerous. With this one's skin in such a condition the stitches would probably tear and refuse to hold. As for the missing eye, all he could do was cover it with gauze. Whoever had the misfortune to identify this little girl was in for one hell of a shock.

Detective Sham returned to the police station. Even before he entered the building it was obvious that some kind of drama was taking place at reception. A flash premonition warned him that his name would be in the cast. Head down, he walked quickly past the desk where a tall, dark-haired, well-dressed woman was tearfully accusing an obviously harassed sergeant of not taking her seriously.

'Sir.'

Damn the man! Why can't he handle it? Sham sighed and turned.

'Sir, this is Mrs Vitry. She wants to speak to

someone in authority.' Behind her back the desk sergeant pulled a face which said, 'Rather you than me.'

Sham forced a smile. 'Please come this way, Mrs Vitry.'

In his office, a small, square, airless room, he indicated a chair for her. 'Have a seat, Madame.' He went around the dossier-strewn desk and sat down. He waited politely while Mrs Vitry tried to compose herself. When it became evident that she was fighting rising hysteria and not likely to get any calmer, Sham, with practised professionalism, asked, 'Now, how may I help you?'

Within two minutes, the detective realised he'd found the identity of their corpse.

'Why did you wait for five days?' he asked the woman, deliberately stamping down the sympathy that welled in him. Mrs Vitry seemed like a nice person – intelligent, sincere and desperately worried. Sympathy wouldn't help her when he broke the news. In Sham's experience, receivers of shocking news needed kindness and controlled impartiality to help them through the first few terrible minutes.

'She . . . we . . . she often stayed out of touch. We haven't been getting along very well lately. Corrine has her own apartment. I did try to phone her but there has been no answer. When I went around there this morning the landlord said he hasn't seen her for a while. Georges, that's her boyfriend, said they'd had a fight and haven't been in touch for a week. She's not been at work either.

30

They assumed she was sick and didn't think anything of it. I . . . I know something is wrong.
Perhaps it's nothing but . . . ' She let it hang, not
willing to voice her fears.

Sham noted down the usual details: name,
address, where she worked, names of friends,
boyfriend's name, et cetera, while Mrs Vitry fid-
geted and wrung her handkerchief into a twisted
knot. He knew he'd get no sense out of her once
she'd been told about this morning's discovery.

'Do you have a recent photograph of your
daughter, Madame?'

Mrs Vitry produced several. Sham's face revealed
nothing, but a rush of anger hit him when he
looked at the fresh-faced innocence of the beautiful young girl laughing at the camera.

'When were these taken?'

'Two months ago.' Tears were forming in the
woman's eyes. 'You know something, don't you?
Something has happened to Corrine. What is it?
For God's sake, what is it?'

There was no other way, 'I'm very sorry,
Madame, but a young girl matching these photographs was found dead on a beach this morning.
I'm afraid I'll have to ask you, or some other member of your immediate family, to come with me to
the morgue.'

The woman broke down. Sham found himself
hoping that Dr Prost, in the process of making the
body presentable, had had the forethought and
sensitivity to do something about the missing eye.

ONE

A grey and distinctly unappetising dawn fil-
tered through fogged windows of the
Cremorne Point cottage Holly Jones called
home. It had been a wild night. A freak storm, normally a summer phenomenon, had ripped through
several suburbs of Sydney wreaking destruction
and instant havoc. Trees were down, power out,
roofs smashed by flying debris, the ground littered
with branches, their leaves glistening wetly in the
rain.

The steaming coffee mug Holly held in her
hands was both warm and comforting as she stared
out at the cold scene. Late winter was drab enough
without this. The morning's view from her lounge,
over the dull waters of Sydney Harbour, was
depressing. Sluggish grey, almost sullen-looking.
On most days dancing wavelets lit by brilliant sunshine sent bright shards of light skittering away to
Point Piper on the far side. It was flat now, cold and
menacing.

She sipped the coffee slowly, reluctant to finish
and brave the pandemonium that still battered the
outside world. It was Sunday morning, at an hour

when most sensible people were snuggled up in warm beds. *Damn you, Quinn,* she thought sourly. *Why can't you sleep late and take Sundays off like normal folk?* As usual, he'd been unwilling to discuss whatever was on his mind over the telephone.

'Come into the office in the morning. We'll have a chat.'

'What time?' she'd asked, knowing it would be absurdly early.

'Seven thirty.' There'd been no apology in his voice.

'Tomorrow's Sunday,' she'd pointed out tartly.

'So it is. See you then.'

Sighing, Holly left her mug beside the sink and went to the telephone. Time to go. The luxury of a taxi was preferable to coaxing life into the draughty old MG, which was unreliable and hated cold early starts as much as its owner. She punched in a number and put the instrument to her ear, cursing when there was silence. 'Damn it! So much for Plan A.'

Although she'd been living in the cottage for just over three months, she was still not completely unpacked. From a cardboard box in the bedroom Holly produced a woollen cap and a fluffy mohair scarf of a garish purple colour she'd been forced to knit by a sewing teacher who'd given up on ever teaching her to do anything more than sew on a button. Holly kept and wore the garment with pride. It was proof of her one and only venture into home craft. 'Too thin,' she told her reflection in the small oak-framed mirror. The face that looked back had a vulnerable quality. Large grey eyes, winged light brown brows, high cheekbones, full lips and a nose she described as long and bony but in fact was just high-bridged enough to save her face from bland prettiness.

Sunday best it was not. Jeans, sneakers and an oversized sloppy joe which hung halfway to her knees and hid the boyishly slender body under it. She jammed the cap over short blonde hair, tucked errant strands up out of sight, didn't like what it did for her face, tried to hook some back with her nails, lost patience and snatched the cap off again. Ruffling slim fingers through the offending hair, she tried again. The process didn't work much better the second time. So she left it. Nothing seemed to work. To Holly, she was too thin and hated her nose.

As she wound the scarf around her neck and pulled on an oiled cotton Drizabone jacket, Holly saw someone flawed, someone who had failed. There was pain and the start of fine bitter lines around the corners of her mouth. 'Screw this,' she muttered at the mirror. 'Who cares?'

Snatching car keys, Holly left the cottage and made her way carefully up thirty-three wet, leaf-strewn steps to the street where the MG was garaged. She had no umbrella. Her last one had disintegrated under similar weather conditions. The steps were stone blocks, old and slippery. Rain lashed down and, before she was halfway up, her cap and jeans were soaked. Water trickled under the scarf and the wind found small gaps in her clothing through which it blew its icy breath. At least the Drizabone worked.

A tree had blown down across from the garage but she figured the MG could get round it. Further up the street, emergency teams were already out with chainsaws, cutting debris into manageable pieces ready to be carted away. At least two houses nearby were roof damaged. Fingers turning numb from the cold and wet, Holly fumbled with her keys and finally unlocked the garage doors. They were the old-fashioned kind, made of wood, which swung outwards and blocked the footpath. She wedged a brick against each so they didn't blow shut and approached the MG. 'Do me a favour. No sulks,' she muttered.

But the car sulked anyway and, by the time she backed out into the street, an understandably miserable paperboy on a bicycle was ready to trade insults with her. 'Sorry,' Holly said, hopping out of the car, which, left to its own devices – but for a recalcitrant choke with its own agenda – promptly stalled. One at a time she kicked away the bricks and managed to wrestle the doors closed.

With the offending obstacles removed, the paperboy – a lad of maybe twelve or thirteen – exercised his limited vocabulary. 'Stupid old cow.' He pedalled away up the footpath, angrily flinging plastic-wrapped newspapers in the general direction of nearby houses.

Holly slid back into the MG, adjusted the rear-vision mirror which, for some inexplicable reason, always seemed to need it, caught sight of herself, screwed up her nose and said, 'Moo.' Feeling slightly better, she played the usual start-or-flatten-the-battery battle of wits with the old car – a test of mental against mechanical tenacity which, more often of late, she lost. The engine hiccupped three times, groaned once, then roared into life and blew blue smoke as fat flatulence tumbled through the exhaust with unmitigated fervour. Holly, from years of experience, knew that this would be her only chance. She slammed the short gear lever forward and accelerated away.

At this hour there was very little traffic. Driving rain that still fell with unrelenting ferocity quickly found its way inside the car. The heating system was basic and had only two settings – too hot or not hot enough. She set it on high and directed its blast towards her feet, knowing that by the time she reached the city, both legs would be toasted but the tip of her nose would need defrosting.

She was heading for Market Street in the inner city and the offices of *Out of Focus*, a monthly magazine which occupied two floors of a high-rise building. Established in 1983, *Out of Focus* was a slightly off-the-wall publication with an investigative journalistic leaning towards the bizarre. Mainstream news was left to such conventional weekly publications as *Time, Newsweek* and the *Bulletin*. The editorial aim of *Out of Focus* was to feature reports of the unusual, the nearly or ex-famous and the far-flung and interesting. Readers of the magazine could be assured of only one thing: if there was such a thing as a BSc in useless though thoroughly entertaining information, *Out of Focus* would be required reading.

The magazine was the whim of its flamboyant and eccentric managing editor-in-chief, the very wealthy Sir Richard Aitken, and began as a bimonthly with an audited circulation of six hundred. To the surprise of everyone and the annoyance of Sir Richard, who wanted to keep it small and manageable, the magazine rapidly gained in popularity to its present official circulation figure of almost two hundred thousand, with thirty per cent of that falling beyond the shores of Australia. Despite its best efforts to steer clear of the popular media arena, *Out of Focus* had actually broken several significant news stories, including the recently acclaimed exposé of a networking child pornography ring that extended around the globe, above and below the equator.

Holly, as a freelance journalist, had worked for *Out of Focus* before. Her father, Quinn Longford-Jones, was the features editor. Not that he gave her preferential treatment – he didn't. In fact, stories that might have gone to Holly were often allocated to others so that there could be no mutterings of favouritism. In typical Quinn fashion, the briefing – and she had to assume that was what she was going to – always took place at his convenience and no-one else's. Despite the fact that this pissed her off totally, there was always a sense of excitement that accompanied a summons from her father. The assignments were never dull. She had covered the landmine issue well before Princess

Diana made it vogue. She did a tongue-in-cheek piece on what happened to old advertising men and women concluding that, since the industry appeared to be run by children barely out of nappies, anyone over thirty who did not get an offer to join one of their clients probably, at best, wrote a bad book of memoirs or, in extreme cases, contemplated donating their bodies to the mechanical expertise of the office shredder.

She had tramped all over Mexico with an eccentric, retired British actor who now collected geodes and was in search of the agate-lined amethyst crystal-encrusted variety to add to his collection. His addiction to the world's geological wonders played second fiddle only to the one abiding passion in his life. He had an absolute *thing* about strange men in bars. Holly had spent a great deal of time drinking coffee, or tequila, depending on the time of day or night, while she waited for him to fall out of love. Fortunately, he seemed to do this at the same speed with which his heart first succumbed, otherwise the article might never have seen the light of day.

Out of Focus seemed to have a bottomless pit of crackpots with missions just interesting enough to be different and a profile just different enough to be interesting. Earlier this year, she had spent time in Japan, in the company of two scientists with stars and research grants in their eyes who were investigating the plight of the macaque or snow monkey. Nothing unusual in that except the dedicated duo intended to publish a controversial paper, in which they had stated in a blare of publicity preceding their departure, that DNA findings would prove conclusively that the macaque was man's closest relative.

The trip was cut short when the two men could not agree on the wording of their conclusions. One wanted an academic paper that was slanted exclusively towards scientists, the other argued that since their findings would cause considerable media interest, the paper should be presented in such a way that it held appeal for a broader readership. Neither man would budge and, in an outburst of surprisingly childlike pique, they abruptly cancelled the study.

Returning to Sydney, two days before expected, Holly surprised her husband in more ways than one. Dennis had been in bed with one of her best friends. Holly had a lot of friends. She wasn't going to miss one. But she only had one husband and the split from him had been painful.

She was driving across the Harbour Bridge now and the little MG was fighting hard to go where the wind blew it. Holly was fighting just as strongly to prevent it. Her legs were on fire and hands frozen. The windows had misted over and she repeatedly wiped at the condensation to see where she was going.

She wondered if Dennis was still in bed and with whom? The pain and shock of his betrayal was never far from the surface. Although he'd pleaded with her to give him another chance, she'd been unable to remain under the same roof. She moved into a unit, wanting time to think. That was when the full extent of his deceit became clear. Friends, unwilling to speak out before, told of his ongoing infidelities. He'd been unfaithful to her from the beginning, even before they married.

Holly didn't know which hurt more: his breach of her trust or her own blindness to it.

The divorce went through uncontested. Dennis, when he saw how much pain he had caused, knew he'd never get her back. Holly bought the two-bedroomed cottage in Cremorne Point and moved in. She had as much work as she wanted and threw herself into it, leaving little or no time to dwell on the past. When she wasn't working, she was renovating. Time passed quickly but Holly wasn't healing.

The streets of Sydney were practically deserted, a change from the normally congested narrow thoroughfares of the week. She drove to the underground car park and ignored all the deserted bays to park right next to her father's new BMW. Silver grey, sleek and solid, the dripping MG by comparison had a dejected, sad appearance.

An express lift sped Holly to the twenty-second floor, where the reception area was deserted. Quinn Longford-Jones occupied a corner of the floor which gave sweeping views over the city, Pyrmont Bridge and Darling Harbour. The office was as impressive as his car and, indeed, as Quinn himself. Holly's father was tall, with a thick thatch of silver-grey hair. He kept himself fit and tanned with regular rounds of golf and twice-weekly tennis. His only child had inherited her grey eyes and full lips from him and wished she also had his beautifully aristocratic nose. Actually she did, but couldn't see the similarity. Quinn's voice was a boom and his laugh a deep, raspy chuckle. Where Holly's feelings were always reflected in her eyes, Quinn's sparkled with enjoyment and mischief, irrespective of inner emotions. Both Holly and her mother adored him.

She knocked briefly and opened the door. He was on the telephone and waved her to a chair. Listening to him convince a hard-nosed and highly experienced journalist, whom Holly knew slightly, to tone down the political angle on a story he was writing about Bosnia and to concentrate on the effect the unrest was having on art and artists, she wondered how, with a role model like Quinn, it had been possible to marry a rat like Dennis.

Holly hadn't waited for her divorce before reverting to her maiden name. Unlike Quinn, who revelled in the double-barrelled surname, Holly had always resisted it. When she was fourteen and her peers' opinion of her had mattered more than any later-developed tendency to revel in her independence, she had taken to calling herself Holly Hyphen in a kind of inverted show of snobbism. These days she usually dropped the Longford, but only because Jones was easier for others to remember.

'Hi, Big Shot. Hang up that wet jacket.' He pulled a face at the receiver as he put it down. 'Damned fool never listens to the brief.'

'How long have you been here?'

He looked at his watch. 'Couple of hours I suppose, why?'

She shook her head. 'I don't know how Mummy stands it.'

Quinn laughed. 'She doesn't. When I left she was flat out in bed, fast asleep.'

Holly smiled.

'How you doing?'

'Fine.'

'Bullshit. You look like hell.'

'Thanks.'

'And take off that ridiculous hat. It makes you look about ten.'

She whipped it off and shook out her short hair.

'That's better. Now you look about fifteen.'

'What's with the age thing?'

'You're twenty-nine next month. I'm just trying to make you feel better.'

'I feel fine about my age.'

Grey eyes twinkled at her. 'And the rest of it?'

'It's . . . still difficult.'

Quinn nodded. 'How'd you fancy an assignment that every journo on our books would kill for?'

'Preferential treatment?'

'For your own sake.'

'Your detachment is slipping.'

'So what. You're my daughter.' He rose suddenly and extended his arms expansively. 'Hug time.'

Holly went into his arms. She felt him lay his

cheek against her head. They stayed like that for nearly a minute.

Finally, Quinn pulled back. 'Your mother said I must invite you to lunch.'

Holly sat down. 'I don't suppose it occurred to you that you could have briefed me at the house?'

He looked surprised. 'Good God, no! Ruin a splendid lunch!' He grinned. 'Besides, you know how your mother gets when I bring work home.' He sat down opposite her and leaned forward. 'Well? You haven't answered my question.'

'About the assignment? Yes.'

'Know what I like about you, Big Shot?' He didn't wait for her to reply. 'You sure as hell know your own mind.'

Finally, Holly laughed. Quinn could always get around her defences.

Eyes alight with satisfaction and pleasure, Quinn began the briefing. 'Ever heard of Connor Maguire?'

'Australia's answer to Richard Branson? Sure.'

'Is that disapproval I hear?'

'Well . . . ' Holly defended her tone. 'The guy is born wealthy, fancies himself as an entrepreneur, has businesses all over the country, and always seems to come up smelling like a rose.'

'Is that a crime? He's never hurt anyone.'

Holly inclined her head in agreement.

'He does a lot of good work for a host of different charities.'

'Sure. And he always milks the publicity machine like hell whenever he does. Look at that

43

ride he did on horseback across Australia a few years back. Raising money for kids with cancer. Okay, I agree, he raised a lot of money but I'd like to see the guy get honest and admit that he's a publicity-seeking adventurer at heart.'

'What's wrong with that?'

Holly thought about it. 'Nothing, I guess.'

'You appear to dislike him on principle rather than performance.'

'What principle?'

'That he doesn't have to slog for a living.'

'It's not that. It's just that . . . well, he seems so frivolous.'

Quinn wagged a finger at her. 'Do you want this assignment or not? I can't send you to cover this one if you don't approve.'

Holly sighed. 'What's he up to this time?'

'Looking for lost treasure in the Sea of Zanj.'

Holly's eyebrows showed interest.

'Know where it is?' Quinn often tested her general knowledge. It was a game they played, to see who could catch the other out.

'Kind of.' Holly knew he hated vague responses. And he'd obviously forgotten how she used to devour stories of the *Arabian Nights* as a child.

'Where?'

'Um, somewhere between the Tropic of Capricorn and the equator, off the coast of Africa, ah . . . full of islands, coral reefs and atolls . . . Madagascar, the Seychelles, Mauritius, somewhere around there.'

Quinn took it philosophically. 'Good girl. Go to

the top of the class. But don't take your books cos you'll be back.'

'It's all part of the Indian Ocean. The Arabs called it the Sea of Zanj or, to be more precise, Bahr-el-Zanj, which means sea of the blacks. But it hasn't been called that for centuries.'

'Okay. Take your books.' His eyes approved but Holly could almost hear the wheels turning behind them as he tried to figure a way to get even.

'What the hell is Connor Maguire up to this time?'

'I told you. Looking for lost treasure.' Quinn watched her, waiting.

'Pirates,' she said eventually. 'The place was once crawling with them. I suppose it's just possible . . .'

Quinn inclined his head. His daughter had won that round. 'Maguire thinks it is.'

'So where is he now?'

'Mauritius.'

'Mmmm. Sounds interesting. I've always wanted to go there.'

'Excellent. Ah . . . one thing though, this time he doesn't want the publicity.'

Holly folded her arms and sat back. 'Super. A crackpot philanthropist is one thing. A reluctant crackpot philanthropist is quite another.'

'The organisation that will benefit if he finds anything has asked us to cover it.'

'Here we go again. What charity is it this time?'

'Not a charity. AIDS research.'

Holly gave a cynical laugh. 'Connor Maguire

and Elizabeth Taylor. He probably wants to meet her. Good publicity and all that.'

Quinn shuffled some papers around. 'He already has met her.'

'Okay, okay. The guy is a modern-day knight in shining armour. He doesn't need the money. He's doing this out of the goodness of his heart. And, just for a change, he doesn't want publicity. Why?'

Quinn didn't answer the question. 'Did you know that I've met him several times?'

'When?' She was surprised. Her father loved to talk about interesting people.

'Last year when he launched that Flower Power thing. You know the one. In competition against Interflora. It's doing very well.'

'Everything he touches does well.'

'Not everything. I saw him again a couple of months ago. He was telling me that some shipping deal had just gone horribly wrong. Lost squillions, I gather.'

'He can afford it.'

'He's never asked for publicity. It just seems to follow him around.'

'Okay, Quinn. Okay. He really is a nice guy. So, where do I find him?'

'With a bit of luck he'll still be on Mauritius. If not, I gather he plans to head for Rodrigues. You'll find him easily enough.'

'You're talking a bloody big area here.'

'Piece of cake.' Quinn grinned at her. 'Fancy something to eat? They do a great continental breakfast downstairs.'

Over croissants and coffee, Quinn filled her in on a bit more detail. 'Early in the eighteenth century, the Dutch pulled out of Mauritius. Apart from the garrison and officials of the Dutch East India Company, there were about three hundred settlers on the island, mainly retired pirates. They weren't too enthusiastic about being left behind. Local Creole people were a cut-throat bunch and the pirates were afraid of them. Many fled to whichever country they had originated from to try for a pardon. Some never returned. For example, the English would not hear of clemency and so-called reformed pirates foolish enough to set foot back on British soil soon found themselves at the wrong end of a rope. It's a known fact that most of these men hid their fortunes, buried them, stashed them in caves, that sort of thing, while they were off pleading their case.

'A few years later, the French offered amnesty to any pirate who surrendered. The pirates were suspicious. Not many jumped at the chance because they thought it was a trick. But a few of them, those inclined to take up the offer, also buried their treasure while they were back in France trying to convince anyone who'd listen that they were really nice guys at heart. It's possible that some never returned to dig it up again. Picture it, three hundred terrified pirates living with untold riches they couldn't spend fast enough. They'd all be wary of each other too. What with the law, disease and feuds, why, the whole island is probably knee deep in buried treasure!'

Holly laughed. Her father usually reached a

wildly enthusiastic stage when he was briefing someone. 'You're getting the bug.'

'When did Connor Maguire ever take on anything without first going into it thoroughly?' Quinn asked.

Holly picked up her croissant and nibbled at an edge.

'Don't prejudge him. He's actually a good man. Life hasn't always been kind to him. He lost his half-brother a few years ago, which knocked him sideways.'

'I didn't know that.'

Quinn nodded. 'Brian, I think his name was. He was killed in the Seychelles during a coup attempt. Probably in the wrong place at the wrong time. It happens. Anyway, Maguire took a long time to come to terms with his death.'

'How do you know this?'

'It was in the newspapers. The first time I met Connor was about six months after it happened. When I offered condolences it was pretty obvious that he still couldn't talk about it.'

Images of the good-looking playboy adventurer flashed across Holly's mind. She found it difficult to picture him grieving. 'Married twice, wasn't he?' she said, more tartly than she'd intended.

'You've been married once,' Quinn reminded her gently.

'Yes . . . but . . .'

'But nothing. How do you know the reason for each divorce was his fault?'

Holly changed the subject. 'When do I leave?'

'You fly to Melbourne this evening. The Air Mauritius flight takes off at eleven thirty tonight.'

'That's cutting it a bit fine. I've got things to organise.'

'Can't help that. There's only one flight a week, unless you'd prefer to go via Singapore or fly to South Africa and then back to Mauritius.'

'No.' She made up her mind quickly. 'I'll go via Melbourne.' She glanced at her father's plate. 'Finish your breakfast. We've still got work to do.'

'Done that,' Quinn mumbled, leaning into a mouthful of crumbly pastry. He swallowed, wiped his mouth and put down the napkin. 'Cover Maguire's search. Aussie icon's latest challenge. Push the haves and have nots as well – you know the sort of thing. See if you can throw in a little danger – sharks, cyclones, corrupt politicians, whatever.' He waved his hands vaguely. 'That's your brief.'

'Thanks, Quinn,' she said dryly. 'As usual, you've been a mine of information. How many words do you want?'

'As many as it takes. If the piece is what I hope, we'll serialise it.' He stood up. 'Finished?'

She hadn't.

'Good. I'll walk you to your car.'

Holly, from many years of experience, knew her father's mind had shifted gear and he was anxious to get back to his office. Little things like air tickets, expenses, where to stay in Mauritius, how to locate Connor Maguire, would, no doubt, have been taken care of by his secretary. 'Got an envelope for me?'

He delved into a jacket pocket and passed over a fat package.

There was no need to check it. Quinn's secretary was the best. Everything she needed would be in it, including a full briefing.

'When are you going to replace this thing?' Quinn kicked absently at one of the MG's wire-spoked wheels.

'Careful. It's likely to collapse on your foot.'

He had that father's look on his face, the one that was both full of pride and anxious at the same time. 'You're a funny little monkey, sweetheart. I love you very much. See you at lunch.'

She watched him walk away, knowing he was hurting at her hurt. He was very loyal. When she told her parents of Dennis's betrayal, when the full extent of her misery became known to them, Quinn had to be restrained from, as he put it, 'rearranging the bastard's features'. He'd have done it, too. Only Holly's reassurance that it wasn't worth the effort had prevented a more than likely assault charge.

Sighing, Holly settled into her car. 'Start,' she snapped. 'It's not as if you're still cold.'

But the MG fired and died, coughed and spluttered half a dozen times before holding its burbling rhythm. 'Quinn's right about you,' Holly threatened. 'It's time for the scrap heap.' Thus warned, the car behaved impeccably all the way home.

Quinn and Delia Longford-Jones lived at Castlecrag, overlooking Sugarloaf Bay. Built halfway down the sloping land, their home was virtually invisible from the road and was engulfed by lush vegetation planted many years before. It was a neat and modest-looking house from the outside, but it dropped through four levels to a deck that sat right at the water's edge. Surprisingly large inside, the house radiated light and warmth, was furnished with exquisite antiques and glowed with a subtle blending of honey and cream tones. It had a comfortable lived-in feel and, although some of the furniture would fetch a small fortune at auction, managed to avoid pretension or showiness.

Holly, packed and ready to fly, stuffed her one case onto the passenger seat and secured it with the seatbelt. She'd leave the MG at Castlecrag and go straight to the airport from lunch. If her parents took anything seriously, it was entertaining. A casual invitation to lunch probably meant there'd be a dozen or more other guests, all hand-picked to ensure a good working mix. The food would be beautifully presented, absolutely delicious and more often than not, quite unusual – a talking point in itself. Lunch could stretch from midday to five in the afternoon. The wines were always superb, often from little-known boutique estates. Sampling them was undertaken with dedication and enthusiasm as Quinn urged, 'No, you must try this one, it's still young but it's going to be a winner.' More than one guest would inevitably go home by taxi – in fact, those in the know usually arrived in one as well.

Holly deliberately arrived early in case her mother needed any help.

'Hello, darling.' Delia Longford-Jones was an unusual woman who managed to look both bohemian and sophisticated at the same time. Grey curly hair caught at the back in a silk scrunchy was allowed to flow around her shoulders. She wore no make-up, barring eye shadow and lipstick, both of which were skilfully applied. Earlier beauty, though faded, was still very much evident in a flawless and practically line-free complexion. Wearing a barely pink linen trouser suit, with a rich and regally purple silk tailored blouse, she was both elegant and casual.

Holly felt positively dowdy dressed in clothes suitable for travel. 'Hi, Mum.' She sniffed. 'Mmmm, something smells delish.'

'Greek,' Delia said succinctly. She usually stuck to a single theme for any gathering, formal or otherwise.

Holly kissed her mother's cheek. 'I won't ask who's coming. Might spoil the surprise.'

But she was told anyway. About fourteen in all. Among them, two well-known actors, one television presenter, several journalists and an author. 'Are you taking the Mauritius assignment?' she asked, not drawing breath.

'Case is in the car.'

'Excellent. It will be good for you.'

Holly pulled a face.

'Oh come on, darling. Just think. Mauritius. Tropical paradise. At least you'll be away from this horrid weather.' The wind had eased somewhat but rain still poured down. 'Wish I could come with you.'

'Uh huh!' Holly smiled. 'Perhaps sending me was your idea.'

'Not at all. Your father thought . . . Anyway, how are you darling?'

'Fine,' Holly said shortly.

'You're not fine. Oh, my darling, look at you. I could kill that bloody man for what he did to you.'

Holly felt the telltale flush of tears, never far from the surface. 'It's taking time, Mum, that's all. I'll get there.'

Her mother's eyes were soft with love and concern. 'Don't let this influence the way you think about all men. Look at Daddy.'

'Mum, did you ever like Dennis?'

'No.' One of Delia's greatest attributes was that she tended to be devastatingly honest.

'Would you have told me that if he hadn't . . .'

'No.'

Holly hugged her. 'I love you, Mum. Don't ever change.'

Delia scrutinised her daughter's face, hating the fine lines of bitterness and the haunted look of betrayal which had appeared overnight and now refused to go away. 'I wish I could say the same for you. You used to find joy in everything. It was one of your most precious gifts. It will come back you know.'

Holly couldn't see that happening.

They were in the entrance hall, moving towards a set of six steps that led down to the next level, a floor comprising a cottage-cosy kitchen, the family lounge and a more formal dining room.

Wanting to shift the conversation away from herself, Holly asked, 'Can I help?'

'All done. We're using the bottom room today. Drinks are set up. Come on, let's get a head start before the others arrive.'

Holly smiled. Her mother only ever drank mineral water, into which she occasionally squeezed the juice of a lemon or lime. The reason, Delia had once admitted to Holly, was a never to be forgotten encounter with champagne when she was an innocent eighteen. The ensuing hangover the next day had been made worse by her father's refusal to allow her any water to slake the raging thirst. 'Suffer, young lady,' he'd told her. 'You've earned the right.' She hadn't touched alcohol since.

Guests began arriving half-an-hour later. They were outgoing characters in the main and, with very little effort, made the lunch an instant party, filling the room with laughter and conversation. Holly allowed herself to go with the flow, avoiding personal questions with practised ease and fobbing off two requests for her telephone number. Quinn was late as usual but everyone forgave him. He breezed in, apologised, kissed Delia and then became the life and soul of the party. As a Longford-Jones lunchtime bash went, this was a good one.

At six-fifteen Holly called a cab to take her to the airport. Quinn walked with her to the taxi. 'Take as much time as you need. Have a bit of fun. The magazine can afford it.'

'I'm supposed to be working,' she reminded him.

'That's okay. I can do a great Lord Nelson when I have to.'

'Thanks, Daddy.' She very rarely called him that. 'But if you turn a blind eye for me you'll have to do it for everyone.'

He ignored that. 'Are you doing the usual with your mail?'

'Taken care of.' When she was away a neighbour collected her mail and held it until Delia picked it up to attend to it.

Quinn kissed her cheek. 'Love you, sweetheart. See you in a couple of weeks or so.'

She climbed into the taxi.

'And don't forget the fun part,' he said, before shutting the door.

Fun! Holly thought a few minutes later, staring at the smeared lights of the city through the rain running down the taxi's windows. *What's that?*

TWO

The Air Mauritius flight offered genuine, friendly service, excellent cuisine, a timetable that was adhered to and the hardest seats of any airline with which Holly had ever flown. Air travel was something she neither enjoyed nor disliked, it was simply a means to an end and a chance to catch up on some escapist reading. There was one stop in Perth, where joining passengers took up every spare seat on the plane, then it was on into a never-ending night. Dawn came slowly, and almost thirteen hours after leaving Melbourne they were dropping towards a lush green island which had materialised out of the Indian Ocean. Holly was convinced that her rear end would never be the same again.

Landing at Plaisance was a treat. The airport was on the south-east coast. Holly had a window seat, and, as they flew over the island in order to come around and land from the west, she was able to have a good look at the country beneath them. Craggy, jagged mountains partly covered by thick vegetation with spectacular outcrops of rock standing in stark relief – a relic of the island's volcanic past – dominated the scenery. At their base, where the land flattened and gentled, the grass-like green of field upon field of sugar cane. A thin band of white sand separated the island's predominant agriculture from an aquamarine lagoon. Surrounding the island, containing it in an almost unbroken ring of coral, was the reef. Incessant waves pounding against this age-old protective circle formed what looked like a second beach. Beyond the reef the ocean became a deep blue, disappearing to the horizon. It was picture book, tropical island perfect.

The airport building – a long, two-storeyed rectangle, painted white – seemed to have an identity crisis. Two signs gave conflicting names – *Welcome to Mauritius* was flanked by *Plaisance Airport* on one side, and *Sir Seewoosagur Ramgoolam International Airport* on the other. The location of the building had a sad but interesting connection. Reading up on Mauritius during the flight, Holly had learned that an English school teacher had found dodo bones on this very site.

Inside the building was light, bright and pleasant which was just as well since both the ceiling fans and the wheels of immigration ground slowly. Finally, it was Holly's turn.

'May I see your ticket.' The man looked at her indifferently.

An inveterate traveller, Holly knew better than to ask why.

'You have not booked an onward flight?'

'No.'

'Why not?'

'I don't know when I'll be going back. It's an open ticket.'

'That is highly irregular.' He frowned at her.

'Really?' Holly found that a breathy 'please help me' ignorance worked well with most forms of officialdom. But this man was having none of it.

'You are not intending to reside here indefinitely?'

'No. A few weeks, maybe a month.'

'You are with a tour group?' His ability to turn a statement into a question was an art form in itself.

'No.'

'Hmmm.' Now he was frowning at her ticket. The word OPEN in the date section was definitely not to his liking. 'You do not wish to make a return reservation now?'

'No thanks.'

'Where are you staying?'

It was on the immigration form but she told him anyway. 'The Merville Beach Hotel.'

'You do not have any other contacts in Mauritius?'

'Fraid not.'

He pursed his lips, clearly vexed. 'And you will not outstay your visa?'

'I don't have a visa. I was told I didn't need one.'

'I will issue one.' He handed back the ticket. 'Passport and arrival card please.'

They were already in front of him. She tapped them.

He studied the documents carefully. 'You are a journalist, Miss Longford-Jones.'

'Yes.'

'Why do you come here?' An open-ended ticket *and* a journalist. Very suspicious. 'What is it you will write about us?'

'Australians like the idea of Mauritius but few know much about it. My magazine wants an informative piece . . . something that might encourage tourists to come here.' Holly looked the man directly in the eye as she lied. 'Your tourist board has been most helpful to date,' she added, hoping that, as in most holiday destinations, mention of the body responsible for satisfied customers would short-circuit what was likely to take some considerable time. It worked.

'How long do you wish to stay?'

'Would thirty days be possible?' She smiled sweetly.

'Ah!' Her passport was stamped. 'If you require a longer period you must go to the immigration department. You will find them at police headquarters in Port Louis.' He handed back her passport. 'Be sure to book your return flight as soon as possible. And you must confirm the reservation at least three days before your flight. Enjoy your stay.'

Holly thanked him and went to move away.

'One more thing.' He was smiling at her now.

She turned back.

'When you write about Mauritius, be sure to mention our friendly service.'

'You've got it.' She gave him her best seriously genuine look.

'Ah! C'est bon.' He dismissed her with an important nod of his head and turned to the next victim waiting in line.

The baggage carousel was broken and luggage had to be manhandled into the hall by sweating airport officials. By the time Holly emerged unscathed from the Customs 'nothing to declare' green channel, she'd been on the ground for just over an hour. She braced herself for the usual throng of eager young hopefuls wanting to carry her bag or find a taxi but was pleasantly surprised to find that, though they were there in their hundreds, they were orderly and confined to one area just outside automatic glass doors.

Holly cashed a traveller's cheque and then made her way to the car rental counters. She managed to keep smiling through the unexpected complexities of a matter as simple as hiring a car. It was a further half-hour before she found herself behind the wheel of a Mini Moke, the only vehicle available. Open to the elements, with a spare tyre she suspected belonged to a different vehicle, Holly was pleasantly surprised when it started first go.

The briefing from Audrey Hammond, Quinn's secretary, had said that she'd most likely find Connor Maguire somewhere in the north, near Grand Baie. She located it on a road map she'd picked up with other background brochures while waiting for her suitcase. 'Nothing like starting at the top,' she told herself. 'That would be the Royal Palm no doubt.' The redoubtable Mrs Hammond had provided useful information about where to stay on Mauritius and Holly had familiarised herself with it during the flight. The Royal Palm was apparently the choice of kings and queens, the jet set and those on bottomless expense accounts. Maguire would be attracted to such a place as a moth is to flame. It was beyond the budget of *Out of Focus*, however, and she had been booked into a medium tariff tourist resort which was almost next door.

Concentrating on driving an unfamiliar vehicle on foreign soil, Holly's first impressions of Mauritius were pretty much as she had seen from the air. Jagged mountains in the distance were both dramatic and beautiful. Field after field of sugar cane, growing right up to the road. Dotted in these fields were stone pyramids, some quite large and all perfectly symmetrical. They had a kind of shrine appearance. Holly made a mental note to ask about them. The recently constructed dual carriageway ran north/west from the airport, climbing up through the Central Highland towns of Curepipe and Quatre Bornes before dropping down to the capital of Port Louis. It was well signposted and, in the main, in good condition. Beyond Port Louis, the sparkling blue sea was never far away and the land flattened and became even more tropical in appearance. In the open Mini Moke, the air had felt almost too cool in the centre of the island, but as soon as the last of the mountain passes had been crossed, the temperature rose and Holly enjoyed the balmy rush of air around her. She almost felt she was on holiday.

The Merville Beach Hotel was set in spacious palm-shaded gardens off the coast road just north of Grand Baie. Accommodation ranged from deluxe to the very ordinary but all guests shared the resort facilities. Privately owned bungalows still fanned the hotel but many others had disappeared as the developers scrambled for tourist dollars. Right in the middle of the Merville Beach resort one old cottage still remained. Slightly run-down but not in the least daunted by the three-sided invasion, it appeared totally unconcerned by its commercial neighbour.

Holly's room – the wonderful Mrs Hammond had booked a deluxe as opposed to a bog standard – had a balcony which looked over the solitary cottage and to a wide lagoon beyond. Despite a sadly out-of-place appearance, Holly could not help but admire the tenacity of the owner of the bungalow. After all, the dwelling had been there first. She unpacked, set her watch back six hours and realised she was hungry.

The spicy aromas of traditional Creole cooking led Holly to The Badamier, a large, thatch-covered bar overlooking the pool and opening onto a terrace scattered with tables and bright sun umbrellas. Set directly above the beach, there was no escaping the sensation that this was one tiny corner of a tropical paradise which had but one aim – to ensure that its guests relaxed. Everywhere she looked, people were doing just that – lazing around the pool talking and laughing or on the beach, some windsurfing, while the more adventurous souls opted to paraglide. *Great place for lovers*, Holly thought, feeling a sudden rush of loneliness.

She chose a table in the sun with a view towards the open sea. The time-zone change meant she was in no-man's land food-wise – somewhere between breakfast and lunch – so she ordered a toasted sandwich. The waiter departed and Holly, sparing no sympathy for those poor cold and wet souls in Sydney, sat back to enjoy the warm sun and stunning view.

'Excuse me,' a male voice said.

Holly looked up. He was tall, fair-haired, almost too thin with skin slightly red from the sun. Early thirties possibly, with an anxious half-smile, and a mole above his top lip. The blue eyes held a degree of uncertainty. Holly liked him straight off. 'Yes.'

He rubbed two long fingers across his brow. 'I heard you speaking English. I wonder, would you mind if I joined you?' The accent was upper-class English. 'If you're on your own, that is.' He looked slightly nervous.

Holly decided he was probably lonely and waved her hand at a spare chair. 'Please do.'

The man sat down, beckoned to a waiter and ordered a Phoenix beer for himself. 'Bit early but what the hell! Have you ordered?'

'Just a sandwich.'

'May I buy you a drink?'

She considered for a moment. Her internal clock was ticking away at a perfectly acceptable drinks time. 'Only if I get the next one.'

'Righto. What would you like?'

Holly said she'd have a glass of dry white wine.

The stranger also asked for a toasted sandwich. With the waiter gone, he smiled shyly. 'Justin. Justin Parker. That's me. I hope you don't mind. One gets awfully fed up with eating alone.'

'I know what you mean. My name is Holly Jones.'

He glanced around the almost empty terrace. 'Are you staying here?'

She nodded. 'Just arrived. You?'

'Yes. Been here nearly a week. I've never *seen* so many honeymooners. When you came in on your own and I heard you speaking English . . . well . . . I hope you don't think I'm trying to pick you up.'

Holly couldn't tell. If he was, he was doing a damned good job of disguising it, but she'd been the recipient of some classic attempts. She decided on a little verbal insurance. 'If I thought that, you wouldn't be sitting here now.'

He blinked at her bluntness but merely asked, 'Are you here on holiday?'

'No. I'm a journalist. I'm working.'

'Oh dear! What a terrible assignment.' Another shy smile. 'I suppose someone has to do it.'

Holly laughed, warming to him. 'It's not all it's cracked up to be. You spend a lot of time on your own.'

'I thought journalists and photographers travelled together.'

'Sometimes, but on this occasion I am it, or should I say, both.' She did not add that one of the field work requirements for *Out of Focus* was that all the journalists had to be handy with a camera. Quinn had a theory that words and visuals needed a single mind to coordinate the two and achieve a balanced blending. 'You can always pick it,' he'd said, 'when two egos try to tell one story.'

Holly wasn't sure he was right. There had been some stunning results from various marriages of artistic endeavours, though she had to admit that more often than not, either the words let the pictures down or vice versa.

Justin was asking, 'Are you from Australia or South Africa?'

'Australia.'

'Forgive me. It's your accent. You don't sound terribly Australian.'

'Is the operative word there *terribly*?'

'Oh no. I didn't mean . . . Well, yes, I suppose I did mean . . . It's just that some people from Down Under are a bit hard to understand.'

He appeared to be getting flustered. Holly changed the subject. 'You're English.'

'Yes. From Bath. Well, Claverton actually.'

'Just outside, is it?'

'Yes.' His face brightened. 'Do you know it?'

'Lucky guess.' She smiled. 'Are you on holiday?'

He hesitated before answering. 'Sort of. I've always wanted to come here.' Another hesitation, as though he were reluctant to say more. Eventually he did. 'Um, actually, I'm looking for dodo eggs.'

Holly's eyebrows raised in interest.

'Yes, I know what you're thinking. But even part of an egg would do.'

'Are you an anthropologist or something?'

'Um, biologist actually.'

Holly was instinctively working again. This bloke could make an interesting addendum to the story she'd been sent to cover. Just the kind of off-beat activity *Out of Focus* liked to print – dedicated biologist hot on the trail of dodo eggs.

Their drinks arrived. 'Cheers!' Justin raised his condensation-covered glass. 'Aahh. Wonderful. Great beer. How's the wine?'

Holly sipped her drink. 'Just like home.'

'Then they've given you South African wine.' He peered at the bar chit. 'Charged for French, though. You have to watch that.' But he made no attempt to recall the waiter.

Holly liked that. She hated men who made a fuss, usually for effect. Dennis had done rather a lot of that she remembered. He'd have upbraided the waiter for cheating them and demanded either a refund or a glass of French wine. All in a very loud voice so that those around him would know he was a man to be reckoned with.

'What kind of article are you doing?'

It was Holly's turn to hesitate. Before making contact with Connor Maguire and establishing just how willing he would be in cooperating with the story, she probably shouldn't say anything to a stranger. 'Just the usual touristy thing.'

Justin had noticed the slight reticence on her part. His eyes flickered briefly, surprise perhaps at her need to think about it. He nodded, only asking, 'Are you a travel writer?'

'If the brief calls for it.'

'Bit of an all-rounder then?'

'Yes. You could say that.'

There it was again. A glimmer of something. Gone as quickly as it came. 'You don't give much away, do you?' He flashed a quick, lopsided smile.

'Nothing to give away,' Holly countered lightly. 'I'm writing a travel piece – beaches, resorts, restaurants, arts and crafts, the usual.'

'I'm being nosy. Sorry. Bad habit.' He shrugged apologetically.

Holly smiled in acceptance and changed the subject. 'How long are you staying here?'

'My visa runs out in three weeks. They'd only give me a month. I just hope it's long enough.'

'You can get it renewed though.' She told him where.

'Really! They didn't mention that when I arrived.' His eyes widened suddenly. 'Wow!' he breathed.

Realising that he was staring intently over her shoulder, Holly turned. Coming towards them was the most strikingly beautiful Chinese girl she'd ever seen. Like a model on a catwalk, head slightly to one side, looking neither left nor right, a small smile on her lips. She walked almost in slow motion, with a languid grace, knowing that every eye in the place was on her. Every eye but one. Holly was more interested in the man behind her. Photographs didn't do him justice. Tall, dark and handsome never even came close. He was better looking than a man had any right to be. And he carried himself with unconscious ease. Connor Maguire in person nearly took her breath away.

'Wow's right,' she muttered. Covering this man's activities was her job. Looking at him was a bonus.

'I do apologise.' Justin was blushing. 'She's beautiful, isn't she?'

'Very,' Holly agreed. *And as hard and cold as pack ice.* Instinct told her that the exquisite exterior of the Chinese girl did not reveal all. Her smile was too set, her eyes too calculating. Arrogance radiated from the way she held herself. Realising that an intrusion had to be the last thing Connor Maguire would expect, and that she might benefit from catching him off-guard, Holly rose from the table. 'Will you excuse me a moment, Justin? I must say hello to her companion.'

The beautiful twosome had just been seated when Holly approached. 'Pardon me, but are you Connor Maguire?'

He dragged his gaze lazily away from the Chinese girl. 'Who wants to know?'

'Holly Jones. You know my father, I believe. Quinn Longford-Jones.'

Dark eyes narrowed. 'So what do you want?' He made it plain enough. She was about as welcome as a swarm of angry bees.

Holly ignored his obvious reluctance. 'I've been sent to cover your search –'

'No publicity,' he snapped.

Committed, she pressed on. 'The organisation who might benefit want –'

'I said, no publicity.'

'Unfortunately –'

'You're the unfortunate one, Miss Jones. You've come a long way for nothing. Now, if you'll excuse us.'

Holly stood her ground. The Chinese girl was watching her with amusement, which irritated the hell out of her. 'I don't like this any more than you, Mr Maguire, but unfortunately I don't get to choose my assignments. You can cooperate or you needn't bother, but one way or the other, the story will be written. Take your pick.' She turned without waiting for a response, bright pink spots of indignation and embarrassment burning hotly on her cheeks.

The toasted sandwiches had arrived and provided a welcome diversion. Justin correctly guessed she was angry and wisely held his tongue. All he said was, 'Food's good.'

Holly attacked her snack as though it was responsible for Maguire's arrogant dismissal. A refusal to cooperate was standard fare for any journalist who covered the rich and famous, so how had this bloody man raised her hackles without even trying? She was aware of Justin's glances and grateful for his silence. Downing the last drop of the now warm wine, Holly thanked him for his company and left, saying that she had to make a phone call. She deliberately avoided walking past Maguire's table.

It was only when she was passing through the foyer that she realised Justin had been left with the bill. In her room she called Quinn, forgetting the time difference of six hours. It was eleven fifteen in the morning in Mauritius, five fifteen in the afternoon in Sydney. Her father, however, was still at his desk.

'Hi Big Shot! How's Mauritius?'

'Give me a break, I've only just got here.' She sank onto the bed, rubbing fingers at the tension headache which was developing.

'Met up with Maguire yet?'

'That's why I'm calling. He's not interested.'

'Make him interested, sweetheart. That's your job.'

'Thanks, Quinn. I knew I could rely on you.'

'So what do you want from me? A lever?'

'That might help.' Her father usually had one or two up his sleeve.

'Couple of free ads for one of his companies.'

'Not good enough.'

'A feature article on the AIDS research program over and above the one we're writing about him. He knows the score – he's newsworthy but readers are a little jaded when it comes to AIDS research. Maguire might jump at the chance to get them some publicity.'

'That might do it.'

'Okay, see what you can do. By the way, what do you think of him?'

Holly minced no words. 'He's an arrogant asshole.'

Her father's chuckle came down the line. 'Knew you'd like him, sweetheart.'

Talking to Quinn was calming her down.

Maguire was simply a problem. Problems could be solved. She hadn't liked him much before and their brief meeting had changed nothing. *To hell with him*, Holly thought, remembering Justin and his rather strange mission. 'Could you use a piece about a biologist looking for dodo eggs?' she asked, knowing her father would probably say yes. It was just bizarre enough to be right up his street.

Quinn did not disappoint. 'Yeah! Great stuff! Is he famous?'

'I have no idea.'

'Be better if he were. Is he a bit dippy?'

'Seems normal enough.'

'What's he after dodo eggs for? DNA testing or something? Find out, it might be interesting. Listen, I've had a thought. See what you can dig up about Robert Surcouf – you know, the pirate king. Late eighteenth century, I think. Try to tie it in with Maguire's treasure. You must keep on the Maguire story. You can do it, I know you can. Okay, must go. Got two calls waiting. Talk to you soon. Bye.'

The connection was broken, leaving Holly with the familiar feeling that she'd only said half the things she'd meant to while her father's nimble mind leapt effortlessly from one subject to the next – a sure sign that he did not actually wish to hear what it was that he suspected she wanted to say. When it suited him, Quinn tended to talk *at* you, rather than *to* you. It was a tactic that worked well for him, and despite the fact that she was very used to it, one that inevitably left her feeling she'd been outsmarted.

Holly went back to The Badamier to offer Connor Maguire a carrot for his cooperation. He'd gone, and so had Justin. She decided to walk along the beach and suss out the exclusive Royal Palm. If Maguire wasn't there she could always leave a message.

Holly was about to find out the hard way that walking from one small inlet to another needed the agility of a mountain goat. True, the jumble of black volcanic basalt round the point wasn't high, but it seemed to go on forever and there wasn't a flat surface to be seen. It would have been quicker and easier to walk the long way round, along the road.

The foyer of the Royal Palm was so plush, so exquisitely furnished and decorated that Holly felt out of place, fearing she'd be asked to pay for simply drawing breath.

'I believe you have a Mr Connor Maguire staying here.'

The receptionist turned to her computer screen and paused. 'What name again please?'

'Maguire. Connor Maguire.'

'We have no guest by that name,' she said, without touching the keyboard.

'Are you sure?'

'Yes, madam.'

Surprised, Holly rock-hopped back to the Merville. She'd have bet on Maguire staying at the Royal Palm. Perhaps he was. It was a big hotel. The receptionist hadn't actually looked him up and she could hardly remember the names of all the guests.

It was probably hotel policy not to pass out information of that nature. She'd telephone later, act like she knew he was there. Now what? She checked her watch. Half-past twelve. 'Sod it.' The tropical blue water of the lagoon looked so inviting. 'Swim time.'

A neatly folded message was waiting with her room key in reception.

'A Mr Maguire will call you in the morning.'

Well! A change of heart perhaps? An apology? Not his style. No point in speculating, just have to wait and see. There was nothing she could do until he called. She changed into a swimsuit, collected up a towel, sunglasses, sunscreen and book, and took herself off to the beach, satisfyingly convinced that Maguire must have remembered his manners.

'Miss Longford-Jones. It's Connor Maguire.'

She ruled out an apology, his voice held no trace of one. 'Jones will do just fine.'

'I'm prepared to speak to you.'

She bit back a sarcastic response. 'Where are you staying? The Royal Palm, I suppose.'

'Why on earth would you assume that?' He sounded quite taken aback. 'I'm renting a room with a private family.'

It was Holly's turn to be startled. If not the island's premier hotel, she'd have expected four stars at least. 'Where?'

'Just down the road in Grand Baie. Why don't we meet for lunch?'

'Suits me. Where do you suggest?'

'Sunset Cafe. It's on the new boulevard where the deep sea fishing boats berth.'

'I'll find it.'

They arranged a time and said goodbye. Holly hung up wondering what had caused Maguire's change of heart.

Despite having a Grand Baie address, the Merville was not actually inside the bay itself but just outside the mouth. To reach the main shopping area required a twenty-minute walk along the congested and narrow Royal Road. The footpath came and went, mainly the latter, and self-preservation took on new meaning as Holly ducked backwards off the road into yet another hedge to avoid being swatted by a passing bus. However, the weather was balmy, exotic flowers bloomed in profusion, spicy food aromas filled the air and fellow pedestrians called a friendly 'bonjour' as they passed.

The centre of Grand Baie was designed for tourists. Holly spent the morning wandering through the curio, craft and clothing shops. There was an amazing variety of goods for sale but by far and away the most interesting find for Holly was the Model Ship Gallery, where the manager took her into the workshop itself. For nearly an hour she observed, enchanted, as old sailing ships, like the *Bounty*, were re-created in miniature, bringing alive every tiny detail under the dexterous fingers of the model builders. Finally, after glancing at her watch and promising to return later, she reluctantly left to meet Connor Maguire.

He was there already and automatically rose to his feet as she approached. 'Miss Jones. A woman who is punctual. A rare treat.'

'A man who is early. Even rarer. Please call me Holly.'

'Connor.' He indicated a chair. 'Please.'

Holly sat down and got straight to the point. 'Yesterday your refusal to speak with me bordered on hostile. Today you invite me to lunch. What changed your mind?'

Dark eyes probed hers as if he were seeking confirmation or reassurance. Holly stared back, waiting. He seemed wary, almost distant. She did not anticipate his apology.

'It was rude of me. I'm sorry.'

Holly relaxed and leaned forward. 'I'm used to it. It goes with the territory. But thanks anyway.'

His eyes softened a little. 'You don't look tough enough to be a journalist.'

'I didn't know it was a prerequisite but I'm tougher than I look.'

He smiled at that, then grew serious again. 'Do you know much about me?'

The question took her by surprise. 'Only what I've read.'

He pulled a face. 'Then my behaviour yesterday must have confirmed your impression.'

'What impression would that be?'

He didn't answer but looked down at his hands and said, 'I really don't want the publicity this time. Not on a personal level.'

'Oh come on! Everything you do attracts

publicity, invited or otherwise. If you don't want it, try doing something ordinary.'

Holly noticed how thick his lashes were. She leaned back, watching him until he looked up. At close range, what she had taken as perfection had minor flaws. One eye was set ever so slightly higher than the other. There was a tiny scar above the left eyebrow and another on his chin. She remembered reading something about a ski-boat accident, which might account for them. His two front teeth overlapped fractionally, but when he smiled at her any dental flaw was completely overridden by the sudden appearance of dimples on both cheeks. 'Ordinary?' he quizzed, amused.

Holly smiled back. 'Toned down, anyway.'

Connor gave an elaborate shrug. 'I am what I am.'

'Then why be shy of publicity this time? It's not your style.'

He didn't respond immediately, seeming to weigh up how much to say. Finally, he reached a decision. 'If you agree to stick to the treasure I'll cooperate.'

'That's why I'm here. The treasure, the AIDS research program which, incidentally, Quinn is prepared to feature on its own, pirates generally, that sort of thing.'

'Nothing about me?'

Holly wouldn't go that far. 'Anything I write will be run past you first. How's that?'

He nodded slowly. 'Okay,' he said eventually. 'I'll tell you a story.'

Got him! 'Should I start the tape?'

'If you like.'

A waiter hovered and they each ordered a light lunch and coffee.

'Three hundred years ago,' Connor began, 'this whole area was crawling with brigands and cut-throats from just about every seafaring nation in the world.'

'I know.'

The interruption drew a brief frown. 'My story concerns only one of them. An ancestor, Captain William Maguire.' He paused, waiting for comment. When she remained silent, Connor continued. 'He was born in the latter half of the seventeenth century into an Irish aristocratic family, but being the youngest son, he could only hope for a settlement and a modest allowance. As was the custom in those days, William was expected to take up the cloth and join the priesthood. I guess the prospect didn't appeal to him. The lad ran away and went to sea. He must have been a bit on the wild side though, because within a very short time he'd gone from legitimate sailor to pirate.'

'How do you know all this?'

'I'll get to that. William began his predatory adventures in the Caribbean, but as soon as he had command of his own ship, set off for the west coast of Africa. He was obviously very good at what he did and became exceptionally wealthy.'

'Is that where your family fortune originated?'

'Some certainly benefited from his activities in this part of the world.'

'Not a fact you'd want generally known, I imagine.'

Connor shrugged. 'Doesn't bother me one way or the other. I wasn't there. Not many wealthy families could withstand a vigorous investigation into where their inheritance came from.'

'Doesn't it make you just a little uncomfortable? You said it yourself, brigands and cut-throats. They didn't stop at theft. They murdered and raped as well.'

His dark eyes were unreadable but she sensed it might be a sore point. 'As I said, William Maguire headed for the warmer waters of the Indian Ocean and established a semi-permanent base here in what was then called Maurice.'

'The Sea of Zanj.'

'You know about that, do you?'

'I had a thing about stories of the *Arabian Nights*.'

He grinned lopsidedly and a dimple appeared.

Holly had to force herself not to gaze at it. 'Why are you telling me this?'

'It's interesting. Far more so than simply following me around the place.'

She let that go. Besides, he was right, it was interesting. 'Please go on.'

'The British East India Company had a Captain Mackra commanding their ship, the *Cassandra*. When William Maguire started to plunder every trader that passed his way, the Poms fitted out a fleet and placed Captain Mackra in charge. After several close encounters with his pursuers, William decided to lay up in Madagascar for a while. But Mackra found him and the chase was on again. It was only Maguire's skill as a seaman that enabled him to avoid capture. Eventually he settled here, more or less permanently.

'For a spot of rape and pillage no doubt?'

'More like trade and running repairs.'

Holly raised her eyebrows and he inclined his head, acknowledging her point.

'What year are we talking about? Mauritius was still Dutch then, wasn't it?'

'No. The Dutch left in 1710. The French arrived in 1715. William settled here five years after that. It was another two years before French colonialists started arriving in any great numbers.'

'I read a bit about the history of Mauritius on the flight. It seems to have been passed around quite a lot.'

'Correct. This island has had a variety of colonial masters. Every time it changed hands, so did the name.'

'Can you remember them? It's good material for the tape.'

He nodded. 'Arab seamen discovered it in the tenth century. They called the island Dinarobin but made no attempt to settle here. Then the Portuguese came along and called the island Ilha do Cerne.'

'Swan Island. I like that.'

'You speak Portuguese?'

'No. But it's sort of like Spanish.'

'Spanish then?'

'I can muddle through.'

He raised his eyebrows appreciatively. 'A lady of many talents.'

'What happened next?'

'Not a lot. Virtually no-one actually lived here. About a hundred years after the Portuguese found this place, the Dutch arrived and claimed it for the Netherlands. They named it Maurice after the then Prince of Orange. The Portuguese didn't seem to mind, no-one contested ownership, and the Dutch set up a base station for their Dutch East India Company ships.'

Holly chipped in. 'They brought in slaves from Africa too.'

'Yes. For labour. They established sugar cane and tobacco here.'

'Exit the dodo.'

'No. Not straight away, and it was not strictly the Dutch who were to blame. The Portuguese had found them to be almost tame. And why wouldn't they be? They lived undisturbed on an island with no natural predators. Because there was no need for escape, pigeons, parrots and doves had virtually lost their ability to fly.'

'The dodo was a kind of pigeon, wasn't it?' Holly asked, thinking briefly of the article she planned to write about Justin Parker. No harm in killing two birds with one stone. She grinned inwardly at her own pun.

Connor nodded. 'About the size of a turkey.

They were killed for meat and sport. The Portuguese even tried exporting them to Europe but none survived. Monkeys and hogs, released on the island to ensure a steady supply of food, loved to eat dodo eggs. So did the rats that escaped off the ships. The poor bloody bird didn't stand a chance.'

'But the dodo disappeared during Dutch occupation, didn't it?'

'Yes. Only because they did nothing to protect it.' He gave her an approving glance. 'You've certainly done your homework.'

'I'm a journalist. What would you expect?'

'I've met some pretty thick members of the profession.'

Despite herself, Holly grinned outright. So had she.

Connor continued. 'The territory wasn't all that profitable and the Dutch simply lost interest and left. When William Maguire first arrived, he found the island deserted, save for a few other pirates who'd set up house here, a couple of hardy settlers and the slaves. As cut-throat a bunch as the one-time sailors may have been, they were frightened to death of the marrons . . .'

'The slaves?'

'Yes.' He fished a packet of cigarettes from his pocket. 'Do you smoke?'

'Only when I'm on fire.'

He put the packet back without lighting one. 'Enter the French. Once again, the island had a name change. Île de France. This time the place was used as a way station for the French East India

Company. About ten years later, immigrants started arriving from France. They developed the existing sugar and tobacco plantations, built a sugar mill and established an infrastructure of roads, ports, medical care, all that sort of thing.'

'The French East India Company collapsed, didn't it?'

'Late in the eighteenth century.' He nodded. 'The British navy claimed numerous islands in the Indian Ocean but, so far, they hadn't bothered with this place.'

'But your ancestor, William, was obviously dead by then. Did he stay here?'

'He took a fancy to the area around Grand Port. Lived to a ripe old age, too. He's buried there.'

Holly remembered the conversation she'd had with Quinn. 'Do you know anything about a self-proclaimed pirate king in Port Louis?'

'After William's time, but yes, Robert Surcouf was his name. He created a sanctuary for the pirates. Literally hundreds of them settled on Île de France. Bloody awful place by then. They liberated the slaves then released bloodhounds and hunted them down for sport. The poor devils didn't stand a chance. Some made for the centre of the island where they were reasonably safe, planting a few of their own crops but basically living a hunting and gathering existence. A few of the women, perhaps to save their own skins, married pirates. It was a common enough practice back in those days. William had also taken a slave wife. Being married and having children didn't seem to slow him down though. He continued to loot any ship passing. It was only about fifty years after his death that the British East India Company had had enough and sent in the Royal Marines.'

'Hang on.' Holly's brow furrowed, trying to remember. 'The Treaty of Paris in 1814 gave Britain Île de France, Rodrigues and the Seychelles. Am I right?'

'One hundred per cent.'

'Good. We seemed to flash through a few centuries there. I just needed to get my bearings. So the Brits changed the name again?'

'Back to Maurice. Though they insisted on calling it Mauritius. A lot of the French settlers were deported back to France. That included the pirates. Most were executed, although some returned with a full pardon.'

'And many buried their treasure before leaving.'

'Everyone did, whether they were sent away or not. They didn't trust the marrons, the British or each other. Taking their fortunes with them just wasn't an option.'

'So you think there are still places here where buried treasure . . .' She broke off. 'It sounds a bit far-fetched. Surely it's all been found by now?'

'More than likely. There's just one thing.'

'What's that?'

'William Maguire kept a journal. It was supposed to have been sent home to Ireland just before he died, to his sister, the only person in the world he felt he could trust. Unfortunately, life hadn't been all that kind to her. She lived well enough, on the family estate, but was – how can I put it – emotionally and mentally –'

'Gaga,' Holly offered pointedly.

He smiled. 'Politically incorrect, I fear.'

'So what?' She shrugged. 'It sure as hell beats playing footsy with words.'

The waiter returned with their meal and fussed around the table for a while. When he'd gone, Holly said, 'This journal. I take it you have it now?'

'Correct.'

'How did you find it? For that matter, where did you find it?'

Connor speared a piece of tomato with his fork. 'The Maguire clan has its share of historians. The family tree is comprehensive and up to date. My mother keeps in touch with dozens of my father's distant relatives who she's never even met. She's obsessed with keeping tabs on the Australian Maguires. It's a disease with her.' The tomato found its way to his mouth and he chewed reflectively for a while. Swallowing, he went on. 'I took time out earlier this year –'

'When your second marriage broke up.'

He blinked but did not otherwise comment. 'I went to Ireland, to the family estates.' The smile was sardonic. 'It was quite an experience.'

'Not all good by the sound of things.'

'Some good. The Irish make loyal friends and dedicated enemies.'

Her eyes invited an explanation.

'One side of the family welcomed me with open arms. The other regarded their antipodean relative with the deepest of suspicion, although they were scrupulous in their efforts to hide it from me.'

'Why? Why the hostility?'

'It goes right back to William and a cousin of his called Kavanagh. Yes,' he added, when he saw her look of disbelief, 'back to the eighteenth century. I told you they are a dedicated lot. Not one of them knows the truth but for generations they've managed to keep the feud alive. As recently as seventy-odd years ago, a girl from one side of the family had the misfortune to fall in love with her cousin from the other. Her parents were so shocked they had her committed to an asylum where the poor creature eventually went mad. That's how real it still is.'

'That's insane,' Holly burst out.

He grinned. 'You're not listening. The girl went insane.'

'Sounds like a bad B-grade movie.'

'Is there any other kind?'

They were getting off the track. She redirected their conversation. 'Which side of the Maguires are you from?'

'It gets kind of convoluted but I'm directly descended from William's side.'

'From William himself?'

'No. From his brother, the eldest son, Gilchrist.'

'Oh.'

'You sound disappointed.'

Holly shrugged. 'Tying you in with a pirate would have been good. Nice story angle.'

'Sorry. Gilchrist, as far as I can tell, was landed gentry. Probably as boring as hell.'

'So where did you find the journal?'

'In an attic.'

Holly waited.

'The house belonged to the wrong side. Kavanagh's family.'

'Ah. And I don't suppose you told them by any chance?'

'No.' His eyes challenged her. 'I didn't know what it was then, and anyway, I didn't like them.'

She paused, fork halfway to her mouth. 'You didn't *like* them?' she repeated slowly.

'I'm a Maguire,' he excused himself.

Holly's food waved in the air. 'That's it? You justify blatant theft because they were the wrong Maguires?'

'They stole it from William's family.' Connor must have realised that his excuse sounded petulant. 'Well,' he amended quickly, 'the journal was entrusted to someone for delivery but that person inadvertently handed it to the wrong family. They should have given it back. It's part of William's history, not theirs.'

'You said a while ago that William was supposed to have sent the journal back to Ireland. I take it then that he didn't.'

'He couldn't have. He'd hardly have sent it to the wrong family. Besides, there was a note tucked into the front from someone called Aroon saying she was sending it back to Ireland for safe-keeping. The date on it was 1873. That's over a hundred and twenty years after William died.'

'And Aroon was?'

He shrugged. 'Haven't a clue.'

'I thought your family tree was up to date.'

'Not the Mauritian side, not William's descendants.'

'Okay, so the journal stayed here until the middle of last century and was then delivered to the wrong side of the family.'

'I'm guessing a bit, but it seems likely. And I'm also speculating that whoever received the journal read it and then hid it away without saying anything to anybody.'

'What makes you think that?'

'Stories they told me when I was there, obviously handed down through generations, that bore no resemblance to what William had written in his journal.'

'What exactly were you doing poking around their attic?'

'When my mother heard I was going to Ireland she suggested that I ask both sides of the family for any information that might help her fill in a couple of remaining gaps in our family tree. No-one over there thought it strange. They were probably relieved that I was occupied and nobody had to spend too much time entertaining me. Took me to the attic and told me to help myself. I don't believe that the present generation have any interest in what's up there. Judging by the cobwebs and dust, no-one had been in the attic for decades. It's my guess that nobody knew about the journal.'

'But why don't you like them? It's got to be more than old Maguire feuds.'

Connor considered his answer for some time. 'I didn't actually like either side very much. The whole damned lot of them are inbred, arrogant and selfish.'

Holly's eyebrows went up.

'It's true. Not one of them had a nice thing to say about another. Not even those on the same side of the family. I don't know how they can stand being around each other.'

'Still, you took what doesn't belong to you.'

'They don't need the money. Look, call me a perverse Aussie if you like, but the idea of snatching William's treasure from under their noses appeals to me.'

Holly was beginning to feel irritated. Connor Maguire would, no doubt, receive a huge amount of positive publicity if he did find the treasure and donate it to charity. The public would never know that his generosity was driven by a desire to pull a fast one over his Irish relatives. She forced her thoughts back to the interview.

'So did William's journal explain what really happened between him and Kavanagh?'

'Oh yes. When William arrived in Maurice to settle, Kavanagh was already here. Kavanagh stole William's ship and sailed to Bourbon, leaving William and two others stranded here. The Dutch had deserted but the French were yet to settle. Life must have been very hard.'

'Wait.' Holly wagged her finger sideways. 'Go back a bit. Where is Bourbon?'

'It's the name the pirates gave to Réunion.'

'Okay.'

'Kavanagh lived the good life on Bourbon. He gave up pirating when he was in his early forties and returned home to Ireland. His contribution to the Maguire coffers ensured that future generations would be well cared for. He told the rest of the family that William had been killed.'

'And then, a hundred and twenty years later, William's journal turns up.'

'Yes.'

'Hold on a minute. This makes no sense. Three hundred years ago, give or take a couple of decades, one cousin rats on another. This sets off a family row even though none of them seem to know exactly why. When some form of evidence does eventually come to light, one side of the family learns the truth and they keep it to themselves. What the hell are the current generation fighting about? Seems to me neither side has a bloody clue.'

'Whose version would you prefer?'

'Both.'

'Okay. The Kavanagh lot claim that when their boy returned with untold riches, William's family accused him of treachery. That in itself was enough to cause a rift. On top of that, Kavanagh fell for one of William's sisters. The two eloped. She was shunned by both sides and eventually committed suicide.'

Holly nodded. 'That would do it.'

'William's family relate a story that is similar except they claim that Kavanagh abducted the sister and held her his prisoner until, in desperation, the poor girl took her own life, leaving a letter to her parents telling that Kavanagh had boasted about tricking William.'

'But Kavanagh's family would finally have learned the truth when the journal arrived.'

'Some of them, certainly. But remember that the feud had been going on for such a long time by then that I suppose they simply couldn't admit to being wrong. Do try to remember that they're Irish.' He shrugged. 'Besides, there was still the matter of William's sister. Kavanagh's family accused her of lying.'

Holly wiped her mouth with her napkin and checked that the tape was still running. 'Why put yourself to all the bother of finding William's treasure, if it exists? You don't need the money either. Wouldn't it be simpler to write a cheque for AIDS research and be done with it?'

Connor raised one eyebrow. 'How romantic,' he said at last. 'Here I am living a boyhood dream and you suggest I simply write a cheque.'

'Is that what this is? Nothing but an adventure?'

'Of course.'

'Well,' Holly said tightly, 'it must be nice for some.'

'I get the impression you don't approve. What's your problem?'

A glint had appeared in his eyes. Holly didn't know if it was anger or amusement. Nor did she care. Irritation boiled over. She had said to Quinn that Maguire was frivolous, now she knew he wasn't. He was downright childish. Shaking her head in disbelief, the words came slowly. 'Something as important as AIDS research is not a game. You could . . . could . . . afford to help –'

'There's no harm in having a little fun while I'm helping.' His tone was mild, he even smiled, but the look in his eyes intensified.

Holly stared back, undaunted by what she was fairly certain was rising anger. 'Just think about this,' she gritted. 'While you're out there having fun, people are dying of AIDS. Your cheque could make a difference. You're playing with people's lives.'

His voice went hard. 'Choose your words carefully. You're not in a position to judge and I'm not accustomed to criticism from someone who hasn't a clue what she's talking about.'

'You're not accustomed to criticism. Full stop.'

He shrugged, signifying that her opinion of him didn't matter.

Holly threw down her napkin and stood up. 'I'm sorry, Mr Maguire. I've just decided your cheap thrills are not worth the paper a story would use.' She stalked from the restaurant forgetting, in her anger, to pick up the tape recorder.

THREE

She literally bumped into Justin Parker. He turned from the reception desk and Holly, who was kicking herself for her unprofessional behaviour with Connor Maguire, ran straight into him. She nearly snapped 'Watch where you're going,' before she saw who it was. Instead, she said, 'Sorry. My fault.'

'I was just trying to phone your room. Thought you might like a swim.'

He'd already had too much sun. His nose and cheeks were bright red and cream was smeared over his lips. Wearing sandals, brown shorts and a red and white striped shirt, Justin looked absurdly out of place, sort of defiantly English. Irrational as her annoyance might have been, Holly gave in to it. 'I really don't think you should get any more sun.'

He looked ruefully at his arms. 'Mad dogs and Englishman . . .' He laughed self-consciously.

Her anger dissipated and she smiled. It wasn't Justin's fault that Connor Maguire was a shallow thrill-seeker who, far from being the compassionate benefactor he wanted the public to see him as, was an arrogant, self-centred plutocrat, seeking amusement for his own satisfaction. 'I wouldn't mind a swim but I have to make a phone call first. Meet you at the pool in about fifteen minutes.'

From her room she called Quinn at home. When he came on the line she got straight to the point. 'This is not going well. How you can take him seriously is beyond me.'

'Simmer down. What happened?'

Holly told him. 'The story's interesting enough,' she concluded. 'I can probably get him to change his mind and let me cover the search. I was pretty rude to him but someone with a hide that thick may not even notice. My problem is, I'm not sure I want to give him the publicity. He doesn't bloody deserve it. He's an asshole, Quinn. He's playing God with people's lives and doesn't care who knows it. I can't stand the man.'

Silence was loud on the line while Quinn chewed on his daughter's outburst. Finally, 'He does, you know. Deserve the publicity, that is.'

'Then you must know something you're not telling me.'

More silence. Quinn was not normally indecisive. Holly braced herself.

'Look, I must insist this time. Get back to him. Grovel. I don't care how you do it, just get the story.'

'Why? Why is it so important?'

The line remained ominously quiet for a good ten seconds. 'I can't tell you.'

Holly brushed a hand through her hair. 'You're not listening to me, Quinn.'

'I hear you loud and clear.'

She doubted it and said so.

'I mean it, Holly. Cover the man any which way you can. Get close to him and stick with it. I'm afraid I insist, sweetheart.'

Jeez! Holly pulled the telephone away from her ear and stared at it. Quinn certainly had the wind up over this one. Her professional mind knew he was right. What was wrong with her? She'd covered other stories where she had not been particularly fond of the people involved. She was allowing Maguire to get to her and it both surprised and irked her.

'You still there?'

'Okay. I'll put my personal objections aside and go after the story. I get the distinct impression that he's lying about not wanting publicity. He was keen enough to tell me how he came to learn about the treasure. I've got a funny feeling about this one, Quinn. Maguire uses journalists all the time. I think he's playing with us.'

Quinn made no comment. Her father knew something she didn't, Holly was sure of it. But she'd never get it out of him. Quinn's ability to keep a secret was awesome. Better to put it out of her mind, at least for now, and concentrate on finding a way round Maguire's pretence that he didn't want publicity. She had a thought. 'There's one tack I could take.'

'What's that?'

'Promise him that the story won't break until he's ready.'

'It's worth a try.' Quinn sounded regretful.

'You'd honour that?' She'd seen her father conveniently forget promises in the interests of a scoop.

'Of course.' Now he was indignant. 'What do you take me for?'

'Don't ask, I might just tell you.'

Quinn laughed and changed the subject. 'What's the weather like?'

'Perfect.'

'Lucky you. It's still pissing with rain in Sydney.'

She glanced at her watch. 'Got to go. I'm meeting the dodo man in five.'

'Don't waste too much time on that,' Quinn advised. 'Get after Maguire.'

'I will, I will. I just need to calm down first.'

They said goodbye. Hanging up, Holly wondered what it was that Quinn wasn't telling her. And why.

Justin Parker sat in deep shade slightly back from the water. He was also in deep conversation with the striking Chinese girl who had been with Connor Maguire yesterday. Holly draped her towel over a chair and dived into the pool, swimming up and down ten times before climbing out. Justin was watching. The Chinese woman had gone.

'Very professional,' he called out.

'I've done a bit of training,' she admitted, walking towards him towelling her hair. 'Lacked the commitment to take it further.' She sat down opposite him. *Will he explain the Chinese woman?*

'I ordered you a drink. Fresh lime juice and soda. Okay?'

'Great. Thanks.' *Will he hell!*

'How'd you go today?'

Holly pulled a face. 'Don't ask.'

He looked surprised. 'Problems? Surely not. Publicity can only be good for tourism.'

Holly remembered that she'd told Justin she was doing a tourist piece. 'A freelance journo doesn't stick with one story. I'd like to cover your dodo search too, if you've no objection that is. The holiday destination article is easy but I'm also supposed to be covering some high-flying wacko's search for buried treasure. The gentleman I need to interview doesn't want the publicity. The publisher who sent me won't take no for an answer. I've been told to grovel.'

There was a sudden uneasy look on Justin's face which, despite his best attempts, he was unable to conceal. 'Buried treasure?' he finally drawled mockingly. 'How very droll.'

Holly mentally cursed herself. She was supposed to be offering Maguire privacy until he was ready. 'A place with a history like Mauritius always has rumours,' she said lamely.

'I'm sure.' He smiled suddenly. 'Can't see you grovelling, though.'

'Oh I've done it before. And it won't be the last time. Goes with the job.' She changed the subject. 'What about you? Any luck?'

'Not today.'

'I meant what I said. A story about your search

and what happens if you find anything could be fascinating. Do you mind?'

Justin was a fraction slow in replying. 'No. Of course not.'

His hesitation alerted Holly's journalistic instincts. 'Is it supposed to be classified information?'

'Not exactly.' He looked away. 'No more than any other scientific endeavour. It's . . .' he searched for the right words, 'it's just that so much of what we do results in nothing more than a waste of time. The press love to pick up on how much government money is spent on what they think is a wild goose chase.'

Holly grinned at his unintentional pun.

He looked back at her, shrugged and spread his hands. 'You lot don't seem to appreciate that for every success, every major breakthrough, there are hundreds, even thousands of failures. That's the way it works.'

'Not to mention the competitiveness of your business,' Holly guessed out loud. 'You do rather like to make a grand announcement once everything is neatly sewn up.'

Justin nodded. 'I suppose we do.'

'So why be coy about your project? Science cracked the transference of genetic characteristics decades ago. I assume you're working on a DNA experiment of some kind. Please correct me if I'm wrong.'

He didn't answer, just looked at her.

'Jesus!' The penny dropped. 'You're going to try

and twin with the helical chain of a pigeon, aren't you? This goes much further than Dolly the sheep. You want to bring back the dodo.'

He frowned. 'It's not that simple.'

'I'll just bet it isn't but that's the guts of it, isn't it?'

'Yes,' he admitted. 'Put frankly, that's exactly what we're attempting to do.' He seemed to relax suddenly. 'Okay, I'll talk to you provided you give me a fair hearing and a sympathetic verdict. Too much is written about the cost of research.'

Holly shook her head. 'The direction of an article is dictated by the person writing it, Justin. Convince me your work is worthwhile and that's what I'll say.'

He didn't like that and let it show.

Holly went on. 'It's a chance you'll have to take.'

'Then perhaps we'd better forget it,' he said tightly. 'There's too much riding on the outcome for misinformed publicity to diminish the importance of this search.'

She hadn't expected that.

'Besides,' he went on. 'I'd have to clear it with my colleagues first.'

'Suit yourself,' Holly responded airily. The cat was out of the bag anyway. She had her story. Time spent in Japan on the snow monkey assignment had resulted in pages of unpublished but thoroughly researched information about DNA and its potential ramifications. A couple of days' further investigation, a chat with a biologist acquaintance back home and some background on the dodo was all she needed. The piece would virtually write itself. All Justin had to provide was the name of the institution, or university, funding his project. That could wait. He probably wouldn't tell her if she asked now.

The silence between them was not a comfortable one. Holly sought to break it. 'I left you with the bill last night. Sorry. Let me buy you dinner.'

'I'm not sure I'm free.'

Holly wondered if his churlishness was due to the realisation that she already knew enough to write her story about him. 'I may see you later then. Must go now. One more swim then it's back to work.' When she climbed from the pool, Justin was gone.

The priority now was to locate Maguire. He'd said he was staying just down the road. Where to start, though? Couldn't exactly knock on doors until she found him. She was on the point of leaving her room when the telephone rang.

'Holly Jones.'

'Don't get mad and hang up. This is Connor Maguire.'

Holly wasted no time. 'If we guarantee not to publish until you are ready, will you allow me to do the story?'

Maguire was not inclined to waste it either. 'You left your tape recorder on the table.'

She ignored that. 'Straightforward story. The research program, high-profile adventurer and hidden treasure. Nothing private. No mention of the journal or how you came by it.'

'You'll probably want it back. I'll bring it over if you like.'

'Are you listening, Maguire? Look, give me a break. I'm sorry. I run off at the mouth sometimes. I was out of line at lunch.'

'That's one each then.'

She knew what he meant. 'How about it?'

'You give your word? Nothing published until I say so?'

'Mine and my father's.'

'That's a worry.'

Holly grinned. Sometimes he could be downright likeable. 'Trust me.'

'Okay.' She'd give him this. When he had to make up his mind quickly, there was no hesitation. 'And yes, I'd like it back.'

'Have dinner with me. I'll bring the journal, you might like to read it. I don't mind if you mention it in your article.'

'Yes to both. Thank you.'

'Don't mention it. I'll come to the hotel. Meet you in the bar at seven thirty.'

Connor was perched at the bar talking to a man Holly didn't recognise. Tall and attractive in a flamboyant kind of way, he was the sort of person people notice. Hair was partly grey, partly silver, as though some remnant of earlier colour still clung stubbornly on. He wore it long, caught back into a ponytail by a thin strip of leather. The tan was natural, built on time, his skin stretched tight over well-defined cheekbones and a high-bridged nose. A snowy white shirt with fuller than usual long sleeves was tucked into faded blue chinos and set off by a red and white kerchief tied at a jaunty angle around his neck. Connor saw her approaching and waved. 'Holly Jones, this is Raoul Dulac. Raoul, Holly Jones. Raoul's a local farmer,' he added.

Holly found her hand held between two giant paws as the French-Mauritian bent low and kissed her palm. Connor looked on, seemingly amused. 'Charmed,' murmured Raoul. 'Where are you from, ma cherie?'

She retrieved her hand and looked into pale blue eyes which regarded her with more than passing interest. 'Australia.'

'You are a friend of this reprobate?' he asked teasingly.

'Not really.' His gaze made her uncomfortable.

'Holly's covering my wanderings for a magazine piece,' Connor cut in. His stare told her that he'd prefer it if the exact reason for his presence on Mauritius was not mentioned.

'So, a journalist.'

'Freelance.'

'Which publication are you working for?'

'This time? *Out of Focus.*'

'Mmm. A pity. An article about our beautiful island would not be of interest to them.'

Despite its healthy overseas circulation, Holly was surprised that he'd actually heard of the magazine. She'd have thought Mauritius too far off the beaten track. 'I'm doing a tropical holiday paradise piece as well. There is a big demand for leisure time material. I can always sell it to the Sunday papers.'

'Then you must meet some real Franco-Mauritians. I will organise a lunch or dinner. You must come as well, Connor, I insist.'

Connor looked less than pleased. 'Thanks. I'd be delighted.'

After a few more minutes of small talk, Raoul left them saying, 'I'll be in contact in a day or so.' With a wave, he was gone.

'Quite a dynamo,' Holly commented. 'I get the impression he doesn't take no for an answer.'

Connor laughed. 'Like somebody else I could mention. But you're right, it's not part of his vocabulary. Probably never even heard the word. He's very used to getting his own way – most French Mauritians are. They've run things here for a long time.'

'And always at the expense of less fortunate individuals.'

'It was the way of things back then.'

'Still is, as far as I can see.'

'You disapprove?'

She considered her answer. 'Don't know,' she admitted candidly. 'I'd have to know more about it.'

The busy barman finally asked what they would like to drink. 'How about a bottle of champagne?' Connor suggested. 'We can have it brought to the table. This place is getting a bit crowded.'

'Sounds good to me.'

The barman snapped his fingers and a waiter

appeared immediately to show them to their table. Holly was aware that several women were watching Connor with open admiration. If he noticed, he didn't react. As soon as they were seated he took her tape recorder from his pocket and passed it across the table. 'Mustn't forget this.'

'Thanks.' Holly dropped it into her handbag.

'What, no taping this evening?'

'Not unless you have more on William.'

'I have his journal.' He passed over a plastic bag bearing the logo of a Grand Baie supermarket. 'That should answer most of your questions.'

Holly jiggled the bag. It wasn't very heavy. 'Must be pretty small.'

'Not a man of words, our William.' Deftly changing the subject, Connor told her about the family who were renting him a room.

Watching his face in the flickering candlelight, Holly was aware of two things. One, there was a sensitivity to it, a degree of uncertainty she had not previously noticed. Two, his quiet voice and easy manner had somehow awakened her own femininity – not a bad trick considering her recent betrayal and subsequent re-evaluation of the opposite sex.

Connor had ordered a sixty-eight vintage Dom Pérignon. When their champagne arrived he checked the label, felt the bottle with the back of his hand, nodded that the temperature was right and indicated that it may be opened. 'Here's to the mysteries of life,' he said, raising his glass.

Holly felt him watching her over the rim of his

tall-stemmed glass. She wondered what he was thinking. His words took her by surprise. 'Do you always dress to hide yourself?'

Certainly Holly hadn't taken any trouble with her appearance. Just pulled on the first blouse that came to hand – a loosely fitting blue cotton number which fell to her thighs – over white linen trousers. No make-up, barring lip gloss. She'd combed her hair with her fingers. 'I beg your pardon!' The comment was too personal.

He looked boyishly uncomfortable. 'Oops!'

'Please explain.' She set her glass down carefully, but found herself grinning at the words which had become part of Australian diction thanks to the would-be politician Pauline Hanson.

He ran a hand over his chin, a half smile, half grimace on his face. 'It's a gift of mine. Dive in, say what's on my mind, live to regret it. Did I offend you?'

She simply looked at him.

'Okay. Every time I see you, you look as though you're wearing clothes two sizes too big. Kind of makes me wonder what you think you're hiding. And . . .' he held up a hand when she opened her mouth, '. . . and fetching as it is, current fashion aside, it makes you look as if you need a bloody good hug.'

Holly's mouth formed a perfect 'O'.

'How am I doing?' The boyish questioning look was strangely appealing.

She swallowed hard. How had he done that? Subconsciously, Holly was frantically searching for a response to steer him away from her own personal demons. He'd just swept aside her armour and put his finger right on the button. She was unnerved by it. The only refuge was to use her profession as an excuse. 'I'm working. I like comfort. I'm not here to win any fashion award.'

The smile faded. There was something akin to regret in his dark eyes. 'Have it your way.'

Holly sought the safety of a subject change. 'How long do you intend to look for William's treasure?'

'A month, tops.'

'And then? What if you don't find it?'

'Go home, write another cheque, forget about it.'

'Write another . . . but I thought . . .' He was doing it again. He had her off balance. 'You said –'

'No. You assumed.'

Holly ducked her head. When she looked back he was grinning.

'Like I said on the phone: Jones one, Maguire one.'

'That's very magnanimous.' An edge had crept into her voice.

'What can I say? I'm nice like that.'

She owed him an apology. 'I'm sorry.' It was hard to say.

'You're forgiven. More champagne?'

Holly found it difficult to work out her emotions. Angry that he was making fun of her, embarrassed she'd jumped to the wrong conclusion and surprised that, despite this, she was actually enjoying his company. He was making her see a funny side that, she knew, she could never have found on her own. 'I mean it.' This time it was easy to say. 'I really am sorry.'

'You speak your mind. Nothing wrong with that.'

Quinn may have been right. Connor Maguire was a nice man. 'May I ask you a personal question?'

'You're the journalist.' He pulled a wry face. 'Just when I was beginning to like you.'

'That Chinese girl you were with at lunch yesterday. Who is she?'

With no change of expression, Connor said, 'Gretchen von Brandenstein.'

Holly burst out laughing.

'Why do you want to know?'

'I saw her again this afternoon. She was with someone I know slightly.'

'And you have a nose for news.'

'Actually, I hate my nose. No, it's just that there's something about her . . .'

Connor went serious suddenly. 'Stay away from her, Holly. She's a powerful lady. Her name is Madame Liang Song. She's about as friendly as a cornered honey badger.' When Holly looked surprised, he added, 'I mean it. Don't try sniffing around her. She'll eat you alive.'

Little did he realise that his words were only making Holly more interested.

'I'm going to Rodrigues next week,' Connor said suddenly. 'You can come if you like.'

'Flying?' Holly asked.

'Probably, although Raoul has offered to take me in his boat.'

'That would be fun.'

'Takes too long.'

'Is Raoul an old friend of yours?'

'Not exactly. More of a business colleague.'

He was not going to say more so she didn't push it. 'Why Rodrigues?'

'William lived there for a while. It's all in the journal. I just want to look at it.'

'How did he get there? He was supposed to be stranded here. Rodrigues is . . . what . . . six hundred kilometres north-east.'

'Came up with another boat. You'll see when you read it.'

Holly shook her head in amazement.

'What?' he quizzed. 'You don't believe me?'

'It's not that. I was just thinking how different life was back then. You want something, you go for it. Rodrigues? No problem. Grab some leaky old craft and set sail – it's up that way somewhere. What a life! No regulations, no form filling, no bureaucracy. Just do it. Scary but free.' She shook her head again. 'I'm not sure if they were mad in those days or we are now.' She hesitated. 'That's not a bad angle actually. Kind of ties William in with your lifestyle.'

'What?' Connor appeared genuinely puzzled.

'You do the same thing. Get a grip on life and yank with all your might.'

'And sometimes it collapses all round me.'

'Life's like that,' Holly said flatly.

He cocked an eyebrow at her but made no comment.

Holly quickly steered the conversation away from life and its little idiosyncrasies. 'This story is taking on a different shape from the one I had in mind originally.'

'William, you mean?'

'Sounds like there's some good meat in the journal.'

'If it's colour you want pull whatever you need from it. Quinn likes that sort of thing.'

'You've met him a couple of times, I believe.'

Inner amusement showed briefly in his eyes. 'A couple. He's quite a character.'

'You've featured more than once in *Out of Focus*. Becoming quite a regular.'

He took the comment seriously. 'I know what you think of me. That I'm nothing more than a bored, wealthy adventurer.' He shrugged. 'What can I say? It's true I get up to some unusual pranks. The media seem to like me. But it's all for a good cause.'

'Quinn said something like that too.'

'Life should be exciting. There's nothing illegal about having a bit of fun.'

'Fun,' she repeated, remembering Quinn's advice. She had no idea how wistful she sounded.

'Don't you have fun, Holly?'

They had opted for the set menu. Two steaming bowls of shark fin soup arrived. Holly was glad of the diversion and the question remained unanswered.

Perhaps sensing her discomfort, Connor kept the conversation reasonably impersonal throughout their meal. Holly learned surprisingly little about Connor Maguire. He was exceptionally good at saying nothing. Even direct questions such as, 'What do you do in your free time?' were deflected.

'Same as anyone. Relax. How about you?'

He had a knack of turning the conversation away from himself. At times, Holly felt that *he* was interviewing *her*. Over coffee and liqueurs, she said so, pointing out that if she were to write a piece about him it might be helpful if he didn't turn all his answers into questions.

'Boardroom tactics. I'll try not to. Won't be easy, though,' he added. 'People interest me. By the way, you still haven't said if you'll come to Rodrigues.'

'Yes. Yes I will. If I'm covering your search for William Maguire's treasure then I'm sorry to say you're stuck with me until I get the story.'

'Good. I'll make the arrangements.'

I wonder, she thought after they had said good-night and she made her way back to her room. *Is he interested in people? Or is he just dodging the questions?*

The journal of William Maguire was not much more than a ledger of seized booty, but it also included random snippets of his pirate years, a half-hearted apology for past activities and a scathing attack on his cousin Kavanagh. Couched in flowery terms and full of clichés, the faded brown writing remained surprisingly legible. Considering his unusual and interesting life, it was disappointingly short, with long gaps, sometimes years, between entries. There was a formal introduction, obviously written at a later date, inside the front cover:

Grand Port, Île de France, 25th November in the Year of Our Lord 1746

My name is William Makepeace Maguire, born in County Cork on the twelfth day of June in the Year of Our Lord 1679 the third son of George and Kathleen Maguire. My eldest brother, Gilchrist, so named after our paternal Grandfather, fell sole heir to the Maguire Estates. George, second son, secured a royal commission in the Irish Dragoon Guards. Thus it fell as my destiny to serve the Church but this expectation was not to be. I went to sea on the square-rigged trader, Isabella, only to be taken prisoner by Spanish corsairs off the straits of Bab-el-Maneb. In time, my endeavours earned sufficient respect to be released with my own vessel – the Serpent. The notes hereafter are my personal account of incidences and adventures as they occurred in subsequent years.

There followed a meticulous account of numerous successful engagements off the West African coast and vessels looted on the way south, round the Cape of Good Hope to the Sea of Zanj. The list of riches seemed endless – golden guineas and pieces of eight, Spanish silver ducats, personal jewellery confiscated from luckless passengers, pearls, amber and jade, Ming Dynasty china, Kang Hsi porcelain decorated with enamel and gold, Delft porcelain and pottery – and each had been carefully identified: where it came from, the ship's name and the year it had been seized. Holly noted that against some items, William Maguire had added an asterisk. Was this to indicate booty he kept for himself? If so, and assuming the treasure remained intact, it would be worth tens of millions of dollars today.

According to the dates against the inventory in the journal, William's life as a pirate stretched over a period of nearly forty years, from 1703 until 1739. And what a life it must have been, full of danger and excitement. Such a pity he didn't see fit to keep a more detailed account of his experiences. The few glimpses were tantalising, to say the least, but impossible to put together a full understanding of how things were back then. Reading the diary, Holly felt she'd been given limited access to a window into the past.

After reading through the cold, hard facts – pages and pages of riches captured – she settled down to learn more of the man. William began his account with an explanation of exactly where the Sea of Zanj lay and a generalisation about some of its characteristics.

Sinbad knew this sea. Bahr-el-Zanj, the sea of the blacks, the Sea of Zanj extends from the shores of Africa to 80 degrees longitude and is contained between the Equator and the Tropic of Capricorn. Within its warm waters lie many island groups – the Mascarenes, Madagascar, the Seychelles, Comoros, Aldabra Islands, Amirante, Galega to name but a few. A sea of treacherous currents and reefs, trade winds and cyclones but a sea of remarkable beauty and a bounty of marine creatures. It is a sea of magic and legends, of strange land creatures and even stranger people. It is the forgotten sea.

Having got that off his chest, William was then content to allow his inventory to do the talking for him. The next entry was to do with the unexpected arrival of one Captain Mackra and a fleet fitted out by the British East India Company with express orders to rid the Sea of Zanj of all pirate activity. William had been caught unawares and nearly lost his life. The event was sufficiently worrying to force a run down the west coast of Madagascar into open water, and back to the relative safety of Île de France. After a brief, though not very complimentary introduction of Captain Mackra, William wrote:

28th July 1720, off St Augustin's Bay
Three days sailing from the Comoro Islands. Have not sighted Mackra's sails for nearly sixteen hours. God, in his great Providence, has given us fair winds. All leaks are caulked and our jury rigging holds up well. The Engagement has left five

*dead and fourteen wounded with two not expected
to reach port. A musket ball wound to my own
head troubles me little, though it might so easily
have been a different story. Mackra is a devil. How
did he find me?*

That was it. No description of the battle or any
damage William might have inflicted on Captain
Mackra. No mention of other ships or, indeed,
whether Captain Mackra had been alone or in the
company of his fleet. Presumably, the journey was
without incident for nothing more was recorded
until William reached his base near the small
French way station at Grand Port and trouble
reared its head in the form of his cousin, Kavanagh
Maguire. In William's own words:

*Much to my surprise a somewhat dilapidated
British man-o'-war rode at anchor in Warwyck
Bay. I feared we were discovered but they showed
no hostility and despatched a cutter in our direction. The captain proved to be none other than my
young Cousin Kavanagh who greeted me well
enough and offered refreshment aboard his ship,
the Dancing Queen. She was a vessel of thirty-
four guns but most had been thrown overboard
during a storm. The main mast lay in splinters
and the ship was in great need of repair.*

The journal went on to state how they joined
forces, first restoring the less badly damaged *Serpent*
then working on the *Dancing Queen*. William's

own men helped replace the broken mast and the two ships' companies enjoyed several months on shore, living on the beach and mixing freely with the local marrons, happily impregnating every maiden who would – and in some cases, wouldn't – prove willing. William was quite graphic in his descriptions of the women. He also made the point that the small French garrison turned a blind eye as long as the pirates kept to themselves. Of Captain Mackra they saw no further sign and the *Serpent*, along with the *Dancing Queen*, was soon back in business. William and Kavanagh made a formidable team judging by the ledger but, at some point, William began to suspect his cousin's motives. The next entry, with no preamble, read:

Last night, well after the company had disbursed or fallen into drunken stupor, I selected three of my most trusted men, rowed out to the Serpent and, making seven trips in all, transferred our share of the Treasures still held on board to a safe if temporary haven on shore. When Kavanagh makes his move, as surely he must, it will be to discover that the spoils so ardently coveted have been considerably depleted. From tonight, one of us will stand watch.

And a postscript: *It is a sad and sorry day indeed when a man cannot trust his own kith and kin.*

The telephone rang suddenly, startling Holly. She answered impatiently, keen to get back to the journal.

'Did I wake you?'

'Justin. No, I wasn't asleep.'

'Sorry I couldn't make dinner. Something came up.'

'That's all right. I was tied up myself.'

'Another time perhaps?'

'Sure.'

'Fancy a nightcap?'

'Thanks but no thanks, Justin. Early start in the morning.' That was true enough. She'd arranged a visit to the Historical and Naval Museum in Mahébourg with Connor.

He sounded disappointed. 'Okay. See you around then.'

'Goodni –'

He broke the connection before she finished the word.

She returned to the journal. The next entry confirmed Kavanagh's treachery:

The swiftness of Kavanagh's attack almost caught us by surprise. Not satisfied with seizing the Serpent and all that he thought she held, my dear Cousin sought our eternal silence. Twas Thomas Capstick who raised the alarm as the scoundrels made their way up the beach towards us. The four of us fled inland, towards the mountains, leaving our precious stash to the mercy of any who might undertake a search. Young Capstick took a musket ball in the neck and died instantly. We could do nought for the poor devil as we were fleeing for our very lives. Kavanagh and his cut-throats pursued us for two days and two nights until we were near dead with the exhaustion. He was like a man possessed in his eagerness to conceal this vile treachery.

Several pages followed which were devoted to the hardships of evading Kavanagh and his men. William also mentioned earlier memories of his cousin in which he made it clear that, even as a boy ten years younger than himself, Kavanagh had been quite devious and was not to be trusted. Perhaps Kavanagh's final betrayal clouded William's recollections because, for a couple of pages at least, past and present combined in a confusing jumble of unrelated events. Reading between the lines, Holly could see that what outraged William more than anything was the complete lack of loyalty shown by one family member to another. A rift had been created that could never be bridged.

It was unclear from the diary how long the men stayed hidden in the mountains. The next entry simply recorded their return to the beach:

Returning with care to Grand Port we were pleasantly relieved to find our booty untouched. Of the Dancing Queen, the Serpent and the crew of both there was no sign. We could surely have used young Capstick's strength at that time but employed our own to bury the poor laddie, a task neglected by my dear Cousin.

Being unexpectedly marooned on the island we had little choice but to join forces with the French

garrison and assist with preparations to receive the
first settlers from France. The arrival of their ships
ultimately provided the opportunity we had sought
for so long. In 1725, by Royal Charter from King
Louis the Fifteenth himself, a fine vessel and crew
were made available and we eagerly took to sea as
legal corsairs under the flag of France.

There were very few entries after that. Hardly
any were dated and Holly could only guess at the
time span between them. The treasure spirited off
the *Serpent* was removed from the beach to a more
secure hiding place, undisclosed but apparently
several miles inland. Then, this one:

The main island of Rodrigues is a small miracle.
Barren, yet softly green, rugged, yet delicate.
Topped by fern and flower, grass and tree, the like
of which I have never seen before. Bays and inlets
in the folds of cliffs. Curious sea birds unafraid by
our presence in this Garden of Eden. Reefs of coral
abounding with all manner of life and colour, a
beauteous display like the bursting of stars or the
flash of sunshine on a barrel of the finest gem-
stones. Caves abound, the depths and darkness of
which are well suited to our purpose. Surely here,
we have found Paradise. I shall build my house on
one of the smaller islands which may be reached
on foot at low tide, for I am done with life at sea.

Left on Rodrigues with two loyal followers,
William seemed as disinclined as ever to keep a

daily record of his life, or indeed, explain how and why he came to be there or give any reason for retiring. Entries were sporadic and dealt mainly with catastrophic events. If it hadn't been for the fact that two were dated, William could well have been oblivious of the passage of time. The first of these was dated 1745, when William would have been sixty-four:

16th February 1745
A terrifying cyclone has laid waste to the island. It raged for four days. I have much work ahead to repair my shelter. A sorrier sight would be hard to find. The hills are littered with fallen trees, their great trunks snapped like tinder, branches and leaves scattered and strewn so that all is carpeted with them. The sight is depressing. It is the Will of God that my remaining water barrels have survived.

2nd October 1745
I have been ill with the fever these past days. This accursed place, crawling with rats and spiders, no water. What use is a man's wealth here? How I long for home.

Isolation was finally getting to him. One of the other men had died of natural causes, leaving William and a fellow called Tim Ainsley. The journal seldom mentioned Ainsley so Holly deduced that the two were not close. William seemed more fascinated by the dodo, which he referred to as a solitaire:

*I have observed that the solitaire has intelligence,
the like of which is not apparent in other birds.
However, it cannot fly. When captured, it will shed
tears. Something causes it to refuse all manner of
food so that it dies of starvation rather than endure
captivity. Tis fine eating though, despite its
appearance. Ungainly, with feet and beak not
unlike a turkey and nary a feather on its rump.
Today I watched another marriage. A new fledged
bird came, with its parents, and was introduced to
another. As many as thirty others accompanied
and, after a period, all left and the two young ones
remained alone.*

Suddenly, William was back on Île de France. As
usual, he did not make clear how he arranged the
journey. He simply mentioned a couple of
hardships:

*Ile de France
The journey took eight days and never have I
been so pleased to see land. We experienced
extremely foul weather and our food was soon
sodden with sea water. Pushed by the winds we
struck land too far north and nearly ran aground
on the reef before reaching Grand Port. The sight
of this place, home for so long, left me nostalgic for
Ireland. I have lived fairly to other men for seven
long years. A pardon could surely be arranged.*

Whether he ever sought a pardon was unclear.
He never mentioned it again. Tim Ainsley

drowned, an event recorded dispassionately. Likewise the fact that a marriage took place between William and a woman only referred to as 'my wife'. By Holly's reckoning, William was sixty-five when he married. Followed by the subsequent arrival of two daughters whose names were as ignored as his wife, and then the birth of a son called Thomas. One clue to the identity of his wife had been a laconic 'I had thought that Thomas, at least, might carry the Maguire blood but no, he's as brown as the other two.'

William became totally obsessed with the developments that had taken place. In particular, of a safer harbour on the western side of the island at Port Louis. The French had decided to move the capital from Grand Port to Port Louis in 1729. William, after seven years on Rodrigues, was obviously amazed at progress. He went to great lengths to describe a fort being built on Coopers Island and into raptures over the erection of a brand new hospital. However, the new capital ceased to absorb him for too long. The journal was reduced to such notations as 'Ducros died of the pox.' There was one final undated entry:

My time draws near. The past three years have been pleasant enough. Each ship brings more French settlers and I enjoy jovial company as and when I please. Word comes that Kavanagh has returned to Ireland. I will send this journal to my sister that its content may denounce the evil treachery of his ways. The map I have drawn will

*provide her with a not insignificant inheritance.
But lest my directions fall into the wrong hands,
let it be known that any who have no right to it
will die a most horrible death with their spirit
cursed for all eternity.*

A spidery signature followed the last entry.
William Maguire presumably, having put his affairs
in order, then expired. Holly turned the page. The
back page of the journal, the one on which
William had drawn his map, had been neatly cut
out.

Holly closed the book and put it carefully into
her bedside drawer. What kind of a man had
William Maguire been? Kind, cruel, certainly not
forgiving. His ramblings gave no real clue to his
personality. A bit on the cold side it seemed,
though that could have been the way most men
were back then. She could see how, having read
such an account, someone like Connor Maguire
would have found the challenge to find William's
treasure quite irresistible.

Is that all there is to Connor Maguire? she wondered. Somehow, it seemed unlikely.

FOUR

The next morning, after a light breakfast by the pool, Holly telephoned the hire car people and asked them to collect the Mini Moke. She left the keys at reception and wandered outside to wait for Connor. Since he seemed happy enough for her to tag along with him, there didn't appear to be much point in keeping the car. Mauritius was well served by public transport and taxis were everywhere.

She was wearing baggy khaki trousers, a white tank top under a sleeveless jacket with four large button-down pockets, and walking boots. Camera bag slung over one shoulder, the tape recorder peeped from a breast pocket, a notepad from the other. On her head, a bright blue baseball cap with the words *totally awesome* embroidered in gold on the front. Small, round, wire-framed sunglasses perched atop the cap's peak.

If Holly was aware that she looked like a foreign correspondent down on her luck and stranded in some war-torn third world country, it didn't seem to bother her. She slid into the car next to Connor, pulled out her notebook and said, 'Thanks for dinner last night. How old are you?'

'Thirty-two.' He eyed her with amusement.

Holly knew very well that he was used to being seen in the company of immaculately dressed women. It was for this precise reason that she had chosen the clothes she was wearing, believing that, since she couldn't compete, she might as well go the other way. 'How old were you when you made your first million?'

She was all business this morning, adding notes against a list of prepared questions.

'Twenty-six.' He pulled out onto the road and accelerated to get ahead of an oncoming bus.

Holly waited until he'd slowed, wrote down his answer, then carried on. 'You've been married twice. Any children?'

'No.'

'Think you'll try it a third time?'

'Maybe.'

'Anyone in mind?'

'Yeah!' He glanced in the rear-view mirror, changed down a gear and overtook a wildly lurching lorry. Safely back on the left side of the road, he added, 'A combination of saint, angel and earth mother would just about do it for me.'

'Choose a wife with your ear, not your eye?' Both his wives had been quite stunning.

'Something like that. Next time, if there is a next time, I'll be quite sure there is no hidden agenda.'

She heard wryness, not bitterness. 'Is that what went wrong?'

'Is this really relevant?' Connor's voice was still light but tightness had crept into it.

'I'm trying to find a personal angle.'

'Then ask about what sport I play, what books or movies I've enjoyed.'

'I'm getting to that.'

He sighed. 'My most recent ex-wife has said enough to fill your notepad. I don't need to add anything.'

'Except your side of the story.'

'I'm a self-centred cad. Will that do?'

She was making him angry. Good. Angry people were often less cautious. Holly kept her voice impersonal. 'Pressure of work must have come into it. That and lifestyle.'

Connor swerved to the side of the road and pulled up. The lorry, then the bus, trundled past. 'Shit!' He rested his wrists on the steering wheel and looked hard at her. 'I don't talk about it because it's nobody else's damned business. Get hold of *her* interviews. Read between the lines. Just don't expect me to make excuses or accusations, okay?' Throwing a look over his shoulder, he pulled back onto the road.

Well! She'd certainly made him angry. But not inclined to discuss deeply private issues. When she thought about it, Holly realised that through both divorces Connor had kept a dignified silence. She also remembered that his last wife had remarried within a couple of months. Had she used him to further her own ends? Was it all a question of money? Holly looked over at Connor, trying to gauge his mood. Judging by his white-knuckled grip on the steering wheel, he probably wouldn't welcome any speculation in that direction. She decided it might be prudent to drop the personal angle for now. 'What happened to the map at the back of the journal?'

'Your guess is as good as mine. Did you bring it with you?'

'It's in the camera bag.'

They were travelling south from Grand Baie, towards the capital Port Louis. Holly had studied a map the night before, trying to locate places mentioned in the journal. Mahébourg was near Grand Port. There were two ways of reaching the southeast of the island. They could stay with the national highway, which would take them up through the central highlands before dropping back to sea level near the airport. From Plaisance, Mahébourg was a mere eight kilometres north. Or they could cut across on a secondary road further north and follow the coast south. They took the more direct route. Either way, it wasn't going to take long, no more than an hour or so. She lapsed into silence, fascinated by the jagged peaks which seemed to rise almost vertically from the lush green fields of sugar cane.

At Curepipe, the tea industry capital of Mauritius, crowds of people on the road forced them to a crawl. After five minutes, Connor wound down his window and asked a Creole man near the car what was going on.

'Ah!' The man shook his head. 'It is a funeral.'

'Must be someone important,' Connor said. The wall of people was unbroken, a solid mass.

'A young girl. She was murdered.' The man's shock was evident.

'Did you know her?' Connor asked in sympathy.

Another head shake. 'She was white. Some knew her, not many.' He was clearly eager to talk. 'The whole town is here. It is a disgraceful business. She was only nineteen. We come to show the family our respect.' He waved his hand over the heads of those in front of him. 'The cemetery is only a little way ahead. We will soon be out of your way.'

A slimly built Indian man in a dark blue suit walked past the car, his eyes scanning the crowd, a frown on his face. Detective Sham was attending the funeral of Corrine Vitry to see who else was there. He knew that a murderer very often attended the victim's funeral to gloat. Sham had been dismayed to see how many people had turned up for Corrine's last ride. He supposed there was an element of curiosity over the inevitable rumours, which would account for such a crowd. Sham had his suspicions about who had murdered the girl but in this mob, whether his suspect was there or not, the chances of Sham being able to study his face seemed unlikely.

Sure enough, as the Creole had told Connor, the funeral procession soon turned off the main road and they were able to proceed south.

Mahébourg showed its age. Holly's trusty guidebook informed her that the town, pronounced

'Mayberg' in English, was the first settlement of any size to be established in Mauritius, a fact reflected in its black basalt buildings and dated architecture. They located the Historical and Naval Museum without difficulty and Connor parked at the imposing wrought-iron gates.

'Looks shut,' Holly commented.

Connor went to investigate. Several pedestrians stopped and spoke to him. 'Temporarily closed for renovations,' he announced, getting back into the car. He started the engine. 'Bit of a pity but there's nothing we can do about it. It was a long shot anyway.'

'So what now?'

'Fancy some lunch?'

Holly threw him a puzzled look.

He glanced back, a question in his eyes.

She shrugged and turned her head away.

'What? What have I done now? It's not my fault the place is shut.'

She looked back at him. 'How did you get to be so successful?'

'What's that supposed to mean?'

'You've come all this way and just because the museum's closed you give up and think about lunch.' She checked her watch. 'It's too early anyway.'

'Okay. What do you suggest?'

'What about Births, Deaths and Marriages?'

'I've checked. Nothing about William but there were a succession of Maguires in this area. Mainly dead ones.'

She should have known better. Making assumptions about Connor Maguire was not a good idea.

The cheque issue for AIDS research was a case in point. Maguire might sometimes seem like an irresponsible schoolboy but he sure as hell wasn't. Holly knew he'd have covered it before she asked the question. But she asked anyway. 'Phone book?'

'Done that as well. Found one.'

Connor seemed to be driving aimlessly as they turned along the seafront. He stopped the car. 'Let's walk. Stretch our legs. Take in some sea air.'

'Anywhere in particular?' Holly fancied his intentions were more precise than they appeared. The Connor Maguires of this world were simply not that vague. And, as she was learning, this particular Connor Maguire left little to chance.

'That looks a likely place for lunch.' He pointed across the road. 'We can come back later.'

The Restaurant le Phare did indeed look good. Holly noticed how closely he studied it as they passed. There was something . . . she couldn't quite put her finger on it . . . something a bit staged about Connor's behaviour today. But for now, since he seemed determined to explore, she might as well go along with it. 'Mind if I tape as we go?'

Holly threw in questions as they strolled, deliberately keeping away from sensitive personal issues. In the next hour, they walked and talked, doing a complete circuit of the town without really paying too much attention to it. Connor, like too few people being interviewed, appreciated and was good at the technique of the question-and-answer process. She liked the way he kept his responses concise. It meant she wouldn't have to wade through hours of irrelevant waffle.

They were back outside Restaurant le Phare.

'My treat,' Holly announced, as they walked under an archway onto the open-sided patio. A waiter hurried towards them. 'Table for two.'

'Certainly, Monsieur, Mademoiselle. Would you prefer inside or outside?'

'Out –' Holly began.

'Inside,' Connor cut in firmly.

She was about to object but glanced inside and immediately saw his reason. The beautiful Madame Liang Song was seated at a table with two Chinese men.

The waiter tried to steer them towards a window table but Connor chose one against the wall, literally no more than a metre from where his lunch companion from earlier in the week now sat. The two showed no sign of knowing each other.

What's his game? Holly felt like a pawn on a chessboard, especially when he took the seat closest to the trio, facing the door and looking out to the bay beyond. This left Holly a fine view of nothing but the back wall. *How rude!* If he was aware of the breach of etiquette, *and*, she thought, *he bloody-well should be*, he showed no sign of it.

Connor seemed to be eavesdropping on the conversation behind him, which was being conducted in Chinese, but in quite a loud voice he asked Holly what personal information she required for her story.

Taken by surprise, since she'd already told him

what she was after, it didn't take a genius to work out that he was not actually listening to her. *Right, you bastard, cop this.*

'. . . and so if we can wrap up the question of your sexual preferences with one or two saucy anecdotes we can then turn to your search for pirate treasure.' She smiled at him sweetly.

He nodded absently. 'Of course.' But her words suddenly sank in. He blinked and shook his head as if to clear it. 'Sorry?'

The expression on his face was one she would dearly have loved to photograph. Connor Maguire, stunned into silence and filled with incredulity. It was a very sweet moment. 'Just testing.'

He swallowed hard. Both eyebrows were doing a little dance around his forehead. She had quite taken the wind out of his sails.

'Tell me.' She leaned towards him and lowered her voice. 'How many languages do you speak?'

'Not many.'

His eyes glittered with an emotion she couldn't fathom – amusement, excitement, anger? She observed him closely. There was certainly more to this man than she'd first thought. She had the feeling that whatever lay beneath the surface was not reflected in the facade. He might claim to be in Mauritius for the reasons given but Holly was prepared to bet they weren't the only ones.

'What are you thinking?' he asked suddenly.

'Not a lot. Probably that I hate that question.'

A dimple appeared. He passed her the menu without another word.

An argument seemed to be developing at the next table. Voices were raised and one of the men was gesticulating with both hands. Only Madame Liang remained calm and poised, her expressionless eyes unfathomable, a small smile on her face. Abruptly, the more agitated man rose, flung down his napkin and stalked quickly from the restaurant. With an apologetic shrug, his companion followed, leaving Madame Liang alone yet not noticeably moved by their sudden defection. She called for the bill, paid it, then walked leisurely from the restaurant.

Connor's eyes followed her all the way to the street. As soon as she was out of sight, he said, 'You must be wondering . . .'

'Yes, I am. I'm filled to the brim with wonder.'

He gave a wry grin. 'The Chinese are a tight-knit community on Mauritius. They run a lot of the businesses here and operate by a code of "you scratch my back and I'll scratch yours". Madame Liang's family own supermarkets and wholesale operations all over the island. When you saw us together, we were discussing a possible joint venture in Australia. The reason we didn't let on that we knew each other is really quite simple. She's interested in branching out, acquiring business interests outside Mauritius. Her family is not exactly opposed to the idea but they would never deal with a Westerner. The two men with her were connected – uncles, I think. If any of her relatives discovered that she was negotiating with someone outside the Chinese club, well, you've heard of the Triad.'

'The Chinese Mafia? Yes, of course.' She wondered how long the farce would continue and was beginning to feel a, by now, familiar rise in her irritation level. What kind of a fool did he take her for?

Connor correctly read her scepticism. 'I'm not joking. Some members of the Liang clan are quite ruthless. She'll be threatened, or worse.'

Holly knew of the Triad's reputation and wondered why, under the circumstances, Madame Liang openly flirted with danger. 'Surely meeting you in public was taking a huge risk?'

'Yes. Although sometimes it's easier to conceal something when it's right under the noses of those you wish to hide it from.'

'Agreed. But if her devoted family knew about your lunchtime get-together wouldn't they be suspicious that you pretended not to have met?'

'They don't know. If she thought they did, Madame Liang would have greeted me.'

'What makes you so sure?'

'I don't do business with people until I'm confident that nothing nasty will creep out of the woodwork.'

Holly's eyes narrowed. 'That's some network you've got behind you.'

He stared back unflinchingly. 'Standard practice.'

She let it go. 'What *were* they arguing about?'

'As far as I could tell, distribution of profits.'

He was being evasive but she let that pass too. 'If what you say is true, she's running a hell of a risk going outside the family. What's her reason?'

'Who knows? She's arrogant and ambitious. Perhaps she needs to prove something. She's just been made a director of the Liangs' parent company. Maybe she's trying to impress.'

Holly recognised blatant lying when she heard it. She just couldn't figure out why it was necessary. 'There is a Swahili superstition in East Africa that if a person stands up and his clothes stick between his buttocks then he is in the habit of telling lies.'

Connor's eyes twinkled. 'Or he has a terrible tailor.'

She waited, but no explanation was forthcoming. All he said was, 'If the waiter arrives while I'm gone I'll have the sole. Excuse me.' He stood up and walked towards the toilets. Holly noticed that his trousers fitted perfectly.

She sipped her beer, trying to mull over and make sense of their conversation, but her thoughts were in the men's room. Connor Maguire was an enigma. A rich adventurer, a tough and clever businessman, and something else. Was he simply one of those people not satisfied unless dicing with danger? Or did he have a darker side? That talk of Triads. Was it to impress? Or warn her?

She beckoned the waiter and ordered for both of them. Then she went back to her musings.

The Chinese organisation had a ferocious reputation. The secrecy of the modus operandi of the Triad Society and the Mafia bore remarkable similarities. The Triads, formed two thousand years ago for the sole purpose of ridding China of the detested Manchu overlords, had, more recently, developed a minority criminal element. Branching into narcotics, protection rackets, gambling, prostitution and murder, small but organised gangs had brought disgrace to the very name Triad, tainting the reputation of all its members who were, in the main, honest, upright citizens. These fringe elements now operated wherever Chinese communities existed throughout the world.

The rapid rise of Triad power was due to the Chinese people themselves. Holly didn't know a lot about it but remembered reading that an innate and thoroughly justified fear of retribution, expectation to pay for the slightest favour or service, and a tight-knit clan system all served to protect the identity of Triad members. In a population known as *lao-pai-hsing* – the Old Hundred Names – it was generally acknowledged that most Chinese were related one way or another. They would rather die by their own hand than turn against a family member, irrespective of how tenuous the connection.

Holly glanced at her watch. Connor had been gone for at least ten minutes. What on earth was he doing? After fifteen minutes she began to get annoyed. The waiter appeared with their food. Holly indicated that he should put it on the table.

'I can keep the gentleman's plate warm in the kitchen, Mademoiselle.'

'Don't bother. He'll be here soon.' *And if he isn't he can eat his bloody food cold.*

The food was served but the waiter kept coming back and offering to keep Connor's warm. Holly, now thoroughly put out, insisted he leave it where it was. When a full half-hour had passed, and she had finished her own meal, Holly called the hovering and indecisive waiter. 'Did my friend leave?'

'No, Mademoiselle.'

'Please, would you check the toilet. Perhaps he is unwell.'

The waiter quickly returned. 'No, Mademoiselle. There is no-one in the toilet.'

'Is there a back door?'

'Yes. It is through the kitchen. But no-one passed that way.'

'The toilet windows?' Holly was feeling a little ridiculous.

'They are barred.' The waiter was eyeing her suspiciously. 'Would Mademoiselle care for the bill?'

She nodded curtly. 'And take this with you.' If Connor Maguire reappeared he'd find his meal had, more than likely, been eaten by the staff. Served him right.

Holly paid and left the restaurant. She could not believe that Connor had walked off, just like that. *What a rat! How dare he? Who the hell does he think he is? How did he leave?*

The car had gone. She made her way along the street to where crowds of people gathered at the bus station, caught a bus to Curepipe, then another to Port Louis and finally, a third to Grand Baie. Only the last was an air-conditioned express. Both the others, despite their open windows, were hot and overcrowded and the wait between stages seemed interminable. Finally reaching the Merville Beach Hotel in a taxi, Holly was in a foul temper. She had a tension headache she could barely think around, and an overwhelming desire to plunge into the aquamarine waters of the Indian Ocean. Which was exactly what she did.

Forty minutes later, feeling somewhat more relaxed and refreshed, Holly returned to her room to find a message waiting light flashing on the telephone. She checked with reception, half-expecting more lies from Maguire but the message was from Raoul Dulac, with a number for her to get back to him. A woman answered. 'Solange Dulac.' The French accent was light but detectable.

'This is Holly Jones. I'm returning Mr Dulac's call.'

'Miss Jones, I am Raoul's wife. He's had to go out. You've just missed him, unfortunately.'

Holly heard the rattle of ice cubes in a glass.

'We are having a little lunch party on Sunday. Raoul and I would be delighted if you could join us.'

'That's very kind. Are you sure it's no bother?'

Solange Dulac gave a tinkling laugh which sounded strangely forced. Ice cubes rattled again before she spoke. 'Bother? Of course not.'

Her words were slightly slurred and Raoul's wife sounded as if she couldn't care less whether Holly came or not. She heard a man's voice in the background, then Solange Dulac muttered, 'One moment please,' and Raoul came on the line. Holly wondered whether Solange had deliberately lied about Raoul not being there or if she'd made a genuine mistake.

'Holly. Thank you for returning my call. Solange has mentioned our lunch? Good. Connor too.'

'It's very kind of you both.'

'No trouble at all.' He gave her complicated instructions on how to find the estate which, as far as Holly could establish from her scribbled notes, was somewhere in the middle of the island. 'You can't miss it,' he concluded with more optimism than she felt. 'We'll expect you around midday.'

'Thank you. I'm looking forward to it.'

'Can I leave it to you to invite Connor?'

'Of course.' No point in telling him how the bastard did a runner from the restaurant and she had no idea where he was.

'Fine. We'll see you –'

Holly heard a loud crash and a woman scream.

Raoul said hurriedly, 'Excuse me, see you Sunday,' and broke the connection.

But not before Holly heard someone sobbing. She put the receiver down thoughtfully. Raoul Dulac was not the sort of man she would instinctively trust, there was something too flamboyant, too hale and hearty about him. Some sort of drama was taking place at his end of the line. Holly shrugged it off. It was nothing to do with her.

A little after seven thirty, as Holly was about to go for dinner, there was a discreet tap on her door. Madame

Liang stood there, proud eyes defying Holly's obvious surprise. 'Madame Liang!' She stepped back and the Chinese woman entered her room.

'So, you know my name.' She swept the room with a penetrating look. 'Where is he?'

'Who?'

'Connor Maguire.'

Good question. 'As you can see, he's not here.'

Madame Liang's acuminous inspection flicked almost insultingly over the baggy, bottle-green slacks and dark blue T-shirt, before returning to stare at Holly's face. 'Answer my question.'

Holly hadn't been spoken to like that since her school days. 'I have no idea.'

'Why did you follow me today?'

Boardroom tactics seemed appropriate. 'Why should I follow you?'

Long, red-painted nails tapped against the milky whiteness of her upper arm. Madame Liang took a deep breath as if to emphasise her intolerance of fools. 'I'm referring to Maguire, not you.'

Holly could accept the arrogance – just. She'd seen it often in the rich and powerful. But she could not tolerate the contemptuous dismissal in the woman's voice. 'You'll have to ask him that.' She kept her voice even with an effort and was totally unprepared for Madame Liang's next words.

'What is the man doing?' It came out as a desperate whisper, her composure suddenly gone. For a moment, she looked quite vulnerable, on the point of tears even. But she recovered rapidly and snapped, 'Tell Maguire to stay away from me.'

'I'm not his secretary, or yours,' Holly snapped back. 'Tell him yourself.'

Madame Liang remained unmoved by Holly's tone. 'I take it you're a journalist. Who do you work for?'

'Myself.' Holly could see that the woman didn't understand. 'Freelance,' she explained.

'Ah!' She turned slowly, as if deep in thought, and walked to the desk where Holly had set up her laptop computer. Still saying nothing, Madame Liang picked up the notepad and flicked it open.

Holly was more amused than anything else. The arrogance in this woman had probably been injected at birth. An infallible belief in the inherited right to act as she pleased. Another's privacy might well be sacrosanct but the rules didn't apply in her case. What must it be like to feel so exclusively superior?

The pad was tossed carelessly back on the desk. 'Personal questions. Westerners!' Madame Liang shook her head. 'You cloud reality with the weakness of human emotions.'

Considering that it was Connor Maguire who had upset Liang Song's equilibrium, Holly only just managed not to smile.

'Who is this article for?'

There was no harm in telling her. '*Out of Focus*.'

Madame Liang looked relieved. 'You cover his treasure hunt? The man's a fool. There is no treasure. The whole island laughs at him.'

'That's his problem.' She was getting sick of this haughty creature. 'Why are you so concerned about Connor Maguire?'

139

Liang Song slowly crossed to where Holly leaned against the wall. 'He does not understand our ways,' she said softly, her beautiful face an expressionless mask. 'If he makes trouble it will only be for himself. You too, if you are fool enough to associate with him.'

'I don't like being threatened, Madame Liang.'

'Threatened?' She seemed surprised. 'It was no threat. I speak the truth.'

Holly wondered if she would know the truth if it bit her on a slender ankle. 'I'm writing an article. If that unnerves you then you must have something to hide.' She stared the Chinese woman down. 'I wonder what that could be?'

The tiniest reaction registered in Liang Song's eyes. Was it fear? It was gone in an instant and the woman smiled. 'I refer to my family's network of associates, built over the years from mutual respect, trust and our own unique culture. We do business differently from you. Maguire doesn't understand. Some of my people could, ah . . . misinterpret.'

It was a measure of Madame Liang's conceit that she expected such a flimsy explanation to be accepted. Holly, however, was not one to miss an opportunity. With the Chinese woman momentarily on the back foot, it was an ideal time to suggest an interview.

'You make a very good point, Madame Liang. Misinterpretation often leads to misunderstanding. As well as writing about Connor Maguire, I'm also doing a piece about Mauritius itself. I'll be covering all the ethnic groups. Perhaps . . .' She left it hanging, but her smile was the end result of many years' practice – hopeful, tinged with humility and professional interest.

Faced with Holly's proposal Madame Liang could hardly refuse. She reached into her bag and produced a card. 'If you want a Sino-Mauritian angle, I'd be happy to talk to you. Make an appointment with my secretary.' Turning, she let herself out of the room, leaving Holly more than pleased with herself. She looked down at the card. *Madame Liang Song, Director, Liang & Associates – Importers.*

Holly slid the card into a small pocket on her camera bag and made her way to the Badamier.

Justin Parker was dining alone. He caught sight of her, rose to his feet and waved. 'Come and join me.' Holly slid into the chair opposite him.

'Do you mind if I finish this? How was your day?' He cut steak as he spoke.

'No and different, in that order. How about you?'

'Bloody frustrating.' He forked a piece of steak into his mouth and chewed vigorously, swallowed, and added, 'I'm going to run out of time. Typical bloody Oxford. They should have sent a team ahead of me. I'm a biologist, not a bloody archaeologist.'

Holly filed Oxford away for her article. 'You could try Rodrigues. The solitaire flourished there.'

'Solitaire?' He looked puzzled.

'The dodo.'

'Oh! Yes, of course.'

A waiter hovered. Holly ordered her meal and a glass of wine. She thought it exceedingly strange that Justin appeared unaware of the name French sailors had given to the dodo. But, between bites of food, his conversation had taken a new tack. 'You must visit the Pamplemousses Gardens. There are something like eighty different species of palms growing there and they've got these giant tortoises, some more than one hundred years old. If you're free, I could show you tomorrow.'

Well, she probably would be free since Mr Bloody Maguire had vanished, presumably through a crack in the floor of the gent's toilet and into thin air. 'Sounds interesting. I'd like that.'

After dinner, Justin proposed a walk along the beach. It was a beautiful night, balmy and calm. They took off their shoes and wandered in silence, listening to the gentle lapping of water on the sand and, by contrast, the almost intrusive rhythm of the *sega* blasted out by bands playing at resorts along the shore. She liked the way Justin didn't try to fill the silence with meaningless words, seeming content to enjoy the evening and her company.

Beyond the drawn up and deserted deckchairs, the beach descended into near darkness. All but three of the private bungalows appeared unoccupied. Holly found herself wondering how it must have been in William Maguire's day. Months away from home, no roads, no electricity, no running water, nothing familiar. A haven it might have been but survival depended on self-reliance and a total dependency on the strength of one's own body. The sense of isolation must have been strong. If he could only see it now, what would he make of it? Hotels, bright lights, happy tourists, all modern conveniences and home just a few hours away across the ocean.

Preoccupied with thoughts of the past, of loneliness and danger in unfamiliar lands, Holly shivered suddenly. For some inexplicable reason she felt vulnerable, that some kind of threat lurked in the shadows. She tried to shrug it off but the fear would not go away. 'I think we should head back, Justin. It's too dark to see where we're going.'

'Just to those rocks.'

There was a shape up ahead but that was all she could make out. They walked slowly on. It turned out to be a sea wall. Above was privately owned land.

'Okay,' Justin agreed. 'Let's go back.'

Turning, they made their way towards the friendly, twinkling lights. Seeing them so close was reassuring. Not usually given to flights of fancy, the premonition that some kind of menace waited in the darkness had been strong. She had just started to relax when a soft pounding of running feet alerted her that someone was approaching from behind, very fast. As Holly turned to look over her shoulder a blur of movement collided with them, knocking her flying. She heard Justin shout and the sounds of a scuffle. Holly tried to get up but a bare foot lashed out with vicious intent, sending pain shooting through her side. She slumped back onto the wet sand, breathing with difficulty. More voices, not only Justin's this time. Shadows running as the night subsided into silence. Holly heard Justin groan and she tried to sit up, but the pain in her ribs was too intense.

'Bastards!' Justin gritted. 'Jesus Christ. Holly! Are you all right?'

'Ribs,' she managed to croak. 'Might be broken.'

Sand scrunched and the dark shape of Justin stumbling, like a drunk, to where she lay. He knelt beside her. 'Can you get up?'

It was the last thing Holly wanted to do. 'I'll try.'

'Which side hurts?'

'Left.'

Though her teeth were clenched, she could not avoid crying out with pain when he went to help her. 'Sorry. Here. Is that any better?' He placed an arm around her shoulders.

It was, but only marginally. 'Let's go.' She had to get away from this place. Every shadow seemed to dance threateningly towards them. Her side ached abominably, though whether from internal damage or from the intensity of the kick, she wasn't certain. Together, they stumbled back along the beach. Reaching the lights, Holly saw that Justin had blood on his face. 'You're hurt.'

He touched his face gingerly. 'Superficial, I think. My room's on the ground floor. I always keep the key with me.'

They cut through the floodlit garden, screened from sight by shrubs and flowerbeds. The door to

Justin's room stood ajar. 'Oh Jesus!' he groaned, as light flooded the interior. The place had been trashed. Bedclothes strewn everywhere, the mattress pulled onto the floor and slashed, drawers and cupboards open, a suitcase cut to ribbons, a torn toilet bag on the bathroom floor. Even his clothing had not escaped the knife. Linings ripped and hanging in tatters, the heels prised off his shoes.

'Justin!' Holly managed, as she took in the carnage. 'This is more than petty theft. Someone was seriously searching for something.'

'I'll worry about it later. Let's call the hotel doctor first.'

'What about the police?'

'I guess so.' He sounded doubtful. 'Though what they can do about it I don't know. We didn't really see them.'

'Them? I thought there was only one.'

'No. I saw two outlines.' Justin picked up the telephone which had been knocked to the floor and dialled reception. In a concise, even voice he gave his name and room number, asked for a doctor, reported the break-in and requested that someone come to inspect the damage.

The doctor arrived first. With no comment on the chaos or words of sympathy, he felt Holly's ribs, said two might be cracked but, as far as he could tell without an X-ray, not broken. Justin, with old-fashioned courtesy, turned his back when the doctor helped Holly out of her T-shirt and taped her ribcage. 'Leave that on for as long as you can stand it,' he said, assisting her back into the garment. 'I will give you a referral for an X-ray.'

Holly twisted her torso gingerly. 'It feels much better already.' She wasn't sure she wanted the hassle of medical attention. From past experiences outside Australia, it was usually more trouble than it was worth.

The doctor, an Indo-Mauritian, nodded briskly. 'The damage should mend quickly. How did this happen?' He directed the question at Justin, who still stood with his back to them. 'You can turn around, young man.' The doctor examined his face carefully. One eye was closing, a nasty bruise had appeared just under it and his lip was split. 'Headache?'

'A bit.'

The man held up two fingers. 'How many?'

'Two.'

'Good. No concussion. Couple of days and you'll be right as rain. Where were you attacked?' He was pouring something from a bottle onto a wad of cottonwool.

'On the beach,' Justin mumbled as antiseptic lotion stung his lip. 'We went for a walk.'

The doctor tutted and shook his head. 'Disgraceful. I apologise on behalf of my countrymen. It happens now and then, but not often.' He glanced at Holly briefly. 'And the room?'

She shrugged, then wished she hadn't as a pain stabbed through her. 'It was like this when we got back. Someone broke in.'

'Tut. Once this island was a safe place. Now

there is crime. Regrettable but the way of the world I fear. Not even Mauritius is spared. Hold still, young man.'

Justin winced as the doctor turned his attention to the bruise. 'Ouch!'

There was a commotion at the door and the night manager marched in. A horrified 'Mon dieu!' burst from him. He clapped hands to his cheeks as he surveyed the damaged room. 'This is terrible. I am so sorry, Monsieur. We will find you another room immediately. How did they get in? Did you leave the door open?'

The doctor, obviously an amateur sleuth, beckoned and pointed. 'I don't think so, Monsieur. Look, the lock is broken.'

The night manager was scandalised. 'This has never happened before. What is coming to this world?' He placed a hand over his heart and spun theatrically on the balls of his feet to face Justin, whose eye was disappearing rapidly into puffy folds of bluish-green flesh. 'Guests attacked in their own rooms, Monsieur. Those responsible should be hung.'

Holly began to feel tired and slightly hysterical, a combined reaction no doubt to the ordeal on the beach and the night manager's histrionics. She rubbed a hand across her eyes and said slowly, 'We were not in the room when this happened. We were attacked on the beach.'

The night manager looked vastly relieved. Clearly, the beach did not constitute his domain. 'Do you wish to report this break-in, Monsieur?'

Justin shook his head. 'As far as I can tell, nothing has been stolen, simply torn apart. Perhaps it was vandals?'

'Perhaps.' The man seemed doubtful and comforted at the same time. Holly guessed that Justin's refusal to report the matter to the police, and the night manager's relief, probably had something to do with the ridiculous amount of red tape connected to any criminal activity in a territory once administered by Britain. In Holly's opinion, having come up against it several times in the past, the British legacy of official procedures should have been the first thing dropped by any country the instant it gained independence. It would be a lengthy enough experience reporting the attack.

'I will leave a full report in the manager's office,' the night manager was saying. 'If you would care to see him in the morning, Monsieur, he can advise you the best places to go to replace your possessions.'

'Thank you,' Justin said.

'If you don't mind,' Holly cut in, 'I'd like to go to my room.' She was desperate for a stiff whisky. That, and to take the weight off her legs, which had begun to tremble with shock.

The doctor left with her. 'Mademoiselle, I will come with you.'

'There's no need,' Holly declined. 'I'll just pick up my key and –'

'I do insist, young lady.'

His tone invited no further protest. In any case, she was glad he was there. Although the lights were on, opening the door of her room was not something she wanted to do alone. The doctor checked cupboards, under the bed, the balcony and the bathroom. 'All clear,' he announced rather proudly.

Holly declined the offer of a sleeping pill and locked the door carefully behind him. She poured herself a large J & B whisky, courtesy of Downtown Duty Free at Melbourne Airport, threw in three ice cubes and a splash of bottled water from the refrigerator. Sitting on the bed, she nearly jumped out of her skin when the telephone rang.

'Yes.' Her tone was irritable.

'It's me. Did I wake you?'

She took a long pull at the glass and banged it down on the side table. 'The concern is touching. Thanks for today, Maguire. I particularly enjoyed the scenic bus trip back.' When he said nothing, she added, 'Where the hell did you go?'

'Would kidnapped by little green men do it for you?'

His attempt at humour didn't work. It was Holly's turn to remain silent.

She heard him sigh. 'I saw someone I had to speak to.'

'Crap, Maguire. You knew Liang Song would be there. You set the whole thing up.'

'Yes,' he admitted.

'That doesn't explain your disappearing act. Just how *did* you get out of there?'

'I walked.'

'Hello, Maguire. Remember me? I was sitting there.'

'There's a little passageway runs along the dining room. It's visible from the tables, but not very.'

'So you just tiptoed down it and hurtled after the Chinese ice queen. Lurking outside men's toilets doesn't seem like Madame Liang's style.'

'Madame Liang!' He sounded genuinely surprised. 'It wasn't her. I'm sorry, but I can't say any more.' Silence was loud on the line. Connor broke it. 'I apologise.'

'That doesn't do it for me either, Maguire. What are you up to? This chasing after buried treasure story is bullshit. You're messing me around and I don't like it. Perhaps it's time I did some independent digging.'

'No!' He nearly yelped the word. 'Don't do that, Holly.'

'Listen, Maguire. I want a story. That's why I'm here. Cooperate or I'll get it my way.'

'Jesus!'

'And He certainly won't help you.'

'Look . . . okay . . . what's your room number?' Holly gave it to him.

'I'll be there in ten.' The connection was broken.

He made it in seven.

'Come in.' Holly looked at him. He appeared distracted and edgy.

'Come for a walk.'

She folded her arms carefully. 'No thanks.'

'Just for a drink.'

'We can have one here. I've got some scotch.'

'I'd rather go to the bar.' He leaned towards her

and whispered softly, 'Your room could well be bugged.'

'Oh, please!' She was in no mood to argue.

'Are you coming or not?' He didn't look as though he was in any kind of mood to argue either.

Holly threw him an exasperated look, picked up her room key and they went to the bar.

At that hour the place was quiet, but Connor chose a seat well away from anybody else, ordered two scotches, and stared expressionlessly into space until they arrived. Once the barman moved away, he leaned towards Holly and spoke softly. 'I can't tell you much.'

'Can't or won't?' She realised suddenly that he was angry.

'Dammit! What was Quinn thinking to send you here?' His eyes glittered. 'You're getting in the way.'

'Thanks.' She glared at him. 'Just as I thought. My father does know what you're up to?'

'Yes and no.'

'What kind of an answer is that?'

Connor sat back. A pulse ticked in his cheek. Either that or he was clenching his teeth so hard that a muscle was in spasm. Seeming to reach a decision, he leaned forward again. 'I am looking for William's treasure. It's the kind of thing that appeals to me. But I'm doing something else as well. Quinn thinks he knows what it is. He doesn't. Even so, the story I leaked to get him off my back should have been enough to keep you out of it.'

'Maguire,' Holly said flatly. 'My father accepts what you seem unable or unwilling to go along with. I'm a big girl now, so will you stop stuffing about. As I said on the phone, there's a story out there. If I can't get it from you –'

'Remember what I told you at lunch?' he cut in. 'About the Triads?'

So! He had been warning me.

'Keep away from it, Holly. They play rough.'

'You're telling me nothing, Maguire. Tossing out a few crumbs, that's all. It's not good enough.'

'Drugs.' Conner said the word with reluctance and anger. 'That's all you're getting.'

'Is that Quinn's version or your own?'

'It's the truth.' He tried to stare her down but she held his gaze. 'Quinn doesn't know.'

Their eyes were still locked. Holly nodded slowly. 'Okay,' she breathed softly, knowing honesty when she heard it. 'But I'm still doing the treasure story.'

Relief showed on his face. 'Do you mean that? No sticking your nose into anything else?'

She smiled slightly. 'A journo who goes after a drug story needs certain insurances in place before asking questions. People who know where they are and why, a cameraman or two covering every move, contact with the Australian Embassy or, if there isn't one, the British. I'd be mad to go it alone. I'm no fool or heroine, if you'll pardon a particularly bad pun. You have my word.'

'Thank God!'

'So if you don't mind, Maguire, I'd appreciate it

if you could be a bit more up-front in future. That way I won't blunder across your wires. I'm doing an interview with Madame Liang soon. Now I know what subject to avoid.'

'You're what?'

'You heard.'

'Don't do it, Holly.'

'A look at Sino-Mauritians as part of a tourist piece! Where's the harm? Anyway, she's agreed.'

'When? When did you speak to her?'

'This evening. She was here earlier. Came to my room looking for you.' Holly smiled wickedly. 'Oh yes. Said to tell you to stay away from her.'

Connor closed his eyes. 'She was checking up on you.'

'She sure was. Had a good snoop through my notebook.'

'That won't hurt.' He looked at her soberly. 'Promise me, Holly. Stick to the tourist angle when you do the interview.'

'I've already given my word.' She remembered Raoul Dulac's call. 'Lunch on Sunday at the Dulacs'. It's confirmed. Midday. I've got directions.'

'Fine.' He nodded absently. 'I'm going back to Mahébourg tomorrow. Want to come?'

She thought it over. She needed one more session with Justin Parker to tie up loose ends – background stuff on him mainly, questions she could ask without raising any suspicions. With Justin and his dodo search out of the way she would be free to concentrate on Connor Maguire. 'No thanks. Once bitten twice shy.'

He looked surprised but all he said was, 'Another day then.' He noticed her empty glass. 'Want the other half?'

'I don't think so.' Her sides were aching badly.

Connor drained his glass, stood, and put out a hand to help her up. An expression of pain crossed Holly's face as she rose. 'What is it?'

'Nothing.' She was tired, in pain, and desperate to lie down. 'Just a twinge.'

He looked at her closely. 'You don't seem very well. What's wrong? You're quite pale.'

She went to tell him, then changed her mind. His concern had her perilously close to tears. Holly was too proud to cry in front of someone she hardly knew. 'Been a long day, that's all.' Thankfully, her voice was steady.

'I'm sorry,' he apologised again, thinking she was referring to the bus trips. 'I'll make it up to you.'

They walked to the door of her room. 'Good night.' He bent his head and kissed her cheek. 'Sleep tight.' A quick grin, and he turned and walked away.

FIVE

Holly spent an uncomfortable night. If she tried to turn over, the pain woke her. Shadowy figures with evil intent ran amok in her mind. Finally, she found the most comfortable position – flat on her back – and fell into a deep and dreamless sleep. The telephone rang what seemed to be only minutes later but the sun was well up.

'It's Justin. Did I wake you?'

'Yuh!' she mumbled, wondering why her ribs felt tight then remembering the bandaging. The bedside clock showed seven twenty. Far too early for Holly.

'Sorry, the police have just called. The manager reported the break-in. Something to do with the hotel's insurance claim. I'd hoped to avoid this but it can't be helped. The police are sending a car. I have no idea how long it will take. We might have to do Pamplemousses another day.'

She should have realised something like this would happen and regretted turning down Connor's invitation. 'It's okay. I think a day of rest is called for anyway.'

'How are the ribs?'

'Bit sore. You?'

'Not too bad. Looks worse than it feels. I'd better go, maybe see you later.'

Holly lay staring up at the ceiling. Great! Now what? Madame Liang maybe? No harm in trying her, though she might not agree to being interviewed at such short notice. Holly was thinking ahead. She could start with the Chinese-Mauritian angle and follow up with the French-Mauritian perspective on Sunday. That left the Indian and Creole population. Some of Connor's relatives might come in handy and there was always that nice doctor who taped up her ribs. Nothing too in-depth, but Australians would be fascinated by the multicultural melting pot in Mauritius. Bit of history, some anecdotes. It would certainly add flavour to her piece about the island itself. Maybe even do something similar on Rodrigues. There were several magazines in Australia that would buy an article like that and there were always the Sundays to fall back on. Split the story between two islands. Two cheques instead of one. Perhaps she could slip down to Réunion and across to Madagascar once this assignment was finished. Do a four-piece thing on the Sea of Zanj.

The day was looking better already. But first the problem of ablutions had to be solved. A shower was out of the question, but using the base of it as a shallow bath might avoid getting the bandages too wet.

Twenty minutes later it was obvious that she might as well have showered. Holly doubted that the protective strapping would last. It was driving her mad already. Anyway, she'd read somewhere that these days, the medical profession in Australia preferred ribs to heal with no support. Something to do with pain being an essential element in not overdoing things, she supposed.

There was just enough complimentary instant coffee for one strong cup. Waiting for it to cool, Holly fished out the card Madame Liang had given her. The address was in Port Louis. She checked her watch before dialling. Eight twenty-five. Business hours ranged from anywhere between six in the morning and seven in the evening. She took a chance and dialled the number.

'Liang and Associates.' The telephonist sounded professional, well bred and bored.

Liang Song had told Holly to make the appointment with her secretary. To hell with that! 'I'd like to speak to Madame Liang please.'

'Which Madame Liang?'

'Madame Liang Song.'

'Who's calling please?'

'Holly Jones.'

'Hold please.'

Piped music entertained her for nearly a minute.

'Miss Jones.' Holly didn't know how she did it but Madame Liang's voice was a reflection of her face – hard, sort of like setting cement.

'You agreed to an interview.' Holly wasted no time. 'I'd like to set it up.'

'When?'

'Today.'

'Today!' Amusement crept into Madame Liang's tone.

'I know it's short notice.'

Silence. Good sign. She was thinking about it. Then, 'I have meetings this morning. If you'll hold on a moment I'll check with my secretary. We might be able to meet for lunch?'

Slapped wrist! Holly was reasonably certain that the Chinese woman would already know if she were free for lunch. She was being punished for the bypass.

After a lengthy wait, Liang Song came back on the line. 'It is possible to reschedule one or two things. We can meet for lunch.'

Okay, now I know how important you are. 'On one condition.'

'Condition?' She made no attempt to hide her disapproval. Conditions were things Madame Liang imposed on others, not the reverse.

'Lunch is my shout.' Holly grinned. In her experience, success with people like Liang Song was more likely if their control of people or situations was temporarily out of reach. For some reason, Holly didn't quite know why, the more arrogant and commanding an individual, the more important it was to try to keep them off balance. Given the upper hand, some of them seemed to feel morally obliged to be uncooperative.

'Shout?' Puzzlement was clear in the Chinese woman's voice. She had evidently never heard the expression.

'An Australianism,' Holly explained. 'It means I'd like to buy you lunch.'

'There's no need.' Liang Song didn't like it. Power play was everything. Even something as small as being taken for lunch removed some of her authority.

'Oh, but I insist,' Holly said cheerfully. 'Incidentally, I'll be taping the conversation. You don't mind, do you?'

'I suppose it's necessary?'

It was working. A small concession, yet you'd think Madame Liang had been asked to give away her personal fortune. 'Would you care to suggest a restaurant?' Give her back control.

This was more to the Chinese woman's liking. 'Labourdonnais Hotel. Meet me in the foyer. It's on Caudan Waterfront.'

'I assume that's in Port Louis?'

'Of course. Your taxi driver will know how to find it. I'll book a table, you'd never get in. One o'clock.'

Holly said that would be just fine. Madame Liang hung up without further comment.

It took most of the morning to prepare her questions. At eleven thirty she caught a taxi to the capital.

The Caudan Waterfront was new, stretching around three sides of the harbour and separated from the frantic city centre of Port Louis by a pedestrian underpass. The boulevards were free of traffic and far from crowded. Large shopping centres housed boutiques, handicraft markets, art galleries, duty-free shops, hotels, restaurants and a cinema. Holly had plenty of time to enjoy playing the tourist before making her way to the impressive Labourdonnais Hotel. She chose a chair from which she could observe the entrance and settled down to wait.

Liang Song was only twenty minutes late. Holly had anticipated thirty. She made an entrance like a movie star in a bad mood – head up, coldly gracious to anyone crass enough to greet her, fixed smile and a look in her eyes that said, 'I'm here, I'm performing, but don't ask me to like it'.

'Sorry I'm late.' She wasn't, her tone made that quite plain.

Two words competed for attention in Holly's head. Regal was one. Bitch the other. The latter triumphed. 'You have lipstick on your teeth.'

She didn't, but Liang Song wasn't to know that. In fact, she looked breathtaking in a sea green cheongsam of embossed satin, slit up one side to reveal a silky thigh. Glossy black hair hung, thick and perfectly in place, to her shoulders. Pale flawless skin glowed with health. Ruby-red lipstick, expertly applied, gleamed. Her shoes, which matched the dress, must have cost a small fortune. A white clutch bag completed the picture. Holly felt rumpled, dowdy and boring.

As good starts went, this one was not perfect. Holly's opening words hit home and the game was on. Madame Liang blinked and scrubbed a forefinger across her teeth in a quick and furtive movement, uncertainty suddenly evident on her normally expressionless face. 'Gone?'

Holly nodded, her conscience bothering her not at all. Composure returning, the Chinese woman, with a withering look at Holly's linen trouser suit, asked with feigned concern, 'Aren't you hot in that jacket?'

Okay! 'Not at all. I'm quite used to the heat.' In point of fact, with the air-conditioning apparently having a bad day, Holly's bandages were acting like a thermal vest. She was damned nearly expiring from the temperature but would rather die than admit it.

Abruptly, Liang Song turned and strode away leaving Holly to follow. The restaurant was extremely busy but somehow the Chinese woman had managed to get them a table.

In rapid French, she ordered for both of them. Holly said nothing. The maître d'hôtel, who materialised the moment they had been seated, was doing his impression of obsequious with all the fervour of a squirming puppy. Madame Liang Song was probably his idea of royalty. He was star-struck, turning himself inside out to cater for her every whim. *Either that*, Holly thought nastily, *or a visit from the family thugs is something he'd rather avoid*. Her guest brought the performance to its conclusion with the wave of a hand and the man melted into thin air. She turned and stared expectantly at Holly.

Holly decided to be brisk. The tape recorder lay on the table between them. Holly turned it on. 'How old are you?'

Madame Liang looked surprised, not expecting such a blunt personal question, but she answered with no hesitation. 'Twenty-eight.'

'Young to be a company director.'

'It's a family business.'

'So I gather. What exactly do you import?'

The Chinese woman flipped one hand back and forth. 'Specialist foods from around the world. Furniture. White goods. Cars. Building products. Agricultural machinery. Alcohol – wine mainly. Textiles.' She broke off. 'Just about anything.'

'Would you say you are the biggest importer in Mauritius?'

'No.'

Holly raised her eyebrows. 'One of the biggest then?'

Madame Liang smiled slightly. 'If you like.'

Holly changed tack. 'How did your family come to Mauritius?'

With no sign of rancour, the response came back. 'Indentured labour, as with most of the Chinese here.'

'Does that make you resentful?'

'Why should it?'

Holly wasn't going to be led. 'Are all Sino-Mauritians practising Christians?'

'No. But most of us are.'

'You're a Christian?'

'Yes. Roman Catholic.'

A waiter brought Madame Liang the fragrant tea she ordered.

Holly leaned forward on her elbows. 'What do you do when you're not working?'

A surprised blink. 'Go to the cinema. There are many parties. See my friends.'

'Are these questions too personal for you?'

'No.' The answer was slow in coming.

'But you're having a problem with one or two of them,' Holly probed. 'Why?'

'I thought you wanted general material on Chinese Mauritians.' Madame Liang's eyes narrowed. 'I don't see the relevance of my age or what I do privately.'

'Allow me to be the judge of that,' Holly said in a cold voice. 'You pointed out to me yesterday that Sino-Mauritians are different from Westerners. This is an article for Australians. I think I'm qualified to know what they like to read.'

Madame Liang didn't like that much but merely inclined her head.

Holly went on, knowing the Chinese woman would not expect, and most probably hate, the next question.

'Do you have a boyfriend?'

'No.'

She didn't hesitate, Holly had to give her that. She pushed further. 'Have you ever had one?'

'No.'

'Why is that?'

'My husband wouldn't like it.'

Holly was about to laugh but killed it when she saw that Liang Song was not trying to be funny. Her eyes dropped to the Chinese woman's hands. Ringless.

Madame Liang noted the brief inspection.

'Surely,' she said coldly, 'your French is good enough to know the difference between madame and mademoiselle.'

'You don't wear a wedding ring,' Holly defended herself.

'I will when the time is right.'

It didn't make sense. 'What do you mean?'

Liang Song looked uncomfortable. Eventually she said, 'It is difficult for a Westerner to understand. My family is of a certain class. It's impossible for me to marry beneath it. On Mauritius there are few families considered to be suitable. The Liangs are one. My husband will be the sole beneficiary of their not inconsiderable interests. It's business. He is young. We do not yet live as man and wife.'

'How long have you been married?'

'Nearly two years.'

'How old is he?' Holly thought he might be in his early twenties.

'This really can't be of interest.'

'I assure you, it is.'

'Why?'

'Because it's totally alien to the Australian way of life.'

Madame Liang speared Holly with a defiant look and answered the question. 'Sixteen.'

It was Holly's turn to blink. That's all she did. She knew when to stop pushing. But her thoughts were a different matter. Sixteen! The poor little bastard had been saddled with this cold creature since he was only fourteen. Jesus! There must be a law against it.

Madame Liang sipped her tea, waiting for the next question.

Very deliberately, Holly changed tack. 'Why do you want me to warn Connor Maguire to stay away from you?'

With no change of expression, the ice maiden again showed her mettle. 'I thought we'd covered that last night. In any event, it has nothing to do with your article.'

'Okay. Answer this. Why do the Chinese community stick so closely together?'

'We're no different from any other group. A segregated society has developed on Mauritius and no-one sees any reason to change it. The Chinese are very clannish.'

'Surely every now and then someone from outside breaks through? It must happen.'

Madame Liang gave an elaborate shrug. 'Sometimes. Not often.'

'What would be the consequences? Let me put to you a hypothetical scenario. A beautiful Chinese girl, such as yourself, meets and falls in love with a French-Mauritian man. What's the outcome?'

'As I said,' Madame Liang answered tersely, 'it can happen. She would probably be ostracised by her own family.'

'And the French?'

'She'd be accepted but only after a fashion.'

'What if she were French and the man Chinese?'

'Then neither side would accept them.'

'Why not?'

The Chinese face was unreadable. 'It's hard to explain. Each of the ethnic groups has its own customs. If someone from mine, male or female, went outside of it they would be shunned. That is our way. The French?' Another expressive shrug. 'Their men's word is law. They get away with murder. But women must be at least seen to conform.'

Holly nodded, then referred back to her notes. 'What is the inflation rate in Mauritius?'

The answer came so quickly that Holly wondered if Liang Song had just looked it up. 'Under seven per cent.'

'You mentioned the class system. Is there much poverty?'

'Some, but we also enjoy high rates of employment.'

'What does Mauritius export?'

Again, the answer was self-assured and immediate. 'Sugar, mainly. Tea, tobacco, fruit and vegetables. We can compete against Europe because of the seasonal differences.'

'I've seen some big name clothing labels that have apparently been manufactured here. How does that work?'

'The government offers tax incentives for companies to set up here. Wages are low and our people work hard. The textile and wool industries have been particularly successful. It's mainly for export but tourists buy a lot also.'

'South Africa has invested heavily in the tourist industry.'

Madame Liang nodded. 'So have others,

although we get most of our visitors from the African mainland. Many of the big hotels are South African owned.'

'GDP?'

Madame Liang's brow wrinkled. 'I'm not sure. The Reserve Bank would give you up-to-date economic indicators.'

'Okay. So, would you say that Mauritius is booming?'

Madame Liang came close to a genuine smile. 'Very much so. We all work hard to make it so.'

Their first course arrived and Holly switched off the tape. 'Thank you. After lunch, time permitting, I'd like to ask just a few more questions.'

Madame Liang's look gave nothing away. 'Certainly.'

Holly turned her attention to the food. Madame Liang had ordered Filets de Sole Marguery for them both – fillet of sole ringed by mussels and shrimp and then covered with a white wine sauce. It was delicious. Their main course was Selle d'Agneau Armenonville – roast saddle of lamb with green beans, cocotte potatoes and artichoke hearts stuffed with tomato. A bottle of *petit* Chablis rather let the side down. It was five years old and well past its prime. Madame Liang seemed not to notice but then, she barely touched her glass, preferring the tea which the waiter kept topping up.

'Dessert?'

'Not for me.'

'As you wish.' Crêpes Suzette made its way

down Madame Liang's throat. Holly wondered how she kept her figure.

The interview resumed. Holly asked about the effects of tourism, whether Mauritians were concerned about global warming and the ozone layer, what was being done to protect the indigenous flora and fauna, wildlife reserves, the crime rate and finally, was there a drug problem. To all but the last question, Madame Liang answered patiently and directly.

'There's no drug problem here,' she said sharply.

'I'm told they are freely available. Whatever you want.'

'Isolated incident. We can't keep them out altogether. Every now and then you'll see a piece in the newspaper about someone caught carrying drugs into Mauritius. It is generally believed that we are used as a halfway house where drugs can be held before being moved on to Europe. I think you'll find, Miss Jones, if it's a drug angle you're after, that Mauritius is fairly clean.'

'I'm not set on any specific angle, Madame Liang. I'm looking for one.'

Liang Song's face remained expressionless.

Holly returned to Chinese-related specifics. After a further fifteen minutes, Madame Liang checked her watch. 'I'm sorry, I have to go.'

Holly turned off the tape. 'Thank you for your time.'

'Will you be speaking to other Chinese from here?'

'If time permits. The article must be informative

for potential tourists. This is largely background material.'

'In your country, do you have many Chinese people?'

The question surprised Holly. It was the first time the woman had shown even the slightest interest in anything other than herself. 'Yes, we have a large Chinese population. Have you been to Australia?'

Liang Song shook her head.

Holly pulled a card from her bag. 'If you ever get there, this is where I can be contacted.' She pushed the card across the table.

Almond eyes examined it. The card was picked up and slowly, very deliberately, ripped in two. Madame Liang rose. 'Now why would I want to do that?' With a curt nod she left Holly sitting at the table.

A laugh bubbled up and Holly had to put a hand over her mouth to silence it. She might have bulldozed the woman into an interview but Madame Liang had certainly enjoyed the last word. Holly couldn't help but admire her exit line. When she called for the bill, Holly discovered that Liang Song wasn't above turning the screws as far as she could. Their meal had been paid for.

Since she was in Port Louis, Holly decided to explore some of the old city. The central market, only minutes' walk from Caudan Waterfront, was a jumble of stalls, seething with people and selling everything from food to curios. Not looking for anything in particular, she ended up buying a beautiful handmade tablecloth for her mother.

Wandering the labyrinth of narrow cobbled streets seemed like stepping back in time. Although Port Louis was laid out in a grid pattern, shops made full use of the footpath to display their wares, leaving little or no room for the thousands of pedestrians who were forced to duck between traffic on the road. It was easy to lose a sense of direction. But, with the help of a map, Holly was able to orientate herself. She was on Jummah Mosque Street heading up and away from the bustling, overcrowded centre of town. About to turn back, where the buildings finished Holly noticed an old flight of steps leading up the grassy hillside to a dark stone fortress set high and alone above the city. Thinking it would provide a good view of Port Louis, Holly set off. Over one hundred steps later, and short of breath, she reached the top. The effort caused considerable protest from her left side and it took some time for the sharp pain to subside.

A plaque above the fort entrance revealed that the peeling structure was called Fort Adelaide and had been built by the British garrison in the reign of William IV. Inside the walls, several of the old chambers had been refurbished and turned into craft shops, otherwise the place had a dejected air of abandonment. A friendly assistant in one of the shops informed Holly that the fort was generally referred to as the Citadel and that it was linked by tunnels – closed to the public – to other forts down by the harbour, which were called Victoria, William and George. She added the gruesome information that about thirty years ago two children had been murdered in cold blood up here.

The steps to the battlements were closed, so Holly went back outside. Looking out over Port Louis, the reason for the city's overcrowding was obvious. It lay in a basin. Hemmed in by mountains on three sides and opening onto the harbour, there simply wasn't room for urban sprawl. Steel and concrete jutted skywards, dwarfing older buildings of wood and wrought iron. Suburbia looked distinctly working class with box-shaped houses set cheek-by-jowl. Of shady trees and colourful gardens there was little sign. By comparison, outstanding in size and park-like in appearance was Champ de Mars, the oldest horseracing track in the southern hemisphere and evidence of Mauritians' passion for gambling. The Caudan Waterfront looked tiny and the harbour, the island's only safe haven for boats during a cyclone, didn't seem big enough to turn around a Manly ferry.

A road winding down the side of the hill appeared to be the more usual way to reach the Citadel and probably explained why the steps were in such bad repair. Several children hung shyly back but their eyes were alert for any sign that begging might prove fruitful. A jogger, who had run up the steps with ease, continued his exercise along the road. *Bloody show-off*, Holly thought, admiring the man's trim and taut body.

By contrast, two other people, stooping hands on knees by the top step, were recovering from their exertions. Holly felt sympathetic, her gaze travelling past to the ocean beyond before recognition snapped her eyes back to them. They were Chinese. It took only a moment to remember where she'd seen them before. Mahébourg. Yesterday. Lunching with Liang Song. One of them noticed her watching. He looked away and said something to his companion, whose eyes flicked briefly towards Holly.

A prickle of fear ran through her. What had Connor said about them? They were Madame Liang's uncles. Holly pretended to look at the view but her mind was racing. The children were still there. A couple – honeymooners by the way they were glued together – stared down at the harbour. A taxi arrived carrying a middle-aged man and woman, who spent two minutes taking photographs then got back into the vehicle, which sped off down the hill again.

The Chinese men loitered by the steps. Holly reached a decision. It was broad daylight and there were too many people around for her to be in any danger. She would simply go back down the steps. Steeling herself, she made her way past the pair.

Don't panic. Holly forced herself to walk slowly. There was a group of school children with their teacher struggling up the steps. *You're safe*, her mind said. *Don't panic.*

Even so, in the humid heat her linen trouser suit and silk shirt were made even more clinging by the sudden stickiness of fear. She felt itchy under the bandages around her midriff. She dared not risk a look back. When she reached the road, it was two blocks before the streets became crowded and bustling. A line of four taxis stood outside a seedy-looking hotel and Holly almost dived into the first. 'Merville Beach Hotel, Grand Baie.' She looked back as the taxi pulled away from the kerb. The two Chinese men were running for the next in line.

Traffic was not merely congested, it was impossible. The driver, an Indian, clucked and fussed behind the wheel, finally apologising for the delays.

'It's not your fault.' Holly welcomed the confusion, confident that in such riotous bedlam the two men following her would never be able to keep up. So, when she checked behind once they were onto the main road heading north, she was both surprised and horrified to see their taxi close behind.

Her driver glanced in the rear-vision mirror, frowning. 'You are being followed, Mademoiselle.'

'I know.'

'The driver is my friend. He is not experienced. His passengers must know your destination.'

Of course! Madame Liang knew where she was staying.

'Would Mademoiselle like me to stop at the police station?'

They can't get to me at the hotel, Holly thought, and then she remembered what had happened to Justin and herself the previous evening. 'I don't think that will be necessary.'

Her driver shrugged.

Why would Madame Liang have her followed? To see where she went, who she spoke to? But why? What was the Chinese woman so concerned about? Holly didn't think Liang Song meant to physically harm her, which meant that she was being followed, none too expertly and perhaps even deliberately ostentatiously, to see where she went and to make sure she knew about it. *Okay, if that's all there is to it they should leave me alone once I get to the hotel.*

With some misgivings over the reliability of her conclusions, Holly paid off the taxi driver and walked inside, deliberately loitering behind a group of tourists trying to check out. The Chinese men did not follow.

There was a note from Justin at reception. *I've been moved to Room 24. Give me a call when you get in.*

Before she did, there was a little matter needing urgent attention. The bandages had to go. Hoping their removal would not cause further damage, she unwound the restrictive binding. Without support, it hurt slightly to breathe and sudden movement was not a good idea. But oh, the relief! Testing gingerly, Holly twisted this way and that until she had a pretty good idea what she could and could not do. What it boiled down to was keep perfectly still and all would be fine.

She showered off the stickiness of Port Louis before dialling Justin's number. He answered on the first ring. 'Holly! Where did you disappear to? Is everything okay?'

'Everything's fine.'

'Like to sit on the beach and watch the sunset?

'Sounds about the right speed. Anything strenuous might severely strain the pact I just made with my ribs.'

'Still sore?' He sounded concerned. 'A gentle dip in the sea is what you need. See you downstairs.'

As she changed into a swimsuit, Holly wondered about Justin. Why had his room been broken into? It hadn't been a simple burglary. Nothing, according to him, seemed to be missing but he hadn't exactly had a good look. It was almost as if he knew what it was the intruder had been searching for. And if so, what was it and had it been found? Now she came to think about it, Justin had been a little too calm considering all his possessions had been destroyed. Was Justin Parker what he said he was? Holly supposed a rival research group might have instigated the break-in but that possibility seemed a little far-fetched. And was the burglary somehow linked to the attack on the beach?

She left the room, still uncertain. Justin was a nice enough person on the surface but who was he exactly? Something about him kept her wary.

He was waiting for her in the foyer, sporting a face that drew curious stares – one eye was completely closed and he had a greenish-black shiner. The split lip had returned to its normal size but there was no disguising the scab that had formed. They walked down to the beach. 'I was back here

175

by midday,' Justin said. 'Thought we could still go to Pamplemousses but I couldn't find you anywhere.'

'I've been to Port Louis. Managed to set up an interview with a Chinese businesswoman called Madame Liang Song.'

'I've met her. Quite a powerful lady by all accounts.'

Holly glanced at him. His voice had held no secrets, his face was impassive. She wondered again why they had been speaking so intently the other day. 'She's only twenty-eight. Pretty young to be a company director.'

'Really?' Justin sounded vague. 'I thought she was older than that.'

'She gave me some good material about the Chinese community. Stuff I can really use.'

'Here do?' Justin stopped, took off his shirt and dumped it, along with a towel, onto the sand.

Holly unwrapped the sarong she'd worn over her bikini, dropping her gear on top of his.

'What happened to the bandages?'

'I took them off. They were driving me nuts.'

His eyebrows raised. 'Was that wise?'

'In Australia they don't even bother.'

'Well . . . ' He looked doubtful. 'Take it easy if you plan to swim. You're quite badly bruised.'

'It's water. What can it do?'

The bay was calm and crystal clear. It was also surprisingly cold, though that could have been because she was unable to swim. The temperature certainly wasn't bothering Justin.

After five minutes, Holly gave up and left the water. Picking up her towel, she inadvertently collected Justin's shirt as well. Putting it back, something slid out of the pocket. A photograph by the look of it. Returning it, she noticed that it was a map of some kind. Probably to do with his research.

Justin joined her a few minutes later. 'You'd never guess that this is supposed to be winter. The sea in Britain doesn't get this warm in summer. Just look at that sunset.'

It was spectacular. Low storm clouds gathered dark against the horizon. Closer to land, ridged layers of altocumulus floated – mixed meteorological signals, since one warned of rain while the other promised sunshine. All were washed with brilliant orange light which drained the sky of blue, turning it instead a silvery grey. This same colour was reflected in the rippled waters of the lagoon, cut only by ribbons of black lines as boats made their way back to their night-time buoys inside Grand Baie.

Holly leaned back on her elbows, quickly wished she hadn't and sat up, hugging her knees. The scenery was fantastic but her mind was on more practical matters. 'How did it go with the police?'

'Bloody tedious.'

'Did you tell them about being attacked on the beach?'

'No.'

'Why not? They must have been curious about your face.'

'If they were, they made no comment. You weren't there. The business with the room was bad enough. It took hours. In the end all I did was make a statement and list what had been damaged.'

'Nothing missing?'

'Not from the room, no.'

'What do you mean?'

'I think something was stolen from my pocket when we were knocked down.'

'You *think*. Don't you know?'

'It was just a sheet of paper. I may have dropped it without noticing.'

'What makes you think it might have been stolen?'

'Competitors. Someone else working on the same research.' He shrugged. 'I'm only guessing.'

'What was the paper?'

'A map. Possible dodo nesting sites. It's not a problem, I've got a copy of it.'

The photograph she'd seen in his pocket? It could have been a laminated colour copy. Maybe not. The map looked quite old. Of that she was certain. All she said, however, was, 'It's getting dark. If you don't mind, Justin, I've had enough of this beach at night.'

'We've got another half-hour. Besides, there are plenty of people about.'

They were right in front of the hotel and in full view of at least fifty people. It didn't make Holly feel any more secure. As they went back through the terraced bar area, she reflected that the attack last night must have rattled her more than she knew.

Holly had declined the offered sundowner. She wanted to play back her interview with Madame Liang and perhaps make a start on the tourist piece. That was the plan. She thought she'd just lie down for a moment first. When the phone woke her it was fully dark outside. Reaching out to stop the incessant shrill a sharp pain suggested sitting up first. She swung her legs off the bed and picked up the receiver. 'Holly Jones.'

'It's Connor. Got some great news. You doing anything tonight?'

'Well, I . . .'

'Good. Pick you up in half-an-hour.'

So much for work! After a quick shower, Holly pulled a pair of brown chinos from the wardrobe, went to put them on, shook her head and delved back into the cupboard. Not much choice but the taupe slacks would look better, especially with a white blouse. She surveyed herself critically. Since coming to Mauritius she'd picked up a little colour on her face. Nothing wrong with adding a shade more. Blusher and lipstick, nothing special. A dab of perfume behind the ears. The hair dryer worked well and her short cut needed no special attention. She looked at her reflection and nodded, satisfied. The suntan had masked the tension lines around her mouth. On closer inspection, she saw that they were actually fading. *Must be smiling more*, she thought. Come to that, and despite last night's little drama, she was feeling happier. Quinn had been right. Perhaps it was the complete change of tempo in this holiday haven, or maybe it was the tropical surroundings, or even something as simple as the perfect weather. Whatever it was, last night aside, this assignment was good for her.

A plain, no-nonsense cafe and bar at Cap Malheureux, north-east of Grand Baie, was Connor's destination. Creole curries appeared to be their speciality. Remembering her large and rich lunch, Holly ordered an entree only.

Connor didn't seem in any hurry to tell her his news. Instead, she found herself listening to enthusiastic talk of future plans. It was remarkable to hear him speak of opportunities just waiting to be tapped. He had a clear-eyed view of what would work and what wouldn't, employing others with the necessary skills or experience to implement his visions. He was also a great believer in the value of the veteran, rather than automatically choosing young, highly qualified but inexperienced candidates for a job. The strategy clearly worked. That, plus leaving day-to-day decision-making to those appointed to make them, rather than interfering and imposing his own instructions. Connor obviously believed in the worthiness of people, and showing appreciation for a job well done.

'It costs nothing,' he was saying. 'It works for you and it works for those around you. In the end, everyone wins.'

'A policy more people should adopt. Those fortunate enough to have the opportunity are so often on their own personal ego trip.'

He smiled slightly. 'Such a waste of energy.'

'I agree, but let's not forget that at least one

person I could mention never had to fight for what he's got.'

Again, a little smile. There was that damned dimple. 'Okay, I may have been born with a silver spoon in my mouth. Is that some kind of crime?'

She smiled back. 'I guess not. Now, are you going to tell me what this great news is?'

Excitement lit his eyes. 'Remember I'd found a Maguire in the phone book? Turned out to be a Thomas Maguire. As soon as I told him my name he insisted I come and see him. Nice chap. When I explained what I was looking for . . .'

'The treasure?'

'What do you think? Patience, dear girl. Information about William. Family tree stuff.'

Holly pulled a wry face.

'Give me a break! I couldn't just tell them I'm here to find their ancestor's treasure.'

'Sorry.'

'As I was saying, when I explained what I was looking for Thomas said that I should talk to his sister. He called her up and she came over. She's a nun. Works at a convent school in Mahébourg. Her name is Kathleen. Like her brother, very enthusiastic at meeting another Maguire. She proved extremely helpful. Filled in a lot of blanks. Even offered to show me the site of William's house. We went there this afternoon. It overlooks old Grand Port. I'd never have found it on my own. Not much to see but there's a kind of atmosphere about the place.'

'And did you eventually . . . ?'

'Holly, what do you take me for? Give me some credit. Of course I told her about the journal.'

'What did she say?'

'Already knew of it. And she wasn't at all bothered by my interest in it.'

'Must have been weird being in her company.'

'It was. Generations ago, her ancestor and mine were brothers.' Connor shook his head. 'Now look at us.'

'Did you experience any kind of emotion? Any bonding?'

'Not really. I think both of us thought we should have but neither of us did.'

'Hardly surprising.'

'We may have nothing else in common, but my civilised mind told me Kathleen is a relative, therefore I will feel connected.'

'And you didn't.'

'I liked her. Connected? Not really.' He laughed at himself. 'I was probably going through some kind of ethical struggle between a learned response and reality.' He changed the subject suddenly. 'How was your day?'

Holly assumed he'd get to the point when he felt like it. 'I was supposed to visit Pamplemousses Gardens. The trip was cancelled so I set up an interview with Madame Liang Song instead.'

Connor's eyebrows registered what he clearly hadn't expected. 'Did you indeed. I'm surprised she agreed.'

'She wasn't given the chance to refuse.'

'So,' he said softly. 'There's a tough side after all.'

'Rock hard.'

His eyes twinkled. 'You wish.'

Holly would have preferred to keep the conversation away from personal feelings. 'There has to be, in my business.'

'Only on the outside, Holly. Underneath is what really counts.' He sensed her discomfort, going on to ask, 'And how was the lady?'

'Immaculate.'

He laughed. 'She is rather.'

'Inscrutable.'

'Madame Liang? Never.'

'A bit like interviewing a wind-up doll.'

'Now, now. Did you get what you wanted?'

'A few quotable quotes, some good business background, a couple of reluctant peeks into her personal life and a bloody good lunch. I had a wander around Port Louis afterwards and found myself being followed by the two Chinese gentlemen whose conversation you were so fascinated by yesterday. They knew I was on to them but it didn't seem to matter. I was followed all the way back to my hotel.'

Connor looked concerned. 'Be careful, Holly. You promised not to rock any boats. Don't gamble with your own safety just for a story.'

'Why follow me though? I'm a journalist. It stands to reason that I ask a lot of questions. Why so paranoid about a tourist article? I'm fairly sure Madame Liang had them find out where I went after our lunch but I fail to understand her reason. Unless it's because she's seen me with you.' Holly waited but Connor made no comment. She sighed and said with heavy sarcasm, 'No, please. I insist you tell me nothing.'

'Holly, I'm sorry. I just can't say any more.'

She shrugged. 'I can probably work it out for myself. Let's see. It's safe enough to assume that your exceedingly long business arm extends right around the world. In other words, you are known in boardrooms from Cape Town to Cairo, Marrakech to Michigan, Leningrad to Lightning Ridge and all points in between. You have an astonishingly high profile, Maguire, and, more importantly, you are very well connected. I'm a little cloudy on your motives since you don't strike me as the type to do anything so stupid you're likely to end up in prison, but a short flight of fancy leads me to all kinds of interesting possibilities.'

'Such as?' His eyes were unreadable.

'You said it yourself. Drugs. Mauritius is in the middle of a bloody great ocean. So we expect to find boats and yachts of every size and purpose. We also have direct flights to and from Africa, Europe, India and Australia. You see what I'm speculating on here, Maguire? This island is ideally placed to act as a clearing house for supplying drugs from the East to the African mainland, Europe and the west coast of Australia. An Indian connection makes sense since about seventy per cent of Mauritians originated from that part of the world. The Chinese hook-up is not immediately apparent but I'll bet anything you care to mention that Madame Liang is in it right up to her pretty little Chinese collar. How am I doing?'

'Way off beam.'

'So help me out, Maguire.'

He reached across the table and gripped her arm, not painfully but with just enough strength in his fingers to say that he was serious. 'Drop it, Holly.'

She snatched her arm away. A waiter appeared with two beers and Holly used the diversion to control her frustration. When the man had moved away, she said, 'You were telling me about your day. We seem to have veered off the subject.' She had no idea how angry her eyes were.

Connor tried to make light of it. 'I'm sorry.' He laughed. 'I seem to spend my time apologising to you.'

Surprising herself, she forgave him, though she did question the sudden lapse into feminine acquiescence. 'Forget it. I hate mysteries, it's as simple as that. Tell me about Kathleen.'

With contentious issues momentarily sidetracked, Connor and Holly stopped skirting warily around each other. 'Like I said, she's a nun. What I didn't mention is her interest in genealogy – must be a family failing.' Connor produced some folded sheets of paper from his pocket and spread them out in front of him. 'Are you ready for this?'

Eyeing them upside down, Holly saw names and arrows going off in all directions.

'I've got my tape with me. Do you mind if I run it?'

'You'd better. I'm not sure I want to go through it all again.'

Holly switched on the machine.

'When William Maguire died, he left, among others, a baby son.'

'That information is in the journal. Thomas, if I recall. He was the youngest of three.'

'Correct. But Kathleen had additional information.' Connor sipped his beer, peering at the notes in concentration. 'Apparently Thomas became a fisherman. Kathleen has no idea what happened to the other two children.'

'How does she know about Thomas?'

'I'll get to that. Thomas married and had four children. His only son, Sean, was born around 1770. While still in his teens, Sean followed in the footsteps of his grandfather and joined the self-proclaimed pirate king called Robert Surcouf. You mentioned him the other day. He operated out of Port Louis.'

'What happened to Sean?'

'He was killed in a skirmish with the British.'

'Did he have a family?'

'After a fashion. Various children littered from here to the Seychelles. About three years after he died, a woman approached Thomas with a child she said was Sean's. Thomas obviously believed her. He christened the boy William and raised him as his own for ten years.'

Holly's head was spinning.

Connor looked up. 'You still with me?'

'Recap for the tape. The first William Maguire had a son called Thomas. His son was Sean and Sean's son was William. Okay, I think that's clear enough.'

'It gets better. There's a third William, another Sean, two Georges and a second Thomas.'

Holly grinned. 'I'll say this for the Mauritian contingent of the Maguire family, they're consistent, if a little lacking in originality.'

'Stick with it. I'll make it brief. When Thomas died, the journal was handed to William. Apparently, Thomas must have seen that the young man could be trusted. He certainly hadn't been close to his own son, Sean.'

'Okay. What happened next?'

'When William died in 1847 – William the second, that is – the journal went to his son, George, and then to his son, Gilchrist. Gilchrist didn't live long, about thirty-five years. He drowned.'

'Any more pirates?'

'No. After Sean, the family settled down and became full-time fishermen.'

'Before you go on, did Kathleen say why no-one followed the map and looked for William's treasure?'

'I expect they did but, back then, it wouldn't have been easy. We have the advantage of accurate maps, metal detectors and other forms of technology, not to mention the convenience of good roads and fast cars. The journal doesn't say where the treasure is hidden. It might even be on Rodrigues.'

'Okay. Where were we?'

'Drowning with Gilchrist.'

'I suppose he had a son?'

'Several, apparently. The only one Kathleen has information on is Sean. He was only four when his father drowned.'

'What year are we talking here?'

'Um,' Connor peered at his notes, 'Gilchrist drowned in 1873.'

'So Mauritius was well and truly British by then?'

Connor nodded. 'Since the Treaty of Paris in 1814. It was Gilchrist's wife who sent the journal to Ireland for safe-keeping. That's the Aroon I told you about, the one who enclosed a note with it.'

'And it went to the wrong side of the family. Who delivered it?'

'Aroon gave it to a missionary who was being recalled to Ireland for health reasons. He died aboard the ship taking him home and he entrusted its delivery to a fellow passenger.'

'I wonder why Aroon felt it necessary to send the journal home? What would prompt her to do that?'

'Kathleen thinks it had something to do with the Free Labour Association. You see, they abolished slavery here in 1835 and very few of the slaves stayed on the sugar estates. Property owners had to look elsewhere for labour. An immigration scheme between Mauritius and India was established and coolie labour became commonplace but conditions were appalling. Wages operated on a double cut system which meant employers could withhold two days' pay for every day a worker took off. Sickness virtually guaranteed that most coolies were actually in debt most of the time. So unrest erupted. There was fear among the Creoles that they'd be forced back into labour. As keeper of

Williams' journal, Aroon probably thought it would be safer in Ireland.'

'And there it stayed until you found it?'

'Yes.'

'Where does Kathleen fit in?'

'The second Sean had a son, William the third. He was killed in 1917 fighting the German, von Lettow, in Tanganyika. His son was George the second and George's son was Thomas the second.'

Holly shook her head rapidly in an effort to take it in. 'Thank God that's all on tape.'

Connor grinned at her. 'The detail doesn't matter. What does is that Kathleen is a sister of the second Thomas.'

'And something of a family historian.'

'Only so far as the original William's son, Thomas, is concerned. She has no idea what became of his sisters. She's restricted her research to a direct link with the first William Maguire.'

'This is all very interesting . . .' Holly broke off as their meal arrived, '. . . as history goes. But you don't appear to know any more about the treasure itself.'

'Oh but I do.' Connor held up a yellowish piece of paper. 'I have the map.'

He spread it carefully on the table. Holly looked at it aghast. It was the original of the copy she'd seen in Justin's pocket.

SIX

A myriad of thoughts swept through Holly's mind. She was certain it was the same map as the one in Justin's pocket. Although she'd only glanced at it, certain features were clear in her mind. Top corner missing, crease marks, signs of a tear almost to the centre. How did Justin come to have it, and why? He'd said the original must have been stolen during the attack or fallen from his pocket. Was the story about dodo research just that, a story? He had a map all right – William's.

And now Connor was showing her that very same page from the journal. Was he responsible for the attack and the trashing of Justin's room? 'Where did you get this?' Holly demanded.

He carefully returned the map to his pocket. 'Kathleen gave it to me.'

'I thought you said it was missing.'

'It was.' Connor picked up his fork. 'Eat before it gets cold.'

'That's it? You're avoiding my question yet again.'

He glanced up briefly from his plate. 'I'm not. I haven't eaten all day and I'm starving.'

Holly thought he was deliberately keeping her waiting. Either that, or stalling for time. She wanted to believe him but found herself suddenly uncertain and sceptical. Had he arranged the attack or was it true that Kathleen gave him the map. Come to that, how did Kathleen get her hands on it? She couldn't have organised theft and thuggery, she was a bloody nun for God's sake! Where did Justin fit into all of this? Should she mention the copy to Connor? *No! Not until some believable answers are forthcoming.*

By the time their empty plates had been removed, Holly was no closer to knowing who she could trust. She waited impatiently to hear what Connor had to say next. He ordered two more beers.

'I want you to meet Kathleen.'

'Why?'

'You doubt me. I can see it in your eyes.'

Damned traitorous things! Holly avoided his gaze. 'How come Kathleen had the map?'

'She found it.'

Holly's scepticism grew. She was forced to look at him again. 'Where?'

Connor raised one eyebrow at her tone but answered patiently. 'I told you about Kathleen's interest in her family tree. She goes to the site of William Maguire's house to get a feel for the past. There's not much there any more. A few foundations, part of a stone floor, half a chimney, some stone steps. But the atmosphere is incredible. Kathleen is fairly spiritual. She can sense things just by being there.'

'You mean she's clairvoyant?'

'Not exactly.' He smiled at her expression of disbelief. 'She's what I would call fey. She's aware of the supernatural, has a completely open mind on the subject, but doesn't run around with a crystal ball. You'd have to meet her to understand. I'm going back tomorrow. Come with me if you like.'

'Are you seriously telling me that she found the map in the ruins of William's house by following some kind of extrasensory instinct?'

'Something like that.'

'And?' Holly prodded. 'Come on, Maguire. There must be more to it than that.'

'Okay.' He reached into a pocket and produced cigarettes and a lighter. 'Do you mind if I smoke? I'm trying to give up but . . .'

'I couldn't care less if you burst into flames.'

Connor grinned wryly and lit a cigarette. 'Kathleen became interested in tracing her family when both her parents were killed in a bus accident a couple of years ago. Her brother, Thomas, had become seriously depressed over the loss so it was Kathleen who had to go through all the personal effects, documents and so on before putting the family home up for sale. What with her duties as a nun and a determination to do the job thoroughly, it took months.'

Holly caught a whiff of cigarette smoke. She'd given up five years earlier but sometimes, like now, the smell was so pleasant that she craved a puff. Without stopping to think she put out a hand. Without hesitation Connor passed the cigarette to her. She dragged in smoke but didn't inhale, blew it lazily upwards and handed the cigarette back. No words. No look. It was the action of two people who knew each other intimately. A fact that struck them simultaneously. Holly looked down at her hands, embarrassed. Connor cocked an eye at his cigarette, as though it had spoken. It took him several seconds to continue.

'She came across some old letters, love letters really, written between Gilchrist and Aroon. There was also a diary, which Aroon apparently started after Gilchrist drowned. But the exciting discovery was a box of old papers. They turned out to be copies of birth, death and marriage records. There were also several sheets of paper where someone had tried to follow the family lineage. That's when Kathleen decided to have a go at it for herself.'

'Quite a find. Fancy all that stuff being kept for such a long time.'

'That's not all. Some of the old records had been posted to the family. I told Kathleen to check the envelopes. An 1847 penny red stamp, provided it's in good condition, can fetch anything up to a million Australian dollars today. It's possible that she is sitting on a fortune in stamps.'

'First the treasure, now the stamps. You must look a bit like Santa Claus to Kathleen.' Holly smiled. The image of Connor Maguire in an over-sized red suit was a bit hard to take. 'Did Aroon's diary mention the journal?'

'No. The only thing of interest was a reference to her house in relation to rock formations, trees and the view from it. Kathleen traced the ruins and discovered that they dated back to the original William.'

'How on earth did she realise that?'

'His initials, WMM, and the date, 1726, are cut into one of the chimney stones.'

'So Gilchrist and Aroon lived in the house that William built?'

'We have to make some assumptions. It seems pretty likely. My guess is she lived there until she died.'

'When was that?'

'Mauritius gets hit by a monster cyclone every twenty-five years or so. Four years after Gilchrist drowned, a big one struck. Kathleen is pretty certain that it killed Aroon. It's one of the family stories. No proof though the date on her headstone tallies, 1877.'

'Refresh my memory, I got a little lost back there. Any children?'

'Four. But Kathleen has only traced one of them. A son – Sean. Must have been about eight when his mother died. We don't know much more about him. Knowledge of the journal and map, at least within the Mauritius side of the family, died with Aroon.'

He stubbed out the cigarette. 'Anyway, Kathleen started to visit the ruins regularly. Apparently she gets the feeling of being welcome there.'

'And the map?'

'She found it quite early on.' He gave her a quizzical look. 'This might stretch your imagination somewhat but she told me she'd been led to it.'

Surprising both herself and Connor, Holly giggled, then found she couldn't stop. Her ribs hurt but she was helpless.

'Is it something you'd care to share with me?' Connor asked eventually. 'Or do you plan to sit there amusing yourself for a while? No, please,' he added, holding up a hand as the mirth that had bubbled up so unexpectedly became a throaty laugh, 'don't stop on my account.'

Wondering what the hell was wrong with her, Holly finally composed herself. 'It wasn't that funny,' she admitted. 'I just had this mental picture of an unseen spirit leading a nun by the nose up a rocky hillside.' She glanced at Conner. 'Sorry,' she added lamely, 'I won't make a habit of it.'

Then Connor burst out laughing. 'That's a very dirty laugh you have there. You should do it more often.'

If only you knew how seldom I laugh. It crossed her mind then how good it felt. 'I interrupted. Please go on.'

'You don't like personal observations much, do you?'

Holly had spent some considerable time erecting a defensive barrier around herself. Many had tried to break it down but no-one had come close. Now here was this man, one she was not even certain she could trust, quite effortlessly standing on the inside. She had no idea how he'd got there. Whatever, however, it was unnerving. Even her much practised defensive responses, those that always provided a quick and cutting rejection, were letting her down. 'Ah . . . well.' *Great stuff, Jones! You've just won first prize in the tongue glued to roof of mouth competition. Where's your bloody brain gone?*

Possibly fearing a mental, if not physical, embolism, the accused bloody brain finally shook off its paralysis and kick-started. It was not a moment too soon as far as Holly was concerned. 'Actually, I don't mind them at all. I just don't like answering them.' *Well! It wasn't top-of-the-class material but it was better than nothing.*

Connor's eyes glowed, reflecting an elusive combination of understanding and regret. He continued. 'Kathleen was where a garden must once have been. It's completely overgrown now but you can still see evidence of it. Trees, shrubs gone wild, that sort of thing. No sense of order, nothing to say how it used to look. She found a well. Said she walked straight up to it, knowing it would be there. She showed it to me. You can't see it until you're right on top of it.'

'And the map was there?'

'Wrapped in oilskin and lodged behind a stone in the wall. Kathleen said it was waiting for her. With the map was a short letter written by Aroon. Kathleen compared the handwriting with the diary. Though at some stage I would like to check it for myself against Aroon's note in the journal.'

'Have you got the letter with you?'

'No. The paper is very thin and I didn't want to risk damaging it.'

'What did it say?'

'I copied it down. Here.' Connor passed a sheet of paper across the table. Holly read:

I have done as William Maguire seemed to desire and sent his journal back to Ireland. It is entrusted to Father Lynch for safe delivery, but these being troubled times and William's sister dead for so long, I have taken the precaution of removing the map lest the information fall into the wrong hands. I pray to God I do the right thing.

'She sounds worried about it.'

'A simple but anxious woman is how Kathleen put it.' Connor leaned forward. 'Do you remember what William wrote in the back of his journal?'

'About the curse? Come on, Maguire. Back then Catholics called on the wrath of God whenever it suited them. Didn't mean anything would happen.'

He sat back, folding his arms. 'There's not a shred of Irish in you, is there?'

Holly didn't get his drift and responded with an elegant, 'Huh!'

He shook his head slightly. 'Kathleen can sense something about the map. A warning of some kind.'

'Don't tell me you believe that shit?'

His eyes reproached her.

'Well,' she shrugged, defending herself. 'It's a bit far-fetched, wouldn't you say?'

'Not so much that Kathleen wouldn't touch the treasure with a barge pole. She wants nothing to do with it or the map.'

'But doesn't mind you running the risk?' Holly rolled her eyes. 'Now that's what I call a truly religious person.'

'There's not much point in telling you the punchline.'

'Try me.'

'She put it strangely, but she believes William's treasure will be found.'

'If she's so clairvoyant, how come she doesn't know exactly where it is?'

'She says it's not her destiny.'

'What did she say about finding it?'

'It will reveal itself.'

The look on Connor's face killed any glib response. He was excited. He was serious. Above all, he was ready to accept the challenge. Holly understood, for the first time, what it was that drove Connor Maguire. He was clever, astute, probably quite brave and adventurous – all those things rolled into one. But touching each and every aspect of his character was a simple boyish enthusiasm, a sort of Peter Pan belief in Tinkerbell. And he was asking her to believe with him.

Holly swallowed hard. It was impossible. She had always been a realist. Now she was touched by cynicism. 'I . . .'

He reached over and took her hands in his. 'Don't think, Holly. Feel. Your brain may have been conditioned, your heart hasn't. Trust what you feel, not what your mind tells you.'

She truly wanted to. To fly with the dream, to experience that long-forgotten freedom of childlike optimism. Holly slid her hands from under his warm fingers. Hopeless! How could she? The child no longer existed. 'Oh grow up, Maguire.' She was cross with him for tempting her, cross with herself for being tempted.

Connor sighed in disappointment. 'For a moment . . .' He left it hanging between them.

She regretted the outburst but it was too late to take it back. Holly had the absurd feeling that she'd just broken the news to a five year old that there was no such thing as the tooth fairy.

The moment passed. 'I'm meeting Kathleen tomorrow, eleven o'clock at William's. Why don't you come with me? I'll pick you up at nine. We could take the coast road. You'd love it.'

'Sounds good to me.' Relieved to have the conversation back to practicalities, Holly sat back, lacing her fingers around the beer glass in front of her. 'I'll wait for you outside reception.'

Connor glanced down at her hands. 'Here I go again.' He grinned at her. 'Sticking my neck out. Your father said you were married, yet you wear no ring. I'm not being personal, just curious. Are you married?'

'I was.' Holly answered tersely.

His dark eyes were unreadable. 'Don't want to talk about it?'

'No.'

'Fair enough. But it does explain a few things about you.'

'Maguire,' Holly said evenly. 'You've done everything possible to make this one of the most difficult assignments I've ever undertaken. When do you stop?'

'Difficult?' He seemed genuinely surprised.

She nodded. 'Reluctance, hidden agenda, disappearing act, turning every question I ask into one of your own, and now you seem hell-bent on poking your nose into my private space.' Even as she spoke Holly knew her last point was likely to backfire. It did.

'You can talk!'

'I'm the reporter, remember?' *Flimsy, Jones. Think of something else.* 'What about the map? Does it show where William hid his ill-gotten gains?'

'Not specifically.' Connor didn't seem unduly perturbed by the switched topic.

'Does it help at all? I only glanced at it before.'

'He's drawn an outline of the coast. Indicated a mountain and given a set of directions.'

'Fifty paces north, twenty east?'

'That kind of thing.'

'Then it should be easy.'

'Not really. There are no longitude, latitude or orientation references anywhere. I've compared it with a map of Mauritius. It doesn't tally.'

'Rodrigues?'

'There's one place that is kind of similar, give or take a fair chunk of artistic licence.'

'How about one of the smaller, uninhabited islands?'

'Nothing. Following William's specific instructions will be the easy part once we've located the general area.'

200

'Know what I think, Maguire?'

He raised his eyebrows.

'I think you'll be writing that cheque.'

'Oh ye of little faith,' he said lightly.

Holly shifted position and the movement caused her to wince.

'What's wrong?'

She hesitated. Connor would hardly have invited her to meet Kathleen if he hadn't acquired the map exactly as he had said. Which left Justin Parker's explanation questionable. She had to trust one of them. Holly made her decision.

'Last night, one of the hotel guests and I went for a walk along the beach. We were attacked. My ribs are bloody sore.'

'Holly! Why didn't you tell me before?'

'That's not all. We made it back to the hotel only to find that someone had broken into his room and systematically trashed the place. It wasn't random theft, someone was looking for something. His room had been thoroughly done over.' She was watching for guilt. She could see only concern.

'This afternoon we went for a swim. I came out of the water first and when I picked up my towel I dislodged something from his shirt pocket. I didn't get a good look at it but I'm fairly certain it was a copy of your map.'

Connor was frowning. 'Who is this person?'

'His name is Justin Parker. He's English, a biologist, or so he says. Claims to be part of a research project trying to find dodo remains for an experiment with DNA twinning. Funny thing is, he didn't seem aware that, on Rodrigues, the dodo was called a solitaire. Even more interesting is that he seems to know Madame Liang. When I asked if anything had been taken from his room he told me that nothing seemed to be missing although a map of possible dodo nesting sites had either been stolen or lost during the attack. Said it didn't matter though, as he had a copy of it.' Holly took a deep breath. 'Now my dilemma is this, Maguire. Which one of you is lying?'

He was nodding. 'I see. Fag time.' Connor lit a cigarette and tapped the lighter on the table, turning it end over end. His eyes hadn't left hers. 'Not me,' he stated finally.

'I rather thought you'd say that.' Holly found she believed him. 'But you don't sound too surprised that someone else might have a copy of that map.'

'It might not be the same one.'

'I'll lay odds to even it is.'

'If that's so, then yes, I'm surprised. It might be interesting to check up on this Justin Parker. It would explain something Kathleen said today as well.'

'What was that?'

'I know you doubt her ability to sense things, but she also told me that she can feel the thoughts of one, if not two others, focused on the map. I thought it had to be you.'

'My thoughts are focused on you, Maguire, not the map.' She was glad of the subdued lighting because when he grinned and those dimples appeared she realised what she'd said and couldn't prevent a sudden rush of colour to her face.

Connor watched the drifting cigarette smoke, aware of her sudden embarrassment. 'Did you see a doctor?'

It took Holly a moment to register what he was talking about. 'One was called to the hotel last night. I'm fine. Nothing seems broken. I'm just a little sore.'

'Even so.' He caught the waiter's attention and made a scribbling motion to request the bill. 'I'm sure an early night wouldn't go astray.'

As they left the restaurant, a voice called out in greeting. Turning, Holly saw the French-Mauritian, Raoul Dulac, striding towards them. 'What a pleasant coincidence. I was just thinking about you both.'

The two men shook hands then Raoul advanced on Holly and kissed her three times on alternate cheeks. 'You have told him of my invitation, yes?'

'Yes.' Connor replied for her. 'Thank you.'

'Come early. We can have a look over the farm.' Raoul appeared to be in a hurry, glancing at an enormous diving watch on his wrist. 'Forgive me. I must not keep you. See you both on Sunday.'

Connor made no move towards his car, but stared thoughtfully after the retreating figure of Raoul Dulac. It was only when the Mauritian melted into the darkness that Connor said curtly, 'Let's go.'

They crossed the road quickly. Connor had

parked in an open area between a small, red-roofed church and a building identified by the words Mauritius Fishermen's Co-op. Beyond it was the beach where Raoul had disappeared. Leafy branches of a large fig tree screened the car from illumination by a nearby streetlight. Holly followed Connor's intense stare to where Raoul had vanished and saw the flare of a lighter ignite a cigarette, move a short distance and light another.

'He's met someone,' Connor observed softly.

'It might not be him.'

'It's him.'

Holly glanced at Connor's silhouette. It was too dark in the car to see his expression but there was a tense set to his shoulders. The faint glow of a cigarette was moving towards them. 'He's coming back,' Connor hissed, sounding surprised. With a whispered, 'Sorry for this,' he leaned over and kissed her, his arms going around her as he slid closer, one hand snaking up to press her head firmly towards him. She realised he was putting on an act in case Raoul – and she had to assume it was Raoul coming towards the car – recognised them and wondered why they were just sitting there. Holly lifted her hands, placed one on either side of Connor's face, and played her part. As she did, it crossed her mind that she should have been furious.

Whoever it was turned towards the darkened co-op. Connor relaxed and moved back from Holly. She thought fleetingly, almost hysterically, that, as kisses went, this one was about as passionate as a slap in the face with a wet noodle. The main thing was that it looked real. As well as being surprised that an angry, or, at the very least, sarcastic response to Connor's cavalier actions seemed to be eluding her, Holly was aware of something else. He had acted swiftly and instinctively but, for all that, he'd still had a cool enough head to remember her ribs. They hadn't hurt a bit.

It had been Raoul. As they watched he approached a side door to the co-op, unlocked it and stepped inside. They waited in silence. It wasn't long before he reappeared.

Connor whispered, 'Whoever Raoul met on the beach gave him a key. Now he's got to return it.'

Here we go again, Holly thought, as Connor's arms folded around her. Prepared this time, she strived to keep her lips as motionless as possible. It was harder than she expected.

'He must come back to reach his car,' Connor warned.

It wasn't until Raoul had passed them a third time that Holly wondered why Connor hadn't driven off while Raoul was on the beach returning the key.

Silence was loud in the car. Holly broke it. 'Are you going to make me ask?'

She heard him sigh. 'He's not exactly what he seems.' The seat creaked as Connor moved. 'That's all I can say.'

Holly assumed they were heading back to the Merville but Connor drove past the entrance and on through Grand Baie itself, turning off several kilometres later to follow a secondary road which ran around the bay. Stopping on a grassy promontory, he cut the engine and killed the lights. Looking out across the dark expanse of water, Connor wound down his window and waited. 'See the Royal Palm over there?'

She looked. The luxury hotel occupied its own small cove. Two brilliant security lights skewered the periphery.

'Take a direct line from the hotel towards us. About a third of the way across is where I'm looking.'

'It's pitch black.'

'Be patient. Keep looking.'

The strain of staring at black nothingness made Holly's eyes water.

'There,' Connor said suddenly.

She'd have missed it. A tiny light where before there was nothing.

'Has to be him,' Connor muttered. Five minutes later the light began to move.

'Where would a boat be going at this hour?'

'That,' Connor said with feeling, 'is something I'd very much like to know.'

They watched until they could no longer see the light. It was heading towards the mouth of the bay and a gap in the reef to open sea beyond.

Instead of starting the car, Connor turned to Holly. 'Back there. I'm sorry.'

'It's okay,' she said lightly. 'I could see why it was necessary.' She stared straight ahead. 'At least I know why you suggested dinner at Cap Mal-heureux?'

'Look, seeing Dulac was a complete coinci-dence. I'd have preferred it if you hadn't been there.' There was silence for a moment and then he gave a rueful chuckle. 'Well done, Maguire. That's probably the diplomatic comment of the decade!'

Holly laughed. 'You're forgiven. Can we go now?' She wanted to be on her own.

They drove to the Merville without speaking. Once there, all he said was, 'See you at nine. Bring the journal with you, Kathleen would like to see it.'

Holly climbed out of the car, leaned down and spoke through the open door. 'Okay. Thanks for dinner. Sleep tight.'

Alone in her room, she poured a neat scotch then curled into a single armchair and stared into space.

Connor Maguire. She believed him when he said that Kathleen gave him the map. He'd shown her two sides of himself tonight, facets she hadn't suspected were there. A boyish enthusiasm for that which most people would dismiss. And level-headed consideration when instant action was required. *And here's me thinking he was a work hard, play hard, but otherwise vacant post! Just goes to show how wrong you can be.* Several times she'd found him on the inside of her defences. *He's sensitive to that too.*

What about his downside? The drugs thing was a

worry. Was Connor Maguire a legitimate business-man? Or a person embroiled in something he regarded as just another adventure? Or worse? Was he lying? Could it be that he had a direct involve-ment in drug-trafficking? He'd said that Raoul Dulac was a business acquaintance. Was the Mau-ritian also connected to the drug thing? And then there was Madame Liang.

Holly sipped her scotch. Quinn obviously respected Maguire and she, in turn, respected her father's opinions. Perhaps it was time for another chat.

How about Justin Parker? Nice enough in a dif-fident kind of way. That might just be a normal English reserve. Two things about him bothered her: the copy of William's map and how he was connected to Madame Liang.

She'd call Quinn in the morning, she decided, finishing her drink.

Staring upwards, waiting for sleep, Holly ruefully concluded that the decision to call her father was the only positive outcome of her wool-gathering.

She woke at six thirty, twelve thirty in Sydney, and immediately phoned Quinn on his direct line, hoping he was not having one of his regular Thurs-day business lunches that seemed to run from midday until anywhere up to midnight. He answered on the second ring.

'Longford-Jones.'

'It's me.'

'Hello Smee. How's it going?'

'I'm getting the story, if that's what you mean.'

'Good. Keep at it.'

'I need some more information.'

'What sort?' Quinn sounded guarded.

'Jesus, Quinn. I'm not asking you to divulge state secrets.'

The silence coming down the line had a profound depth. Quinn wasn't saying a damned thing and yet Holly could hear him loud and clear. 'Come on, Quinn. Don't expect me to believe that Maguire is involved with security matters. He's too well known.'

'Don't jump to conclusions, Big Shot.'

Holly didn't need her father's conspiracies. She told him about the map. 'The bloody thing hasn't been seen for over a hundred years and now your mate, Maguire, has the original and some Pommie boffin comes up with a copy. So what I need to know, Quinn, *if* it's not too much trouble, is just how cautious I have to be of Connor Maguire?'

More silence. Quinn was not normally this reticent. Then, 'You don't have to be cautious of Maguire. Trust me.'

'Is that all you can say?'

'Isn't that what you asked?'

'Dammit, Quinn . . .'

'Why are you so worked up about this?'

So she told him about the attack. 'Bit of a coincidence, wouldn't you say?'

But he wasn't listening to her question. 'Are you okay, sweetheart?'

'Shaken, not stirred. I'll live.'

'Holly!' Quinn sounded genuinely miserable, a rare emotion for him. 'Should I send someone else?'

'Only if I croak,' she said cruelly.

'Jesus, sweetheart! Don't joke about this.'

'You're not exactly helping,' she ground out. 'You know something I don't. Connor Maguire is behaving like a half-baked James Bond over here and all you can say is to trust him.'

Quinn rarely played the heavy-handed father. He had always shown respect for Holly's right to make her own decisions. 'You're there to cover a treasure hunt. Do not, under any circumstances, involve yourself in anything else. Do I make myself clear?'

The outburst certainly got Holly's attention. 'Yes, Daddy.'

'I mean it, Holly.' He indulged in some noisy breathing, a sure sign of agitation, though he might have been trying to resurrect a cigar, hard to say. Whatever, it restored him to something approaching normal. 'Besides, if anything happened to you, your bloody mother would kill me.'

Holly laughed and promised to behave. She was glad he couldn't see her crossed fingers. 'Could one of the researchers do something for me?'

'Shoot.'

'Check up on a Justin Parker. He's from Claverton, just outside Bath in England. Also try to find out if Oxford University has a research project on the go to do with DNA twinning. I'm not certain my dodo man is all he says. Get Mrs Hammond to e-mail anything you find out. Don't fax it. Parker is staying at the Merville.'

'Is this Parker connected with the university?'

'I'm assuming he is. He let something slip about Oxford.'

'Okay. I'll get someone on it.'

'Thanks, Quinn. How's Mum?'

They spoke for several more minutes. After his initial authoritarian display, Holly's father seemed content to go along with her own judgment. She knew that he doted on her and would never knowingly place her in danger. He accepted, as features editors responsible for sending journalists around the world to cover all sorts of stories had to, that accidents did happen. A reporter might just be in the wrong place at the wrong time. It happened more often than people realised. Journalists were shot at, beaten up or imprisoned. They died in plane crashes. They picked up all manner of exotic illnesses, especially those with gastrointestinal leanings, or the broad range of little darlings carried by that highly specialised and indiscriminate killer, the mosquito. News correspondents were regularly arrested or taken hostage. Only the previous year, two well-known reporters had been executed in China.

Several years ago, Holly had spent six days in a Guatemala hospital with blackwater fever. She'd had a close encounter with an armed elephant poacher in Zambia, been on board a helicopter when it needed to make an emergency landing on a storm-battered oil rig in the North Sea and, earlier this year, when she couldn't have cared less because of her misery over Dennis, narrowly avoided being swept away by an avalanche in the Italian Alps. All part of a day's work. Danger went with the territory. Journalists the world over tended to display a studied nonchalance when it came to the question of their own safety. Once caught up in the business of getting the best possible story, personal security became a secondary consideration.

Whatever Quinn thought Connor Maguire was up to, and however newsworthy his real agenda turned out to be, her brief was clear. Stick with the treasure hunt. For as long as Maguire spent at least part of his time on that particular quest, Holly would oblige. If anything else just happened to come her way . . . well . . . provided she was in no real danger, what Quinn didn't know until she hit him with the finished story wouldn't hurt him.

She looked at the bedside clock. Just gone seven. Connor was collecting her at nine. Quick shower, an hour or so on the computer, then off to meet an Afro-Irish psychic nun. That should be enough for most people.

Connor was late. He looked distracted and had a nasty scratch along one cheek. 'Sorry again.'

'What happened to you?'

He ran a hand through his hair. It was also scratched, as was his arm. 'Did you know that bougainvillea can be positively vindictive?' The grin came easily. 'Especially when you try to run through them.'

'Any particular reason why you tried?'

'They were there. Jump in, we're running late.'

'You don't say!'

Connor ignored the light-hearted sarcasm but couldn't resist a dig of his own. 'You know, I'm getting kind of used to that gear you wear.'

Holly was wearing the same army-style trousers and shirt she'd worn to Mahébourg two days earlier. 'Good,' she responded succinctly. 'It's my best party outfit.'

They both laughed.

She waited until they were on the road. 'You want to tell me about it?'

He glanced at her. 'There was a man in my room last night.'

'Lucky old you,' Holly cut in. 'If that's what turns you on.'

'If you want me to tell you then stop interrupting.'

'I think we'll leave this out of the article,' Holly continued, trying not to laugh. 'Kind of ruins the image.'

He flashed a quick grin. 'Have you quite finished?' When she nodded, he continued. 'He'd come in through the window. I'm not sure if he was someone who saw an opportunity and went for it or if he was looking for something specific.'

'The map?'

'Perhaps, but only you and Kathleen know I've

got it. My camera, a gold pen and some other bits and pieces were in a pillowcase on the bed but, as I walked in, he was ripping the lining out of my suitcase.'

'Sounds remarkably similar to what happened at the hotel.'

'The same thought crossed my mind. He was cool enough, didn't panic. Just legged it through the window and disappeared.'

'And you chased him?'

Connor gave a shrug. 'Tried to. The bloody bougainvillea got in the way.'

'Did you get a look at him?'

'Only for a split second. He was African, that's all I can say for certain.'

'African or Creole?'

'Definitely African.'

'He had to be searching for the map. Bloody lucky you had it with you.' Holly remembered Aroon's note.

Connor must have read her mind. 'He didn't find the note.'

Her thoughts changed direction. 'What if your uninvited guest was after something completely different? Your little deviation into the dark side of life. Someone might want to know who you are working for.'

Connor didn't answer immediately. When he did, his voice was hard. 'Drop it.'

Holly dropped it. She knew a good idea when she heard one.

They cut eastwards, well north of Port Louis,

through sugar cane country where plantation houses, relics of gracious colonial living, stood in beautifully tended tropical gardens. 'I didn't think people still lived like this,' Holly commented.

'You'll find that Raoul does.'

The same square plinths that she'd seen on her way north from the airport, looking like unfinished pyramids of stone, dotted the landscape. 'Mauritius is a volcano,' Connor explained. 'No longer active but rocks keep working their way to the surface. This is how they dealt with them when the estates had more labour than they could poke a stick at.'

They stopped in the village of Poudre d'Or. Non-touristy and quiet, it was surrounded by cane fields. The buildings had seen better days. 'Must have been nice here once,' Holly observed. 'Seriously cute. Have we got time to look at that church?'

'If you'd like to.'

'Please.'

Crossing a sadly polluted river, they parked beside an old but well-tended cemetery. 'Built in 1847,' Holly read out loud.

'This is the centre for anyone seeking pirate treasure,' Connor told her. 'Couple of boys called Olivier le Vasseur and Butin Nageon de L'Estang are rumoured to have buried their combined hoard near here.'

'Has anything ever been found?'

'Not as far as I know. Still, there are those who persist. Did you notice the river bed as we crossed?'

'All the digging, yes. I thought someone had been excavating the sand.'

'According to the rumour, walk about 260 metres north-east from the church altar and you'll come to a sinkhole in the river. That's where the treasure is supposedly hidden.'

'Quinn said something about Mauritius being knee-deep in pirate booty. Perhaps he was right.'

'Perhaps,' Connor sounded doubtful. 'Though in this day and age with sophisticated metal-detecting equipment you'd think they'd have found some by now.'

From Poudre d'Or, they headed down the coast towards Grand Port. It was a beautiful wind-free day and the waters of the Indian Ocean sparkled aquamarine, reflecting the sky. Leaving the sugar cane belt, a winding road took them past numerous tourist resorts and on to the dramatically rugged and fertile valley domain below Bamboo Mountains. No five-star hotels here. Instead, small villages dotted the way, snugged into inlets. Each a separate community perched just above sea level, taking up every square centimetre of reasonably level ground. Twin peaks of column-shaped balancing rock rose majestically to the west.

'The different scenery is amazing for such a small place,' Holly observed, breaking their companionable silence. 'You think you're getting to know the island and pow, along comes something else. Would the real Mauritius please stand up.'

'I know what you mean. Not only the scenery, the people too. It's a melting pot.'

Further south, they rounded the cat-like shape of Lion Mountain. 'That's where William went to hide from Kavanagh,' Connor said. 'Plenty of places to leave his treasure, but the coastline bears no resemblance to his map.'

A few minutes later he swung off the road into an area the size of a tennis court. Blackened stone ramparts separated it from the sea beyond. 'Old Grand Port,' Connor announced as he parked beside an old cannon. 'This way.'

Holly had no time to enjoy the view. She followed as he crossed the road and clambered, agile as a cat, up the steep slope, stopping to help when he realised her sore ribs were hampering her progress. At the top of the slope they halted for a moment. Scattered everywhere around them were signs of a once fortified settlement, strategically important in days when the French and British contested ownership of the island.

Connor led her away from the ruins and stopped beside what had once been a solitary dwelling. 'This is where William built his house. We're meeting Kathleen here. Out there is the Warwyck Bay William mentioned in his journal.'

The coastline swept away towards Mahébourg, flattening out into the serenity of a reef-protected lagoon. The vista stretched to a hazy infinity.

Stone steps, hand-hewn, had once led to the front of William's house. Originally there would have been more but only the bottom three remained reasonably intact. The dwelling had been a simple rectangle about ten metres long and four wide. At one end, part of a chimney leaned crazily sideways. At some stage, the rest had given in to gravity.

Behind the main building, a flagstone floor was all that remained of an outhouse, possibly the kitchen. Grass had taken root between the stones and a rambling rose showed its tenacity, clinging stubbornly to life. When it had been planted was up for conjecture but its trunk was tree-like, woody branches spreading upwards and out in all directions with only the tips showing any sign of life. Starved of sustenance, the few leaves were spindly and withered. Someone had tried to establish a line of trees. Most were smothered by potato creeper and had long since expired. Cyclones must have toppled others as far as the encroaching wilderness would allow. They lay awkwardly, at various angles, waiting for time and the elements to obliterate all evidence of their existence. Holly wondered if William had planted them. How much history had they seen, how many stories could they tell, what lives had come and gone while they grew towards the end of their own?

A diminutive figure, dressed in the traditional penguin colours of a nun, was making her way daintily towards them. Holly watched her, marvelling at the diversity of genes that had combined to make up this one person. Of her Irish ancestry there was little sign. Only a hint of aquiline in the snub of a nose, a dusting of apples on rounded cheeks. The small amount of exposed skin shone like burnished gold, smooth and soft – the skin of a girl. Full lips bore the darker pigmentation of her African heritage, a shade repeated around deep brown eyes. She wore small, round, rimmed wire glasses giving her a quaint, almost delicate appearance. The serenity in her eyes was a pure delight.

'Welcome back, Connor Maguire, welcome back.' Her voice was soft and held an interesting blend of French and African accents. 'And you would be Holly Jones.' The deepening smile of greeting sent a good twenty years scurrying from Kathleen's face.

'Sister.' Not being Catholic, Holly was ill at ease with the term.

'Kathleen, please.' Holly's hands were clasped briefly in warm fingers. 'What a pretty girl you are.'

'Thank you.' Unsolicited compliments usually covered Holly with confusion but Kathleen's frank sincerity was so refreshingly free of guile that her only reaction was one of pleasure.

Those brown eyes were scanning her face. 'A loyal heart,' Kathleen murmured. 'Betrayal cuts deep where there is such allegiance. Who would be so cruel?'

She didn't dare look at Connor and was furious with herself for blushing, grateful when he simply asked, 'Do you mind if Holly tapes our conversation?'

'Not at all. Come. We will sit here.' She led them to a flat, almost polished rock. 'I feel that William used to sit here, watching the ships come and go.' Kathleen folded herself gracefully to the ground. 'What have you been getting up to, Connor?'

He felt his scratched cheek. 'Had a run-in with a prickly bush.'

Kathleen raised her eyebrows but made no further comment. She turned to Holly. 'You have questions for me, my dear?'

Holly nodded. 'About your family, yourself, and how you feel about William's treasure. But first, do you mind telling me about this rather unique ability of yours?' Holly turned on the tape recorder.

Kathleen smiled. 'Not at all. Most people find it fascinating.'

'What actually happens when you sense something?'

'Mental images – brief ones. Feelings. Sounds. Smells.'

'So you have to put it all together? It's not a clear picture or a whole scene?'

'Sometimes it is. There are times, usually when I'm asleep, where a message is so strong it's as if I'm watching a film. At others it's no more than a fleeting feeling, as if I'm eavesdropping on someone else's conversation. More often than not it's just snatches of things.'

'Have you always been able to do it?'

'Yes, although as a child I didn't understand what was happening. It was only when I became a nun that I learned how to interpret the information.'

'Don't the two clash? I mean, being a nun requires some pretty inflexible beliefs. This gift of yours must involve a lot of loose . . .' Holly paused, '. . . more lateral thinking.'

Kathleen laughed. 'These days the church is surprisingly loose and lateral itself.' She adjusted her guimpe so that it spread evenly over both shoulders. 'Besides, messages from beyond the grave are only an extension of the life-after-death doctrine. I admit that until recently the Catholic Church was publicly ambiguous about such things but they've never denied their existence. No, my dear, the two complement each other perfectly.'

For a brief moment, Holly felt a flash of envy for this calm, contented woman. Given only a fraction of her equanimity, she'd be more than satisfied. 'Do you ever resent the intrusion into your head?'

Kathleen smiled. 'Never.'

Holly looked away, over Grand Port. 'How lucky you are then.'

She felt those warm fingers against the skin on her arm. 'You are thinking that if you had such a gift you could prevent mistakes? It doesn't work that way, my dear. I have made many.'

'But surely you could have seen them coming and taken a different direction?'

'To a different set of errors, yes. There are pitfalls on every road. Changing direction does not avoid them. One's destiny is set, though the route taken may vary.'

'At least you could be forewarned.'

'My gift very rarely relates to me personally, I just bumble along like everyone else. You young people have a wonderful expression. Go for it! That's what I do, it's what you should do. Pick whatever road feels right and go for it.' Her eyes twinkled. 'If you hold onto past sadnesses you'll wake up one day and discover a wasted lifetime spent milling around at some unimportant cross-roads. The good Lord would probably regard that as a terrible waste of His most precious gift.'

Holly forced her gaze away from the wide bay and back to Kathleen. She didn't want to be having this conversation, especially in front of a very silent Connor. Such deeply personal issues were not things to be discussed with anyone other than family or very close friends. But the nun's brown eyes seemed to be gazing straight inside her heart. 'How do you know when you're on the right road and are not simply making another mistake?'

'You don't.' Kathleen smiled. 'I think God is a gambling man. A more rigid deity would make our path straighter, don't you think?'

It was time to change the subject. 'When you found the map and Aroon's note, their significance must have been apparent. Did you make any attempt to find William's treasure? And what about your brother? Is he interested even if you are not? After all, if the treasure exists it could be worth a fortune.'

'It was irresistible for both of us to try. We compared William's drawing with a map of Mauritius. Nothing matched. It wasn't surprising. Back in William's day pirates ranged all over the Sea of Zanj. It could be anywhere.' Kathleen looked over at Connor. 'I sensed that I wasn't meant to find it. As for Thomas, he's a bit of a dreamer. Loves the idea but lacks the staying power to look for it. Then, when this young man appeared from nowhere a few things fell into place.'

'Are you saying that Connor will succeed?' Holly shot him a look but he seemed more interested in the view than their conversation.

'There are degrees of success. He will find it, yes, only to discover that there is much to be said for leaving it where it is. These are just feelings, you understand, but I have a very strong sense that the treasure and one other are destined to meet.'

It seemed a strange way of putting it.

Kathleen went on. 'I'm not getting a clear picture. All I can say for certain is that there is danger.'

Holly was glad she'd mentioned the curse. She asked about it. Kathleen's answer surprised her.

'William's warning. Connor told me about it.' She shook her head. 'A bit of melodrama, I fear.'

'But I thought you . . .'

Kathleen looked down. 'There is something about the map, certainly,' she cut across Holly's words, a hand fingering the crucifix that hung around her neck. 'Evil can be summoned and used. Curses have been known to lie dormant for centuries. Look at the extraordinary events affecting those who violated the tomb of Tutankhamen. A curse? Or simply coincidence? Science argues for the latter but do we really know? I believe it was something more. I don't get that feeling with William's map. There is danger, but not from supernatural sources.'

'I have the journal with me. Would you like to see it?'

'I would indeed. It might make the messages I'm getting clearer.'

Holly passed the journal to her. Kathleen sat quietly for a while, her fingers brushing the cover, eyes shut. Then she sighed. 'Nothing. Nothing else anyway. Certainly no curse, just a feeling of danger.'

'What kind of danger?'

'As I said to Connor, the mind of one, possibly two others is also on the treasure. One will do anything to find it.'

Justin! 'Kathleen, has the map ever been out of your possession?'

Shrewd eyes invited elaboration.

Holly obliged. 'It's just that I think I've seen a copy of it.'

Kathleen's eyes flicked to Connor, who spread his hands and shrugged as if to say, 'I suppose it's possible.' Then she looked back at Holly. 'Where?'

Holly told her.

The nun's serene face showed concern. 'Be careful, my dear. Anyone who has that map, other than Connor, of course, is not to be trusted. It was stolen last year.'

'But you must have got it back. How?'

Again, Kathleen looked at Connor before responding. 'I stole it back.'

Holly stared at the nun. 'You *what*?' Out of the corner of her eye she could see that Connor was grinning.

Kathleen smiled serenely. 'One of the advantages of my vocation is that, to most people, I am invisible. I knew who had it. It was simple enough to wait for him to take his family on holiday, which he did at least twice a year. I broke into his house and found it in a safe.'

'For which you just happened to have the key,' Holly thought out loud.

'Of course not, my dear, I picked the lock.' Kathleen looked pleased at the memory. 'It wasn't a very good one.'

Holly could hardly believe what she was hearing. 'Surely, when the person returned and found the map missing he must have realised that it could only have been you, or a member of your family taking it back?'

'Oh no. I cleaned out the entire safe.' She was really worrying the crucifix and her face had taken on a slightly defiant expression. 'Just so it looked like a proper burglary, you understand. The . . . ah . . . jewellery . . . fetched a tidy sum. For the church, of course. I can only pray that the good Lord has forgiven me.'

Holly's eyebrows gave a very good impression of twin Sydney Harbour Bridges. 'Who took the map from you?'

Connor spoke for the first time since they'd sat down. 'Raoul Dulac.'

Kathleen's face confirmed Connor's revelation. 'I'm afraid Monsieur Dulac is not all he seems.' She closed her eyes briefly. 'I have known him since he was a baby. He was pampered and indulged right from the start. Raoul quickly learned that he only had to demand something and he got it. Sadly, the one thing his mother consistently denied him was her attention. He grew up starved for affection. I tell you this because it explains much of the man as he is today.' Kathleen was looking back in time, the slight smile on her face tinged with bitterness.

'Raoul's mother was a beauty. On the surface she had everything going for her – a handsome and wealthy husband, a lovely home, a glamorous life, travel, jewels, good education and an aristocratic background of her own. But she was emotionally fragile, hiding her insecurity behind a mask of cold arrogance. A deeply unhappy woman, I suspect. Any early love for her husband had been squandered by him – probably right from the beginning. I have no doubt that she loved her son, she just seemed unwilling or unable to show it.'

Holly was thinking of her own mother. Delia's love, affection and support had been unstinting, there for her to draw on whenever needed. She had provided a sense of security and strength. To have been without it didn't bear thinking about.

Kathleen went on. 'Raoul's father was a devil. Took what he wanted and gave nothing in return. He had a filthy temper and controlled others through their fear of him. His treatment of Raoul was no exception. He expected much of his son and was quick to punish even the slightest failure. I remember him saying, "You are a Dulac. You have no weakness." By the age of ten, Raoul was so terrified of disappointing his father that he'd lie, cheat or steal just to please him.'

'What perfectly horrible parents,' Holly said with feeling.

'They were indeed, and are probably paying for it now. The good Lord called them to account only last year. They died in a fire that destroyed the original Dulac home.' Kathleen's eyes dropped to her neatly folded hands. 'I try very hard to forgive them but I must confess, when I heard about the tragedy my first thought was not very charitable.'

She looked up. 'By the time Raoul was fourteen the pattern of his life had been set. He had no regard for anyone. His mother's outward lack of love made him quite incapable of loving, though he always demanded it from others. In his mind, attention equates with affection and, from the little I've heard, that remains true to this day. If he fails to attract recognition with his manners or the way he dresses he'll get it some other way, even if he has to buy it. Since dishonourable behaviour brought approval from his father, he sees no reason to change that. A Dulac wins at any cost. He is not to be trusted. The man has no conscience. He's arrogant and believes himself to be above the law, untouchable. One should pity him really. In essence, he's a very weak man.'

Kathleen fell silent. Holly could see that she was struggling to juggle her personal dislike of Raoul Dulac with a spiritual attempt to see good in him and she was finding it hard going.

'How is it that you know him so well? Forgive me for saying this but I have seen no sign of the French and Creoles mixing in friendship.'

Kathleen seemed relieved by the diversion. 'My mother worked at the big house. My brother and I lived there with her.'

'She was a servant?'

'Yes. In service with the Dulacs for nearly fifteen years. Thomas and I virtually grew up in the servants' quarters.'

Connor leaned over and placed an arm around Kathleen's shoulders. 'You don't have to say any more if it brings back bad memories,' he said gently.

Kathleen smiled at him, squared her shoulders and looked at Holly. 'I promised to tell him my story. It's time it was told.' She looked down at the tape recorder. 'I'd prefer it if you didn't record this, or even write about it. It has nothing to do with William's treasure.'

Holly stopped the tape. 'I'll honour that.'

'Thank you.' Kathleen turned back to Connor. 'You are connected to Raoul Dulac in some other way, I can feel it. Be careful of him, he's a dangerous man.'

Connor went to say something, shook his head and remained silent.

'I understand.' Kathleen nodded. 'You cannot speak of it.' She stared off into the distance and it seemed to Holly that the wind which had sighed through the overgrown ruins since they arrived was suddenly still with anticipation. 'I have never spoken of this to anyone save my own mother. Not even Mother Superior knows the full story. There is something . . .' Kathleen hesitated, '. . .

something out there which compels me to do so now. Forces within forces. I cannot get a clear picture but the message that keeps coming back is very strong. It is imperative that you both learn the truth. It is the past that warns us of the future. Perhaps that is why you must be told, to help protect you.' She smiled slightly. 'God's wisdom does not need to be understood in order for us to accept it. I don't question His intention even though the reason for it may remain clouded. This is what happened.'

SEVEN

'I was five and my brother three when our mother was employed as a maid by Raoul's father. Thomas and I went with her. Daddy had always been a fisherman. Some years were better than others but we never had much money. When the chance to work for the Dulacs came up, my parents saw it as an opportunity to secure a more reliable income. Mummy worked six days a week. Most Sundays the three of us caught a bus home to see our father. Those visits were wonderful. We seemed to laugh all the time. My parents were very close. I think the separation brought them even closer. Having only one day a week together, they made every minute count. Thomas and I were sent outside to play while they . . . ah . . . well, they said they were cleaning the house.' Kathleen smiled. 'In the afternoons we'd have picnics, see friends, swim, go to church. Sometimes, if he'd had a good week fishing, Daddy would take us all out to tea. Then we'd have to get a bus back to the north and return to the Dulac estate. Not that we didn't like it there, you understand, it was just that we missed our father. The first eight years were good.' Kathleen's voice was soft as she looked back over half a century.

'Along with all the other employees' children, my brother and I were educated in a little school on the estate. We were fortunate. Our teacher was Chinese – a Mr Po. A truly gifted man. He was not satisfied simply imparting knowledge – he managed to do it in such a way that most of us wanted to learn more. Mr Po wasn't a qualified teacher, in fact he wasn't very well educated. In some ways he was still learning himself. That's what he communicated to us, his own enthusiasm to acquire knowledge. For eight years, all the children – Creole, Indian and Chinese – benefited from his dedication.' She laughed softly. 'Even if he couldn't pronounce his r's and l's properly. He would say things like "fright" instead of "flight". It didn't matter, we knew what he meant.'

Kathleen hesitated, as though reluctant to pass on from happy memories. 'I would say that my childhood was a good one. We had the security of a roof over our heads, food in our tummies and clothes on our backs. We were more fortunate than many. The estate even had its own chapel. A special place, peaceful and quiet, where I could thank God for His many blessings. It was the one place where the Dulacs and all their employees seemed to find common ground. Every Sunday, nearly everyone on the estate collected there. It was a kind of ritual. No-one was allowed inside until the Dulacs arrived. They would come in their Sunday best and speak with all of us. I didn't like it much. To me it seemed as if God was just their excuse to show off. Fortunately, being Mother's free day, we didn't go very often. I preferred having the chapel to myself.'

A shadow passed briefly over Kathleen's face. 'I was thirteen when our teacher was told to leave. We had no warning. One day he was there, the next he wasn't, replaced by an Indian woman who could barely speak French or English. Monsieur Dulac came to the schoolhouse and told us that Mr Po had filled our heads with nonsense, that we were destined for work in the fields or the big house, and that a few of us might as well start now. I was one of those he selected, and I was put to work in the kitchen. At night, by the light of a candle, I continued my studies. It was difficult. Kitchen duties were hard and the hours long. More often than not I would fall asleep over my books. But Mr Po had done one thing for me. He'd taught me to read and write. Armed with that, I was determined that I could educate myself.' Kathleen glanced at Holly. 'Motivation is the student's greatest ally. Remember that, both of you, when you have children.'

Holly risked a brief peek at Connor, embarrassed, but he did not look her way.

'I worked in the kitchen for two years. Then, one day, Madame Dulac sent word that I was required to serve at table. I didn't want to. I'd heard gossip . . . it was safe in the kitchen. The girls who waited at table . . . some of them . . . Monsieur Dulac . . .' Kathleen broke off, her eyes downcast. She took a deep breath. 'Sorry. I'm telling this badly.'

'Take your time,' Connor said in a gentle voice, so full of understanding and sympathy it brought a lump to Holly's throat.

Kathleen flashed him a grateful look. When she resumed the tale, her voice was steady. 'They had a big lunch party. I was very nervous and spilled a little soup on the tablecloth. Madame Dulac became very angry. She slapped my face in front of all her guests. One of them laughed. I was terribly embarrassed, which made things worse, and I kept on making mistakes. It became a cruel game. Madame Dulac would call out, "Here she comes again, be careful everybody." She was deliberately drawing attention to me. I know why now but, at the time, it seemed that she was just amusing herself at my expense. Monsieur Dulac sat smiling at the head of the table. When I went to remove his plate he put a hand on my bottom and pinched it, hard. I realised that he, like everyone else, was drunk. They all saw him touch me but no-one thought it strange.'

Holly found her hands clenched in anger. *The bastard! How could anyone inflict such humiliation on a helpless fifteen year old who was in no position to object?*

Kathleen continued. 'It was a Sunday. My mother and brother had gone to see Daddy. I had about two hours between shifts and should have gone back to my room. But I'd missed church. The family and their guests were still busy at the house. I thought it would be safe enough to visit the chapel.'

Connor's eyes met with Holly's over Kathleen's head. Both thought they knew what was coming.

'Monsieur Dulac found me there,' Kathleen said simply. 'He raped me.' She shrugged slightly. 'It had happened to others. All of us lived with a fear that, one day, it would be our turn. We were nothing more than animals, to be used at will. Monsieur Dulac acted as if the young girls were his to do with as he pleased. When it was over, all I could think about was that he had desecrated sacred ground.' For a brief moment her voice wavered. Holly realised that the rape was less distressing to this deeply religious woman than where it took place.

'That was the start of it.' Kathleen fell silent again, remembering. Then, 'You might ask why I stayed? I was fifteen, where could I go? My mother . . . had been aware of the danger. It was always her intention to send me away if Monsieur Dulac made any improper advances. She never forgave herself for not being able to protect me.'

'But surely she . . . ?' Holly's fists were still clenched.

'Secrets,' Kathleen whispered. 'So many secrets.'

A flurry of breeze disturbed the moment, disappearing as swiftly as it had come. 'Odd,' Kathleen observed. 'It's the wrong direction for trade winds at this time of year.' They watched as its passing ruffled the smooth waters far below. Then Kathleen resumed her story.

'You were about to ask why my mother didn't then send me away. She couldn't. Monsieur Dulac made it impossible. Oh, she was quite prepared to walk away from her job, but he threatened to tell my father that she had been his mistress for the last ten years. Mummy couldn't risk –'

'That's outrageous!' Holly burst out, unable to stop herself.

Kathleen continued, ignoring the interruption. 'It wasn't true. But she had been raped by him many years earlier under almost identical circumstances to my own. My mother had a mole on the inside of her thigh. He used his knowledge of it to blackmail her. She loved Daddy very much. She'd never told him.'

'So you were sacrificed,' Holly whispered in horror.

Kathleen's expression was matter-of-fact as she said, 'Sacrificed? No. Life is a series of compromises, don't you think? My mother had made many to provide Thomas and me with a future. What happened was not unusual. Mummy would have known the risks, if not before she went to work for the Dulacs then very soon afterwards. She took the chance for the sake of her children.' Kathleen sighed. 'The hardest cross to bear is often the weight of family responsibility. People look at things in a different light now but, back then . . . Anyway, staying was my decision. I'd heard the threats and seen my mother's fear. It was too late to protect me. I loved Daddy too. Monsieur Dulac quickly lost interest in any one girl. It would only be for a little while. Mummy was so upset that she agreed.' Kathleen gave Holly a gentle smile. 'I don't think of it as a sacrifice.'

'Oh, you poor dear,' Holly murmured. 'What a terrible story.'

'That's not the end of it,' Kathleen said softly. 'It's only the beginning.'

Connor put his arm around her again.

'At least we got Thomas away before he heard of it. He was only thirteen and probably could have done with a bit more education but we used the excuse that Daddy needed help. He went happily enough. Becoming a fisherman was all he ever wanted to do anyway.' Kathleen leaned over and tapped Holly's knee. 'And the myth continues that we are the weaker sex,' she said almost playfully. 'We know differently, don't we dear?'

'What was your mother frightened of?' Connor asked, anger on Kathleen's behalf making his voice harsh. 'That your father would blame her?'

'No. She was scared of what he might do. A gentle and loving man he might have been but he lived according to a fisherman's code. Simplicity, honesty and mutual respect for others, but Heaven help any man who violated those standards. If he'd known what his wife and daughter had been sub-jected to, he would have reacted out of a terrible need for revenge. Where would it have got him? Or any of us for that matter? He'd have gone to the gallows. It was the last thing my mother needed.'

'Kathleen's right,' Holly put in. 'What man would not feel it his duty to demand retribution? It would have served no purpose to be without the main breadwinner in the family.'

'I think he might have been given the benefit of the doubt,' Connor said mildly. 'Not all men –'

'The New Age guy had yet to be invented,'

Holly replied tartly. 'Besides, a woman knows how her man will react.'

Kathleen favoured them both with a long stare of reproach.

'Sorry,' Holly apologised meekly.

'Me too. We interrupted. Please continue.' Connor looked suitably contrite.

'The abuse continued for more than four years. Monsieur Dulac terrified me. I was in some kind of emotional straitjacket, too frightened to do anything except submit. It wasn't so much his threats to tell my father as an inability to think rationally. I became so scared of him that whenever I thought of refusing, or running away, this terrible, numbing dread would render me incapable of doing anything. Does that sound silly?'

Holly shook her head. She'd done a piece about battered women a few years ago and recalled the reason why many stayed with abusive and violent men. Most admitted that they'd simply been too scared to leave. It would have been especially difficult for Kathleen – a teenager in a servant and master situation, compounded by an inescapable fear for herself and her mother. 'It's not silly. The longer someone controls you, the harder it is to break from that hold, especially if fear is the weapon you are facing.'

Kathleen nodded. 'The stupid thing is, once you've made the break you realise it wasn't nearly as difficult as that fear would have had you believe.' She took a deep breath and continued. 'The only positive thing about it all was that I didn't fall pregnant. It seemed like a miracle – none of the girls did. None, that is, until Raoul . . .' With trembling hands, Kathleen clung to the crucifix around her neck.

'When I was nineteen my life changed forever. Raoul was fourteen. He was a big strapping lad and had already been in trouble over accusations by one of the young girls in the kitchen. She was only fourteen herself. We found her half dead. She'd been flogged, sodomised and raped. There was a big fuss, the police came, but they were powerless to do anything. Half of them were in Monsieur Dulac's debt – money here, a favour there – and the rest were just too scared of him. The Dulacs gave their son an alibi and that was the end of the matter. Raoul got away with it. Nine months later she gave birth to a son.' Kathleen pulled off her glasses and rubbed at them vigorously with a handkerchief. 'The baby was stillborn.'

She seemed to be steeling herself for the next bit. 'The Dulacs had a huge row about Raoul. Monsieur Dulac wanted to send him to school in France but his wife wouldn't hear of it. Not long after the fight, Madame Dulac sent word that she wanted to see me in the drawing room. I thought I'd done something wrong but she smiled and told me to sit. She didn't beat about the bush, just got straight to the point. Raoul was growing up with the usual young man's desires and that, as his mother, it was up to her to arrange suitable recipients. That was her word. Recipients!'

Once again, Connor and Holly's eyes met.

'You must understand how it was back then. I was already used goods. No decent young man would look at me. People talk. The things that went on were common enough knowledge. I was still young, in awe of the whole Dulac family and in no position to refuse. Madame Dulac made it clear that my job depended on cooperation. Then she left the room. Raoul came in through another door. I was locked in there with him for what seemed like hours.' Kathleen shook her head vigorously and the guimpe around her shoulders flapped wildly. 'I don't remember much about it.'

She blinked a couple of times. 'Three months later, I discovered I was pregnant. Madame Dulac found me ill with morning sickness. I expected her to be angry. Instead, she seemed pleased . . . no, not pleased, more like relieved. Oh, she pretended to be shocked but it was all part of a game to her. She deliberately blamed her husband, ranting on about it being bad enough that he flaunted his little floozies under her nose, now he'd made one pregnant. There was the shame of it, couldn't he have been more careful and what were they to do with his bastard child. Monsieur Dulac just told her to shut-up and said that if she let him into her bed every now and then he wouldn't have to go looking elsewhere. Instead of being embarrassed, he seemed quite proud that I was pregnant.'

These memories were more than painful. Holly could see that Kathleen's gentle soul had been as violated as her body.

'They said I could stay on. Even offered to pay

any medical expenses. After a few more weeks, it became clear that my condition was not going to stop either Monsieur Dulac or Raoul. I couldn't stand it a moment longer. Going home wasn't an option. I went to my mother and told her everything. Although she was aware of Monsieur Dulac's continued interest in me she had no idea about Raoul or that I was pregnant. I'd kept that from her. We agreed that I couldn't possibly stay at the house. So . . . she . . . she . . . decided to call Monsieur Dulac's bluff. Mummy got me safely away and then resigned. Monsieur Dulac made all kinds of threats but my mother stood up for us. It worked. Daddy never found out.'

Holly had been aware, by the tone she used whenever she spoke of him, that Kathleen had been particularly close to her father. It had also been apparent that the little nun had not enjoyed a similar depth of feeling for her mother. Now she thought she knew why. Whether she agreed or not, Kathleen's happiness had been sacrificed by the one person she should have been able to count on.

'But where did you go?'

'We waited until the Sunday when everyone was at church, then we simply walked out. There was a small convent near Port Louis and the nuns agreed to take me in. Daddy was told that I had decided to become a nun and no contact with family or friends was allowed for twelve months.' Kathleen looked wry. 'Funny how things work out. As a young girl I dreamed of a husband and a family. The convent offered sanctuary. I felt so safe there. The world outside was harsh and cruel. Perhaps I went a little crazy but, for a while, I believed that all men must be the same as Raoul and his father. It was easy to wrap the atmosphere of the convent around me like a security blanket. Before I knew it, it became my way of life.'

'Years later I discovered that Monsieur Dulac was unable to father children. Raoul obviously wasn't his son, and the older he became the less he looked like a Dulac.'

'And the baby?' Holly asked gently.

'My daughter was beautiful.' Kathleen's lips trembled. 'The Dulacs found me. They offered money for her. When I refused, Madame Dulac said that since the baby had been fathered by her husband . . . she would never acknowledge that it had been Raoul . . . a court of law would grant them custody. I didn't know what to do, it was an impossible situation. The nuns urged me to accept and I . . . I signed a piece of paper giving my baby over to the Dulacs. One condition was that I would never approach the child, never attempt to make contact. To all intents and purposes, she no longer existed. At first I couldn't see it but it seems to me now that destiny was at work on my behalf. All that had happened seemed to be pushing me in one direction. I never left the convent. I studied, took my vows and became a nun. The husband and family were not to be. Our good Lord had other plans. Sometimes I wonder, what if I hadn't been asked to work that Sunday? What if my mother had sent me away?' Kathleen smiled slightly. 'I do

241

hope,' she said softly, 'that somebody up there has a satisfactory explanation. When my time comes, I certainly intend to ask for one.'

A muscle ticked in Connor's jaw.

'I honoured my part of the bargain. As the years went by my daughter began to appear in the society pages. They called her Anne-Marie. I was able to . . . to follow her progress a little. She enjoyed a lifestyle I could never have provided. I worried about her though, growing up in that terrible place with such arrogant and cruel people. I feared she would become just like them.'

Kathleen looked over the bay and pointed. 'Then, in 1997, both my parents were killed just over there. The bus they were travelling in left the road and went into the water. They were on their way to Ile aux Cerfs to see some friends. It was only when I was sorting through their private papers that I learned a little of our family history. I had never even heard of William the pirate until I read Aroon's diary and traced the house where she and Gilchrist had lived. Finding William's map gave me an idea. Just once I wanted to see my daughter, touch her hand, hear her voice. Suddenly I had something to bargain with.'

Tears rolled down Kathleen's cheeks. 'But it was too late. Anne-Marie had grown up. She was a Dulac through and through. She refused to see me.'

'And by then you'd shown them William's map?' Connor guessed.

'Yes.' Kathleen shrugged. 'I offered it in exchange for a meeting with Anne-Marie. It was no use, they said I was a fool.' Kathleen frowned. 'Perhaps that was true.'

'And Raoul?' Connor prompted.

'I don't know. His parents probably told him about it.'

'And he stole the map.'

'Yes. Oh, not Raoul himself, he got someone else to do that for him. It was in a safe deposit box at the bank. You see, Raoul came to see me. He said he could trick Anne-Marie into a meeting if I gave him the map. It was tempting, but I didn't trust him and I didn't wish to deceive Anne-Marie. I refused. Raoul became angry and threatened to take the map anyway. There was no doubt he could. That's when I put it in the bank. When I went back about a month later the map had vanished. The bank manager said it was impossible but . . .' Kathleen shrugged, 'Raoul has many contacts. The normal rules don't apply to Dulacs.' Her gaze travelled from Holly to Conner. 'And that's what I wanted you to understand. He's devious, corrupt, has no conscience and, above all, is very, very dangerous. Be careful of him, both of you.'

Holly picked up one of Kathleen's tiny hands. 'Where is Anne-Marie now?'

'She lives in France most of the time. You have another question. What is it you wish to know?'

'Didn't you see any of this coming? I mean, with your . . . ability, couldn't you have headed off some of it?'

'Remember, I only learned how to use my gift once I'd become a nun. I could sense things, certainly, but I was still too young to realise what any of it meant. You must understand though, none of us can change destiny.' Kathleen grinned suddenly, a boyish sort of smile that lit up her whole face. 'Our karma you might call it.'

Holly laughed. 'Hindu doctrine from a Roman Catholic nun. Is that allowed?'

Kathleen turned serious for a second. 'It makes sense, though. Think about it.'

'If you believe that fate is fate in any faith, how about extending the idea?' Holly was deeply suspicious of all religions. Not only were their histories steeped in violence and deception. Today, more suffering, intolerance and unrest had religion as its root cause than any other single factor. 'One God, one faith, one holy day, one set of rules.'

Kathleen wagged a finger at Holly. 'I would love to have that argument with you another time, my dear. Unfortunately, I am almost out of time. But I do want to tell you this. You have a remarkable sensitivity.' She turned to Connor. 'In fact, you both do.'

Holly frowned slightly, not sure what Kathleen was alluding to.

The explanation was quickly provided. 'You both hide past hurts behind the face that people see. It is that which makes you so sympathetic to my own facade. Most people would not understand how I can make light of . . . things which they would undoubtedly take more seriously.' She smiled. 'We all handle difficulties in different ways, do we not?'

Something like a snort came from Connor. 'Handle! I wish.'

'Me too,' Holly said softly.

They spent another half-hour together. Holly used the time to question Kathleen on tape about general issues and learned that the Creole population of Mauritius – those who lay claim to African blood, irrespective of how much or how little – was surprisingly small, making up about twenty-seven per cent of the island's inhabitants of just over a million. Within this ethnic mix, those with typically African features were referred to as *mazambic* while lighter-skinned people were called *milat*. The two groups tended to keep separate from each other. They did, however, share a common love of all-night parties, good food, lots to drink, and a generic inability to accumulate either wealth or possessions. Most Creoles lived life to the full and let tomorrow take care of itself. If they took anything seriously it was religion. Most were Roman Catholic with a simple faith in God that they wouldn't dream of questioning.

Holly finally switched off the tape recorder. 'Thank you for that.'

Kathleen smiled. 'I've never done that before. Makes me feel like a celebrity.'

'You were better. All they want to do is blow their own trumpet.' She glanced at Connor. 'Mind you, some of them have no choice.'

He raised his eyebrows and, quite out of character, stuck out his tongue.

Kathleen looked at her watch. 'I must go soon.

Before I do, please tell me about this person you think has a copy of the map.'

'I don't know much about him. He's staying at my hotel. English, about thirty at a guess. He introduced himself the day I arrived.' Quickly, she related all that had happened. 'I've asked the magazine I'm working for to run a check on him.'

Connor nodded. 'I've asked my people to do the same.'

'Good idea.' Holly agreed. 'There's something very suss about Monsieur Parker. And don't forget his acquaintance, Madame Liang.'

'Liang Song!' Kathleen looked startled.

'Yes.' Holly wondered what had surprised the nun.

'Well I'm blessed!' Kathleen gave a chuckle. 'Looks like Raoul isn't as smart as he thinks.'

'What do you mean?' Connor asked.

'Madame Liang Song is his current mistress.'

'Yes, I know. But why should her obvious acquaintance with Parker be significant?'

'Raoul stole the map. This Justin Parker has a copy. That means they might be involved together. Liang Song could be double-dealing. I wouldn't put it past her.'

'Oh shit!' Holly burst out.

Kathleen and Connor looked at her.

'Sorry. It's just that when I interviewed her I put forward a hypothetical question – what would the Chinese reaction be if a girl such as herself became involved with a French-Mauritian.'

'Ouch!' Connor grinned. 'I'll bet that went down well.'

'She didn't like the question but her answer was pretty straightforward. I got the impression that the possibility of such an event happening was so remote from herself that it was almost beneath her to reply. The sly little cow! And here she is married to a young boy of sixteen.'

'Well,' Connor was still grinning, 'underneath she's probably asking herself just how much you know. Interesting. Wonder if she'll be there Sunday.'

'Raoul wouldn't dare,' Holly said. 'His wife will be there.'

Kathleen rose gracefully and brushed off her habit. 'He'd dare. More than likely he'd do it just to annoy Solange. That's the kind of man he is.' She looked at them silently for a moment, smiled slightly, shook her head and simply asked, 'Will I see you again?'

'You tell us, Kathleen,' Connor teased.

'Yes I will.' She waited while Connor and Holly scrambled up. 'But you should be warned. If anyone's a match for Raoul, it's Madame Liang. They have an interesting conflict of interests. Don't get caught in the middle. Come, Holly. I'll show you the well, then I must be on my way.'

After she'd left them, Holly and Connor took their time. Both were reluctant to go. The site of William Maguire's house had a serenity that was hard to leave.

But something was bothering Holly. Kathleen's early years put Holly's own anguish into a completely different perspective. She needed to say it. 'A failed marriage is peanuts compared to Kathleen's story.'

Connor glanced at her. 'So are two.'

'Did you blame yourself?' She held up the tape recorder. 'It's off.'

'For a while.'

'How did you get around it?'

'You move on, Holly. Eventually.'

'Eventually,' she said softly. 'God, will it ever come?'

He went to touch her arm, stopped himself and turned to look over the lagoon. 'Try telling yourself you're better off without him,' he said finally.

'I do. Constantly. It doesn't work.'

'Still love him?'

She went to say no, but drew in a mouthful of air and really thought about it. Yes, it had been love. She'd trusted Dennis with her happiness. The first weeks after moving out had been desperately unhappy. It had been so tempting to give in to his pleading and return to him. But then, as one after another of her friends told of his unfaithfulness, deceit moulded love into anger and beyond. The Dennis she had once loved appeared in a new light. She did not love him, she didn't even like him. 'No.' Holly had no idea how surprised she sounded.

A small grin touched his lips. 'Come on, Holly Jones. Time to go.'

'Where to?'

'Today's Friday. We've got Raoul's on Sunday. You don't accept an invitation in this country without taking a small gift. Let's grab some lunch at that place we passed near Lion Mountain then head back to Grand Baie and see what we can find.' He held out his hand.

With a slight hesitation, Holly took it. She told herself it was because of the uneven ground.

They agreed that a bottle of good French wine and imported chocolates would make the ideal gift for the Dulacs. Connor knew just the place to get them. After a quick lunch they headed north to Grand Baie. When Connor turned into the Merville Hotel it was almost four thirty. He simply said, 'Keep the presents in your fridge. I'll pick you up around eleven on Sunday.'

Which left Holly Friday evening and all of Saturday to get some work done. She transcribed the tape from that morning and worked the Creole information into her draft article about Mauritius. As a separate exercise she wrote up all she knew about Justin Parker and his search for dodo eggs. For some reason Holly avoided her taped conversations with Connor. The diary and other notes provided references for some inspired writing about the life and times of William Maguire. And the Merville's craft shop had a book about a number of the island's more colourful characters, including the pirate king, Robert Surcouf. Holly worked a few of his antics into the story as well.

By Saturday afternoon she was well and truly fed up with her own company. Holly checked her e-mail. No messages. Despite a few misgivings, she dialled room twenty-four to see if Justin wanted to join her in a swim. There was no reply. Deciding to leave a message at reception, she was totally unprepared for the fact that Justin had checked out that morning. She was turning away from the desk when a clerk called her name.

'A fax has just come through for you,' he said. 'Would you like it delivered to your room?'

'No thanks. I'll take it with me.' She glanced at the top of the page. It was on *Out of Focus* letterhead. Folding the sheet in half, Holly made her way down towards the water.

The weather, since her arrival, had been as near to perfect as any climate could be. Today looked to be the same, barring a slight breeze. However, as Holly quickly discovered, there was just enough chill in it to make the beach unpleasant. She changed her mind, returned to a more sheltered spot near the swimming pool and ordered a glass of wine.

The fax was from Audrey Hammond, Quinn's secretary. Scanning through quickly, Holly noted with approval that Mrs Hammond had been reasonably thorough and stunningly obtuse. Starting with an explanation that she'd tried to e-mail but failed to get through, the message read, should anyone glance at it, like confirmation of an assignment. But, hidden among a superfluity of verbiage, sometimes so well disguised that Holly had to look twice to find it, was the information she had asked for plus a little bit extra for good measure: Justin's birth date, schooling details, parents' names, current and previous addresses, university qualifications, employers, driving licence and even his national health number. The man was a biologist, as he'd claimed, working for a small, privately owned laboratory in Oxford – hence his reference to that part of the world. There was no connection to the university. He had a sister two years older than him, married, with three children. His father was an industrial chemist. His mother a librarian. There was just one piece of intelligence that the industrious Audrey Hammond had been unable to conceal, although she did manage to make it read like a reference to Holly's current assignment. Justin Parker's mother had been a Maguire. 'Interesting,' Holly murmured. 'Very interesting.'

'Miss Jones? Call for you.' The waiter handed her a telephone.

She took the instrument, still reading the fax. 'Holly Jones.'

'Hi, it's me.'

'Telepathy,' she said, immediately recognising Connor's voice. 'Has to be.'

'Sorry?'

'I was just thinking about you.'

'That I'm a lovable, huggable kind of guy?'

Holly grinned. 'I've got news for you.'

'I've got some for you too.'

'I'll tell you mine if you tell me yours.'

'Ladies first.'

'Okay. What do you make of this? Justin Parker's mother was a Maguire. Is that a coincidence or is that a coincidence?'

His voice was dry. 'Certainly sounds like a coincidence to me.'

'Maguire!'

'Okay, okay. It's interesting.'

'That's not all.'

'You *have* been busy!'

'Not really. It's just that Justin Parker checked out of the hotel this morning and left no forwarding address.'

'There I can help you.'

'What do you mean?'

'My news is that Justin Parker checked out of the hotel this morning.'

It was Holly's turn to be dry. 'Thanks, Maguire.'

He laughed. 'But I know his forwarding address. My spies tell me he caught a plane for Rodrigues.'

'Just how long is your corporate arm, Maguire?'

'Long enough.'

'And strong enough by the sounds.'

'I'm going to Rodrigues on Monday. Will you come?'

'Already said yes if I recall.'

There was silence for a few moments. 'What are you doing right now?'

'Sitting near the pool drinking wine.'

'Fancy some company?'

She found she did. 'Yes please.'

'I'll be right over.'

He walked across the terrace towards her. Holly had the fleeting thought that nature had taken the best from Pierce Brosnan, Mark Philippoussis and Mel Gibson and bestowed it on Connor Maguire. The combination was a knockout. Not a woman in the place was satisfied with only a single look, they all came back for seconds. Some even indulged in a third look and at least two didn't bother to disguise what amounted to outright lust. His searching eyes found her. He gave a quick wave and made his way to her table.

Settle, settle, Holly thought. *This is not like you.*

'Hi.' He dropped into a chair, completely oblivious of an almost audible increase in heavy breathing around them that Holly fancied she could hear, even if he couldn't.

'Hi,' she said weakly.

Connor ordered a beer for himself and another glass of wine for her. 'Did you get your work finished?'

'Most of it.'

'Good.'

'How about you?'

'Me?' His fingers drummed on the table. 'I've been a bit bored actually. Do you know, this is the first time I've seen you without your protective coating.'

Holly was wearing a plain black one-piece swimsuit, over which a flimsy short-sleeved shirt of the same colour fell halfway down her thighs. An equally thin sarong was tied around her waist. She'd left the blouse unbuttoned and it did nothing to hide the fact that her body, though small, was taut, well-toned and curved in all the right places. His words had the effect of making her feel as though she'd just woken from a trance to find herself completely naked. She plucked nervously at the edges of her shirt.

'Stop it, Holly,' he said gently. 'What are you trying to hide?'

She bit her lip. She was skinny and her nose was too big. Her normal garb was just as he'd said, a protective coating. Dressed like this, she felt vulnerable, fresh out of sarcasm and very nervous. She couldn't understand it. She'd gone to the beach with Justin Parker wearing a bikini for God's sake! That hadn't bothered her at all.

A soft smile brought two dimples. Holly watched the mouth in the middle. It was so . . . kissable. She remembered the evening at Cap Malheureux, she remembered . . . and realised she'd been staring at him for the longest time. 'Uh . . .'

His already dark eyes went a shade darker.

Something suddenly snapped. Connor Maguire had turned her on merely by walking towards her. But Holly Jones didn't trust men. Ergo, she didn't trust Connor Maguire. So why was she thinking words like 'hunk'? Why was her body tingling and her stomach churning? What the hell was wrong with her heart that it had taken up residence in her throat? She didn't trust men, she didn't trust men, she didn't . . . 'This is my body, Maguire. I'll dress it as I damn well please and I'd appreciate it if you'd stop feeling morally obliged to make comments.'

She'd hurt his feelings, she could see it on his face. *Oh God! Why did you say that? Think of something nice.* 'You didn't answer my question.'

'What question?' His voice was a shade harder.

'Did you get your work, whatever it is, finished?'

'Yes.'

Holly looked down at her hands. 'I'm sorry. I had no right to react like that.'

She heard him breathe in – a sigh of relief? Or was he trying to control his anger? He blew out again. 'I don't know what he did to you, Holly, but I'll tell you this for free. Your husband is a fool.'

'He's no longer my husband.' She spoke tightly. 'Anyway, how do you know it's not me? I might be hell on wheels to live with.' She looked back up and her stare challenged him.

His mouth twitched.

'I could be.' She defended her question.

'Yes.' Connor nodded, smiling again.

'What's that supposed to mean?'

He closed his eyes. When they opened, amusement shone in them. 'Yes, you could be.' He leaned towards her. 'But somehow, Holly Jones, I don't think you're nearly as tough as you like to pretend.'

He was back inside her personal space and she reacted in practised self-defence. 'You know nothing about me, Maguire. We can play these stupid psychological games for as long as you like, but you'll still know nothing about me. Don't flatter yourself.' She rose. 'I've changed my mind about company. I don't want any.'

Connor rose to his feet in a single fluid movement. 'Suit yourself.' He turned and walked away, leaving her staring after him and feeling foolish. She could have sworn he was still amused.

Holly returned to her room, picking up a newspaper on the way through reception. Frustration and anger jockeyed for position. Banging the door of her room did nothing to help matters. 'Shit, shit, shit!' she swore at the walls. 'What the hell is wrong with me?' Walls, being walls, had no answer. She flung herself down on the bed, then swore again when her ribs screamed objection. In a futile gesture, she ripped off her shirt and swimsuit, pulling on her now very rumpled khaki trousers and shirt.

Feeling less vulnerable, Holly picked up the newspaper but she couldn't concentrate or connect with the stories. Some government minister was promising action to control a quarter-of-a-million stray dogs inhabiting the island's cane fields. An Indian national who had been arrested last week at Plaisance Airport trying to bring illegal drugs into the country had been charged. The body of a man missing for two weeks and found in scrub country near Kanaka Crater had finally been identified. Acting police surgeon, Francois Prost, stated that he had died of natural causes. A young girl who had been found dead on a beach somewhere in the south had been buried in Curepipe two days ago. The mystery surrounding the death had caused nation-wide interest and, as a mark of respect, the town of Curepipe had closed for business for two hours so that those who wished to attend the funeral had been able to do so. The girl's family had expressed appreciation to the thousands of mourners who had attended. The police were treating the Corrine Vitry case as murder.

It crossed Holly's mind that the funeral procession that held them up in Curepipe must have been the same one, but she was too absorbed in her own turmoil to feel anything more than a passing sympathy. Tossing the newspaper aside, Holly sat massaging her temples. Tears were threatening and she couldn't decide whether to wallow in self-pity or fight them off. A soft tap at the door made her choose the latter. The last person in the world she expected to be standing there was Connor Maguire.

'Oh!'

He took in her change of clothes and the unshed tears. 'Holly,' he said quietly, 'may I come in?' He didn't wait for a response, stepping into the room and closing the door behind him.

She backed up.

One hand reached out and gently tilted her chin.

She had backed into the wall and had nowhere else to go.

There was a softness in his eyes as he lowered his lips to hers. He kissed her very gently. With his lips still on hers he whispered, 'It's okay to feel, Holly.'

A sob rose in her throat. She swallowed it.

He went back to kissing her gently.

Holly returned the pressure. Her head was spinning. The world had ceased to exist except for what was happening here and now. She could feel herself tremble.

His hands were on her shoulders, drawing her closer. As his arms folded around her, he gathered her into his body. The kiss intensified.

'Holly,' Connor whispered when they drew apart.

She shook her head. Not wildly, just a little shake of confusion, nerves, denial, concurrence, a yes and a no. 'Go away.'

He pulled her back. 'No.'

Her tears spilled over, but as he bent his head to her yet again she met him halfway, powerless to control the reaction. It was a very long kiss.

They clung to each other. Connor brushed back stray hair from her forehead, his thumbs carefully wiping away the tears. 'You have a little frown right here,' he said softly, kissing between her eyes.

A muscle ticked in her cheek. Holly sniffed as she stifled a single sob.

'Do you want me to leave?' He stood back slightly.

Again, a tiny shake of her head. She was searching his eyes with her own, looking for reassurance. And it was there. With a shuddering breath, Holly clenched his shirt in her hands and pulled him towards her. This time, *she* kissed *him*.

'Be sure,' he whispered, when they drew apart.

'I'm sure,' she whispered back. There was no hesitation.

He gathered her close. 'If you change your mind now I could just about deal with it. But now would be as good a time as any to say so.'

Holly's answer to that was to kiss him again.

He groaned when they parted. 'I don't have any protection with me, do you?'

'No.'

They stared at each other, faces only inches apart.

Connor closed his eyes, lowering his forehead against hers. 'Oh shit.'

Holly's breath became a series of little huffs. Tension was leaving, departing with indecent haste as the ridiculousness of their situation hit her. She felt Connor shaking and realised he was laughing. She didn't want to laugh. It was the last thing in the world she wanted to do, but couldn't stop herself. They stood, holding each other and becoming mildly hysterical. What went through Holly's mind at that moment was that a man who could laugh at a time like this was a man worth knowing.

'The shops will be shut by now,' Connor eventually managed. He buried his face in her neck. 'I could just scream,' he added, pseudo dramatic.

So could Holly. 'Don't you have anything back where you're staying?'

'Afraid not. I'm a bit out of practice.'

His admission surprised her. Someone as good-looking as Connor Maguire must be beating women off with a stick. She said as much.

'I'm a man, Holly, not a sex machine. I like it to mean something,' he mumbled against her skin, before raising his head and looking at her.

A haunting memory briefly clouded her eyes and realisation dawned on Connor. 'So that was it.' He took both her hands in his. 'Not all men are the same, Holly. Your husband must have hurt you badly but don't condemn all of us. Give me a chance.' Sitting on the bed, he pushed the newspaper aside and eased her down next to him.

Holly leaned her head into his shoulder. 'I'm scared.'

'I know.'

'It makes me angry. Then I open my big mouth and say things I don't mean.'

'I know.'

'And then I hate myself and get even angrier and then you turn up in my room and . . . I'm scared.'

'You don't have to be, Holly. I could never hurt you.'

She sensed his sincerity. It was important, imperative that it be there. 'I don't want to half do this.'

A smile was in his voice. 'I don't believe that's an option. My self-control couldn't take the strain.'

'Don't make fun of me.'

'I'm not. I'm making fun of us.'

Us! 'Dennis really slept around. I don't know if he always used . . .'

'I understand, Holly. It's okay.'

'And I'm not on the pill.'

Connor turned her towards him and cupped

260

her face in his hands. 'It can wait.' He kissed the
end of her nose. 'You are very beautiful.'

'So are you.'

'Very direct.'

'You're not.'

His eyes twinkled. 'Honourable.'

'Stop it.'

'Touchy.'

'Agreed.'

'Funny.'

'Hysterical.'

'Down-to-earth.'

'What *is* this?'

He kissed her nose again. 'You have a very aristocratic nose.'

'Bullshit!'

He let that go. 'And a beautiful body.'

She glanced down at her crumpled clothes.

'But your dress-sense needs attention.'

'Says who?'

Stopping the banter, he gathered her close. 'You
make me want to protect you.'

The slick reply died on her lips. It was actually
quite a nice thought.

'Connor?'

'Hmmmmm?'

'What time do the shops open in the morning?'

It was after midnight when Connor left the hotel.
They'd had a light supper and stayed in the dining
room, just talking. Their conversation came easily.

Connor was open and frank about his two divorces. While he'd been busy out there building an empire, his first wife found solace and company in alcohol and cocaine. He blamed himself. 'All the signs were there but I was too involved in my work to see it happening. She needed me, and I wasn't around.'

'But no-one forced her to take drugs.'

'That's not the point. I should have seen it coming. By the time I did it was too late. She stopped trying to hide things from me and refused to accept help. It was a downward spiral from there. I promised to lighten my workload, spend more time at home, but she blamed me for everything. In the end, it became obvious that she hated me.' He'd breathed in deeply. 'It's the most hideous and painful thing, to see someone you love destroy themselves.'

Holly asked the same question he'd asked on Friday. 'Do you still love her?'

'Not any more.'

'And how about the second one?'

He looked uncomfortable. 'To put it crudely, I was in lust. She was incredibly beautiful. Cold as an iceberg. She didn't love me either, just my money and the social pages.'

Holly saw how the truth pained him. Not an easy thing for a man to admit. 'Yet you kept all this from the media. By remaining silent you took most of the blame. Why?'

'Believe it or not, Holly, I'm a very private person.' He saw she was about to argue. 'I am. Sure, I get up to all kinds of publicity stunts. Everybody knows of Connor Maguire, but no-one really gets close. My private life is just that – dirty linen and all.'

'Aren't you worried about telling me? After all, I'm a journalist.'

'No.'

She'd given a small smile. He was right. Although Holly would go to almost any lengths to get a story, abusing a confidence wasn't one of them. She was pleased he knew that.

'You're very loyal. That's what hurts most, isn't it? Trust being thrown back at you?'

'Psychology at this late hour.' Holly glanced at her watch and yawned. It was twelve fifteen. 'Be warned, Maguire. I'm only tolerating this interrogation because I'm bloody tired.' She was not hiding or dodging the issue this time, simply stating a fact.

He grinned, realising that some kind of understanding had been reached between them.

'Are you loyal?' she asked suddenly.

Brushing a hand through his hair, Connor pretended to think about it. 'I could be,' he admitted. 'Given half a chance.'

They said goodnight outside in the car park. 'I'll see you in the morning,' he whispered into her hair. 'Just as soon as I can get here.'

EIGHT

Misgivings hit her the moment she opened her eyes. The previous evening had occurred with no planning, as naturally as it should have been. But now? Now it was calculated. Connor would arrive at the hotel where Holly, presumably, would be lying in bed just waiting for him. No way! This was definitely not on. But she didn't know how to stop him, how to tell him not to come, that she'd changed her mind. There was something tacky about the whole situation. She couldn't go through with it.

'Jesus, Jones!' she berated herself. 'What were you thinking?'

She flung back the covers, grunting with pain as her ribs reminded her that sudden movement was a bad idea. A quick shower, a cup of coffee, and her worst outfit later, Holly paced the room, still unable to relax. It was nearly eight thirty and she was an emotional mess. 'Jesus, Jones!' she repeated angrily. 'Your bloody libido takes over and your commonsense doesn't just go out the window, it checks itself off the bloody planet altogether.'

A demanding shrill from the telephone scared

her half to death. 'Holly Jones.' She fair barked it out.

'It's Connor.'

Might as well come right out with it. 'Look, I . . . about last night . . .'

'It's okay, Holly.'

She didn't hear him. 'It's just that . . . well, I've been thinking . . .'

'I'm not coming.'

'What was that? What did you say?'

'I'm not coming.'

Of all the cheek!

'I'll pick you up at eleven as arranged.'

'Fine.' Her voice was stiff.

'See you then.' He hung up, leaving her staring at the instrument in her hand.

She was slow to replace the receiver. Doubts crowded her mind. Was he backing off because he had the same misgivings? Or because what seemed like a good idea last night was now a bad one? Did it mean anything at all to him? Was she not good enough? She caught sight of herself in the mirror. Drab grey trousers, loose white blouse, no make-up, the unflattering way she'd combed her hair. Holly sank down on the bed, put her face in her hands, and laughed herself silly.

At eleven, she was waiting for him outside reception. The oyster-coloured linen trouser suit had been resurrected and a touch of make-up applied. She was in brisk mode. So was he.

'Got the directions?'

'Yep. And the presents.'

'Let's go.'

Silence was loud in the car for about ten minutes. Connor broke it. 'We must talk.'

'What about?'

'Today.'

That surprised her.

'Shoot.'

'And last night.'

Holly turned to face him. 'Must we?'

'Yes.'

'Okay.' She squared her shoulders.

Connor stamped on the brakes to avoid hitting a stray dog. 'Sorry. It won't happen again.'

The question popped out before she could stop it. 'Why not?'

If he hadn't been concentrating on the road she'd have seen the amusement in his eyes. As it was, all she had to go by was his voice, which he kept neutral. 'Because it will get in the way.'

'I agree.'

'You do?'

'Absolutely.' She was staring straight ahead.

He glanced sideways at her. 'Good.' His voice was quiet.

'Yep.' She nodded.

'I'm not apologising, you understand?'

'Sure.'

'And I'm not saying I didn't enjoy it.'

'Elephants,' she said, a trifle desperately. She was blushing and it annoyed her.

266

'What?' He was startled.

'Let's talk about elephants.'

'Why?'

'Because.'

'I don't want to talk about elephants.'

'Oh.'

He reached over and squeezed her arm. 'There's no reason to feel embarrassed.'

'I'm not.'

'Good. So don't be.'

'Okay.' She turned away, seeing but not seeing the view through her window.

'Holly.'

'Yep.'

'Look at me.'

She did, reluctantly.

'You look very beautiful today. It's all I can do to keep my hands to myself. I want to throw you over my shoulder, take you to my cave and ravish the daylights out of you. I want you begging for mercy.'

'I'm not in the habit of begging.'

'Would you consider demanding mercy?'

'Demanding is good.' She felt a rush of affection and gratitude. He was trying to lighten her discomfort. She undid the seatbelt, leaned over and kissed his cheek. 'Thank you.'

'Get off me.'

Holly smiled as she buckled up again.

'There's just one more thing,' he said.

'Damn! Just when I thought you'd finished.' She watched his profile, wondering what he was about to say. He was so damned good-looking.

'When we get back to Oz, brace yourself.'

'Is that a warning, Maguire, or are you simply bragging?'

A dimple perched on the edge of his smile. 'I could get unbelievably used to you, Jones.' He shook his head as if to clear it. 'Right, a word about today.'

Holly was sorry for the subject change but didn't object. 'What about it? Raoul has invited us to lunch. It's because he knows you and because I need a Franco-Mauritian angle on my story.'

'Okay. Keep it that simple. Keep everything superficial.'

'Superficial! As far as I know, it's the truth. You let that little word "drugs" escape the other day but since then you've been as tight as a duck's arse on the subject. What about the treasure? Does Raoul know you're after it?'

'Probably. I'm a Maguire and he's not stupid.'

'What if he asks me?'

'If it comes up there's no harm in saying that you know. Madame Liang does and as she's his mistress there's every chance he does too. But be very guarded with your words. Don't mention that fellow Justin, Kathleen, or the journal. If Raoul is after the treasure he'll stop at nothing to beat me to it.'

'You said he's a business acquaintance. What kind of business?'

Connor's tone hardened. 'Shipping. Cost me a lot of money, that little venture. I had a first-rate South African partner but we needed a third man.

Raoul seemed perfect. What a mistake. The man has no professional ethics. Took what he could when he could. No proof, of course. Always some excuse. He knows that I know but it doesn't bother him one iota.'

Holly hesitated, then asked, 'Is Raoul involved in the drugs thing?'

He blew out air. 'I'm beginning to wish I'd never mentioned them. Can't you give it a rest?'

'Is he?'

His answer surprised her. 'It's complicated but I don't think so. Not what I'm . . . No, he's not.'

'I hope you're right. You don't sound very sure. From what Kathleen said, he's a man to be avoided.'

'Oh, I don't know. It might simplify things.'

'What things?'

'Things. Just things. I can't say any more. Just be very careful around him.' Connor's voice was quiet but there was no doubting his sincerity. Whatever the reason for Connor Maguire being in Mauritius, and Holly was not fooling herself that she had been told the full story, Raoul Dulac had him worried.

Their arrival had been announced by shrill, hysterical barking from within the house. Raoul himself opened the door and Holly was nearly bowled over by an eager Afghan hound that pushed past its master to sniff out the scent of newcomers. Realising that Raoul had made no attempt to stop the embarrassing investigation, Holly, who believed that dogs, like children, should be taught good manners from an early age, delivered a sharp slap to the inquisitive pointed snout. Thus rebuked, the hound turned its attention to Connor who, equally unfazed by what Raoul might think, jerked its collar hard enough to get attention, said 'no', quietly but firmly, then patted the animal's chest when it obeyed.

Raoul, like his house, was clad entirely in white. 'Welcome, so glad you could make it.' The expansive smile and outstretched arms were followed by flamboyant cheek-kissing and exclamations of protest when the wine and chocolates were handed to him. He pressed himself too close for Holly's liking and it took a conscious effort to control the frown she knew had appeared between her brows.

Ice tinkling in a glass announced the presence of Raoul's wife. Solange stood a few paces behind her husband, waiting to be introduced. Elegant was the word that came to Holly's mind. Dressed in coral silk trousers and a loose tunic-style top, her blonde hair deceptively simple though expertly cut in a chin-length bob, Solange was a trifle over made-up, yet there was no disguising the fact that she had once been stunning. With age, that beauty had started to blur, her features to coarsen, and the smile accentuated bitter lines around her mouth. Her expressionless eyes were hard and impossible to read.

A crystal glass in her hand held liquid the colour of honey. Her breath, as she approached to press a powdered cheek, advertised cognac. Words of welcome came loud yet strangely halting, making it obvious that their hostess was trying very hard not to slur. Holly speculated that the lady had a lengthy head-start on them liquor-wise.

The Dulac residence was a three-storeyed mansion fronted by pseudo Corinthian columns along a wide, tiled verandah, onto which opened six separate French doors. Inside, ornate ceilings and imported marble floors set off antique furniture and gilt-framed oil paintings of racehorses, sailing ships and scenes from the French Revolution. Kathleen said the original house had been burned to the ground. This one, while reflecting a bygone era, was crass in its newness. Holly felt like she was in a museum. The house had no heart, no warmth – a statement shrieking of the money that had been thrown at it.

Raoul fussed over them, proudly pointing out features and furniture, then insisting on a tour of the garden – all five landscaped acres of it – before the other guests arrived. Solange melted away, murmuring about seeing to the food. Their host could not have been more superficially charming or more transparently flirtatious. By the time they went back inside, Holly's patience had been sorely tried. The last straw was Raoul's stage-whispered, 'The beauty of this rose is matched only by your own, my dear,' which provoked her to respond, 'Thank you, Raoul, and just look at all those wicked thorns.'

Approval gleamed briefly in Connor's eyes.

Raoul had just poured drinks, wine for Holly and a beer for Connor, when people started to arrive. The steady stream kept him busy. Staring up at a painting of Louis XVI's execution by guillotine, Connor whispered, 'Not receptive to good old Gallic charm, I see.' He was grinning.

Holly, also pretending to study the old and obviously valuable picture, delivered a withering look. 'Not when it's conducted with all the sincerity of a hungry cat apologising to a mouse.'

As introductions and polite chitchat gathered momentum, a strikingly beautiful woman in her mid-thirties appeared on the winding staircase. She paused to survey the now crowded reception room and swept down to join the throng. She was dressed from head to toe in cream: a silk scarf wound Bedouin-style around her head, long silk caftan, cream-coloured open sandals. The only break from that single colour was her jewellery. She wore gold, lots of gold, around her neck, on her arms, and dangling from her ears. The cream and gold combined perfectly to enhance the rich amber of her flawless skin.

'Ah, there you are, my darling.' Raoul made an elaborate fuss over the new arrival. 'Come and meet our special guests.'

Even before the introductions were made, Holly realised she was looking at Kathleen's daughter.

Raoul, the woman's father, introduced Anne-Marie as his sister. Holly examined the coldly beautiful face. Of her mother there was little evidence. A family resemblance, yes, if you looked hard enough, but time and arrogance had chiselled the face into something cold and hard. Kathleen's softness might have been there once but now there was no sign of it. Anne-Marie had her mother's eyes, but only in shape. And the look she was giving her father was one of pure hatred.

Raoul left Holly and Anne-Marie together while he greeted more people. 'I understand you live in France.' Holly could have bitten her tongue. That information had come from Kathleen.

But Anne-Marie didn't notice the slip. 'Yes.'

'You grew up here though, didn't you?'

Anne-Marie's eyes swept contemptuously around the walls. 'Not in this house. The original one burned down last year. My parents were killed in the fire.'

'I'm sorry.'

Hostile brown eyes bored into her. 'Why on earth should you be sorry?'

'It must have been . . .'

Anne-Marie's gold-encrusted hand swept aside Holly's unfinished response. 'I wasn't sorry then and I'm not sorry now. Does that satisfy your curiosity?' With a curt nod she moved away, leaving Holly standing on her own.

Connor seemed to materialise out of nowhere. 'Is that who I think it is?'

Holly nodded.

'And did her words match the expression?'

'Afraid so.'

A sudden hush in conversation served to

emphasise the supposedly whispered words of several women in the room. Holly turned to see what had caused the silence. Madame Liang Song stood poised in the doorway, an expression of contempt challenging anyone to question her presence. Solange Dulac appeared frozen in mid-slurp, her knuckles white around the raised glass of cognac. Raoul, wearing the smug smile of a contented cat, threaded his way through the crowd as he called an attention-getting greeting. His eyes, as he bent over the Chinese girl's hand, gleamed with malice.

A woman laughed and resumed her conversation. Slowly, the buzz of voices picked up again. Holly found she'd been holding her breath and let it out in a rush. 'How the other half live,' she commented quietly to Connor.

'I told you, he has no morals. It's like Kathleen said, he believes he's untouchable.'

'I didn't like him when I first met him. After Kathleen's story, I can hardly bear to look at him. He disgusts me.'

'Getting ideas for your article?'

'I don't know,' she admitted candidly. 'This is not exactly typical.'

'You can say that again,' Connor concurred. 'The entire Dulac family are conspicuous by their arrogance. Most French Mauritians are warm-hearted, genuinely friendly people.'

'I'm glad you mentioned it,' Holly said in an undertone, moving to join a nearby group. 'I hope I can find some.'

As Sunday lunch parties went, this turned out

to be a good one. Connor was right, most of the guests were friendly and interesting people. When it came out that Holly was putting together an article about Mauritius for an Australian publication, most people she spoke to appeared concerned that a French-only perspective would be misleading. When she explained that this was not the intention, they were keen to answer any questions or provide quotable anecdotes about life on the island. Several times Holly picked up on innuendo that the Dulac family were not particularly popular.

She was standing momentarily alone, when a young man, aged no more than twenty, introduced himself. 'Welcome to the illustrious palace,' were his opening words. 'I'm Guy Dulac. Been watching you. You interest me.'

'Holly Jones.' He was immensely tall, not far short of two metres, and standing as close as he was Holly was forced to tilt her head back to look at him. 'Are you Raoul's son?'

'Indeed.' He smiled and his teeth were very white against the deeply tanned skin. 'Who and what are you, Holly Jones?'

Unless Holly missed her guess, he was flirting with her. 'I'm an Australian journalist doing a feature on Mauritius. Raoul thought I'd find a Franco-Mauritian angle interesting.'

'And do you?'

'Very. It's an important part of something really quite complex.'

He turned his head to greet someone and Holly

noticed he wore his blond hair long, like his father, and tied back with a strip of leather. When he looked back he made no attempt to hide the fact that he found her attractive. Holly might have been flattered if he hadn't been so disturbingly intense. His blue eyes roved over her face and body and the smile on his lips was intimate and self-assured. His words could have been taken one of two ways. 'This is your lucky day. I'm French-Mauritian and you are welcome to me. I can satisfy your every need.'

A younger girl might have been bowled over by his attention. He was certainly good-looking enough. 'That's very kind of you, but –'

'But nothing.' He bowed deeply, sweeping one arm across the space between them in cavalier fashion. 'I insist you let me help. You will have my undivided attention.' Straightening, he added, 'All day and all night if necessary.'

Holly began to feel uncomfortable. He was charming, she'd give him that, but she had never felt at ease with men who said one thing with their mouth while their eyes advertised something quite different. Guy Dulac was making it very plain that he fancied her. 'I'll let you know,' she said lamely.

He would not be fobbed off. 'What are you doing later?'

'Having dinner with a friend.' The lie came easily enough.

'Can't you get out of it?' Guy looked so disappointed she almost felt sorry for him.

'Not possible, I'm afraid.'

'Tomorrow night?'

'I'll be in Rodrigues.'

'Tonight then. Call me after your dinner.'

Holly was starting to feel irritated. 'It will probably be a late night.'

Guy sighed theatrically. 'He's a very lucky man.'

'Actually,' Holly said, smiling sweetly, 'it's a her. I'm gay.' She wandered off, leaving Guy Dulac staring after her and fresh out of words.

Twenty minutes later, Connor caught up with her as she stood chatting to a neighbour from an adjoining estate. When they were alone he bent his head and asked quietly, 'I've just been talking to Guy Dulac. Did you really tell him you were gay?'

'Yes.'

His eyebrows were raised, dimples in place, and she didn't know whether he was trying not to laugh or cover up surprise. All he said, however, was, 'Charming!' before moving off to circulate.

Holly had been aware that Madame Liang Song kept staring at her, so she crossed the room to find out why. 'We meet again.'

Liang Song nodded briefly. 'So we do.'

'Forgive me for saying so, but at our interview the other day I rather got the impression that the Chinese community, especially someone of your background, didn't mix socially with the French.'

'I never said that.'

'No, but the implication was clearly there. It's something I've included in the article and I'd hate to be wrong.' Holly looked guilelessly at the Chinese woman.

'I'm a business acquaintance. There's a difference.'

'That explains it then,' Holly said softly.

Liang Song changed the subject. 'You seem to be keeping quite regular company with Mr Maguire. I gather he's changed his mind about an interview.'

'Connor Maguire is news. He accepts that.'

A smile, or was it a sneer, crossed Madame Liang's face. 'He won't find any treasure.'

'Perhaps, but he sure as hell is going to try. Anyway, it's for a good cause.'

Raoul joined them. 'I see you two have met. Good.' He looked across at his wife. 'Solange, chéri,' he called, loudly enough for most of the room to hear. 'Do come and talk to us.'

Solange Dulac, with apprehension written all over her face, obeyed. She was charming, gracious and as drunk as a lord. Holly found herself in complete sympathy with the woman. Not that she allowed it to show. Madame Dulac was the kind of person who would despise sympathy when sober. Inebriated, she'd more than likely make a scene. Anne-Marie joined the group.

Great, Holly thought. *Now all we need is the amorous son.*

As if on cue, Guy Dulac appeared at her side.

From the conversation that followed it was obvious that these five people had very little time for each other. Holly endured a few minutes of thinly disguised hostility before excusing herself with polite words and moving away.

The buffet lunch was late but well worth the delay. White-coated servants glided in with silver platters loaded with hot and cold food. Holly remembered Kathleen saying she had waited at table in the old house. Somehow, she couldn't picture the serene little nun in a place like this. Guests piled their plates high and found somewhere to sit. There was nothing formal at this gathering. Holly perched on a sofa and was joined by a portly gentleman who introduced himself as Francois Prost. He turned out to be the acting police surgeon, out from France to do a locum and due to fly home in about a month. Holly wanted to find out about his work but Anne-Marie arrived and sat on his other side. The Frenchman's attention wavered, switched allegiance, then galloped away, leaving Holly to silently wish him the best of luck. Whether it was Anne-Marie's beauty or obvious wealth that had attracted Prost's interest she didn't know, but if the woman's expression and lacklustre responses were anything to go by, Francois Prost's time and energy were being seriously wasted.

Deciding to skip coffee, Holly went in search of a bathroom. There was one off the entrance hall but it was occupied and two people were waiting. Coming back into the crowded reception room, she saw Solange Dulac sitting alone and asked if there was another that she might use. Solange pointed upwards. 'Upshtairs, shecond door on the left.' Holly climbed the curved staircase to the first floor, located the door and opened it. She was in a bedroom. It was large, light and airy with French doors opening on to a balcony. No personal belongings. The room appeared unoccupied. An equally uninhabited bathroom opened off it. Relief! She shut and locked the door behind her.

Holly had only seen such luxuriously appointed bathrooms in the pages of magazines. Toilet and bidet, spa bath, shower raised on a dais, twin vanity basins, mirrors everywhere, floor to ceiling marble, gold taps, exquisitely monogrammed towels – it was almost decadent. She loved it! About to flush the toilet and leave, Holly heard conversation coming from the bedroom – male voices. She hesitated, recognising Raoul's. Making a noise to announce her presence was the logical thing to do, but instinct told her that whatever had brought these two upstairs for a private chat might be interesting. So she did what any self-respecting journalist would – eavesdropped. It took only seconds to discover that the other man was Justin Parker.

'You weren't there long enough to know that,' Raoul barked, sounding angry. 'You knew I wanted you to stay there.'

'I'm telling you, Rodrigues is not the place. Nothing matches.'

'So why is Maguire going there tomorrow? He must have a good reason. And he's taking that reporter girl.'

Raoul was getting closer to the locked bathroom. He went past the door.

'You'll have to go back. You were a fool to leave. I told you to wait for Maguire.'

'I thought I would be of more use back here.' Justin sounded sulky.

'Well don't think.' The voice kept moving. Obviously Raoul was pacing. 'Just do as you are told. And don't come to the house again. What if Maguire, or the girl, had seen you?'

'What if they did? You might have invited me.'

'I'd prefer it if Maguire doesn't connect the two of us.'

Justin's voice sounded puzzled. 'Look, I appreciate you don't want him horning in on the treasure but your need for secrecy over our association is bordering on paranoia. What's the harm in anyone finding out we know each other?'

'Maguire is tough,' Raoul snapped. 'The less he knows the better.'

'What's he going to do?' Justin mocked. 'Kill us?'

'Don't be stupid. And don't underestimate the man. I've done business with him. He's good. Do it my way, Justin, and keep our association to yourself.'

The voice was still moving.

Holly tensed. *Please don't let either of them decide to use the bathroom.*

Justin spoke again. 'I'll get the morning plane. Maguire and Holly will be on it but she thinks I'm looking for dodo eggs.'

'No. Better they don't know you're there. We might need that element of surprise. I've got some business to attend to on Rodrigues. We'll take the boat. Get yourself up to Cap Malheureux. Wait for me on the jetty. I'll be there as soon as I can decently leave here.'

'How long will the trip take?'

'About twenty-four hours.'

'Then we won't be there ahead of Maguire.'

Raoul's frustration was obvious. 'It's the best we can do. If the treasure is on Rodrigues he won't waste time, he'll go straight for it. Dammit, Justin! Why didn't you stay there?'

Justin's voice turned nasty. 'I've already told you, there is nowhere on Rodrigues that matches the map.'

'Then there must be more.' Raoul sounded puzzled. 'I know the man. He's got information that we don't. Maguire plays the odds. Doesn't mind risk but he's methodical, leaves little to chance.' Holly heard him snapping his fingers as he spoke. 'Maguire knows something else. There was rumour of a journal. He might have got his hands on it, or some other piece of evidence. Maybe he's found a copy of the map.' Raoul sighed heavily. 'No matter. You just have to find him and observe, understand?'

'What if he finds it?'

'Let me know. Do not approach him.'

'But half of it's mine.' Justin was sulky again. He didn't like being told what to do.

'Half of nothing, my friend, is nothing. And that's precisely what we'll end up with if you're not careful. You'd do well to remember that. Now, unless there's anything else, I'll see you tonight. I must return to my guests.'

Holly heard the two men leave and blew out a shaky breath. Waiting a good five minutes, she flushed the toilet, quickly crossed the bedroom, cautiously checked the passage beyond and set off in search of Connor. She did not notice Raoul narrow his eyes when he saw her coming back down the stairs.

Connor looked relieved to see her. 'I was just thinking of a search party. Where did you get to?'

'Let's take a walk in the gardens.'

'Nothing I'd like better.' His voice was dry.

She waited until they were well away from the house before relating all that had happened. Connor didn't seem unduly worried by confirmation of Justin's association with Raoul. He was more concerned that Holly might have been discovered eavesdropping on their conversation. 'Did they mention anything other than William's treasure?'

'No.' Holly leaned towards him and lowered her voice. 'You don't think that Justin is involved with that D-word you hate me to mention?'

'It crossed my mind but no, I don't.' His eyes warned her to say no more.

Holly ignored him. 'Then what's going on?'

'Two things. They're not connected.'

'But, if . . .'

Connor turned her to face him, his hands holding her arms. 'Woman, don't you ever let up?'

Holly shrugged. 'There's a story on the wind. It's like –'

'The scent of blood to a hungry lion,' he finished for her, letting his hands drop. 'Are you about finished here? I've had the social scene in chunks.'

'But we're supposed to be the Dulacs' special guests. It's too soon for us to leave.'

'I don't know how to break this to you,' Connor told her heavily, 'but you and I could spontaneously combust in front of Solange and Raoul and neither of them would give a monkey's.'

Holly knew he was right.

They made their farewells using the early flight to Rodrigues as an excuse. Raoul managed to appear disappointed that they were leaving so soon, Solange didn't even know, having already retired. Anne-Marie stood in for her. 'So nice to meet you,' she murmured, offering one perfumed cheek and then the other. Guy Dulac watched them leave with brooding eyes but made no attempt to come and say goodbye.

'Whew!' Connor breathed, as they drove away. 'I just can't believe that she's Kathleen's daughter.'

'What is it you Catholics say?' Holly asked. 'Give a priest a child for the first five years and he'll be a Catholic for the rest of his life.'

'I'm not a Catholic.'

'With a nun in the family and a name like Maguire! Who lapsed?'

'God knows.'

'He's probably the only one who does.'

Connor ignored the comment. 'There has to be *something* inherited from her mother.'

'If there is, it's well buried. Or, more likely, it died a long time ago.'

*

At the hotel, Holly was surprised when Connor parked the car and came with her. She expected him to simply drop her off. 'Going somewhere?'

'Your room.'

'Any particular reason?' *Damn!* Her heart started hammering.

'We haven't discussed Rodrigues.'

'That reminds me. Give me the ticket details and I'll see that *Out of Focus* repays you. Ditto the accommodation.'

'I'm not worried about that. We need a plan.'

'A few days ago you said that there's one place on Rodrigues that sort of matches the map. Surely that's it? Our plan, I mean.'

Connor didn't answer.

There were no messages at reception when she picked up her key.

'Help yourself to a drink.'

'No thanks.'

Holly shrugged out of her jacket, threw it over a chair and kicked off her shoes. Connor had crossed to the sofa. 'Come and sit down.'

She joined him.

'I haven't been entirely honest with you.'

Holly grinned. 'Surprise, surprise! I have to tell you, Maguire, that I find your lack of interest in finding buried treasure outstanding in its intensity. You barely avoid yawning whenever the subject comes up. It's a cover for something else. That D-word keeps popping into my head.'

'And you said it was too risky to do a drug story without back-up security.'

'True.'

'So? What keeps you here? If you don't believe I'm looking for treasure, why stay?'

Holly chewed her bottom lip while she thought about it. 'For some reason better known to yourself, and my father no doubt, you have to *appear* as if you're up to another newsworthy charity stunt. And, in your own inimitable style, you are doing just enough to give it credibility. The uncharacteristic lack of publicity is to make sure nobody looks too hard and discovers another agenda altogether. With your luck, you'll probably find the bloody treasure, but whether you do or don't doesn't actually matter. The mere attempt will make fascinating reading. You are the news, Maguire, not the treasure. The Australian public love you to bits. Anything you do is okay by them. That's the bottom line and the reason I'm still here.'

Connor made no comment. She was stating fact, nothing more. Instead, he picked up on his concerns for her safety. 'Then you'll drop all this hidden agenda stuff?'

She couldn't fathom him. 'Why should I? You're the one who wanted to avoid the subject.'

'I do. It's just that . . .' he looked away, his voice soft. 'It's just that I'm a bit concerned you are getting mixed up in something about which you know nothing and which could prove dangerous to you, or me, or even both of us. That's why.'

'I'm extremely touched.'

His voice hardened. 'This is not a game, Holly.'

'What are you really, Maguire?' When he didn't

answer, she went on. 'Because you're sure as hell not the adventurous playboy you pretend.'

He turned back and grabbed both her arms. His eyes glittered with emotion – frustration, anger? Holly stared back at him, unflinching. She saw his look, almost of despair, as one hand reached for her face and his finger gently traced a line around her jaw. With a shuddering breath he pulled her to him, his lips seeking hers. There was passion and a kind of desperation in the kiss, as though afraid of whatever lay ahead. Through the thin material of his shirt she could feel him shaking. 'Holly!' His voice was hoarse. 'You are the most exasperating woman I've ever known.'

'You have a funny way of showing it, Maguire.' The sting was softened by the fact that she was still in his arms, her lips the merest whisper from his.

Pulling back a little, he gazed deeply into her eyes. 'Go home, Holly. Please.'

'No.'

He sighed, brushed his lips gently over hers, then gathered her close and kissed her again. When they broke apart Holly's breathing was unsteady.

'This is wrong.' Connor sounded anguished. 'Go home, damn you. Keep this on ice until the job is done. Promise me . . . baby . . . Holly. You don't know what you're getting into.'

But Holly was kissing him, not listening. He'd told her to feel, not think. She was full of feeling. If she'd thought about it she'd have wondered what the hell was the matter with her. But whatever it was, it was afflicting Connor as well. Reason fled, commonsense melted away, personal hang-ups were forgotten, past hurts no longer counted. Holly Jones and Connor Maguire might have been forgiven for feeling that they'd been born for this particular moment.

A long time later Connor stirred, nuzzled her neck and asked, 'Are you awake?'

It seemed a funny sort of question to ask. 'You can't seriously think I'm asleep.'

Holly raised herself on one elbow and looked down at him. He was quite a mixture. His love-making had been tender and passionate, and he'd remembered her sore ribs, taking great care not to hurt her. Suave, cheeky yet vulnerable, these traits were all there in his face. And a little bit extra. Sensitivity that was strictly his own. It was an irresistible combination. She realised suddenly that all the empty spaces inside her had been filled. There was no longer the hollow feeling of betrayal, loneliness or anger. She was complete again. It didn't matter if the relationship with this man would last, or if he'd want to take it further, or even, for that matter, if she'd want to. All Holly knew for certain was that he had swept away her inability to trust. With that finally gone, she could take the first step towards the rest of her life. None of these thoughts showed. She simply smiled at him and said, 'Maguire, you are one beautiful man.'

'Jones.' He looked serious. 'You are one beautiful woman.'

'But,' she said, snuggling into him with her head on his shoulder, 'you're not off the hook. I think you have something to tell me. The diversionary tactics were very good but I'm not a guppy. My memory is excellent. As I recall, you confessed to being dishonest.'

'I did not.'

'I haven't been entirely honest with you, quote, unquote,' she repeated his words. 'Same thing.'

'What do you mean, diversionary tactics?'

'You're doing it again, Maguire. Talk to me.'

He was weakening. 'I'll hate myself in the morning.' He tried appealing to her better nature.

'Hard luck.' Holly was damned if she'd fall for it. She had no problem shelving her better nature when the necessity arose.

'My only concern is keeping you safe. That's why I'm prepared to talk.'

'Ta.'

She heard a smile in his voice. 'I'd have told you earlier but you seduced me.'

'Didn't.'

'Shameless. You don't care, do you?'

'Nope.'

He moved to prop himself over her. 'I didn't want this to happen.'

'It's happened.'

'How do you feel about it?'

'I feel good about it.'

'Good?'

'Okay. Better than good.'

He kissed the end of her nose. 'Since it's obvious you're not going to ask, I'll volunteer the information that I feel better than good about it too.'

Connor's lips moved over her cheek to just below her ear and then back, along the line of her jaw to rest firmly on her lips.

'Nice try, Maguire,' Holly mumbled, returning his kiss.

'It's not my fault,' Connor objected, revisiting her ear. 'My diversionary tactic has just developed rigor mortis.'

'I'm not a government agent, a police officer or anyone official, that's the first thing you should know.'

Connor was propped against a stack of pillows, the sheet pulled up to just below his navel, a glass of wine in hand. Holly sat cross-legged next to him, acutely aware of his brown, lean body and how it had felt in her arms. Draped in a beach robe, her wine on the bedside table, she experienced the deepest desire to pounce on this man beside her and kiss him all over. She resisted the temptation. Reluctantly.

It was six in the evening, and as pre-dinner drinkies and some small talk went, this promised to be, in her own words, a lulu. Connor had been amused when she'd expressed that opinion but was now semi-serious. 'I didn't want to tell you, I didn't want to get involved with you and I don't want you with me. So how come nothing seems to be going my way?'

She'd shrugged. 'Some people sure know how to make a girl feel good.'

Half-smile, half-dimple. 'You know what I mean.'

'Agreed. I just don't know why.'

'I could kill for a cigarette.'

'Likewise for some information, Maguire.'

'Okay.' He sighed. 'I'm not a government agent, a police officer or anyone official, that's the first thing you should know. I'm acting on my own, and if it goes wrong, I could be in deep sticky brown stuff. That's why I don't want you involved.'

There was no doubting his concern. Holly felt a rush of appreciation that this man sincerely cared about her safety. That, and apprehension for his. 'I'm listening.'

'My first wife, Diana, was a stunner,' Connor began. 'We were eighteen when we met, twenty-three when we married. She . . . I loved her very much, but I was too young and inexperienced to realise that she needed constant reassurance. As I told you last night, while I was building for our future, she was destroying herself.' He sipped his wine. 'With the booze and cocaine came the inevitable undesirables. We started fighting about her friends. In the end, she ran off with one of them.'

Holly could imagine his confusion and hurt.

'For a while I clung to the hope that she'd come to her senses and return. I blamed myself and wanted to understand what went wrong, to find a way of avoiding the same mistakes. Where to start was a problem. I had no experience of drug addiction or alcoholism. All I knew was that I had to be there for her when she came home.'

Without thinking about it, Holly rose from the bed and picked up Connor's discarded shirt. She found cigarettes, lit one, inhaled with the silent satisfaction of a person who had given up but would really rather not have, and passed the cigarette to Connor. Taking it without comment, he kissed her his thanks.

'One thing led to another. I met with all sorts of groups. Some trying rehabilitation, others counselling the addict and their family. You name it, it's been tried. Tough penalties, educational programs, individuals going into the streets and devoting their lives to saving others, shooting galleries, scare tactics, alternative drugs.' Connor ran a hand through his hair. 'Jesus, Holly! The world has turned itself inside out to help these people but nothing seems to work.'

'I wouldn't say that,' Holly said gently. 'Although I can see how it must seem like that to you.'

'The more I looked into it, the more hopeless it became. I grabbed a few headlines, blamed a few government departments, raised some money for research, generally made a noise, but it got me nowhere. Diana never came back. Then, out of the blue, I received a phone call. This person represented a particular syndicate . . . and no, I can't mention their name . . . that had been extremely active and quite successful in tipping off Customs whenever a large consignment of drugs was due to be smuggled into Australia. Apparently they'd been following my one-man crusade for some time.

They'd seen what I was trying to do. There is nothing vigilante about them but . . .' he hesitated, '. . . let's just say that they are well connected, work outside the usual channels and, in order to succeed, sometimes find it necessary to break the law themselves. They believed that with my commercial connections and networks I could be useful to them. At first I wasn't keen to get involved. It seemed way out of my league. I had businesses to run and, because of my profile, it's not easy for me to do anything without the media getting to hear of it.' He cocked one eyebrow at Holly.

'Guilty.' Holly raised an arm.

He smiled slightly. 'I said no. They didn't push it.'

'What changed your mind?'

'Time passed. I remarried, probably on the rebound and was regretting it within two months. What was it you said? Choose a wife with your ear, not your eye?'

'Not my wisdom. I found it in a book of proverbs.'

Connor offered her the cigarette but she shook her head.

'Events kind of took over. Our marriage broke up, the press learned of it and, for a week or so, it was splashed all over the gossip columns. The group made contact again.'

Holly cut in. 'I know I asked earlier but I'll run it past you again. Is Raoul involved?'

The answer was the same. 'To be absolutely honest, I don't know. He's having an affair with

Liang Song, has the right connections, no conscience, is insatiably greedy. I'm guessing he's
probably involved with her European side of the
business but the Australian deal . . .' Connor
shrugged. 'I'd have expected him to leak something, show off a bit, let me know that he knows.
He's that kind of man.'

'I agree.'

'Liang Song needs my connections in Australia.
Raoul doesn't have them. Up to now, Madame
Liang has been concentrating on Europe and has
established a successful network on the continent.
Now she's looking to expand. Mainland Africa is
not a lucrative option. The Nigerians have got it
tightly sewn up. But the west coast of Australia is
wide open.'

Holly had a flash of insight. 'It would serve your
purpose quite nicely if Raoul were involved. That
way, if Madame Liang goes under in the Australian
deal the rest of her drug business is likely to come
to light and, if Raoul is involved with her, he'll
most likely go under too. Is that what this is all
about? Getting even for the shipping failure?'

Connor's eyes were unreadable but a deeply felt
emotion flickered in them briefly. 'Yes.'

She was disappointed. There was a spiteful element in his plan that she hadn't expected. 'So you
said yes when you were approached for a second
time?'

'Not right away. I had the same worries as
before. Told them I'd think it over and took a long-
promised trip to Ireland.'

'Which was when you found William's journal?'

'Correct. It was like fate had pointed me in this direction. I didn't have much of a plan but it seemed to me that by being here I might be able to dig up enough dirt on Raoul to pay him back. I decided that a search for William's treasure would make the perfect smokescreen. On my return to Australia I said I'd help but only if they had something for me on Mauritius. They did. So here I am.'

'To do what exactly?' Holly thought she knew but wanted it clarified.

His dark eyes bored into hers. 'That's a big ask, Holly.'

'I know.' She held his gaze. 'You can trust me,' she added quietly.

'Yes.' He nodded. 'I suppose you do need to know. You're pig-headed enough to go off half-cocked if I don't explain. Besides, you are already too connected for my liking. If this goes wrong . . .' He let it hang. 'Madame Liang and I are setting up a trading company.'

'To deal in drugs?'

'That's the plan.'

'Wait just a minute here, Maguire. This mysterious group who need you to front for them. How do they fit in? It's all very well for them, you're the one in the hot seat. What if you're caught? Australia would lock you up and throw away the key.'

'Not necessarily.'

'But . . .'

Stubbing out the cigarette, Connor leaned over,

put his arms around her and pulled her down to him. When he had her snuggled to his satisfaction, he said, 'Shut up and listen.'

Holly fumed briefly but decided to do as she was told.

'As I said, there's nothing official about this. *But* . . .' he stressed the word, 'I'm not as far out on a limb as it might seem. If I screw up, the Australian government will deny all knowledge of my activities. If I'm successful, they'll take the credit. I don't exist and neither does the group I'm doing this for. We do, however, have Canberra's unofficial blessing.'

'So all you have to worry about is being dead and discredited.'

He hugged her into him. 'It won't come to that. If the deal goes wrong my name will be kept out of it.'

'You're messing with the Triads for God's sake, Maguire. You don't half live life on the edge.'

'I believe in this, Holly.'

She saw how serious he was. 'For Diana?'

'Yes.'

'And she's too far gone to know the risk you're taking on her behalf?'

'She's dead, Holly. Found in some Kings Cross hotel room a few months ago. Overdose.'

'I'm sorry. I didn't know.'

'Where were you at the time? Siberia? It was all over the papers.'

'A few months ago I wasn't very interested in anything.'

'The divorce?'

'Yes.'

'I can identify with that.'

Holly kissed his bare shoulder. 'I like you,' she said softly.

'Thank you.' He kissed her hair. 'I could get used to this.'

'One more thing.'

'I rather thought there might be.' His lips were still against her hair. 'Are you always so persistent?'

'Always.'

'What's your question?' He was nibbling her ear.

She moved slightly. 'Mmmm. I can't think straight when you do that.'

'I'll bear that in mind.' His eyes smiled at her. 'I get the impression that you'll occasionally need controlling.'

'I'm not a horse, Maguire.'

He grinned.

'How far down the track are you with Liang Song?'

'The groundwork's been done. The company has been established. Arrangements made. Just the last-minute hiccups that usually crop up. Madame Liang is keen for this to proceed but she's understandably cautious. She knows that if anything goes wrong, fur will fly all over the world. It's big, Holly. Liang Song thinks we're setting up a regular trade route but she accepts that our first consignment will be the easiest. Australian authorities would quickly pick up on any increase of heroin in the market and it wouldn't take them long to make the Mauritian connection. For that reason the initial delivery will be massive, bigger than anything anyone has attempted before. The whole stockpile, in fact. And Customs will grab the lot. Madame Liang isn't as clever as she thinks. The link will be made back to her, I can make sure of that. By busting the attempt to breach Australian shores, her whole European network should also break down. It's a one-off hit.'

'What about her family? Are they in on it?'

'A few. Not on the Liang side. Sadly, Liang Song's father-in-law is as honourable a gentleman as you'd hope to find. He hasn't a clue what she is doing. She's got some unsavoury relations, particularly two of her uncles.'

'Those two who followed me?'

'The very same.'

Holly thought for a moment. 'If you pull this off, what guarantee do you have that the Triad won't come after you? They're not exactly known for their forgiving nature.'

'That's been taken care of.'

'How?'

'Better you don't know.'

'Maguire!'

'I can't tell you.'

'Okay,' she said slowly. 'How about this? You are a very clever businessman, well versed in the practice of covering corporate tracks. If the Australian government is backing you, albeit unofficially, some kind of insurance policy must be in place, a watertight safety net perhaps. Am I on the right track? At least tell me that much.'

'Close enough. Now can you please drop it?'

She did. 'Raoul?'

'Hurt him financially. Maybe a spell in prison. Get back at him somehow.'

She gave him a shrewd look. 'That's the only thing that doesn't make sense. It's out of character.'

Again, a deep pain crossed his eyes. 'Trust me, Holly. It's not.'

There was something else, something she couldn't put her finger on. A failed business deal on its own should have been shrugged off. Holding a grudge did not seem like Connor Maguire's style. Holly let it go. He obviously wasn't going to tell her any more. 'So you're not really searching for William Maguire's treasure at all?'

'Well yes, I am actually. It's for a good cause and it's the kind of thing that appeals to me.'

'Rodrigues. Is that treasure or drugs?'

'I've always wanted to go there. Haven't you?'

'Maguire!'

'Treasure,' he yelped, when she dug fingers into his ribs.

'Maguire!' Her fingers were poised for another prod.

'And drugs. There's a connection. My trip there is to meet somebody.'

Holly was absently stroking Connor's chest. 'The other day when you deserted me in the restaurant, who did you need to speak to?'

'A contact. He's Australian, fluent in French and

under deep cover. He's . . . I can't tell you any more, Holly.'

'He wasn't the only reason you chose that particular restaurant. You knew Liang Song was in there.'

'Killing two birds with the one stone. I wanted to rattle her.'

'Why?'

'She's a very good businesswoman. Give an inch and before you know it, you've lost the edge. I just wanted to let her know that she could be found, anywhere, at any time. That's all.'

'Fair enough. But what if Madame Liang had seen you together with this contact?'

'She didn't. As soon as he knew I'd seen him he made himself scarce. We met at a prearranged rendezvous. Anyway, she'd have no idea who or what he is. He's kept well away from her and her associates.'

Holly's hand slipped under the sheet. 'There's just one other thing, Maguire.'

'What?' He breathed in sharply as her fingers found him.

'This was not supposed to happen.'

'No,' he agreed, his arms tightening around her. 'But if you stop now I'll become seriously depressed. Probably never recover.' He grinned. 'Total decline. Can you handle the responsibility?'

She was laughing with him. 'God no, Maguire. I'd hate that on my conscience.'

'Good girl.'

NINE

The flight to Rodrigues left Mauritius at seven thirty in the morning. To reach Sir Seewoosagur Ramgoolam Airport took a good hour and they had to be there one hour before take-off. Connor and Holly had skipped dinner and, what with one thing leading to another, it was after midnight when he left her. Too tired to pack, Holly asked for a four thirty wake-up call and fell into a deep sleep. It seemed she'd only just closed her eyes when the telephone rang and a cheerful voice – so damned cheerful Holly could have choked the girl – announced that it was half-past four.

She was packed, tanked up on coffee and checked out by the time Connor arrived. He looked as if he'd enjoyed eight hours' sleep. Holly felt grouchy and was starving. 'You're late.'

'Sorry,' he said breezily, putting her suitcase into the boot.

Holly half fell into the car, sank back and closed her eyes. 'I hope you realise that I dislike you intensely.'

'No you don't.'

She opened her eyes. 'How dare you look so refreshed.'

He grinned, leaned over and kissed her cheek then started the car. 'I'll buy you breakfast at the airport. Will that help?'

'Marginally.'

'You can sleep on the plane. My shoulder is at your service.'

'Thank you.' A tiny smile touched her lips.

'You'll feel better when the sun comes up.'

'I doubt it. I've never felt more . . . ordinary . . . in my life.'

'You look beautiful.'

Holly suddenly found she felt absolutely fine. She even took it philosophically when they discovered that the airport cafe was shut.

From the air, Rodrigues looked surprisingly large for an island only eighteen kilometres long and eight wide. They came in low over a couple of tree-covered atolls, part of the coral reef that enclosed a shimmering, shallow lagoon and over which the gentle surf foamed, an unbroken frame of white, rolling breakers. Holly caught a fleeting impression of steep-sided cliffs further along the coast before they touched down on the runway at Plaine Corail. The Air Mauritius ATR 42 used the entire convex length of the field before turning back towards the airport building. As the third island of the Mascarenes trio, the other two being Mauritius and Réunion, Holly had expected

Rodrigues to be geologically similar. It wasn't. It was uniquely different from anything she had ever seen.

The small apron lay well away from the terminal, necessitating a leg stretching walk in the warm morning breeze. Although the island belonged to Mauritius and the only way to reach Rodrigues was from the parent island, immigration formalities were mandatory. Also required was confirmation of the return flight. Without that, entry was refused. The delays bordered on frustrating but the friendly service made up for it.

'Are we being met?' Holly asked.

'No.'

'So what happens from here?' The airport perched on the south-western tip of the island, and from what little could be seen there was nothing out there but a gently rising windswept terrain, as devoid of people as it was of vegetation.

'Haven't a clue,' Connor replied cheerfully.

'Where are we staying?'

'Other end of the island. Pointe Coton.'

'How do we get there?'

The look on his face was her answer. He hadn't a clue about that either.

'Just play it by ear, huh?'

'Relax. You've just stepped back a hundred years in time. Something will turn up.'

Something did. His name was Henri and he drove a white transit van with HENRI TOURS emblazoned on the side. He approached as they emerged from the terminal building. 'Cotton Bay Hotel?'

Henri took their bags and threw them, with very little ceremony, onto a lopsided roof rack. Remembering the careless way she had packed, Holly decided that her tape recorder had just been listed as endangered. Three other passengers joined the van and then they were off.

'This could take a while,' Connor warned.

Eighteen kilometres didn't sound like much but when the condition of the narrow, winding road entered the equation, compounded by the state and age of their transport, it was a one-hour trip. The land kept rising, though it fell away sharply on either side. It was as if they were travelling along the island's spine. For the first fifteen minutes it was barren, open and empty country. A few houses dotted here and there, skinny cattle covered with flies, a couple of tiny communities. Holly's first impression of habitation was colourfully hand-painted community rubbish bins. Whoever the artist was, he only had one style – multicoloured dots. The few people they passed waved hello. Henri seemed to know everyone.

Further inland, the undulating country became more dramatic with deeply wooded ravines, terraced cultivation and stunning views away to the sea on both sides of the island. Residential areas, shops and gas bottle depots lined the route. Some houses were surprisingly large, set amid banana plantations, mature mango trees and fields of sugar cane. It had taken them forty-five minutes to reach the village of Mont Lubin. From there the road twisted and turned back to sea level. The last part of the journey wound through rugged farming country with small holdings of onions and chilli peppers. Domestic goats vied for a share of the stunted and overgrazed grass.

Water had to be a problem, judging by the pipes that seemed to snake everywhere. From what Holly could see, pressure relied on gravity. Most houses had flat concrete roofs surrounded by a low parapet. Some still held puddles lying from the previous night's rain. Twice she saw women scooping this water into buckets.

Crouched a mere two floors high above a casaurina-fringed beach and half hidden by gently waving palm fronds, the Cotton Bay Hotel finally came into view. Henri drove over a wooden bridge, past the scrutiny of a security guard, then along a winding paved road that meandered through lush tropical gardens.

Cotton Bay could not seem to make up its mind. En route, they had passed signs to Pointe de Coton, Pointe Coton, Point Cotton, Coton Baie, Coton Bay and Cotton Bay. But the hotel's welcome was straightforward and focused – simple yet effective. A pretty young girl with flowers in her hair offered the new arrivals guava juice in sugar-encrusted wineglasses, while a portly man in a brightly coloured shirt smiled a greeting as he played an unfamiliar but catchy tune on his piano accordion. Reception was small, simply decorated and efficient. Through large glass doors surrounded by tropical plants, Holly could see a crystal-clear swimming pool reflecting the midmorning sun, and beyond that, a deep blue Indian Ocean. The air was sweetly perfumed with pollen, the temperature around twenty-four degrees Celsius, the sky clear and unclouded, waves breaking out on the reef glistened white against the open sea – a tropical paradise.

The accordion player carried their bags, explained about meal times and how to book excursions. Everything was laid-back. The 'Welcome to Rodrigues' sign at the airport should have added, 'stress-free zone'. Despite the relaxed atmosphere in one of the safest, most unspoilt and friendly places on the planet, the Cotton Bay Hotel maintained standards which were up there with the world's finest. It was policy, the acting porter explained, to provide first-class service while, at the same time, maintaining the simplicity and lack of sophistication typical of Rodrigues. 'Our island needs tourists,' he said, 'but not so many that our way of life changes.'

Holly got the impression that if her suitcase were left on the side of the road, not only would it still be there, untouched, a week later, but more than likely, some friendly Rodriguan would be standing guard over it with no expectation of reward.

They were shown to two rooms on the ground floor. Holly took the first, Connor the second. Hers was large and clean, the furniture a combination of local cane and bamboo. Glass doors opened onto a small patio and well-tended lawn. A stretch of brilliant white sand led to the lagoon, which lay just beyond a low rock wall. Holly opened the doors to admit the sound and smell of the ocean. A slight breeze ruffled the curtains.

Connor came out of his room and saw her. 'Will this do?' he asked, waving an arm to take in the surroundings.

'I can just about bear it.'

'Unpack,' he said. 'Then we'll have a drink and some lunch.'

Back in her room, Holly had the sudden and startling thought that just over a week ago she'd been in control of her own life. Miserable and abrasive, yes. Fragile and hurting, definitely. But at least making her own decisions. She'd been alone, independent and in Sydney. Now here she was in the middle of nowhere, with a man she fancied something rotten, full of energy, with a purpose back in her life. If that wasn't enough, he was telling her what to do and she was doing it. Well, most of it anyway. It was just short of a miracle. Nothing had been broken in her bag either. Another miracle. As she sorted out her things it occurred to her that Connor's enthusiasm for the unusual was catching. And, changing into shorts, it crossed her mind that the serious Holly Jones appeared to be taking a holiday.

When Connor appeared at the glass doors, she was humming the theme from *Out of Africa*. 'Ready?'

'Just about. Come in.'

He watched as she finished sorting her things. Then he put his arms around her. 'Last night was rather special.'

'Yes. For me too.'

'But it won't happen again. Not until this is over.'

His face was only inches from hers. Feelings crossed his eyes and he took a deep breath. 'Jesus, Holly. Help me.'

There was no point in having him this close and not taking advantage.

By the time they drew apart, neither was breathing steadily.

'There's no such thing as paradise on earth,' Connor declared, watching a determined line of ants marching up the leg of their table and spilling out to attack any small dot of moisture or crumb of food.

They had opted for the bar menu and found the food delicious.

'What happened to the power of positive thinking? It's only a few ants.'

'A few! Have you seen their reserves?'

Holly looked down. Ants seemed to be coming from every crack in the paved surface around the pool. 'How do they know?'

'They live here. The whole of Rodrigues is probably undermined by ants' nests. These guys aren't stupid, they know where to set up house. They're probably the best fed ants on earth. Let's go for a walk.'

Taking off their shoes, they strolled along the beach. The sand was squeaky soft and made walking difficult in or out of the water. Tepid and crystal clear, the bay looked positively tempting. Outcrops of coral and volcanic rock were clearly visible under the surface but there were plenty of sandy expanses so swimming would not be a problem. Several hundred metres out, a boisterous surf broke over the coral reef but here in the lagoon the water barely raised a ripple. Connor took Holly's hand. 'Australia is over there,' he said, pointing out to sea.

'Five-and-a-half thousand kilometres over there.'

'Yes. But there's nothing in between. No authority, no prying eyes, nothing but sea.'

'Is that how the drugs will get there? By sea?'

'That's the plan.'

'From here?'

'No. From a point midway between here and Mauritius. A rendezvous has been arranged.'

'How much longer will you be involved? I mean, in Mauritius, not just Rodrigues?'

'I'm nearly done, although Australia needs another month to set up.'

'A month!'

'It's a big operation. I won't have to stay here that long. It's all arranged. The drugs leave here in about two weeks. By the time the yacht reaches Australia, Customs will be ready for them. I'll . . . sorry . . . we'll head back to Mauritius on Friday if it's okay with you. We can go home a few days after that.'

'And the treasure?'

'Let's wait till Justin Parker finds us.'

Holly stopped and turned to face him. 'You're playing with him, aren't you?'

Connor's eyes turned serious. 'In a way. I want to see what he does. We know he's involved with Raoul. To what degree is unclear. I don't like surprises, Holly, especially when dealing with the likes of Monsieur Dulac. Parker thinks we know more about the treasure than he does. I'm expecting him to follow us. If he does, I can eliminate him from the rest of it.'

'Justin doesn't seem the conspiracy type.'

Connor shrugged. 'He probably isn't. But the prospect of wealth does strange things to people. Don't forget the Maguire feud. Oh, and speaking of that, I checked out your information on his mother. She is directly descended from Kavanagh's side of the family. Even if he is half-English, I don't think we should underestimate Justin Parker.'

'What about your contact here? When will you see him?'

'This afternoon. I've arranged to hire a car. It won't take more than a couple of hours.'

'So you're planning to disappear again. Thanks very much.'

Connor squeezed her hand. 'Just to let you catch up on some beauty sleep.'

She stepped back from him. 'Oh no you don't, Maguire. I already know the guts of it. The time has come to spill the rest.'

He raised his eyes. 'You sometimes have the most unbelievable turn of phrase.'

Holly kept her stare level, a degree of frost appearing.

Connor returned it unflinchingly. 'You have the most beautiful nose.'

'Maguire!' Self-consciously, she rubbed it. 'Since you are so hell-bent on making life difficult, let's try a little feminine logic. The drugs are on Rodrigues. You are here making sure the consignment is all it's cracked up to be. You'll verify that it's securely stored, probably go through arrangements for getting it off the island. A man checking on his investment. It would appear strange to Madame Liang if somebody with your reputation didn't double-check everything. So what you're doing here, Maguire, is giving a very good impression of a person who trusts no-one and leaves nothing to chance. How am I doing?'

No answer.

'And just in case anyone's looking, you have a pet journalist in tow to cover a soon to be highly publicised search for some ancestor's long-forgotten treasure, which nicely muddies your real reason for being here.' The truth, as she saw it, suddenly hit her squarely between the eyes. How blind could she have been? This bastard was not even remotely interested in her – no wonder he kept saying it wouldn't happen again. She was nothing more than a convenient tool being used to achieve some personal objective. Furious at her gullibility, Holly turned on him. 'Tell me, Maguire, just how low can you get? How much are you prepared to use others for your own selfish ends? That's me, isn't it? A bloody red herring.'

He still didn't answer, although his eyes warned her to stop.

Holly didn't. 'There's a third part to this too. Another bit of the puzzle you've conveniently overlooked. It's got something to do with Raoul Dulac. Why else would you hide the real reason for being here? Madame Liang *knows* why you're in Mauritius.' The more she thought about it, the more sense it made. There had to be another reason why Connor was putting on his treasure sideshow.

He tried to take her arm. 'Come on,' he said tightly. 'I've got to go.'

Holly shook him off. 'You go. I'll stay.'

Without a word, he left her standing at the water's edge.

The crashing sound had nothing to do with surf pounding on the reef. It was her new-found world coming down around her ears. Connor had been using her. Jesus! What a fool to think that someone like Connor Maguire would be interested in her. She suited his purpose, simple as that. But for what reason? Who was he trying to deceive?

That day she first approached him, he'd been dining with the Chinese woman and had been positively hostile at her interruption. She'd assumed that it was because he simply didn't want publicity. But was it? Could it have been a performance for Liang Song's benefit in case his planned cover-up caused her to suspect another agenda? If so, why? It didn't make sense.

Holly walked slowly along the sand.

Ahead was a rocky point forming one end of the bay. It looked as good a place as any to sit and puzzle it out. She made her way towards it, climbing to a flat, grassy promontory, on the other side of which lay a long, empty sweep of wind-blown beach. The absence of people caused a feeling of complete isolation, a sudden fear that she was totally alone, both physically and emotionally. Finding a sheltered place to sit, Holly stared morosely out to sea.

An hour later, she was no closer to working it out.

Madame Liang Song, an established drug dealer, plans to expand her existing activities into Australia. Some secret syndicate is using that fact to try to destroy her international operations.

Connor Maguire becomes the link. A well-known businessman, he has money, connections and a legitimate trading network.

There's no need for an elaborate cover, not on Madame Liang's behalf at least.

Liang Song is Raoul Dulac's mistress.

Dulac shafted Maguire in a shipping partnership – something Maguire has not forgotten. The French-Mauritian might, or might not, know of the drug deal. Maguire thinks it unlikely but doesn't rule out the possibility that Raoul and Liang Song are partners in the European side of the business. Justin Parker and Dulac are connected. And Raoul Dulac is after William Maguire's treasure.

So is Justin Parker.

So, if he can be believed, is Connor Maguire.

Maguire's interest in Raoul Dulac went beyond the treasure. *If* it also went beyond the deal between him and the Chinese woman, and a desire to strike back at Dulac for the shipping swindle, what did that leave? Holly's thoughts went round in circles. She was missing something. It wasn't as if it was there under her nose either. The more she thought about it, the more convinced she became that Connor had something else up his sleeve.

Just to complicate everything further, a little Creole Catholic nun – ex-concubine of both Raoul Dulac and his father, mother of Raoul's daughter and distantly related to Maguire – flits vaguely on the periphery of this puzzle, as does Justin Parker's mother.

Somewhere in that lot exists someone Connor Maguire needs to hide the truth from, whatever the truth is. So he plays up the search for buried treasure.

Enter Holly Jones who, ever so obligingly, gives credence to his publicly declared mission.

But why had it been necessary? Who, on Mauritius or Rodrigues, needed to be fooled into thinking that Connor Maguire was only there to do what Connor Maguire does best?

It struck Holly that the information Connor had supplied was vaguely connected to the truth. He probably told her only so much as he thought it would take to get her on side. Lying by omission. She wondered if the story he'd concocted for her father might also have some echoes of truth about it. It would be interesting to find out. Quinn had been downright evasive with his answers but was undoubtedly convinced of a good, if confidential, reason for Connor being here. Holly knew that her father would not have sent her in cold to cover a drug bust. He'd never send any of the journalists into something as dangerous as that without a safety net. So whatever story Connor told Quinn, it had nothing to do with drugs.

She checked her watch. Nearly two thirty. Eight thirty in the evening at home. Quinn would sometimes work as late as midnight. Might as well try. Holly returned to her room.

Given the isolation and basic infrastructure of the tiny island, she expected difficulties. The call went straight through but her father's direct line just rang and rang. The home number got her mother's voice on the answering machine. 'It's me,' she told the impersonal tape. 'Just phoning to say hi.'

Angry with herself for having been so easily taken in by an obvious con man, embarrassed too that he probably thought of her as nothing more than an annoying necessity, Holly went back to the beach and took her frustrations out on the bay. She swam hard, ignoring the slight pain from her bruised ribs. She duck-dived, floated, played hide-and-seek with fish under boats riding at anchor. It didn't work. Thoroughly exhausted and still out-of-sorts, she showered, dried briskly, turned a beach chair to face west and soaked up the sun's farewell to another day. She thought briefly of having a second browse through William's journal, which was still in her camera case, but decided against it. To hell with William Maguire! To hell with the whole bloody lot of it. Above all, to hell with Connor Maguire!

Mosquitoes drove her inside just on dusk. Still in mutinous mode, Holly decided to eat alone rather than wait for Connor. Remembering that the dining room only opened at seven thirty, she considered a drink in the bar, changed her mind, and eventually resorted to the mini-bar selection in her room and settled on a scotch.

The four course set menu and a delightfully chatty maître d'hôtel, who was astonished that she dined alone, restored her humour somewhat. After dinner, Holly watched a traditional *sega* performed by members of the hotel's staff. The suggestively erotic nature of the dance left her cold. She was back in her room by ten thirty. Of Connor, there had been no sign.

Somewhere around midnight Holly was awakened by a soft knocking at the door. 'It's me. Are you awake?'

It gave her some satisfaction to roll over and ignore him.

TEN

A violent thunderstorm woke Holly before it was fully light and she found it impossible to get back to sleep. Too many thoughts clamoured for attention. The biggest question of all was, what to do from here? The view of the problem, from where she lay staring up at the ceiling, was there were two possible options. One, pack up and go home, forfeit her fee for the treasure hunt feature and forget she'd ever met Connor Maguire. Or two, soldier on and do the job for Quinn, keeping a space between herself and Maguire big enough to engulf the *Titanic*. There was no doubt in her mind that she had been used. Okay, she could also play that game. She would use Maguire for the article.

Holly opened the curtains, made herself a mug of coffee and went back to bed, propped up on pillows, to watch the sunrise. There had been moments when she'd believed that his interest in her was genuine. What a joke! Maguire was a seasoned ball-player, a hard-headed businessman, one who would stop at nothing to achieve his purpose. All that bullshit about wanting to protect her and how perfect their night together had been was nothing more than window-dressing. He needed her onside, knew how skittish she was about men and took out a little insurance. Well he was welcome to his third agenda, whatever it was. Connor Maguire could duck and weave through that little mind game to his heart's content. She would cover the search for William's treasure, but only because it suited her. And if Maguire so much as hinted at anything intimate, she'd deck him.

Showered, she ignored the usual selection of baggy clothes and chose instead to wear a white cotton pants suit. It fitted with figure-hugging allure and the first shirt button was low enough to reveal an eyeful of cleavage. The thinnish material meant it was slightly see-through. To hell with protective coating. Let Maguire see what he was messing with.

She did not wait for him. Breakfast was buffet-style and the choices ranged from light continental to a fully cooked English feast, kippers and all. There was something for every taste, including the cheeky sparrows' that took advantage of the open-air design and hopped from table to table, availing themselves of any crumb they could scrounge. Where possible, the selection of food was securely covered by cling film in an attempt to prevent any nasty little deposits.

Holly helped herself to fruit and yoghurt, following it up with pale scrambled eggs and spicy sausages. She was almost finished when Connor arrived.

'Morning. Sorry about last night. I was invited for dinner.' His stare was an attempt to get her to look up at him.

Flicking eyes briefly to his, she concentrated on stirring powdered milk into her coffee. 'No problem.'

'Fancy a trip to Port Mathurin?' He sounded unsure of himself.

She cut into the last bit of sausage and imagined it was one of his fingers. 'Sure.'

'Holly . . .'

'You have to help yourself. Food's over there,' she waved a hand vaguely. Wiping her mouth with a napkin she rose. 'I'm finished. I'll be in my room when you're ready to go.' Without waiting for his response, Holly left the dining room. She could always have coffee in her room.

It was twenty minutes later when he knocked. She opened the door, camera bag already slung over one shoulder. 'Let's go,' she said briskly.

'Holly . . .' Connor went to touch her then let his hands drop. 'Can we talk for a moment?'

'Nothing to talk about. Come on, Maguire, we have treasure to find.' She tried to step around him but he blocked the way.

'Dammit, Holly.' He moved forward. 'Listen to me.'

Holly spun around, strode back inside, put the camera bag none too gently on the bed and turned to face him. Her voice, she was relieved to find, was steady and hard. 'I don't like being used, Maguire. I don't like being lied to either. So from now on, if you don't mind, keep your bloody distance and your bloody mind on the bloody treasure. That way I'll get my story and be out of your hair. Is that understood?'

His eyes glittered. 'Perfectly.'

'Then let's go.'

'I wasn't using you.'

'Bullshit, Maguire. You still are.'

'Yes,' he admitted softly, 'but not in the way you think.'

'I don't want to hear it. Forget the charm. It's considerable but I'll only fall for it once.' She looked him up and down, deliberately and calculating. 'Not bad either for a one-night stand.'

He sucked in breath sharply. The insult had gone home. He nodded curtly. 'Let's go.'

They walked in silence to the hired four-wheel drive. On the road Holly kept up the professional detachment. 'Exactly why are we going to Port Mathurin?'

'William lived near there.'

'In his journal he said something about building a house on one of the small atolls.'

'I know. Maybe he did. But at some stage, he also lived on mainland Rodrigues.'

'How do you know?'

'Local island knowledge. My contact told me. William built his house at a place called Anse aux Anglais.'

'English Bay. Where is it?'

'About a twenty-minute walk from Port Mathurin. I thought if we park in town and walk we might see . . . get a feel for his life here.'

'Do you have the map with you?'

'Of course.'

'Good.'

Both lapsed into silence.

The only road led up to Mont Lubin then down through a surprisingly prolific forest and series of steep hairpin bends to the capital. Port Mathurin was little more than a village, perched on the water and sheltering in the lee of the mountain. A deep water channel leading to the man-made harbour, one of only two natural breaks in the coral reef through which ships could pass, was clearly visible as they descended. There was a deep-sea game fishing boat alongside the wharf.

Connor parked in shade nearby. 'We'll walk from here.'

She made no comment, stepping from the car and retrieving her camera bag.

'Would you like me to carry that?'

'No thanks.'

They came to a war memorial commemorating Rodriguan volunteers who fought in both world wars. Connor stopped and looked at it. 'Not something you hear about, is it?'

'No.'

'Want a photograph?'

'Nope.'

He shrugged. 'Suit yourself.'

The streets were narrow and old, set in a grid pattern, lined with a jumble of shops that reminded Holly of downtown Port Louis. All were practically deserted. 'Rodriguans get up with the sun and go to bed with it,' Connor explained. 'Most business is done early in the morning. The only petrol station on the island is here in Port Mathurin, and it closes at two in the afternoon.'

Holly thought it time she gave more than a monosyllabic response. She knew her behaviour bordered on childish. This man had severely ruffled her feathers but there was no way she'd give him the satisfaction of revelling in it. 'The banks close then as well. Did you read the information leaflet in your room? The whole place is tucked up for the night by six.'

'There must have been some life here last night.' Connor sounded relieved that she'd made a comment. 'A couple of bars were open.'

They crossed the Winston Churchill Bridge on the edge of town and followed the coast. 'How far is this place?'

'Couple of kilometres max.'

It was very pleasant. Shady trees on one side, ocean the other and the temperature in the mid-twenties. Holly took a couple of photographs looking back towards Port Mathurin and suddenly stiffened, zooming the camera lens to its maximum magnification. 'We have company.'

Connor didn't turn, he kept looking out to sea. 'Who?'

'Justin Parker. He's following us.'

'Let him.' Connor pulled the map from his shirt pocket. 'In fact, let's give him something to think about.' He pretended to study the sketch then shaded his eyes and gazed around, pointing at nothing in particular.

Holly examined it too, which meant standing close to Connor. She couldn't help but notice his aftershave – Hugo Boss – her father's favourite and, not surprisingly, hers too. She moved back from Connor abruptly.

'Come on,' he said, folding the map and setting off again. Ten minutes later they arrived at English Bay.

'Where was William's house?' Holly stood, hands on hips, looking at the few buildings, none of which seemed very old.

'Haven't a clue.'

She frowned, perplexed.

'His house isn't important, Holly. It's the terrain I'm interested in. This is where William's map comes closest to matching anything here or on Mauritius.' He pulled the paper out again, seemingly oblivious of Justin Parker. 'Look over there. With a bit of imagination . . .' He shook his head. 'No, perhaps not. Look at the map. It's reasonably similar, but where are the terraces? It's too different.'

Holly was photographing him. Her tape recorder was in her shirt pocket and running. 'How come you're doing this yourself? I'd have thought some minion would handle the preliminary work.'

'What kind of question is that? You know why I'm really here.'

Do I? 'One that perpetrates a fallacy. After all, Maguire, I've got to write something. Humour me. I'll pretend it's a real question and I'm interested in your answer.'

He looked exasperated. 'When do you stop?'

'When I've got the story I came to cover.'

'That's not what I mean and you know it.'

She was squatting low, photographing upwards, against a backdrop of pure blue sky. A deliberate angle, intended to make Connor Maguire look unassailable, a rock, a skyscraper, a giant in a land of mere mortals. It was an aggressive perspective. Holly thought it was perfect.

'That'll do it.' She stood up. 'As to your question, irrespective of meaning, my answer is the same. I don't give a damn what you're up to. My job is to make it look as though you're chasing long-lost treasure. Isn't that what you want? Isn't that why my presence here is being tolerated?'

A nerve ticked near his left eye. He glared at her for a very long moment before turning his head and looking away. 'No. It is not,' he said carefully.

'Come on, Maguire,' she taunted him, unable to stop herself. 'I'm a big girl. I can handle the truth. In fact,' she added cattily, 'it would make a pleasant change.'

His eyes turned dark with anger, his voice was quiet in an effort to contain it. 'The truth? Fine, you can have it. I didn't ask for publicity, you manoeuvred me into it. Take your bloody pictures and get the hell out of my life. Is that clear enough for you?'

Holly flinched as if he'd struck her. Her face drained of colour. 'You bastard,' she choked. 'Using me is one thing but attacking my professionalism is quite another.' She took a shuddering breath. 'I'd have completed this assignment whether you slept with me or not.'

Connor was breathing hard. 'Holly . . . I didn't mean it like that.'

Tears blinded her. 'I'll wait at the car.' She turned and walked swiftly away.

Connor groaned and closed his eyes. 'I'm sorry, baby,' he whispered to himself. 'I can't have you mixed up in this.'

Justin Parker, had Holly been in the right frame of mind, would have appeared comical in his attempt to hide from her. Wearing red shorts with a white and blue striped shirt, he stepped behind a tree to try to conceal himself. Unfortunately for him, he looked like a walking British flag and was as obvious as a broken leg. Holly drew level and stopped. Almost a minute went by before Justin looked out to see where she had got to. He nearly jumped out of his skin when he saw her waiting on the road.

She spoke through clenched teeth, taking all her anger and humiliation out on him. 'Just so you are up to date, Justin, I'm fully aware that you've been following us. I know you have a copy of William Maguire's map. I know your mother was a Maguire. And while you are indeed a biologist I'm reasonably certain that cloning the dodo has sod all to do with why you're here. That established, I'd appreciate it if you'd stop this ridiculous charade. It's getting positively boring. You're giving me a headache.' Holly stomped away.

Holly Jones had made many mistakes in her life.

Assuming Justin Parker was nothing more than a misguided fool acting on some stupid feud that was 250 years old was possibly her biggest yet. Had she known, had she seen the look on his face as she left, she might have regretted her hasty words.

When Connor reached the car some thirty-five minutes later, Holly was composed enough to remain civil. Hiding behind the job at hand, she spoke her mind in a neutral voice. 'This assignment has become awkward to say the least. I need a few more photographs and one last interview. If we work on that today I'll return the journal tonight and get out of your space. From tomorrow, you'll be free to do whatever it is you are doing. If, by any chance, you do find the treasure, a fax with some details and a pic or two should wrap it up. Other than that, the article will be ready to roll. Is that a deal?'

'I thought you wanted to write a piece on Rodrigues?'

'I do. I'll move out of the hotel and into one of the guesthouses here in Port Mathurin. It's more central.'

'Deal.' He sounded relieved.

She nodded curtly. 'If you don't discover anything the feature will be mainly fiction and hearsay. Is that okay with you?'

His voice matched hers in neutrality. 'As long as you stress the charity angle.'

'It's one of the few truths I've got.'

'I'd like to see the copy before it's published?'

'Quinn will have it.' She realised that her tape recorder was still running and turned it off. 'Can we go back to the hotel now?'

'Not yet. Since we're out and about, let's explore a bit.'

'Come on, Maguire. You don't need my company any more than I need yours.'

Real regret clouded his eyes briefly. 'There's a coast road from here to the airport. It's new. I'd like to have a look at it. Do you mind?'

'Suit yourself.' She picked up the camera bag and stood waiting for him to unlock the car.

He went to say something, stopped himself, sighed and opened the passenger's side.

Holly climbed in, leaned across and released the driver's door. 'Did you see Justin back there?'

'Hard not to. You seem to have scared him off. He was hiding behind a tree.'

'I suppose he'll shadow us all the bloody way to the airport and back.'

'He's welcome.'

'No sign of Raoul, though. I wonder if he's still here?'

Connor shrugged.

Holly didn't ask why he wanted to reach one end of the island via the other. It had nothing to do with the treasure. And that, she decided, was her only interest.

It seemed he really did have sightseeing on his mind. They headed west, almost at sea level, passing through the residential suburb of Oyster Bay nestled in casuarina forests with tree-covered hills rising almost vertically in the background. There was a rather surprising sign high on one which read HOLLYWOOD in exactly the same style of lettering as its somewhat more glamorous counterpart in California.

Holly had her tape running again. She didn't like recording in cars because the machine often picked up more engine noise than expected, making playback difficult to understand. On this occasion, however, she wanted the whole thing over and done with. Besides, work removed the need for more general conversation, something that always seemed to end with bitter words between them.

While Connor answered questions, Holly took in the passing scenery. Here on the north coast, with the coral reef anything up to three kilometres offshore, small sand-ridged islands – the kind cartoonists often drew to depict shipwrecked sailors – seemed to float in the lagoon. The mainland plunged dramatically to the sea below with white beached coves harbouring the occasional fishing community. The road was hardly busy. Once away from Port Mathurin, it became virtually deserted.

Rodrigues had remained an unspoilt destination. A lover's paradise. No diversions, nothing to do but enjoy each other's company. Visitors who did not like snorkelling, scuba diving or just sitting on a beach had very limited options. They could approach the local fishermen to take them fishing. They could walk, ride horses or take one of only three tours on offer – a boat trip to Ile aux Cocos, a bird sanctuary about three kilometres off the western tip of the island; a sight-seeing drive to Port Mathurin and the north coast; or a guided visit to Plaine Corail and Caverne Patate, a cave complex of stalactites and stalagmites some eighteen metres below sea level and nearly a kilometre long.

The road swung inland towards La Ferme, past the airport turn-off and on to the south coast. Seeing a sign for Caverne Patate, Connor suggested they hire a guide to show them through it. Justin Parker, who had given up any attempt to conceal his pursuit, had followed close behind them along a rough track leading to the cave entrance. He did not join the bus group to which Holly and Connor attached themselves. The torchlit walk underground lasted a good forty-five minutes.

Holly, who usually found caves claustrophobic, was relieved that Caverne Patate, although rugged, slippery and in some places downright boggy underfoot, was high and wide enough to prevent any panic. The climb out, up crumbling rock steps, was physically a bit taxing, making it evident just how far underground they'd been.

'I wonder what your friend is thinking?' Connor queried as they returned to the car. Justin Parker was glaring at them, drumming his fingers on the steering wheel. His undisguised surveillance made him look ridiculous and he probably knew it.

'He's got caves and treasure on his mind.' Holly actually felt slightly sorry for him.

'Bit bloody obvious.'

'Well I hope he doesn't try to explore the cave on his own. With no torch and no guide he'd never be seen again.'

'Great place for dodo remains,' Connor remarked. 'Perhaps I should go and tell him.'

'Leave him be. He's doing no harm.' It was incredible how, after their recent argument, they were able to call a kind of truce. Holly speculated on her luck. First Dennis and his philandering, now this. She concluded that it would be just as well to give men a complete miss from now on. Far less trouble and no risk of heartache.

From Caverne Patate, they travelled along the south coast to Port Sud-Est, where Connor suggested lunch. They found a small cafe of dubious character where they chose an outside table. The proprietor, looking terribly pleased that tourists had selected his establishment, took their order personally. Justin Parker was nowhere to be seen, though Holly supposed he was observing them from somewhere.

Offshore was another tiny island. 'That's Hermitage Island. A likely place for treasure if the rumours are anything to go by,' Connor said. 'Maybe we should try to hire a boat.'

Holly looked at him for a long moment before asking, 'Why are you doing this?'

'Doing what?'

'The tourist bit.'

'Just trying to help out.'

Holly shook her head. 'You really must be

desperate to get rid of me, killing two birds with the one stone like this. Finish my interview then pack in as much local information as possible. Tell me something, Maguire, why are you suddenly trying to speed up my departure?' She was beyond anger or disappointment, speaking without bitterness.

His eyes were unreadable. 'I want you out of here, yes. But not for the reasons you think. Believe me.'

'Nice try. You've run that past me before. It didn't work then and it won't work now.'

He spoke softly. 'One day, Holly, I hope you learn the truth.'

'You've already shown me what that is.'

Connor looked down at his hands. 'Yuh!' He spoke as though his throat hurt. 'Truth has many sides. Remember I said that.'

Holly rose. 'Excuse me. I'll be back in a minute.' She went in search of a toilet. She had to get away from him for a while. One minute she hated him, the next he confused her. Sometimes, like now, she wanted to hold him in her arms and smooth away whatever was wrong.

The toilet, an outhouse at the back of the building, was locked but the proprietor had given her the key. She had Connor Maguire on her mind and was in no rush. When Justin Parker stepped out of nowhere and gripped her arms from behind, Holly was completely off guard.

'My car is this way,' he hissed. 'Don't make a fuss.'

She turned, not yet alarmed. 'Justin, what the hell do you think you're doing?'

His eyes would not meet hers. 'You're coming with me.'

'I am not. Let me go.'

He took a ragged breath. 'I'm afraid I insist.'

Holly struggled. 'Let go of me immediately, Justin. This is ridiculous.' The grip he had on her arms was painful. 'You're hurting me.'

'Sorry.' He relaxed his grip slightly. 'This way.' Justin turned and pushed her in the direction he wanted to go.

Holly's mind raced. The ground was sandy. Connor would be able to read the signs. As they reached Justin's car she managed to drop the toilet key. One part of her mind was calmly trying to figure out a means of escape, the rest was wondering how alarmed she should be. Justin didn't look or behave like a man who meant to harm her, but he appeared determined that she do as he wanted.

He wedged her against the car with his own body. 'Put your hands behind you.'

Holly realised he was taping her wrists together. This is not happening! she thought wildly. There must be people about.

Justin forced Holly into the car and secured her seatbelt.

She tried to stay calm. 'Where are you taking me?'

'Port Mathurin.'

'Why? What's this all about?'

'I want to talk to you, that's all.'

'Justin, this is madness. You're kidnapping me. You can't hope to get away with it. Maguire will come looking for me.'

'Shut up,' he snapped. 'Just shut up.' He looked nervously back towards the cafe before getting into the car. Holly could prise nothing more out of him. He remained silent as they drove up and across the island.

Halfway down the twisting descent from Mont Lubin, Justin turned left on a narrow and deeply rutted dirt track. No more than one hundred metres along it he swung into a driveway and stopped the car. A small, once white bungalow, screened from the road by dense shrubs and an overgrown hedge, sat in the centre of a sadly neglected garden. The view over Port Mathurin and the sea was superb, had Holly been in the mood to appreciate it. Justin unbuckled her seatbelt and cut the tape binding her wrists. 'Into the house.'

She had to remain calm. 'Whose place is this?'

'Inside. We'll talk inside.'

The interior was basic and had seen better days. 'Sit down please.'

Holly chose an armchair. Justin turned a straight-backed chair around and straddled it, opposite her.

'I won't hurt you,' he said in a rush, his eyes pleading for understanding. 'Please, don't be frightened. You're quite safe.'

'What do you want, Justin?' His assurances didn't do much for her. Was he simply so desperate to learn what Maguire knew about the treasure that he was prepared to abduct her in order to get it? Or was he capable of worse?

'Information,' he blurted. 'I won't hurt you,' he repeated. 'Unless . . .'

'Unless what?'

He seemed jumpy, unsure of himself. 'I have to make a phone call. I'm sorry to do this.' Using the same roll of electrical tape, Justin secured Holly's hands and feet. Then he left the house, saying only, 'I'll be back in fifteen minutes.'

Holly looked around her. There had to be a knife somewhere. She got up with difficulty and hopped to the kitchen. To one side of the sink were three drawers. Holly made it across the room and, turning her back, groped clumsily for the recessed lip of the first. It was more difficult than she expected. She managed to get hold of it easily enough but, in order to pull the drawer out, she needed to move forward. She finally worked out a distance from the drawer that was close enough to reach it without falling over backwards but far enough away to lean forward and open the drawer a fraction. She repeated the process three or four times before it was sufficiently open for her to look inside. It took minutes to reveal nothing more than several candles and some paper bags.

The middle drawer was easier but contained only string and spare light bulbs. To reach the lowest one, Holly had to lie on her side, then pull and wriggle forward. Nothing. Completely empty. 'There must be something here somewhere,' she muttered. 'Corner cupboard, recently built by the look of it. Try that.' She hopped over, took the doorknob in her mouth, and zigzagged her bound feet sideways, shuffling millimetre by millimetre. Breathing was difficult with the round knob in her mouth. With the door open, she let go for a second to catch her breath. Spring return hinges immediately pulled the cupboard door closed again. After a number of frustrating attempts, she had to admit defeat.

'Try the other rooms.' One door was shut, the handle impossible to reach. The second proved to be a sparsely furnished bedroom Justin was obviously using. That left only the bathroom, which yielded nothing useful. Holly had just returned to the lounge when she heard Justin's car. She hopped over to the armchair and fell into it, hoping that the dirt on her white clothing would not be noticed. He burst into the house looking positively anxious and appeared relieved to find her still there.

'Let me remove that.' His hands shook as he cut through the tape.

Holly gratefully rubbed the circulation back into her wrists and ankles.

Once again, Justin straddled the wooden chair. He looked slightly embarrassed. Holly took a guess that the phone call had been to Raoul Dulac. 'How come you know so much about me?' he asked suddenly.

Holly hesitated and then, because she was growing angry, threw caution to the wind. 'I had you checked out by the magazine.'

'Why?'

'I saw a copy of William Maguire's map in your pocket.'

'That day on the beach?'

She nodded. 'On top of that, you also didn't seem to know about the solitaire. A bit strange for somebody working on a dodo research project, don't you think?'

Justin smiled condescendingly. 'I'm afraid that was just professional snobbery on my part. There is strong scientific evidence to suggest that the solitaire and the dodo are related but not the same bird. I didn't see any point in correcting your assumption that the two were the same. Most people make that mistake.' He made a steeple with his hands and buried the lower half of his face into it so only his eyes were visible. His voice was muffled. 'I didn't want to do this. You brought it on yourself.'

'Really, I fail to see how.'

'You and that man.'

'Connor Maguire, you mean?'

Justin nodded.

Holly allowed her anger to show. 'That's ridiculous. All I'm doing is covering his search for treasure which, incidentally, he has as much right to as you. Why the hell don't you join up with him instead of going through all this cloak and dagger stuff? If anything does exist there should surely be enough to share. As for kidnapping me, Justin, I could have you sent to prison for this.' *Risky, Jones. Why don't you keep your big mouth shut?*

Panic and then determination showed on his face. Given a choice, Holly wasn't sure which she preferred. Either could prove dangerous.

Justin scowled. 'I'm not kidnapping you.'

'Then let me go.'

'I can't. There's someone who wants to talk to you.'

'Raoul Dulac, I suppose.'

His eyes narrowed. 'What makes you think that?'

'You were at his house on Sunday. I overheard your conversation.'

'Then you know too much.'

'Only that you are after the same thing as Connor Maguire. Aside from this little abduction number, you haven't done anything illegal. Are you sure you want to proceed with this?'

'I must.' Justin looked apologetic but determined.

'Does that mean you are prepared to hold me captive until Dulac arrives?'

'He'll be here soon.'

Holly strove to maintain her calm. 'Then while we wait, why not tell me how you know about the treasure?'

His willingness to answer surprised her. 'I don't suppose there's any harm in that. Anne-Marie told my mother.'

'Anne-Marie!'

'Yes.' He smiled mirthlessly. 'Raoul's sister.'

'Daughter, don't you mean?'

It was Justin's turn to look surprised. He dropped his hands away from his face. 'Daughter! Anne-Marie said she was his half-sister.'

'She would. It's a Dulac charade that's been going on for over thirty years.'

'But that would mean –'

'. . . that Raoul Dulac fathered a child with a nineteen-year-old servant when he was only fourteen.' Holly saw an opportunity to distract Justin from his obsession with the treasure. 'He raped her, actually.'

Genuine surprise, coupled with distaste, was evident on Justin's face. 'Good Lord. I had no idea.'

'Nice company you keep.'

But it didn't work. Justin's expression became defensive. 'The past has got nothing to do with me. We're partners, that's all. Anyway, why should I believe you?'

Holly shrugged that it didn't matter if he did or not. 'I suppose Dulac gave you that copy of the map?'

'Anne-Marie did.'

'Same thing. Same family. Why involve you?'

'Meaning?'

'Why would Raoul Dulac want to introduce a third party? He doesn't strike me as the type who likes to share things.'

'He didn't. As I've already explained, Anne-Marie told my mother.'

'And Anne-Marie can't stand Raoul,' Holly said slowly, remembering the look of hate on the French woman's face on Sunday. 'So learning about the supposed treasure and realising that Raoul took it seriously she deliberately set out to throw a spanner in the works. Was it a case of pick a Maguire, any Maguire, or did she already know your mother?'

'Anne-Marie spent twelve months in England as a university exchange student. While she was there she did some digging into her Maguire background.'

'So she knew, even back then, about her real mother?'

'Mrs Dulac took great pains to mention it at every opportunity. She was never very nice to Anne-Marie. Anyway, to answer your question, Anne-Marie found she had a whole host of relatives in the UK. If this treasure thing hadn't come up she probably wouldn't have contacted any of us. When she learned of the map she saw it as an opportunity to repay some old debts. I think her original intention was to let as many Maguires know about it as possible then sit back and watch the fun. Fortunately for my family, we were the first she contacted. A coincidence really. She'd hired a car and planned to work her way up to Ireland, visiting Maguires along the way. We live the furthest south.'

Holly was thinking quickly. Anne-Marie was Kathleen's daughter and therefore a descendant of William. Justin's mother, however, was from Kavanagh's side of the family. Which meant, in Maguire terms at least, that they might well be bitter enemies. Could it be, therefore, that this was Anne-Marie's way of paying back Kathleen for giving her up at birth?

'Why give the map to your mother? She's the wrong side of the family.'

Justin confirmed Holly's thoughts. 'Anne-Marie

didn't know about the feud until my mother mentioned it. When she heard about it she changed her original plan. By giving us the copy of the map she could achieve two things.'

'Get in Raoul's way and get back at her mother, you mean? Why? If the treasure is found –'

Justin cut in. 'She's not interested. It's nothing more than a mind game to her. Anne-Marie doesn't believe the treasure exists.'

'But what if it does? She's cutting off her nose to spite her face.'

'Don't you understand anything?' Justin's voice rose. Long fingers brushed hair off his forehead. 'We're a thorn in Raoul's side, that's all. It's just as Anne-Marie intended. Raoul brought her in to keep her quiet. She did exactly the opposite, which forced him to accept me as a fifty-fifty partner.'

'Listen to me, Justin. Be careful. Raoul Dulac can play very rough and has no conscience whatsoever.'

He shook his head vigorously. 'You've no proof. You're just saying that.'

'No I'm not. You're mixed up in something that's way out of your league. It's not the Maguire treasure, it's Raoul. You seem like a nice enough guy but you're no match for the likes of him. At best, you can expect to be double-crossed.' She had his attention. Holly felt sorry for him. He'd allowed a dream of untold wealth to cloud his judgment and was having serious difficulties with reality. Holly continued. 'Stop this now, Justin. Before any real damage is done.'

'It's too late for that.'

'Of course it isn't. You can walk away right now if you're strong enough.'

'I can't.' He sounded close to despair. 'It's not just the treasure.'

'The feud? Surely not!'

'I'm honour-bound –'

'Jesus!' Holly exploded, suddenly disgusted with him. 'That was bloody centuries ago.'

'It makes no difference. That treasure belongs to my mother's family.'

'Does it? Are you quite sure of that, Justin?'

'What do you mean?'

Holly shook her head. 'Nothing. Just speculating.' Connor Maguire had asked her to say nothing to Raoul about the journal. The same request would apply to Justin.

Justin checked his watch, frowning. Raoul Dulac was taking his time. He rose and crossed to the window, peering out impatiently, before returning to sit opposite her.

'Enter Connor Maguire,' Holly mused, breaking the silence. 'That must have shaken you.'

'I didn't expect that,' Justin admitted. 'And that's why you're here. Your friend seems to know quite a lot more than Raoul and I. We simply want to find out how much.'

'What makes you think I can help?'

'What were you doing at Caverne Patate?' Justin asked by way of a response.

'Playing tourists.'

'Don't expect me to believe that.'

'We had a guide and a bus load of other people with us, remember?'

'Maguire was checking out the place.'

'Didn't seem like that to me.'

He glared at her. 'You'd do well to tell me the truth.'

The truth! Holly had had enough. Justin was not the only one trying to ferret that out. 'Well, let's see what I can do. Connor Maguire is a selfish, pleasure-seeking playboy who revels in self-gratifying publicity stunts. He doesn't actually give a shit whether or not there is any treasure. The idea of it appeals to him. And not being directly descended from either William or Kavanagh, the family argument doesn't bother him. Your major competitor hasn't a bloody clue where the treasure is hidden and he's not exactly knocking himself out to find it. I'm on some wild goose chase with a man who doesn't understand the concept of working for a living and I'm getting *very* pissed off at the waste of my time.' She was unaware her voice was rising. 'Now you come along with a heap of old family melodrama that's of no interest to anybody. That's your unabridged bloody truth. Now can we drop the subject? And please, I'd very much appreciate it if you could see your way clear to let me out of this place before I totally lose it.'

'Very dramatic.' A voice and slow handclap came from the open doorway.

Holly spun around in her chair. Raoul Dulac was smiling as he walked into the room. 'Justin, dear boy, what have you been doing to this charming lady? She seems to be in quite a state.' He directed his attention back to Holly. 'I really must apologise for my partner's high-handed behaviour. The lad panicked. You are free to go any time you like.'

'Try now,' Holly barked, preparing to rise.

The Frenchman shrugged elaborately. 'A few questions first.' He sat on the arm of her chair. 'I gather from your outburst that Connor Maguire is no closer to finding the treasure than we are. Can you confirm that?'

Holly closed her eyes and rubbed fingers across them. A tension headache was threatening. 'I have no idea,' she said.

'Answer the question please.' A hard note had crept into Raoul's voice.

She opened her eyes. 'I can't. I have no idea how close Maguire really is. Personally, I think he'll find zilch but he plays things so close to his chest it's impossible to say. I don't know how close you are either. So, please or no please, how the hell can I answer your question?'

'You were in English Bay earlier. Why?'

'Apparently William Maguire lived there.'

'How do you know that?'

I can't say that Maguire's drug contact told him. Sorry, Maguire. Time to confess. 'Maguire has a journal . . .'

'Ah!' Raoul leaned back, satisfied. 'The journal. So it really does exist. What else does it tell us?'

Holly saw no point in lying. 'Not much. Random incidences. There's a sort of inventory. An account of Kavanagh's betrayal. A bit about

Rodrigues and reference to a map which, incidentally, had been torn out. The journal doesn't say whether William hid his treasure here or in Mauritius.'

Raoul watched her face carefully. 'You tell the truth. Good. But you were consulting a map. Where did Maguire get it?'

Holly hesitated. Kathleen had stolen it back from Raoul's house. She didn't want to get the little nun into trouble. 'I have no idea.'

Raoul shook his head. 'Wrong answer.'

'Tough.'

He spun in an instant and grabbed both her shoulders. 'I said, wrong answer.' His eyes dropped to the bulge in her shirt pocket and he reached for the tape recorder. 'What have we here? Let's see what you and Maguire find to discuss.'

Holly turned cold. She listened with horror as their voices exposed all that Connor would wish to keep secret:

How come you're doing this yourself?

You know why I'm really here.

After all, Maguire, I've got to write something. Humour me. I'll pretend it's a real question and I'm interested in your answer.

When do you stop?

I don't give a damn what you're up to. My job is to make it look as though you're chasing long-lost treasure. Isn't that what you want?

I'd have completed this assignment whether you slept with me or not.

And a little while later at the car: *From tomorrow, you'll be free to do whatever it is you are doing.*

Raoul turned off the tape recorder. 'Well, well. It seems some people would do anything for a story.'

Justin looked upset and Raoul was far from comforted by what he'd heard. 'Let's see now – "you know why I'm really here". Please tell us what that means.'

Holly had to appear spontaneous. A good lie should be eighty per cent truth. 'Connor Maguire is a very successful businessman. Mauritius has some very attractive tax-free concessions for investors. He's setting up a joint venture.' She tried to look conspiratorial. 'I really shouldn't say any more.'

Raoul wasn't sure, she could tell by his face.

'*Out of Focus,* as you may be aware, likes to publish the unusual. Maguire is practically a regular. That doesn't mean their editorial policy is all frivolity. In this case there was a pretty good chance that his search for treasure was secondary to some kind of business interest. We knew that one attempted merger with a Mauritian company had failed.' Holly mentally crossed everything. This was risky. 'It seemed a safe bet that he'd try again. If we could get in on the treasure angle we'd be on the spot and first with any joint venture story. The magazine works that way. They like to be ready with the news before it breaks. Maguire has a very high profile in Australia.'

Raoul shook his head. 'Then why say "whatever it is you're doing"?'

'I know there have been several high-level meetings. It's definitely a joint venture, though Maguire won't tell me any more than that. It's frustrating as hell. I've tried . . . everything. Yet he still insists on waiting until the day the deal is closed. That's why we had the fight.'

The French–Mauritian appeared satisfied. 'I've done business with Maguire. It tallies. He wouldn't want a reporter nosing around secret negotiations. The man thrives on publicity, but only when he's good and ready for it.'

Holly rose. 'Now, if you don't mind, I'd like to leave.' She jabbed a finger in Justin's direction. 'I've a bloody good mind to report you for assault.'

'Just a moment.' Raoul hadn't finished. 'You still haven't told us how Maguire got hold of the original map?'

'He didn't say.'

'Come, come, my dear. You're a reporter. Surely you asked?'

'Of course I bloody asked,' Holly snapped. 'He said it's better I don't know.'

'Perhaps you could use your, how shall we put it, feminine charm to get the information out of him?'

Holly flushed. 'Are you asking me to spy for you?'

'Spy? Really, Miss Jones. A little investigative journalism. That should be right up your street.'

'It can't have escaped your attention that Maguire and I are not exactly friends.'

'You looked cosy enough to me,' Justin spoke up suddenly.

'We're both professionals but, if you must know, speaking frankly, I can't wait for this assignment to end.'

Raoul stood up and handed her the tape recorder. 'I'll run you back to Cotton Bay. Justin, my friend, your enthusiasm is admirable, if a little misguided. Do try to keep it under control.' There was no disguising the warning in his voice. He turned back to Holly. 'I trust you won't try to take this further, my dear. Justin acted without thinking. No doubt he's regretting it now. Should you choose to report the incident I will, of course, take steps to protect my partner. The Dulac name is not without considerable influence in Mauritius and Rodrigues. You'll find a complaint would lead nowhere.'

Holly walked to the door without speaking.

'If Maguire does let anything slip . . . Well, I can be very generous.'

She spun around to face him. 'This may be a little hard for you to swallow, Dulac, but I'll say it anyway. I don't like you. I don't like him.' She pointed at Justin. 'I don't like threats and I don't take bribes. You can shove your generosity. Now, I'd like to go.'

She remained silent all the way to Cotton Bay, despite Raoul Dulac's transparent attempts at conversation. Whatever Connor Maguire's real agenda, Holly was certain he'd told her the truth for a change. It did have something to do with the French-Mauritian.

She ignored Raoul's farewell, banging the car

door hard and striding into reception. Connor's room key was still in its pigeonhole. Holly had no idea how to let him know she was safe but presumed he'd return to the hotel at some stage.

The shower was only lukewarm but it helped. Unsure what to do next, an insistent knocking on the door cut into her confusion. 'Holly, it's me. Let me in.'

She was still angry, still frightened, and when he walked into the room with concern all over his face she did the only thing left. She burst into tears.

Without a word, he picked her up in his arms and laid her gently on the bed. Then he curled himself around her while she sobbed against his chest. The emotional seesaw was out of control. She cried for a very long time.

'All done?' he asked gently, when she had nothing left but the odd hiccup.

Holly nodded.

She felt his lips against her hair. 'I nearly went mad with worry.'

'It was Justin,' she whispered against him.

'I know.'

'He taped my wrists.'

'Did he hurt you?'

'Not really. Just scared me half to death. He took me to a house above Port Mathurin. Then Raoul arrived.'

'I know.'

She pulled back and looked at his face. 'You know! How?'

'I sat around for about thirty minutes waiting at

the cafe. When you didn't come back I went looking for you. It took a bit of time but your
footprints clearly showed that someone else had
been there. It had to be Justin. Then I found the
key. Putting two and two together, I figured he'd
taken you to Port Mathurin.'

'Since you were so sure where I'd gone, what
took you so long to arrive?'

'The car had a puncture and the spare tyre
turned out to be as flat as a pancake. There was no
garage so a little money changed hands and the
cafe owner miraculously came up with a good
wheel to swap for one of ours. That took at least an
hour. Luckily, my guess about the house was correct. I really enjoyed meeting your friend Justin,
although the feeling may not have been mutual. It
didn't take much persuasion to tell me the whole
story.'

'Raoul said I'd be wasting my time if I reported
it.'

His fingers played with her hair. 'He's right.'

'How did you know about the house?'

'It belongs to Raoul.'

Holly pulled back from him and sat up.

'Now what?' he asked with a degree of
apprehension.

'Tell me,' she demanded.

'What?' Reluctant just about did it.

'Tell me, damn it!' she grated.

'I made some enquiries.'

'Bullshit, Maguire.'

'Someone made them for me.'

349

'The puncture didn't happen, did it?'

'No.'

'Another of your famous little diversions. You don't want me to ask who you contacted, do you? Fine, I won't. But I could have been killed. Don't you think I deserve *some* answers?'

'Yes.'

His look told her she wouldn't be getting them from him. Holly stared back, her feelings more mixed up than she'd ever known. He was devious, tender, hard, soft, funny, frustrating, a mystery, an open book and the most attractive, sexy, desirable, unreliable, despicable man she'd ever managed to get her hands on. Two fat tears rolled down her cheeks. 'Go away,' she whispered miserably. 'Go away and leave me alone. I don't need you in my life. I've never been so confused.'

Connor's arms reached out and gently pulled her down, his eyes bored into hers for a long moment. 'I'm falling in love with you, Holly,' he said hoarsely. 'And I'm scared for you.'

She stared at him, shaking her head. 'No,' she said, struggling against him. 'No, not that old line. How dare you.'

She'd have said more but his lips found hers. Holly tried to hate him but her entire soul wanted to love this man. She responded and the desperation of her confusion transmitted itself to him. They made love urgently, passionately, and each thrust of his body was like a knife, wounding her with deceit yet bearing her away with intense longing for it never to end.

'Holly,' he breathed into her ear, over and over as he reached a shuddering climax to join hers.

They lay together, not speaking, for several minutes. Then she remembered the tape recorder. It was important and, as much as she didn't want to spoil the moment, knew she had to tell him. He heard her out in silence.

'Damn!' Connor said quietly, when she'd finished.

'I had to give him something.'

'I know. You did the best thing possible. I've told you he's devious. He's also greedy. A whiff of money and he'll do everything in his power to secure a slice of the action. The more I think about it, the more it seems unlikely he's aware that I've been in negotiations with his mistress. But Mauritius is small, people talk. If Dulac so much as suspects I'm involved with Madame Liang he'll know it means money and he'll use her as leverage to horn in. That would cause delays. I don't like delays, Holly. The longer something takes to set up, the more seems to go wrong. Damn that man! He's getting in the way.'

'Similar to myself,' Holly said in a small voice. Was she still being used? He couldn't possibly have faked the feeling in his voice.

His arms tightened around her. 'Could you handle the God's honest, swear on my mother's grave truth?'

'Your mother isn't dead.' She was pleased with that. It meant her brain hadn't completely deserted her.

Connor smiled slightly and kissed her nose. 'I know you aren't sure if you can trust me,' he said finally, 'but I'll work on that. You will eventually.'

'Don't count on it. You've come up with more lies than a politician.'

'Only because I had to.'

'How about, "take your bloody pictures then get the hell out of my life"?'

'That was no lie. I want you out of here. I didn't mean forever. Anyway, I was pretty pissed off with that one-night-stand crack of yours.'

Holly grinned wickedly. 'That was good, wasn't it.'

'Real show-stopper.' He nuzzled into her neck for a while.

Eventually, Holly dug him in the ribs with an elbow.

Connor came up for air and looked at her.

'About that truth.'

His eyes locked with hers. 'I am falling in love with you. I'm trying not to but I'm losing. That is the truth.'

Holly searched his eyes for insincerity. All she found in them was herself. Her fingers traced his lips. 'I'm not sure,' she admitted, 'you keep sending conflicting signals.'

He rolled onto his back, burrowed an arm under her neck and drew her into him so she lay snuggled against his side. 'That's my inept way of trying to maintain some kind of distance between us. Trouble is, you keep creeping under the barrier.' His free arm closed around her waist. 'So I've decided to stop trying.'

'Does that mean you'll stop using me?'

'No, it means I'll stop fighting a battle I've got no hope of winning.'

'So you admit you're using me?'

'I've admitted it several times but you weren't listening.'

'I'm listening now.'

He kissed her forehead. 'I needed a smokescreen but it had to be done right. Publicity wise, I had to appear reluctant. You came along at the perfect moment.'

'When you were with Liang Song?'

'The timing couldn't have been better.'

'I don't understand. She knows why you're here.'

'It's complicated. And I still can't tell you the whole story.'

'There's another reason why you want to get at Raoul Dulac, isn't there? It's not just the shipping deal.'

'No comment. Look what happened today. You got away with it but telling lies is not exactly your best thing. You're too intrinsically honest.'

'Is it dangerous, this thing you can't, or won't, tell me?'

'It could be.'

Her fingers tensed on his skin. 'Meaning?'

He held her tightly. 'Meaning it could be.'

'What if I continue to pretend to be covering your treasure hunt?'

'No. I'd rather know you're safe.'

'But, if it helps –'

The kiss was long and hard, dominating and full of caring.

'Here's another truth for you,' he said, his breathing a little unsteady. 'I admit I needed a freelance reporter to suit my own purposes. I didn't expect to fall in love with her. Now that I have, I want her out of danger.'

'What if she won't leave?' Holly slipped easily into the third person conversation.

'If she loves me, she'll leave.'

'That's not fair.'

His fingernails traced imaginary patterns down her bare back, making her shiver. 'Won't she?' he asked relentlessly.

'Don't do that. I'm not going anywhere while you do that.'

His dark eyes said it all. 'I want you,' he whispered. 'I've never wanted anyone more.' He saw her look of uncertainty. 'No, baby.' His lips were on hers and he spoke against them. 'I'm not using you now.'

ELEVEN

Holly left Rodrigues on Thursday. She and Connor had spent all the previous day together, combining her interest in the island with an overwhelming desire to simply be in each other's company. Given the circumstances, it had been an extraordinary day. Still unanswered questions could so easily have caused tensions between them, but both were determined to ignore anything even vaguely contentious. They behaved like two lovers with nothing more on their minds than each other. Not even the lurking presence of what was probably a very surprised Justin Parker, given Holly's denunciation of Connor yesterday, was intrusive. In fact, Connor actually remarked that having him underfoot all the time was probably a good thing, since it inhibited his almost obsessive desire to behave like a love-struck, hands-on teenager.

The only time a note of seriousness intervened was when Holly expressed concern that, should the need arise, Connor might not be able to shake off their persistent shadow. To that, he simply smiled and said, 'I'll manage.'

As the Air Mauritius ATR 42 bit into the air and turned westwards over the coral shallows, Holly wondered when she would see Connor again. They had reached a compromise of sorts. She needed more time in Mauritius to finish her feature on the island. Connor would remain on Rodrigues. With fingers crossed Holly agreed not to try to contact him or involve herself in any way in what he was doing. The understanding was reached with grudging acceptance on both sides.

Connor wanted her back in Australia. She could see why. He could operate better without constant concern for her safety. But Holly had to stay closer than that. She had to be on hand in case something went wrong, though what she could do if anything did was far from clear.

As soon as the seatbelt sign rang, Holly angled her chair back as far as it would go and stared out the window, not really seeing anything. She was looking inwards and backwards and felt that she had entered a world of intangibles. Considering all the false starts and misunderstandings with Connor, the fact that she could fall in love with him came as something of a surprise. But falling in love was exactly what she was doing. No. Scratch that. Had done. The process, although still requiring time and attention, was complete. She was no closer to knowing his third reason for being in Mauritius – and considering he'd talked about the drug deal she still had no idea what could be so dangerous that he wanted her out of the way – but she was finally trusting her instincts. When he said he loved her, he did. Yes, he had used her, but making love to her was not part of it.

With her mistrust at last out of the way, Holly knew that she had never enjoyed simply being with a man so much. There were many things about him that touched her. Genuine feelings shown in numerous little ways – ways he couldn't possibly have faked. Just before they went to sleep on Tuesday night, with his arms firmly around her, he'd said, 'Stay close. If you run away, Holly Jones, I'll retrieve you.'

'Retrieve me!' She'd been amused at the word.

'Retrieve you.'

And sure enough, at some stage during the night she'd turned over and left the circle of his arms only to be woken by him searching the bed and sliding her back against his body. His whispered, 'Bad Holly,' and the sleepy kiss on her hair spoke volumes. She was certain he wasn't properly awake and that his actions had been instinctive. A little later in the night, or was it earlier in the morning, he'd turned over and simply taken her with him. Just wrapped her tighter in his arms and over she'd gone. His breathing told her he was still asleep.

In the morning she'd woken to the lightest touch of his fingers on her cheek. She'd opened her eyes and there he was, his face just centimetres from hers, watching. He kissed her tenderly.

'I'm still in your eyes,' she whispered.

'You always will be,' his quiet words came back.

And she was. During the entire day and evening

of Wednesday, the way he felt about her was there, unhidden. Although an enigma in many respects, when Connor Maguire committed himself he left Holly in no doubt that her feelings for him were fully reciprocated. Rodrigues, perhaps sensing a special something, turned on its very finest weather for them.

They talked of so many things. Walking hand in hand along the beach, music – he liked opera, she liked jazz. On the top of a hill behind the hotel, the results of the Republic vote in Australia – he hadn't wanted it, she had. They slithered and slipped their way up Mont Limon, the highest point on the island, to take in the 360 degree vista. A lively conversation about political correctness in journalism revealed they shared the same views on the subject – boutique idealism and ruination of the English language.

Lunchtime found them in Port Mathurin, at Le Capitaine restaurant. Both opted for the creole lamb.

'Goat,' Connor announced, after the first mouthful.

'I don't care,' she replied. 'It's absolutely delicious.'

'Will it always be this good?' he asked suddenly. He was not talking about the goat.

Holly smiled easily. 'Probably not. I can be bloody grouchy sometimes.'

'Really!'

Holly ignored his mock surprise. 'How about you?'

He grinned. 'I'm the most even-tempered man in the world.'

'Good,' she said airily. 'I hate grumpy people.'

That night, Holly was 'retrieved' at least twice and woke in the morning on the other side of the bed. She had no memory of him turning over with her. She'd slept on as he'd taken her with him.

'If I get up for a wee in the middle of the night,' she complained, 'I'm likely to take a wrong turn and walk into the wall.'

'It's okay, my baby,' he'd said. 'I'll come and pick you up.'

Holly emerged from her memories and realised she had an idiotic grin stretched from ear to ear. Connor Maguire was the reason. He was her kind of man. Never having been a devotee of American-style slang, she now, in a complete about-face, loved the way he called her 'my baby'. She adored the taste and smell of him. His sense of humour connected to hers, his hands on her drove her wild, his body joined to hers was pure bliss and, as an added extra, she thought he was so good-looking he probably should be bottled in preservative for future generations to fawn over. Okay, so she was biased. That was allowed. And here she was leaving him on Rodrigues for an unknown length of time on an unknown and dangerous mission for an unknown yet important reason. She had to be out of her mind!

As the ninety-minute flight progressed, so too did Holly's thoughts.

They had a great deal in common but sufficient

differences of opinion to ensure a debate that was both challenging and enjoyable. Connor Maguire was not afraid to be different. And if she pushed him too far, he was more than capable of giving as good as he received. Holly knew she needed that in a man. Pushovers might be easier to live with but their willingness to acquiesce when the chips were down would quickly lose its appeal.

She sighed. When would he return to Mauritius? At what point should she return to Australia? Would Connor get in touch with her? He knew she was returning to the same hotel.

Touching down in Mauritius, Holly's thoughts were still 650 kilometres away on Rodrigues. She had to admit though, it had been a long time since she'd had such nice ones.

With a bit more local knowledge than before, Holly decided it would be a waste of time hiring a car. The Merville Beach Hotel had a bus service to and from the airport. Once through to the baggage hall, she made inquiries and found that the next international flight was not due for two hours. That meant at least an hour before the hotel bus would arrive with departing passengers. She found a seat from where she could see the hotel buses arriving and settled down to wait.

'You weren't being entirely honest with me on Sunday.' The voice so close behind her made Holly jump. Oblivious to everything external, she'd had no idea of his presence.

She spun around. Guy Dulac had a kind of triumphant gleam in his eyes.

'Son of Raoul,' Holly said, trying to sound friendly.

He sat on the plastic seat next to her, leaned close and murmured confidentially, 'You're not gay.'

'How would you know?' Holly would have moved away but she was already on the end seat.

'My spies tell me everything.'

His proximity was positively intrusive. He was making her uncomfortable. Perhaps he was used to girls who didn't mind him taking up a large chunk of their personal space. Holly was not one of them. 'Would you mind sitting back a bit, you're crowding me.'

'Sorry.' He moved, but not very far. 'So when can I see you?'

The over-the-top youthful enthusiasm made Holly smile. 'You can't. I'm too busy.'

He didn't smile back. His voice became a shade harder. 'Come on. You journalists are all the same. All you ever do is sit around drinking.'

Holly sighed. Time to see him off. 'Sorry, Guy. I'm not interested.'

He blinked. He hadn't expected her to say no and mean it. 'Just a drink. No harm in that.'

She rose. 'I said no. Thanks anyway.'

'Just a minute.' He stood up and used his dominating height to again invade her space. 'What's your problem?'

Holly stepped backwards. She'd tried to be nice

and it hadn't worked. Let's see how he handled a sterner line. 'My current problem is people like you who can't take no for an answer.' She turned and walked away, regretting the fact that, since she had her pull-along suitcase to contend with, the departure lacked pizzazz.

Holly did not notice, and neither did Guy Dulac, a slightly built, smartly dressed Indian loitering beside a flower stall just inside the building. In fact, Detective Sham was carefully observing the two of them. When Holly walked away with her case he subconsciously released a sigh of relief. He'd noticed the tourist earlier and couldn't help but think what an attractive woman she was. When Guy Dulac made his approach he experienced a feeling of disappointment. Usually a good judge of character, Detective Sham would have put money on her having better taste. However, it was soon obvious from the woman's surprise and body language that she was not enjoying the encounter. Sham felt some concern. Guy Dulac was not the kind of man who took kindly to rejection.

Detective Sham had been hard at work on the floater case ever since Francois Prost confirmed that the girl had died of a massive overdose of heroin, most probably administered against her will. Extensive bruising where the needle had entered her arm and damage to the vein itself were good indicators that Corrine had struggled desperately to avoid the injection. She had probably died a peaceful death but she sure as hell hadn't wanted to. She'd had sex just before the overdose and all the signs pointed to her being a willing participant. An earlier snack consisted of a chicken leg and a few bits of cheese. She had been a young, good-looking girl in peak physical condition and some bastard had denied her old age. And Sham, who had a nose for such things, was reasonably certain that Guy Dulac was that bastard.

His inquiries had led him to a single suspect, but he had no proof, nothing that would stand up in a court of law. It had not been difficult, just frustratingly slow. A process of elimination, interviewing, cross-checking family and friends, everyone in fact who knew her. Corrine's boyfriend had been first. Detective Sham believed the lad's obvious grief. The boy had been devastated, quick to blame himself for an argument which meant they hadn't seen each other for a week.

'What was the row about?' Sham had asked.

'Nothing really. There was this fellow always hanging around her. At first, she didn't pay any attention to him but lately . . .'

'His name?'

'Dulac. Guy Dulac.'

'She was okay,' Corrine's boss had said. 'A bit unreliable but that's quite normal with our casuals. I think she enjoyed partying too much to take work seriously.'

'Did she play the field?' Sham asked.

'Not really. She had a regular boyfriend but I believe there was someone else she saw occasionally.'

'His name?'

'Guy someone. Don't know his last name. Blond, very tall, good-looking boy, around twenty I would say. Wealthy family if his car was anything to go by. French, I think.'

One of the permanent staff, an older woman who claimed that Corrine had been like a daughter to her, added more. 'She didn't get on with her mother, you see. If anything was bothering her, she came to me.'

'And was anything bothering her?'

'No. Well . . . yes. She had man trouble.'

'What kind of man trouble?'

'She couldn't make up her mind. You know how it is with these young girls. She had a nice boyfriend and she loved him, I'm sure. But there was this other boy too. She was flattered by his attention, dazzled by the money he spent on her. He never stopped buying her presents.'

'His name?'

'Guy Dulac.'

Then from Corrine's best friend. 'I told her Guy Dulac was trouble. I wouldn't be surprised if he had something to do with it. He's wild.'

'Wild how?'

'He drinks. Smokes pot. I don't know about hard drugs. Corrine was fascinated by him.'

And then, from Guy Dulac himself. 'Who?'

'Corrine Vitry.'

'Never heard of her.'

'I can produce a dozen reliable witnesses who say you knew her quite well.'

'What was that name again?'

'Corrine Vitry.'

'Oh, Corry. Sure, I know her. What's she been up to?'

'Not a lot. She's dead.'

'Well, well, how sad. Do I need my lawyer now or later?'

Detective Sham wanted to slam a fist into that softly supercilious face and wipe out the mocking smile. He had met his kind before. It was inevitably the rich and influential who could fabricate a watertight alibi from one hundred per cent fiction. Sure enough, Solange and Raoul Dulac supported their son's story that he was at home, sick, throughout the entire duration of Corrine Vitry's last few hours on this earth. Sham's nose was itching. Guy Dulac was his boy, he was sure of it.

He needed a reliable witness, probably more than one, or evidence so incriminating that, alibi or not, the defence would collapse. But his case would have to be good. The Dulacs of this world believed themselves above the law and were not adverse to lying when it suited their purpose.

Being the meticulous and thorough kind of policeman he was – dedicated to an unshakeable belief that, regardless of life's lottery, decent people should be able to live in peace, without fear of violence or intimidation – Sham began collecting information about Guy Dulac. From a reluctant snout in Port Louis he learned that his prime suspect regularly bought brown sugar – Indian heroin.

Two prostitutes and an ex-girlfriend told him that Guy Dulac did more than dabble in the darker side of life. Group sex, glue sniffing, cannabis, speed, heroin, snow, drug dealing, bondage, bribery. You name it, he was into it.

Sham discovered that Guy Dulac had no conscience when it came to women. Nor did he particularly care what age they were. One estranged husband had even quoted the boy's words when he found him in bed with his wife of fifteen years. 'If you can't keep it wet and happy, I can.'

It became abundantly clear that no-one liked Guy Dulac, or any of the Dulac family for that matter. Initially, however, most people he spoke to were reluctant to be specific, obviously afraid of the consequences. It was only when they learned that it was a murder inquiry that tongues loosened.

In the course of his investigation, Sham gathered enough evidence to put the Dulac boy away for ten years. But he wanted more. He wanted to wipe the smug smile from the upstart's face. He wanted to do the kid for Corrine Vitry's murder. It was the least he could do for her family.

The detective made no attempt to hide when Guy Dulac looked over and saw him. He nodded briefly when the boy's eyes registered his presence. Instead of acknowledging the gesture, Guy Dulac rose and made his way over to the flower stall. 'Tailing me?'

The same mocking tone that grated on Sham's nerves. 'Should I be?'

'If making sure I meet my mother's flight turns you on, go for it. It's a free country.' Dulac studied the fingernails on one hand.

'We'll see about that,' Sham said, turning away.

Guy Dulac made no response.

The Merville Beach Hotel put Holly back into the same room she'd had before. She unpacked and then sat at the desk with a map of Mauritius, planning her strategy for the next few days. Little more was required on the Chinese, Creole or French perspectives. She needed material on the Indian community. She had seen Mahébourg, Grand Baie, Cap Malheureux, Poudre d'Or, the Flacq district, Bamboo Mountain and Port Louis, she now needed to concentrate on southern and western Mauritius and the central highlands.

She glanced at her watch. Twelve twenty. Twenty past six in Sydney. Thursday. Business lunch day for Quinn. He usually went back to the office. Holly made the call. Quinn was still working.

'It's me.'

'Hello sweetheart. We got your message at home. How's it going?'

'Good. I've been on Rodrigues for the last couple of days. Connor is still there. There's not much more I can do on the treasure front. Maguire's unlikely to find anything, he's hardly bothering to look.'

'How does it read?'

'Don't know. I haven't written it yet. Should be

okay. There's some solid background material on his ancestor.'

'The mad pirate? Good stuff, I like it.'

'Daddy?'

Silence. Quinn had suddenly switched to defence mode.

'What else did Connor tell you about his reason for being here?' She shouldn't be asking, she knew she shouldn't be asking. Holly anticipated and got a one word, stone wall response.

'Nothing.'

This time she pushed it. 'I know he told you something.'

'What makes you think . . .?'

'Because he let slip that it should have prevented you from sending me to cover the story.'

More silence.

'Well? Come on, Quinn. What did he say?'

'Why do you want to know?'

'I think he's in danger.'

'He has my word . . .'

It was time to turn the screw. 'Maguire wants me out of Mauritius. He doesn't want me mixed up in whatever it is.'

'Then you do as he says, Holly. Get out.'

'Sorry. I'm not ready to leave yet. That's one of the reasons for this call. I'm staying on at my expense, ostensibly to gather material for a travel piece. But I keep tripping over undesirable mates of Maguire's. So you see, Quinn, it would save an awful lot of angst if somebody . . . that's you, Quinn . . . told me exactly what he was up to. That way, if a story blows, I know what I'm up against. That way, I keep my scalp. That way, I know what to avoid and what to go for. You with me here, Quinn?'

This time, he didn't hesitate. As Holly was anticipating, professional ethics ran a poor second to his daughter's safety. 'He didn't say much. It's got something to do with an organisation called Scylla.'

'Scylla! As in the mythological monsters Scylla and Charybdis?'

'The very same.'

Holly recalled the saying 'between Scylla and Charybdis'. It had something to do with a place between two equal evils where, in order to avoid one, a person must face the other. 'Who are they? What do they do?'

'It's an international network for hire to governments anywhere in the world. They operate as a legitimate trading company. Concessions in return for services rendered, that kind of thing. Mercenaries basically. There's an office in Western Australia that recruits a lot of ex-South Africans. They have land in the north-west which is used for training.'

'So where does Maguire fit in?'

'Didn't say.'

'Quinn . . .'

'Truly, sweetheart. He didn't.'

'And you didn't think to ask?'

'No.'

'Why not?'

She heard him expel breath. 'This might sound

strange coming from me, but I like the man. We've got a good rapport. If he couldn't tell me then there must have been a good reason. That's all I know. I didn't see how it could affect you.' A slight hesitation. 'Are you really in danger?'

'Let me put it this way, Quinn. Because of this damned story I've been attacked, kidnapped –'

'Kidnapped!' Quinn yelped.

Holly relented. 'Sort of. Look, the treasure story is as ready for writing as it's ever going to be. Maguire won't let me in on whatever else he's up to but there's a story there and you've just confirmed it. If I keep my distance, I'll be fine. I really did need to know what else he was up to so I didn't blunder into any more trouble. Thanks for telling me . . . finally.'

He ignored her sarcasm.

'When is Maguire returning to Mauritius?'

'I don't know.'

'I don't like this, Holly.'

'Quinn, a few days doing the tourist thing isn't exactly high risk.'

'How did you get kidnapped?'

'Quite easily, actually. Grabbed from behind, hands tied, shoved into a car, that kind of thing.'

'Holly!' Quinn really had the wind up.

Again, she relented. 'There are two other people also looking for the treasure. They're working together. One is Justin Parker, the dodo man Mrs Hammond sent me the information on. He got it into his head to try and find out how close Connor is to finding the treasure.'

'Did you tell him?'

'*Them* as it turned out. And you know me, Quinn. I'm a pushover for bullying tactics.'

'Were you hurt?'

'No. They let me go after I'd told them what I knew. It wasn't much.'

'Bastards!' Quinn swore angrily. 'Where was Maguire?'

'It wasn't his fault. He's been trying to get rid of me for days.'

'Terrific!' Despite his concern, Quinn saw the funny side. 'Fat chance. He doesn't know you like I do.'

'I think he's getting the message.'

'You sound as though you've changed your mind about him.'

'Really.' She tried indifference but she could never fool Quinn.

'Well?' he prodded.

'Well what?' She was smiling and knew he'd hear it in her voice.

'Ah!' He sounded satisfied.

'What's that supposed to mean?'

'What it means, Big Shot, is that yours truly took one look at Connor Maguire and decided how perfect he would be for one hurting little girl. That's why I was so insistent that you get him to agree to an interview. I wanted you to meet him. I couldn't tell you that, could I?'

'I guess not. But why all the mystery?'

'The AIDS research people came to me and asked if we'd cover his search. I agreed on the proviso that Maguire was willing. I set up a meeting with him.'

'And he wasn't willing?'

'That was the strange thing. I couldn't figure it out. Normally he'd have jumped at it. Then he told me that the treasure was a cover-up for something else. He mentioned Scylla. I didn't push for more information. Like I said, I trust him. So I decided to send you. Knowing Maguire, he'd do enough to make the treasure story interesting. And, I also decided it wouldn't hurt to have a journo around in case anything broke on Scylla.'

'Why didn't you tell me this before? How am I supposed to cover something I've never heard of?'

'Maguire asked me to keep Scylla under my hat.'

'Guess what?'

'What?'

'You've been had.' Holly was smiling. Quinn was astute but he'd walked right into Maguire's manipulations.

'What do you mean?'

'He wanted the publicity. Just didn't need it to look that way.'

Quinn gave a short laugh of admiration. 'Sneaky bastard. I'll get him for that.'

'I think you've met your match, Quinn.'

'The question is, sweetheart, have you? I mean, forgive me for asking, won't you? It's not like I care or anything. Your ever-loving father wouldn't dream of interfering. No ma'am. He knows his daughter has the stubborn streak of a brumby, a temper like a Tasmanian devil, and the independence of a moggy.

But a man can always hope. Given the tropical island paradise, and the unusual nature of the treasure hunt, and boys being boys and girls being girls, and throw them all together, well . . . Let's just say I had my fingers crossed.'

Holly was smiling broadly. 'You interfering old goat.'

'So? Give.'

'Not on your nelly. You can bloody-well wait until I get home. Bye.' She hung up, still hearing his spluttering protestations.

She began to pace, trying to remember about Scylla. That was it! The monster had been turned into a rock, a dangerous outcrop on the Italian side of the Strait of Messina. And Charybdis became a whirlpool on the opposite Sicilian side. The two faced each other, forcing sailors to make a choice – the rock or the whirlpool. Two evils. To defeat one you exposed yourself to the other. Scylla. Not a bad name for a company offering the services of mercenaries. But how was Maguire involved? If indeed he was. Could it be that Scylla and the secretive anti-drug vigilantes were one and the same?

Holly felt a pang of conscience. She shouldn't have asked. She'd promised to stay well away from Connor Maguire's clandestine activities. Even so . . . Holly had a feeling that she'd just prised open the jar that held the most important reason why he had come to Mauritius. It didn't tell her much and she had no intention of taking it further. All she could do was hope that he stayed safe.

TWELVE

Having put off writing about Connor on a number of occasions, now that she had finally and unconditionally allowed him into her heart, Holly was eager to make a start. Alone in her hotel room, working on the piece brought him closer. She needed that. Once started, the words flowed easily. Dipping into tapes of interviews, her notes, remembered conversations, it was no trouble putting together nearly six thousand words without using anything from William Maguire's journal. By the time she included previously written material from that source, Holly ruefully realised that the *Out of Focus* editorial department would more than likely have a fit when they saw the length of her article, their blue pencils working overtime to streamline it.

Unfortunately, the only thing missing was the treasure itself. A pity it hadn't been found. Holly didn't doubt that it had once existed. Whether it still did was up for speculation. Surely, with modern technology and the degree of development taking place in Mauritius, it would have been discovered by now.

She debated whether or not to include the interest of Raoul Dulac and Justin Parker, but decided against it. Connor wouldn't welcome any mention of the French-Mauritian and besides, the addition of a cloak-and-dagger element could prove distracting. Discipline was required when writing about Connor. She had to force herself to be impartial. It was tempting to write more about him, rather than his activities.

Work finished for the day, Holly organised a taxi for eight the next morning. There were parts of Mauritius she still hadn't seen. They could probably be covered in one day. Another to finish writing the tourist article and then what? The Indo-Mauritian perspective was important since that particular group made up seventy per cent of the island's population. Perhaps a few of the hotel staff would be willing to speak to her. After that, Réunion was an option but Holly dithered. She was, she felt, in some kind of limbo.

At seven, hunger drove her to the restaurant. Settled at a table, Holly glanced around the open-air area. The bar was fairly crowded but she spotted Guy Dulac immediately. He was watching her closely. When their eyes met, he raised his glass to her. It was a mocking gesture and Holly nodded briefly before looking away.

Seconds later, she sensed his presence at her table. 'We meet again. Must be fate.' He pulled out a seat opposite her.

Fate? Holly didn't think so. She couldn't shake off the feeling he'd been waiting. It made her uneasy. 'You don't give up, do you?'

He smiled. 'Not when a beautiful woman is concerned. Anyway, you're dining alone. Wouldn't you prefer company?' Guy sat with one arm draped over the back of his chair – a deliberate pose to expose his chest. Three shirt buttons had been left undone.

Short of making a scene, Holly was stuck with him. But she was going to make damned sure he knew that the evening would start and finish in the dining room. 'Suit yourself,' she gave in ungraciously. 'Dinner only.'

'Of course. What else?' His eyes said what else.

Despite his good looks and attention, Holly was beginning to actively dislike Guy Dulac. She hoped he wouldn't prove difficult to get rid of.

He leaned over the table towards her. 'Where's lover boy?'

'Who?' She stared at him coldly.

'Maguire. The one you were with on Sunday.'

'I have no idea.' Well, it was true enough. He could have been anywhere on Rodrigues.

A waiter hovered. Guy asked him for a menu, ordered a bottle of red wine and instructed the man to put it and their food on his account. The waiter turned to do as he was bid.

'Just a moment.' Holly spoke coolly. 'I'd like a glass of dry white wine.'

The waiter looked uncertain.

'Share my bottle of wine,' Guy said.

'I prefer to be consulted, not told,' Holly said firmly. She looked up at the waiter. 'Dry white please.'

Dulac shrugged, but his expression was unpleasant. 'Change the order,' he said tightly. 'Make it a Chardonnay.'

Holly frowned as the waiter hurried away.

'Lighten up,' Dulac's voice was clipped. 'It's only a drink.' He was smiling, outwardly very sure of himself. 'Anyone would think I was trying to get into your pants.'

Holly felt a rush of annoyance. She hadn't been this harassed sexually since she was seventeen and in the clutches of inexperienced enthusiasm. Guy Dulac was, it seemed, attractive only on the surface.

She'd just opened her mouth to tell him where to go when Guy glanced past her and made a noise of disgust. 'This is going too far,' he gritted, his expression furious.

Surprised, Holly turned to see what had upset him. A slim Indian in a blue suit was observing them from a table nearby. His expressionless eyes flicked to Holly, then back to Guy Dulac. He tapped two fingers against his forehead in a lazily mocking salute.

Dulac's response was immediate. He rose swiftly and moved to stand aggressively, hands on hips, at the Indian's table. Holly had never seen someone get so angry so quickly. Whoever the Indian was, he certainly had Guy Dulac rattled. She watched the two men carefully. So did most of the people nearby. As yet, no words had been exchanged but there was no doubting that a drama of some description was unfolding.

Guy had stooped to lean his knuckles on the

table, his face thrust aggressively towards the seated man, eyes bulging in a face contorted with rage. By comparison, the Indian seemed unperturbed. He stared back at Dulac, unflinching, unafraid, a touch of challenge in his dark eyes.

Guy finally found his voice. At a pitch high enough to qualify as near hysteria and loud enough to attract the attention of those few diners who hadn't as yet noticed the impending confrontation, he burst out, 'Get off my back, you bastard! This is harassment. I'll get you for this.'

The Indian's response was too quiet for Holly to hear, but judging by his expression, he was unmoved by the threat.

Without warning, Dulac grabbed the man by his shirt front, lifted him from the chair and shook him roughly. Then, so fast that Holly wasn't sure she could believe her own eyes, Guy head-butted the man in his face. Looking wildly around, eyes glazed with fury, Guy literally threw the limp form from him. The Indian fell into his chair like a rag-doll, his momentum causing it to tip backwards, sending him sprawling. Blood streamed from his nose.

Reason was slow in returning to Guy Dulac, but when it did and he realised that every horrified eye in the dining room was on him, he turned quickly and blundered through the restaurant. His departure coincided with their shocked waiter bringing the bottle of wine.

'Leave it here,' Holly said. 'Put it on my bill.'

She rose and went to assist the unfortunate

Indian, who was struggling to sit up. Other diners, immobilised by the sudden vicious attack, were also rallying to his side.

'No, no, please, I am all right,' he insisted. 'Just a misunderstanding. Please, I do apologise.'

One by one, those who came to help returned to their own tables. Without waiting to be asked, Holly sat opposite the man who dabbed delicately at his nose. 'Is it broken?'

'I don't think so.' He looked at her quizzically.

She sensed his curiosity over why she had been in Guy Dulac's company. 'I hardly know him,' Holly volunteered. 'He's been making a nuisance of himself. Won't take no for an answer.'

The Indian readjusted his jacket. 'Typical.'

'He acts like the law doesn't apply to him.'

Dark eyes appraised her. 'He'll find out it does.'

She noticed that he was shaking slightly. 'Are you going to be all right?'

'I think so.' He ran a hand through his hair, brushing it back from his forehead.

Holly pointed to her table. 'I seem to have inherited a bottle of wine. Like some?'

'That would be my pleasure.'

She beckoned to the waiter who brought the ice bucket, wine and glasses to their table.

'My name is Sham,' he offered. 'Thank you for your concern.'

'No problem. I'm Holly Jones.'

Sham nodded.

'Is Sham your first name, or is it Mr Sham?'

He didn't answer immediately, watching the

waiter open and pour the wine. The waiter kept glancing at Sham. He was quite a sight. His nose blue black and blood had blotched his white shirt. 'Will that be all, Mademoiselle?' the waiter asked.

'For now, thank you. Leave the menu, I'll order food later.'

He backed away, not taking his eyes off Sham, probably wondering, as Holly was, how the man could take such a belt on the nose and then casually accept a drink.

'Cheers.' Sham raised his glass and sipped. Putting it back on the table, he said, 'Just Sham. That's what everyone calls me. It's my last name.'

'Cheers, Sham.' Holly toasted him.

'I'm a policeman,' he said suddenly.

'Oh!' It was all she could think of saying.

'I saw you with that boy at the airport.'

'I wasn't *with* him. I met him quite by chance. He asked me to have a drink with him and I turned him down. Tonight, though . . . I don't know . . . I got the impression tonight was deliberate, that he was waiting for me. He's becoming a pain in the . . . backside.' She'd read somewhere that Mauritian Indians were incredibly polite. Arse didn't seem appropriate.

Sham smiled slightly.

'Couldn't you have him arrested for assaulting a police officer?'

'I could.' His expression told her he wouldn't.

'But you won't? Why not? Because he's a Dulac?'

Sham's smile was grim. 'His name won't protect him for much longer.'

'You're following him, aren't you? And making damn sure he knows it. May I ask why?'

He looked uncomfortable. 'Sorry.'

'Fair enough. Let me ask you this then. Am I right not to trust him?'

'Most definitely. Better to keep well out of his way.'

'I would if I could.'

Sham put the bloodied handkerchief away in his pocket and changed the subject. 'What are you doing in Mauritius?'

Holly told him about the tourist article.

He nodded when she finished speaking. 'How much longer will you be staying?'

'I don't know,' Holly admitted. 'A couple of days, I think.'

'How did you meet Guy Dulac?'

'Is this part of your inquiry?'

'It might be. Depends.'

'A friend of mine who is currently on Rodrigues knows his father. We were invited to lunch at the estate last Sunday. That's when I met him.'

Sham was still nodding. 'Ah!' He appeared satisfied. 'This friend of yours, is he from Mauritius?'

'No, he's Australian.'

'How is it that he knows Raoul Dulac?'

She remembered Connor's words, 'lying isn't exactly your best thing', and decided to tell the truth. 'His name is Connor Maguire. He's a businessman from Australia who has had some dealings with Raoul Dulac. I don't think they are still involved with each other. He certainly doesn't seem to like the man.'

'Good taste, this friend of yours.' Sham smiled at her. 'Not many of us warm to the Dulacs.'

'How are you feeling?' Holly asked, concerned. Smiling had obviously hurt him.

Sham felt his nose gingerly. 'I've had better evenings.'

She felt genuinely sorry for him – he seemed sincere. 'Are you going to try and find Guy Dulac again tonight?'

'He'll go straight home.'

Holly raised her eyebrows. 'You know him pretty well then?'

'He's rattled,' Sham elaborated. 'It's not the first time I've shaken him up a bit. The boy's like a wounded animal, heads straight for the protection of his den.' He shrugged slightly. 'Anyway, I think I've had enough for one day.'

'I'm sure you have. That was quite a knock.'

Sham lowered his eyes. Holly would have been startled to see the sudden look of anger that flared in them.

Guy Dulac's attack had not surprised the detective in the least. A dossier he had meticulously compiled on the boy gave testimony to the fact that Guy was given to sudden and violent acts, over which he appeared to have no control. What angered Sham most was Dulac's arrogance. Tonight was a perfect case in point. His violence had been the spontaneous reaction of someone completely out of control. Who but the mentally deranged could afford the luxury of believing themselves beyond the reach of consequence? Sham did not presume Guy Dulac to be insane, which left him with one of two options. The boy was either evil – and in Sham's experience, true evil was no more or no less than a complete lack of conscience – or, more likely, he was a self-indulgent weakling who believed himself untouchable. Either way, combined with the boy's unpredictable temper, Sham considered Guy Dulac to be extremely dangerous. Particularly so since his surprisingly influential family appeared perfectly prepared to cover for him.

Dulac's alibi about where he was the night Corrine Vitry died had, so far, held up well. No-one had seen the two of them together. Sham was reasonably certain that she had been dumped in the sea from a boat. Had she gone into the water from land, Corrine would have been found earlier. Fishermen, any one of literally hundreds of pleasure craft, helicopter pilots on joy flights, windsurfers, the waters in the lagoons around Mauritius were too shallow to conceal something as large as a body. So Sham concentrated on that one premise. But no-one had seen the girl on board Raoul's boat and Sham had yet to find a single witness who might have noticed the craft leave Grand Baie or return to its mooring. Guy Dulac seemed to be getting away with murder. What worried Sham now was that having done it once, the boy might be tempted to do it again. And this young woman could very well be his target.

He looked up at Holly, instinctively liking her. 'Beware of Guy Dulac,' Sham said, reaching for his glass. He finished the wine in one swallow and stood up. 'The boy is not to be trusted.' He went to say more and stopped, giving Holly a brief and painful smile instead. 'Good night. And thank you for the drink. It's against my religion but tonight . . .' a shrug and a glance skyward, 'I am sure I shall be forgiven.' With a quick formal bow, he left.

Holly wondered what it was that Sham had been about to say. His warnings were appreciated but unnecessary. After tonight's little show, she wouldn't trust Guy Dulac with an onion. Hopefully, she'd seen the last of him.

Alone again, Holly picked up the menu. The waiter noticed her action and rushed to the table, order pad in hand. She selected a light meal of grilled fish with caesar salad and sat, sipping wine, gazing out over the darkened water. Her thoughts slipped, quite naturally, to Connor Maguire. The word Scylla kept pace. How were they connected? Even more interesting, why were they connected? What was Connor really up to?

Her waiter reappeared. Instead of food, he placed a telephone on the table. The object of Holly's thoughts was at the other end.

'Just touching base,' he said.

'The deal is no contact, Maguire. What do you call this?'

'Imagine I'm not here.'

'That's a big ask.'

'Come on, Jones. You can do it.'

'Okay.' Holly was smiling. 'I'm sitting here all on my lonesome *not* having a conversation with someone who is *not* on the other end of a telephone which I'm *not* really holding. That makes me kind of curious about why everyone in the place is staring at me. Will that do?'

'Good girl. Know why I called?'

'Haven't a clue.'

'Just wanted to hear your voice. Are you okay?'

'I'm very okay.' She was too. Scylla, drugs, Guy Dulac, the treasure, had all slipped silently into second place. Her universe became contracted to the instrument she held against her ear. Nothing else mattered.

'How was the flight?'

'Good.' This was ridiculous! A telephone call hadn't been so significant since God knows when. 'What have you been up to?'

'Tch! When will you learn?'

'Sorry. I'm scratching around for something to say.'

He laughed. 'Do you feel as silly as I do?'

'Probably. It's been a while since a conversation going nowhere held my attention. You have the strangest effect on me, Maguire.' Holly's head was down because she was trying to hide what she knew must be the dopiest of grins.

'What did you do this afternoon?'

'Wrote up the treasure piece. It's good. Quinn will love it.' She cleared her throat, then added, 'She said modestly.'

'So when are you going home?'

'When are you?'

'Oh no you don't, Jones. That's my trick.'

'Saturday week.'

'Why so long?'

'I've left it too late to get this Saturday's flight. Besides, I need a bit more information for the tourist story. I'm also thinking of having a look at Réunion. I might go there on Monday.'

'One thing you should know.'

'What's that?'

'Raoul Dulac put to sea this afternoon. Justin Parker was with him. They should be back in Mauritius late tomorrow. Keep away from them, Holly.'

'I will.'

'Promise?'

'Promise.'

'Holly, I . . . I guess I'd better go.' He hesitated. 'Take care.'

'You too.'

They said goodbye.

Still clutching the receiver, Holly felt dissatisfied, empty somehow. She had deliberately kept quiet about Guy Dulac because she didn't want to worry Connor. But there had been words she wanted to hear and things she'd like to have said. The newness of their relationship inhibited both of them, had them behaving like adolescents. Why couldn't she have said that she missed him, that she was scared for him and that she loved him? Holly had to conclude that she didn't really know him well enough to state her true feelings. It was weird. She wondered if Connor felt the same way.

The taxi was going to cost a thousand rupees for the day, about sixty Australian dollars. Money well spent, Holly thought. The driver turned out to be a chatty Indian. His name, he informed her, was Mr Herro. She asked if he'd mind her taping some of their conversation. An Indian taxidriver's view of Mauritius would do nicely. He appeared reluctant.

'Why would you want to do such a thing?'

'I'm a journalist, writing an article about Mauritius for an Australian magazine.'

'Australia!' He seemed daunted by the very name.

'It will bring tourists here.'

'Ah! Tourists. More work for me.'

'Correct.'

Mr Herro frowned. 'But you should ask your questions of someone more clever. I am a humble taxidriver. I am not knowing many things.'

'Were you born here, Mr Herro?'

'Indeed.'

'And was your father born here?'

'Yes. And his father and grandfather.'

'That makes you perfectly qualified. I promise you, my questions will not be difficult. All I want to do is find out about the Indian population.'

He became cautiously amenable. 'Such as?'

'Well, let's see. Do you, as an Indian-Mauritian, consider yourself as belonging to India or Mauritius? Or do you perhaps feel that you are a part of Africa?'

Mr Herro responded with no hesitation. 'First, a part of Africa, then Mauritian.'

'How about India?' Holly switched on the tape, making sure he knew.

He eyed it with suspicion before saying slowly, 'I have never been to India.'

'But you are Indian. Don't you feel connected at all?'

He answered with a question of his own. 'You are Australian?'

'Yes.'

'From where did your ancestors come?'

'Britain.'

'Do you feel British?'

Holly laughed. 'Point taken. Another question?'

Mr Herro shrugged.

'Are you Hindu, Tamil or Muslim?'

'Hindu. Most Indians here are.' He glanced at her. 'Ask another please.'

'I have seen red and yellow flags in some gardens. What is their significance?'

'It is our belief that if we build a shrine to the gods, our house will be protected. We always put two flags behind the shrine.'

'Why?'

'Tradition.' He looked troubled. 'Is that good enough?'

'Perfectly fine. Are you happy to continue?'

He was still hesitant, but at least he agreed.

The road they followed was the same one she'd travelled when she went to Mahébourg with Connor. Holly took the opportunity to concentrate on her interview. Mr Herro soon relaxed, finding the questions involved more of a personal opinion, rather than any in-depth factual response on Mauritius itself. He talked of his ambitions, of his wife and children and extended family. As he warmed to the theme, he told Holly about some of the religious festivals celebrated by all Hindu people. They sounded colourful and different. Holly was sorry that most took place during the summer months so she would miss seeing them.

'Thaipoosam Cavadee,' Mr Herro explained, 'is to call on Subramanya, the son of Lord Shiva. We fast for ten days, then carry cow's milk on a wooden arch to our temple. It must not curdle on the journey. The arch is decorated with fresh flowers.'

'What is the purpose of this ceremony?'

'To ask forgiveness and seek spiritual cleansing. At that time we pierce our skin with many skewers.'

'Doesn't it hurt?'

The driver wagged his head. Holly was uncertain whether she'd been given a yes or a no.

'I will take you to Grand Bassin,' he offered helpfully. 'It is a holy lake. Each year we must wash in its waters. We wear white clothing and make offerings to . . . do you know the word *guru*?'

Holly nodded. 'Spiritual leaders.'

Mr Herro beamed at her. 'Just so. They are custodians of the lake. It is a very important celebration for us.'

'Does it have a name?'

'Maha Shivaratri. In honour of Lord Shiva.'

'Why is the lake holy?'

The answer was delivered with such seriousness that she realised Mr Herro would not dream of questioning the tale. 'When Lord Shiva went to India and created the world, he allowed some water from the Ganges to rest there. For this reason you might see people paying homage, even though today is not a holy day.'

'What will they be doing?'

'Lighting candles and sending them across the water on leaves.'

Holly found herself fascinated. Talk about diversity! Within the Indian population alone there were three major and distinctly different religious groups, each divided further by caste, home language and from where in India their ancestors had originated. The Chinese claimed family or clan differences. Despite a long association with Britain, nearly all white Mauritians were of French origin. And if that wasn't enough, the word *Creole* covered anyone of mixed blood, but even that group was split into two distinct categories – those who looked African and those who did not.

'You should be here to see the firewalking ceremony,' Mr Herro was saying. 'It is called Teemeedee. Visitors are very welcome.'

'When does this happen?'

'Near to your Christmas. It is very famous in Mauritius. Many tourists come.'

'I've read about the firewalkers in India. They don't appear to suffer any burns.'

Again, the driver wagged his head. 'This is true. I myself have seen it many times. They feel no pain, even when they lie on the coals. True believers are protected by their faith.'

He went on to talk about some of the other Hindu traditions. Holly had to stop him often to check on the spelling of a word or to explain about one of the gods. Mr Herro happily obliged.

They were approaching the highland town of Curepipe. Its name, in English, translated as 'pipe cleaner'. Holly asked why.

'I am not knowing,' Mr Herro responded. 'But French soldiers stopped here on their way between Port Louis and Grand Port. Perhaps it is here they rested and smoked tobacco.'

It was feasible. Many men carried pipes in those days. The first thing soldiers might well do at the end of a day's march would be to clean and refill them.

'Have you been to the Trou aux Cerfs crater?' Mr Herro asked.

'No. I'd like to see it, though.' Holly was delighted with Mr Herro. A driver, an interview and a tourist guide all in one. 'Where is it?'

'Not far.' He turned into a narrow street.

There were no signs, nothing that even mentioned a crater. They climbed a steep hill and came out onto a road that ringed the hundred metre deep, long extinct volcano. As craters went, this one was nothing special. Not particularly large, its inverted cone shape was so classic it might have been moulded from fibreglass. Densely wooded down the steep slope with a small, green, slime covered lake at the bottom, the caldera was about three hundred metres wide. What interested Holly more than the crater, which she dutifully photographed, was the view. It was a beautifully clear day and the panorama extended over most of Mauritius.

To the south-west, Mr Herro pointed out a blurred, dark shape far out on the horizon. 'That is Réunion,' he explained. 'The mountains there are higher than ours.'

Holly was totally impressed. Réunion was two hundred kilometres away.

From Curepipe they continued south on the main road towards Plaisance and Mahébourg before, a short while later, turning right to Souillac. Holly was now in new territory. Mr Herro made his promised detour to Grand Bassin, the sacred Hindu lake. It turned out to be another old crater, this time filled with crystal-clear water. Surrounded by forest, the landscape had an almost picture book alpine appearance. Then it was down to the coast at Souillac, where Mr Herro made a point of showing Holly La Roche qui Pleure – the Rock That Cries – its shape supposedly that of a man in tears. Further on they came to Le Morne, where he related the story of a band of starving slaves who, on the run from their masters, managed to climb the six hundred-metre lump of black basalt to hide. Reaching the top, they were horrified to see a line of soldiers climbing towards them. Rather than face capture, the men jumped to their death. The irony was, the soldiers were coming to tell them that slavery had just been abolished and they were free to come down from the mountain.

From Le Morne, they followed the road north. 'You will wish to see the coloured earths,' Mr Herro said.

'Silly not to,' Holly replied. Mr Herro was a gem.

They stopped at a small area of volcanic deposits where the sand seemed to twist together to form patterns in shades of red, blue, purple, grey and yellow. Hawkers tried to sell Holly a small glass bottle of mixed sand, the main thrust of their selling pitch was that you could shake the bottle as hard as you liked but the sand would always settle out again in different colours. At Cascade Chamarel, a twin waterfall dropped down into the Riviere du Cap. Mr Herro again had all the facts. 'Ninety-three metres,' he said. 'The river flows from here to the sea.'

'Lunch,' Holly declared, as they reached the town of Tamarin. 'My treat.'

Mr Herro wagged his head.

'Where's the best place?' she asked.

'Do you like fish?'

'Love it.'

Their meal was just beautiful, freshly caught and cooked to perfection. Mr Herro declined wine but accepted a beer. 'We will visit the Tamarin Falls,' he declared as they set off again.

They drove through sugar estates along a gravel road. Once again, Holly was grateful to have such a good guide. She'd never have found the place on her own. Mr Herro parked the car, explaining that they would have to walk the remaining distance. On the ground, Holly noticed what appeared to be pools of blood.

'It is the flower of the nourouk tree,' she was told. Holly had never heard of such a plant but saw that their branches were laden with pea-shaped scarlet flowers. She had seen similar trees in Bali, where the locals called it the coral tree.

Quite suddenly, they came to the falls. Over-hung and hidden amid lush vegetation, the volume of water was nothing more than a trickle.

'The hydro-electric scheme has destroyed this river,' Mr Herro explained. 'People do not come here any more. Sometimes the estate managers turn tourists away.' He was encouraged by her interest. 'See where the water first drops? That is called the window.' He pointed further down. 'Look carefully. There are seven steps to this water-fall.'

But Holly's attention was not on his words. Her scalp was tingling. William Maguire's map, it had been assumed, was of a portion of coastline. He'd indicated a scallop-shaped cliff descending down through various levels, at the bottom of which were several wavy lines denoting water. What if his drawing was of something inland? Like this water-fall. The escarpment called the window was, as far as she could remember, identical in shape to that shown on the map. And there were the levels – a series of steps. Jesus! She'd found the site of the treasure. Down there somewhere, in all that thick green stuff, William's treasure had lain buried for 250 years. She had to let Connor know.

'That's enough for one day, Mr Herro. You've been more than helpful.'

Mr Herro beamed and pulled a card from his wallet. 'If you need driver some more, maybe I can make cheap price.'

'Thank you. I'll let you know.' She looked at the card. The man was quite an entrepreneur. As well as driving a taxi he appeared to own a shop called Just Shirts and, if the card could be believed, also rented out accommodation. Holly asked him about that.

'I own the building,' he explained. 'There are two, one-bedroom flats on the first floor and a small studio above them.'

She found herself wishing him every success. He deserved it.

On the way north, Mr Herro wanted to show her the Casela Bird Park near Bambous, the World Spiritual University in Vacoas and a Hindu temple in Port Louis. He seemed so keen that Holly curbed her impatience to speak to Connor, finally arriving back at her hotel a little after five in the afternoon.

There were two messages waiting. Guy Dulac would meet her in the bar at eight that evening. *Would he, hell!* And Madame Liang Song would ring back later.

From her room, Holly got through to the Cotton Bay Hotel, asked for Connor and was not particularly surprised when there was no answer.

She left a message for him to return the call. Looking up the telephone number of the police station in Port Louis, Holly dialled it and asked to speak to a policeman by the name of Sham.

'Detective Sham?'

'If that's what he is.'

'May I ask who's calling?'

'Holly Jones.'

'A moment please.'

Several clicks and a few seconds later, 'Sham.'

'Hi, this is Holly Jones.'

'How can I help you?' He sounded surprised to hear from her.

'Guy Dulac left a message at the hotel. He wants to meet me at eight this evening. I thought you'd like to know.'

'Do you intend to keep the appointment?'

'No. Though I don't quite know how I can avoid him.'

'Don't worry. I'll be there and make sure he sees me.'

'Thank you. Are you sure that's okay? I mean, do you feel up to it?'

'All part of the service, Mademoiselle. I'll see you later.'

Right! she thought, replacing the receiver. *That takes care of the little boy.*

Holly had just lathered her head with shampoo when the telephone rang. 'Bugger!' She dripped a soapy trail across the bedroom. 'Holly Jones.'

'This is Liang Song. Where is Connor Maguire?' No messing around with this female.

396

'Rodrigues.'

'Ah! Thank you.' Without another word, the connection was broken.

'Rude bitch!' Leaving the receiver off its cradle, Holly finished her shower. She had just replaced it when another call came in. Expecting it to be Connor, she eagerly answered. 'Holly Jones.'

'It's me.' It was Guy Dulac.

The last person in the world I need! 'Got your message. Thank you, but no.'

'About last night, I can explain –'

She cut him off. 'I doubt it. Anyway, last night has nothing to do with it. It's no, always has been, always will be. Now, if you'll excuse me –'

'I can't stop thinking about you.'

'That's your problem. I would appreciate it if you'd stop bothering me.'

An edge crept into his voice. 'If I decide to bother you, you'll know about it. All I want is to buy you dinner.'

She'd had him in chunks. 'I don't fraternise with hooligans, Mr Dulac.' Her voice was steely. 'Frankly, you disgust me.'

Dulac lost it. 'That cretin got what was a long time coming. You don't know the half of it –'

'Nor do I wish to. This is a complete waste of time – yours and mine. Goodbye.'

'Wait.' His voice was urgent. 'Don't hang up. I . . . I've got some information . . . about the treasure. You'll find it interesting.'

'I don't think so.' He was lying, she was sure of it.

397

Guy Dulac was an immature spoilt brat who did not know how to handle being turned down. 'Listen, Miss High-and-Mighty, you're no prize. Just who the hell do you think you are?'

'I could ask you the same question,' Holly countered. 'Please don't contact me again.' She banged down the receiver.

The call had unnerved her. Guy Dulac was obviously unstable. Coupled with a quick temper, a capacity for violence and Detective Sham's warning, Holly felt vulnerable. She had no idea why Sham wanted to keep track of Guy, but it had to be serious if he was prepared to waive the attack last night in order to pursue some other crime the boy may have committed.

It was almost six o'clock. Would Dulac still turn up? She wouldn't put it past him. Perhaps an early dinner was called for. That way she could be back in her room by seven thirty, at the latest. It irked her intensely that a twenty-year-old boy's unwelcome attentions were ruling her life.

Should she let Sham know? Probably not. If Guy Dulac did put in an appearance at eight it would be nice to know the police were there. Fifteen minutes later, Holly was pleased she hadn't contacted the detective. Guy strolled through the restaurant, his eyes searching until he found her.

'I thought you might do something like this.' He sounded angry, as if she'd somehow betrayed him.

'Like what?' Holly shook her head when he went to pull out a chair. 'Don't bother. I've already said that I won't be having dinner with you.'

He went ahead anyway, sat down and leaned over the table on his elbows, shoulders hunched. 'Do you make all men work this hard?'

Holly experienced a sudden surge of anger. What exactly did it take to get this arrogant child off her back? What he was doing amounted to stalking. Sexual harassment. In a deceptively soft voice, Holly allowed resentment to rule her commonsense. 'Men? No.' Her eyes flicked over him. 'Boys? Now that's different.' *Oh you bloody fool!* As soon as the words were out she realised her mistake.

The barb hit home. Guy Dulac's eyes narrowed and he breathed in heavily. 'You'll be sorry you said that.' He rose and looked down at Holly. 'Very sorry.' Turning, he strode away, but only as far as the bar, where he swung onto a high stool and sat staring at her.

Holly could not believe her own stupidity. With his influence he could easily get the number of her room and quite probably a pass key as well. A quick bribe would do it. Then what? Wait in a shadowy alcove? There were enough of them. Get there before her and hide? Hang around until she had to be asleep and then . . .' She checked her watch. Only six twenty. Sham was at least an hour and a half away.

Feigning an indifference she was far from feeling, Holly ordered a glass of wine. Thinking quickly, her mind raced over possible ways out of the situation she'd placed herself in. She could check out of the hotel in the morning and find another. That wouldn't do any good. Guy Dulac had found her at this one easily enough. Perhaps an apartment, or a room with a family as Connor had done. Mr Herro might be able to help there. One of his flats could be empty. Or would she be safer where she was, surrounded by people?

Although her thoughts were in chaos, outwardly Holly remained calm, ordering a meal, chatting to the waiter and generally behaving as though she didn't have a care in the world. Without looking directly at Guy Dulac she could sense his obsessive stare. She heard him demanding scotch after scotch. With a bit of luck the bloody boy would drink himself to oblivion.

Twenty minutes before eight, Dulac abruptly rose from the bar stool and made his way unsteadily towards reception. Holly briefly considered making a bolt for her room, but discarded the idea in case he was waiting for her. She sat back, hoping like hell that Sham would show up.

He did, God bless him. Not only did he show up, he had a uniformed police officer with him. Guy Dulac had not reappeared and Holly, who had found his morose vigil at the bar unnerving, was even more concerned now that she couldn't see him.

Sham came straight to her table. 'Is he here?'

'He was. Left the bar about twenty minutes ago full of whisky.'

Sham looked concerned. 'Was anyone with him?'

'No.'

The detective indicated her empty plate. 'Have you finished? I'll walk you to your room.'

Holly nearly kissed him.

For the second time since her arrival at the Merville Beach Hotel, her room was completely checked out. She couldn't help but think that for the peaceful island Mauritius proclaimed to be, and generally was, it had to be her misfortune to need such protective service twice.

Problems slept on can sometimes solve themselves. In the morning, Holly had a plan. For as long as she was in Mauritius she'd stay at the Merville. There were two good reasons for this. Safety in numbers being one, the other that Connor expected her to either be here or on Réunion. His continued silence was of concern but she assumed he'd be in touch when he could.

Today was Saturday. A week to kill before flying home. She called the Air Mauritius office, booked herself onto the following week's flight to Australia and enquired about schedules to Réunion. For as long as she stayed in tourist areas, Guy Dulac couldn't touch her. With luck, he'd get sick of trying.

Putting him out of her mind, Holly spent most of the morning working on her travel piece. At around eleven, the telephone rang. It was Justin Parker. 'Please don't hang up, I must talk to you.'

Surprising herself, Holly found she was quite pleased to hear from him. Despite his dramatic actions on Rodrigues, chances were he was relatively harmless. 'Where are you?'

'Back at the Merville. I arrived last night.'

'Go on.'

He became flustered. 'What do you mean?'

'You said you wanted to talk.'

'Oh . . . yes. To apologise really. Look, can you meet me at the poolside patio?'

She agreed to see him at twelve.

In retrospect, Holly wondered if she was doing the right thing. Connor had said to stay away from him. 'Go with your instincts,' she told herself. Even if he had abducted her in Rodrigues, his company was a hell of a lot preferable to that of Guy Dulac's.

Justin rose to his feet with a tentative smile as she joined him at the table. She noticed that the marks of the attack on the beach had all but disappeared. A slight discolouration under one eye was all that remained. He looked strained and nervous. He jumped straight in and got what was obviously bothering him off his chest. 'I apologise for what I did. It was very stupid. I don't know what came over me.'

'Greed?' Holly's tone was matter-of-fact. Her instincts told her she could trust him but that didn't mean she was going to make it easy.

Justin took no offence. 'Probably.' Long, sensitive fingers brushed hair back from his forehead. 'I'm giving up on this. I don't trust Raoul Dulac. You were right, I'm no match for him.' He leaned towards her confidentially. 'You were wrong about one thing, though. I really am looking for dodo remains. It's a project very close to my heart.' Sitting back, he added, 'You can do the interview if you like.'

Holly realised he was attempting to make up for his treatment of her. She tapped a fingernail on the table, trying to make up her mind whether or not he was telling her the truth. 'It's practically written actually. A few personal details wouldn't go astray though, what drives you, that sort of thing.' She decided to test him. 'What were you talking to Liang Song about the other day?'

Justin's eyes stayed on hers. 'Raoul didn't want to be seen with me. When he bumped into Maguire he put two and two together and came to the conclusion that your friend was also looking for William's treasure. It worried him to say the least. He sent a message through Madame Liang to meet with him. That was all.'

'Where?'

Justin appeared confused. 'Where what?'

'Where were you to meet him?'

'Cap Malheureux. Behind the fishermen's co-op.'

'Connor and I saw Raoul up there one night last week. He met someone on the beach, then let himself into the building. Was that you?'

'Yes.'

'We assumed that the other person gave him a key. How did you get hold of one?'

'That wasn't me. Someone else was there as well. An employee. He had the key.'

That made sense. There had been two cigarettes in the darkness and Justin didn't smoke.

'Why did Raoul need to get inside?'

Justin shrugged, his eyes embarrassed. 'I have no idea. All I can say for sure is that he appeared well satisfied when he came out. He told us to wait for him on the beach. He was only gone a matter of minutes and then returned the key. The other man said nothing and simply disappeared. That was when Raoul warned me about Connor Maguire, told me to be careful what I said to anybody, then left. Why he couldn't do that over the telephone is anyone's guess. He even made me wait in the dark until I had heard his car leave. He seems obsessed by a need for secrecy. I'd taken a taxi to Cap Malheureux. I had to walk back, but that didn't bother Raoul.'

Holly knew it was the truth. 'Does Raoul have any idea that you've given up on the treasure?'

'No.' Justin looked miserable. 'I don't know how to tell him. He won't be pleased.'

'I'm bloody sure he won't. Right now, all he's got to do is sit back and let you do the work. Very convenient.'

'At first I didn't mind being used. We're partners and he has so many other interests. Raoul's very persuasive but I don't think Anne-Marie thought things through too carefully. Her intention was to annoy him but she has no idea . . .' Justin lowered his voice and went on. 'There's a lot more to Raoul than most people realise. He's into all sorts of projects and hates it when people know too much

404

about him. He can become quite beside himself if he doesn't get his way. On the trip back from Rodrigues he revealed a side of himself I'd never seen.'

'What do you mean?'

'Raoul keeps all kinds of documents in a locker on the boat. I came into the cabin while he had one out on the table. He went ballistic – accused me of spying on him, threatened to throw me overboard, then made me swear on my mother's life that I'd tell no-one. Eventually he calmed down and told me it was a confidential business plan. I said nothing but I knew it was a lie.'

'How?'

'I saw the front of the file. It was from the Central African Republic's Ministry of Defence and stamped Top Secret. Someone had written "Scylla Only" in one corner. At least, I think that's what it said. Raoul tried to cover it with his hand as soon as he knew I was there.' Justin shook his head. 'I have no idea what it means or why I wasn't supposed to see it.'

Oh, but Holly did! Several pieces of the Connor Maguire puzzle had just slammed into place. Which made his disappearance just a little more sinister.

THIRTEEN

Scylla was suddenly much more than simply a carrot dangled in front of Quinn to whet his curiosity. It tied in with her suspicion that Connor had yet another reason for being on Mauritius. Raoul Dulac had a Scylla file on board his boat. Was this the real reason for Connor's interest in the French-Mauritian? And if so, why? Did it slot in with the treasure search and whatever was going on with Madame Liang Song? She was sure of one thing. The common denominator running through the whole web of deceit, intrigue and double-dealing was Connor Maguire.

Holly thought about that. Where did it leave her in terms of trusting him? *Make up your bloody mind once and for all and stick to it. I trust him, I trust him not, trust him, trust him not. Oh sod it! I trust him.* She'd been silent too long. Justin was looking at her questioningly. 'What are you doing after lunch?' she asked.

'Nothing. Why?'

'How about Pamplemousses?'

He seemed delighted with the idea, though

probably more for her apparent forgiveness than an opportunity to see the gardens.

It was a pleasant way to spend the afternoon. Tree-lined avenues led from one manicured floral attraction to the next. The famed pond in which giant Victoria regia water lillies floated like over-sized flan dishes did not disappoint, looking exactly as it did on postcards and publicity brochures. Huge, hundred-year-old Aldabra tortoises from the Seychelles showed their displeasure at being con-fined to enclosures by hissing at those who came to stand and stare. Palms of all shapes and sizes were a feature of the gardens, including the rare talipot that flowers only once between forty and sixty years of age, then dies.

Strolling at a leisurely pace, Holly used her tape recorder to gather background material on her companion. It was easy enough to put aside past events. Justin was being especially cooperative, witty and informative. When they returned to the hotel at four thirty and he suggested they meet for dinner, Holly readily agreed. There was method in what, she supposed, others might view as foolish-ness. In Justin's company, she would be safe from Guy Dulac.

Once again, she was handed two telephone mes-sages. Detective Sham wanted her to ring him back and Quinn had called. He would try again in the morning. Holly shuddered at that one. Her father was more than likely to ignore the six-hour time difference and she'd get his call in the middle of the night. Back in her room, she dialled Sham's number. The detective sounded relieved to hear from her.

'I've been trying for hours to reach you. Where have you been?'

Holly bit back a sharpish reply. The man must be worried about her. Under the circumstances, it was a comforting thought. 'Pamplemousses.'

'I phoned to warn you. Guy Dulac has been stowing provisions on his father's boat and taking on fuel. He seems to be making ready for a long trip. Do not allow him to talk you into going on board.'

'Don't worry, he won't. I'm having dinner with a friend at the hotel this evening. I'll be quite safe.' As intrigued as she was by Justin's revelation about Raoul and the Scylla documents, there was no way Holly would risk being alone with his son on the off-chance that she might get a peek at them.

Detective Sham sounded satisfied. With a final, 'Be careful,' he was gone.

Holly wondered what Quinn wanted. Just after ten forty-five at home. She tried the house and he answered immediately. 'What were you doing, sitting by the phone just waiting for it to ring?'

'No. I was about to try you again. Are you okay?'

'Any reason why I shouldn't be?'

'Several.' The word came back heavy with irony.

Holly grinned. Quinn was going to love this. 'Actually, I'm having dinner this evening with the man who abducted me in Rodrigues.'

'You're what?'

She knew he'd love it. 'He's not a bad person

really. Just mixed up in something he doesn't like too much. It's the dodo man. Did an interview with him this afternoon as well.'

'Have you lost your marbles?' Quinn's voice had risen.

'Probably. It's the tropical island effect. Oh, yes. And while you're on the phone you might as well hear the rest of it. I've got a nice Indian policeman concerned for my wellbeing, Connor Maguire has done a bunk and Scylla is real.'

'I know Scylla is real. What do you mean about the policeman?'

'It's a long story, Quinn.'

'I've got all night.'

So she told him about meeting the Dulac family, of Raoul's interest in William's treasure and of Guy's persistence. He heard her out and remained silent when she finished. 'Hello. Are you still there?' Holly asked finally.

'I don't like this.'

'Don't worry. I'm keeping well away from the kid. By the way, I think I've found where the treasure might be. Only trouble is, I can't get hold of Connor to let him know.'

'Sweetheart, I've been doing a little digging of my own. I think you should come home.'

'I was planning a visit to Réunion next week to finish my tourist piece. However, you'll be glad to hear I'm booked to fly back next Saturday. What sort of digging?'

'Scylla.' Quinn hesitated, then went on. 'Have you ever heard of SATCOM SIGNIT?'

'What is it? A computer game or a theatrical comedy?'

'Please. This is serious stuff, Holly. It's a satellite communications and signals intelligence station up near Darwin. They call it Larkswood. The place is part of an electronic eavesdropping network with Britain and America. Recently they locked onto transmissions from Mauritius to the Scylla offices in Western Australia. The Mauritian end originated from Raoul Dulac.'

'Quinn, how the hell do you know all this?'

'Contacts,' he said succinctly.

Holly didn't question that further. Quinn had proved in the past that when he needed information, he had only to make a couple of telephone calls. His web of contacts was vast, and not confined to Australia.

'Just what the bloody hell are you getting mixed up in?' her father asked.

'Frankly, I don't know. I'm trying very hard to stay out of whatever it is.'

'Then how did you discover that Scylla is real?'

So she told him that too. 'Justin hasn't a clue about Scylla. He just knows he wasn't supposed to see the file.'

'And he's the one you're having dinner with tonight? The one who is in partnership with Raoul Dulac? The one who thought nothing of kidnapping you? Are you totally insane, my girl?'

Holly ignored his outburst. 'Talk to me about Scylla.'

She heard him sigh. 'It's like I told you before,

410

they are the recruiting and training arm of an international mercenary operation. Raoul Dulac is head of their African operations. Our intelligence has picked up certain communications which would indicate that something rather big is happening in the Central African Republic.'

Holly knew a bit about that country from an elephant poaching article she'd worked on. French speaking, landlocked, the CAR shared borders with some of the most volatile countries on that continent: Chad, Sudan, the Congo, Zaire and Cameroon. It tended to keep a low profile. But if mercenaries were required in any of the neighbouring territories the CAR would be a perfect base and training ground. There were parts of the country so remote, so rugged, that the only way in was on foot. Communications, away from the capital, Bangui, were non-existent.

'That's not all,' Quinn was saying. 'I did a bit of poking around in Connor's life too.'

'And?'

'Remember I told you his half-brother had been killed in a coup attempt in the Seychelles?'

'I remember.'

'Seems he was a mercenary with Scylla.'

'Ah!' *That might do it. If Maguire blamed Raoul Dulac for his brother's death he might well seek retribution.* 'So you think that Connor may be here on a kind of vigilante kick?'

'It's possible. I don't know the details, but the brother, Brian Anderson incidentally, had a wife who died in a car accident at around the same time. Bit of mystery surrounding it all. That's all I've been able to find out. The police could never come up with an explanation for her accident. Maguire could be planning revenge. He was very badly affected by their deaths. The business thing with Dulac that went wrong may have been Connor's way of getting close to him.'

'Are you sure of all this, Quinn?'

'Positive.'

'I don't see how any of it puts me at risk.'

'It shouldn't, sweetheart. But I still don't like it. And what did you mean that Maguire has done a bunk?'

'He seems to have disappeared.'

She could hear Quinn lighting a cigar. 'It might mean he's gone to ground. The shit could hit the fan at any stage.' A pause and a faint crackle of tobacco as her father drew in deeply came down the line. Holly fancied she could smell the smoke. 'When did you say you're going to Réunion?'

'Monday or Tuesday. Coming back Thursday. I'll stay in the hotel until I do. It'll be quite safe.'

'The policeman doesn't seem to think so.'

'That's different. He's trying to protect me from a child with an overactive libido and a tendency to dump a little violence on anyone who thwarts him.' Holly changed the subject. 'Why are the Australians listening to conversations between Raoul Dulac and Scylla?'

'They're a bit paranoid as a result of the Sandline fiasco in New Guinea. Australia didn't see that one coming. Anything remotely interesting Dictionary picks up –'

'Whoa! Dictionary?'

'Sorry. It's a computer software program capable of eavesdropping on international phone calls, faxes, even e-mail. It picks on key words. Once that happens the communication is accessed. Anything of interest is forwarded to the DSD.'

'Speak English, Quinn. What's the DSD?'

'Defence Signals Directorate.'

'But surely their only concern is Australia's wellbeing?'

'True. But, as I said, since the Sandline incident they're a bit jumpy. Dictionary picked up the Scylla communications and the DSD listened in until they were absolutely certain that it had nothing to do with our national security.'

'You're a bloody marvel. You probably know more about Australia's security than the Prime Minister.'

'I doubt it. The information is easy enough to access.'

'Okay, Quinn. Thanks for that. It's got nothing to do with me.'

'Be careful, sweetheart. You're too close to this thing for my liking.'

Holly wondered what he'd say if she told him about Connor's connection with Madame Liang! 'I'll call you from Réunion.'

'Love you.'

'Love you too. Bye.'

*

That evening there was no sign of either Guy Dulac or Detective Sham. Justin was relaxed but determined to talk about issues that Holly would have been quite happy to let go.

'How are your ribs?'

'Still bruised but not bad. They only hurt if I move suddenly. You seem to be healing nicely.'

'The eye is still a bit tender, that's all. It was doing okay until Maguire . . .' he broke off. 'There was no need for rough stuff,' he said eventually.

Holly wasn't about to let him get away with a complaint. 'Connor obviously thought there was. After all, I had been in his company when you abducted me. He was worried.'

Justin looked away.

'Surely you can see that,' Holly pushed.

'I suppose it must have looked . . .' He hesitated, then changed to a safer subject. 'Raoul organised that attack on the beach. He even bragged about it. And the break-in. He wanted my copy of William's map.'

'Did he say why?'

'Too many of them floating around, or so he claimed. I did wonder if he . . . Well, he might have been planning to go back on his word. Without a map, I'm stuffed. Good job I'd thought to bring two laminated copies and not just one.'

'What made you do that?'

Justin shrugged. 'Just a precaution in case my luggage went missing. I had one in a suitcase and the other in hand baggage.'

'Did Raoul know you brought two?'

'No. When nothing was found in my room he assumed I was carrying it. That's why we were mugged on the beach.'

'Where was the other copy?'

'In the hotel safe.'

'That was fortunate.' Holly leaned back, tapping a fingernail absently on the table. The sound of it eventually got through to her. She frowned and stopped. 'What made Raoul tell you? It's not the sort of thing most people would brag about.'

Justin took his time answering. Holly wondered why, but when he did speak she realised he'd been reluctant to raise the subject of his actions on Rodrigues. 'When Raoul returned from taking you back to the Cotton Bay Hotel he was pretty furious. Called me a damned fool, or words to that effect. Then he saw the map . . . my duplicate. He was quite surprised. Said he thought he'd taken care of any spare copies. When I demanded to know what he meant he, as calm as you please, told me the burglary and subsequent attack had been at his instigation.'

'Arrogant bastard!'

'I agree.' Justin took a deep breath. Holly could see that despite his outward calm, Raoul's actions had shaken him. 'I can't work him out. He needs to be in charge, never explains anything, and expects total obedience.' His voice went hard. 'I don't trust him.'

'Hang on. You said you were giving up on the search. Sounds to me as if you're still involved with him.'

Justin's eyes slid away. 'In a way, I am. But only

through Anne-Marie. I can't avoid the man completely.'

Holly wondered if he was telling the truth. 'Connor Maguire also had a break-in.'

Justin nodded abruptly. 'That was organised by Raoul too. He was trying to find out why Maguire had come to Mauritius.'

'Why not just ask him? Connor wasn't exactly hiding his intentions.'

'That's the way Raoul operates. The man thrives on secrecy and deception. Probably thinks everyone else does too. Look at my involvement with him. Don't take this the wrong way but the reason he was so annoyed with me in Rodrigues had nothing to do with you. He was angry because our association had been revealed.' Justin sipped his beer. 'I've tried, but I can't think of a single good reason why he kept insisting that no-one know we were partners.'

'I can.' Holly turned cold as she thought about it. 'What if you had found the treasure? If your partnership was still secret he could so easily have arranged for you to disappear.'

Justin considered her words, then shook his head. 'Anne-Marie knew.'

'Anne-Marie is family. As much as she hates her father . . . Can't you see, Justin? Raoul is more than capable of getting rid of you so he could keep everything for himself. It would not be difficult for him to arrange a little accident.'

Justin looked sceptical. 'That's a bit dramatic, isn't it?'

'Raoul Dulac plays rough.' Holly repeated Connor's warnings. 'I wonder why he's so hell-bent on finding the treasure. Okay, it's supposedly worth a fortune but he's not connected to the Maguire family, I wouldn't have thought he'd qualify for a share. Ah!' she broke off, understanding. 'Anne-Marie. That's why he invited her on board, isn't it?'

Justin nodded. 'He didn't want to. She found out about it and threatened to contest his right to it if anything was found.'

'Why go to all this trouble and secrecy? It's not as if he's destitute.'

'Apparently the Dulacs are not as wealthy as they make out. Anne-Marie said something about massive debts. The sugar industry is an on-again, off-again roller-coaster. Raoul gambled on future high prices and lost heavily when the market slumped.' Justin finished his beer. 'He has expensive tastes and so does his wife. That estate can't be cheap to run.'

'My heart bleeds for them,' Holly commented dryly.

Justin smiled slightly. 'Anne-Marie's okay.'

'I'll have to take your word for that.'

He glanced at her glass. 'Another?'

She shook her head. 'Not yet, but thanks.'

Justin caught a waiter's eye and ordered a beer. With the man gone, he said, 'You made a lot of sense in Rodrigues. About the feud being so old, I mean. Before that I hadn't really given it much thought. I grew up with the story – it was always very real.'

'The journal tells it a different way.'

Justin frowned. 'I know both sides. My mother believes Kavanagh's account.'

'She would.'

'William Maguire might have been lying.'

'In his journal? I don't think so.'

'He could have made it up. How do you know he didn't?'

Holly had no answer. It was entirely possible that William, who intended that the journal be sent back to Ireland, had invented an account to cover his own treachery. She shrugged. 'Does it matter? It was such a long time ago. Who really cares?'

Justin looked horrified. 'Every living Maguire, that's who. Our family cut its teeth on the stories. They've been handed down from one generation to the next. God! They're better than Captain Hook, monsters, Superman and Biggles put together. Doesn't the notion of pirates and treasure stir you up?'

Holly raised her eyebrows. 'Must be a bloke thing.'

He smiled. 'More like an Irish thing. We are a bit on the emotional side.'

'Who was it said that an Irishman is never at peace unless he is fighting?'

'I don't know. But someone else said that if you put an Irishman on the spit there will always be another Irishman around willing to baste him.'

Holly laughed. Justin Parker was good company when he relaxed.

Then he went and spoiled it. 'Tell me honestly, has Connor Maguire found anything?'

'Here you go again. I thought you'd given up on it.'

'Just asking. Curiosity, nothing else.'

Was it? 'As far as I know, he's no closer than you.'

Justin looked satisfied. 'Maybe there isn't anything. Or maybe there was but it's long gone.'

'I said something like that to Connor about a week ago.'

'So he still believes it's there?'

'Connor Maguire is a romantic at heart. He likes the idea.' She had no control over the softness in her eyes.

Justin frowned when he saw it, and changed the subject. 'I know I've said this before, but I do apologise for Rodrigues.'

'Thank you.'

'Can you . . . will you forgive me?'

'I don't know. You frightened me.' There didn't seem to be much point in lying.

He looked down at the table, then back at her. 'I know I did. I've never frightened a woman in my life. I feel terrible about it.'

To Holly's horror, tears welled in his eyes.

'I really am most desperately sorry.'

'So I see. Please don't upset yourself. I'll get over it.'

He blinked rapidly and the tears disappeared. Reaching across the table, Justin covered her hands with his own. 'I wish I could make it up to you.'

Holly pulled back and twisted the stem of her glass in her fingers. She had no intention of encouraging Justin into thinking there could be anything between them, but that wasn't the reason. She'd just seen something in his expression that sent out a warning signal. A calculation of some kind. It was gone in an instant, but for one brief moment she had the feeling that Justin Parker was playing a part. If that were so, then everything he'd said since returning from Rodrigues could be a lie. Holly decided that whether it was or wasn't, it would be prudent to treat Justin Parker with due caution. To fill the silence that had fallen between them, she asked, 'How much longer will you be staying in Mauritius?'

'Another two weeks.' If he was surprised by the subject change he didn't show it. 'How about you?'

'I'm going to Réunion for a few days. Back here on Thursday and then off to Australia on Saturday.'

'Why Réunion?'

'Part of the travel article. Since I'm so close I might as well include all three of the Mascarenes.'

'How about the story you were doing on Connor Maguire?'

She searched for guile but saw none. 'It's written. If he finds the treasure I can slot it in. If not,' she shrugged, 'it's interesting enough as it is.'

'Are you going to write about . . . about Raoul and me?'

'No. It's Maguire the magazine wants to cover.'

Justin nodded. 'Fair enough. And thanks. I

wouldn't particularly like to be portrayed as a villain.'

Was he? Holly didn't know.

She said goodnight at ten fifteen, still unable to make up her mind about him. On the surface, he appeared genuinely sorry for his stupidity in Rodrigues but that one brief moment, where she saw something else in his eyes, kept her wary. Not that it mattered. If she made the trip to Réunion it was possible she wouldn't ever see him again. He'd said something about going to Port Louis the following day. He had heard about a small museum attached to the Mauritius National Institute which had a skeleton and stuffed replica of the dodo.

Holly had not handed in her room key and the lights were on as she left them. Guy Dulac still had her worried. An envelope had been slipped under the door. She picked it up. One corner carried the hotel's logo. Inside was a single sheet of paper with a message: *Mr Connor Maguire telephoned at nine twenty. He asks that you meet him at the church in Cap Malheureux. It doesn't matter what time. He'll be waiting for you.*

Holly read the message twice. She thought it strange that the telephone hadn't been brought to her table, the hotel had always been pretty good on that score. However, clandestine probably being Maguire's middle name, the message itself didn't surprise her. Nor did the fact that he'd left Rodrigues. But there was something about the note that did. She just couldn't figure out what it was.

The church she remembered – it was across the road from the restaurant she and Connor had gone to the night they saw Raoul Dulac at the fishermen's co-op. As a matter of fact, it was right next to the co-op. What was Connor doing up there?

Could this be a Guy Dulac trick? Holly read the message again. No. Guy did not know that she'd been to Cap Malheureux and the way the note read indicated that it had been left by someone who knew she would remember the place.

Satisfied that it could only have come from Connor, Holly went back to reception and asked for a taxi. When it finally arrived she was delighted to see that it was driven by Mr Herro. She explained where she wanted to go and he looked doubtful. 'It is late. There is nothing to see at this hour.'

'I'm meeting someone.'

That seemed to satisfy him.

Mauritius by night, once away from the tourist areas, was as dead as the poor dodo. The roads became deserted, houses showed no lights and very few people were out and about. Holly found herself wondering why Connor couldn't have come to the hotel.

The trip to Cap Malheureux took only ten minutes. Mr Herro pulled into a parking area between the church and the co-op. There was one other vehicle there, but as the taxi's headlights played over it, Holly could see no sign of any occupant.

'I will wait until the person you are meeting arrives,' Mr Herro offered.

'There's no need,' Holly said. She wasn't sure if

Connor would show himself until he was certain she was alone.

'Well . . .' Once again, Mr Herro appeared doubtful.

'I'll be quite safe.' She pointed to the empty car in front. 'That's his car. He's probably waiting on the beach.'

'Ah!' Mr Herro beamed at her. 'I did not understand.'

Holly let that go. If Mr Herro wanted to think she was on some kind of romantic tryst of an illicit nature, that was fine with her. She paid the fare, hopped out of the car and stood waiting for him to leave. With the taxi gone, she went momentarily night blind. She was keyed up and excited at the prospect of seeing Connor again. As her vision began adjusting to the dark night, Holly realised what had bothered her about the message. It hadn't been on the hotel's usual stationery. She heard a soft footfall behind her. A prickle of alarm turned to terror as arms folded around her waist, pinning hers to her side. Struggling wildly in the iron grip, a dark shape loomed in front of her. Holly took a deep breath ready to scream and inhaled the not unpleasant odour of ether as a cloth soaked in the anaesthetic was rammed over her nose and mouth.

Hard as she tried to fight against it, Holly felt herself losing consciousness.

Harsh light from an overhead fluorescent tube registered reality when her eyes fluttered open. She turned sideways to get away from the intense glare. Disorientated, her mind raced. Where was she? Which country, which town, which hotel? Then she remembered.

Everything hurt – ribs, head, arms – and she could taste the clinical residue of ether in her mouth. As memory returned, so did fear.

Holly realised that she was free to move. Sitting up gingerly, she swung both legs over the side of the double bed. The movement increased her pain and added a wave of nausea. Despite this, she looked carefully around, searching for some clue about where she might be. The room offered few answers. It was plainly furnished and decorated, and as impersonal as many an hotel.

She sat massaging her temples, unable to recall anything that might help her work out where she was and why. Unseen hands, a silhouette, silence save for sounds of the scuffle, no voices. No clues there. The car had been nothing more than a shape. She'd been half expecting Connor's hired vehicle, but for the life of her she could not remember a single detail about it. Vivid was the smell of ether. Then the horrible feeling of her knees buckling, of falling into blackness. Who had grabbed her? Holly tried not to panic. Guy Dulac's name kept crashing through her mind.

She rose and made her way unsteadily towards the door. Bending and listening intently, she tried to identify noises coming from the other side. Someone was either watching television or listening to a radio. Holly cautiously turned the handle and was pleasantly surprised to find the door unlocked. It opened silently. She stepped unsteadily out of the room, fighting off waves of nausea. Whoever anaesthetised her had been somewhat heavy-handed.

Holding one hand flat against the wall for balance, Holly looked around and realised she was in a private house. The hallway where she stood had four doors, a wall at one end and opened off into what was probably a lounge at the other. A soft illumination glowed, made mobile by the flickering light of a television set. Moving carefully, Holly tried the other three doors. All were locked. She turned back to the first room and eased open the curtains. It was pitch black outside. The windows had burglar bars but were open. There was a slight smell of seaweed in the night air. Holly sucked in the refreshing aroma, trying to work out what to do next.

'You're awake. Good. Come through.'

Holly spun around. Madame Liang Song was standing in the doorway. She gave a curt nod and left. Holly didn't know whether to be relieved or scared. Certainly, given the choice, she'd rather be faced with the Chinese woman than Guy Dulac. But, she told herself, that was only because if she were going to be killed she'd prefer not to be raped first. Holly followed, moving slowly towards the far end of the hall.

Madame Liang stood dead centre of the room, her arms folded. The television had been turned off. 'Please be seated.'

Holly chose a padded sofa with serpent and dragon motifs. 'Where am I?' she demanded.

'That doesn't matter.'

'It does to me.' Anger lent her strength. 'How dare you treat me this way!'

Liang Song crossed to a chair opposite Holly and sat down. 'I dare,' she said quietly, 'because I can.'

'What's that supposed to mean?'

'I think you know.' There was no expression at all in those almond eyes. 'Where is Connor Maguire?'

So that's what this is all about. 'Rodrigues. I told you that over the phone.'

'I've been unable to reach him.'

'That's your problem.'

'I have many contacts,' Liang Song continued as if Holly hadn't spoken. 'He's been missing for two days.'

Fear was replacing anger. 'Then I can't answer you. My work with him is finished.'

'You're lying.' Cold eyes pierced Holly. 'You slept with him. Of course you know where he is.'

How does she know that? Raoul might have told her, she could be guessing, or she might have been spying on them. Holly managed to keep her voice steady. 'Sleeping with a man does not mean you own or control him. I'm sure you know what I mean.'

Liang Song's eyes hardened.

'For example,' Holly was pleased with herself, her voice was under control, almost conversational, 'do you know where Raoul Dulac is right at this moment?'

Madame Liang glanced swiftly over her shoulder. 'Be quiet,' she hissed. 'You have no idea what you are saying.' She looked back at Holly. 'You were prepared to meet Maguire tonight. Does that mean he's back? Tell me the truth.'

Holly gave an elaborately casual shrug. 'I have left two unanswered messages for Maguire in Rodrigues. When I received your note I assumed that he was back here. I'm not the man's keeper. I repeat, I have absolutely no idea where he is.'

Two distinctly oriental individuals appeared from what Holly assumed to be a kitchen and spoke to Madame Liang in their own language. She responded in English. 'Our guest says she doesn't know. We'll have to flush him out.'

Holly wasn't certain but she was fairly sure they were the same pair she'd seen in the restaurant with Madame Liang and again when they followed her in Port Louis. Connor thought they were uncles. He'd also said they had no idea that their niece was doing business with him. Were they Triad? How were they involved in the Chinese woman's drug dealing? Had the game shifted? Liang Song must have taken some trouble to get hold of Holly, and despite an arrogant indifference to the law, ran a considerable risk by doing so. This was more than a bit of melodrama. These three were deadly serious.

The conversation, now conducted totally in Chinese, was becoming heated. Holly interrupted.

'Just what do you mean, flush him out? He's not a bloody fox, for God's sake!'

Both men fell silent and looked at her with disapproving frowns. Holly presumed she must have breached some form of Chinese etiquette but was too scared and angry to care. 'How does forcibly bringing me here help?'

The Chinese woman glanced at her. 'Bait,' she said dismissively, as though Holly were some disposable object of no value. 'We'll make sure he knows where you are.'

'If you can't find him how on earth do you expect to do that?'

'We'll put the word out. It will reach him.'

One of the men stepped up to Liang Song and spoke quietly to her. She listened carefully, nodding agreement, then turned back to Holly. 'You will stay here. Your degree of comfort is up to you. For now, you are free to move about the house and garden. Any trouble and you will be locked in a room.' Madame Liang dismissed the two men who bowed and left. 'Would you care for something to drink?'

It crossed Holly's mind that, in this predicament, she was at least safe from Guy Dulac. 'Why are you so desperate to reach Maguire that you have to hold me prisoner?'

Holly had not responded to the offer of a drink but Liang Song moved to an obviously well stocked liquor cabinet, poured a glass of white wine from an opened bottle and handed it to her. 'I am in the process of some rather delicate business dealings with your Mr Maguire. I don't like the fact that he's disappeared. It makes me think I can't trust him.'

'They must be pretty important if you're prepared to hold me against my will. Let me give you a piece of advice. Australians don't do business this way. Your actions are going to backfire. After this, I can guarantee it is Maguire who will not trust you.'

The Chinese woman didn't answer but she was listening.

'You're running the risk of having whatever you and Maguire are working on collapse completely. Is it worth it?'

'Shut up! You have no idea what is at stake.'

'No, I don't. But nothing is worth so much that –'

'Just be quiet, you silly little girl.'

Liang Song was rattled. Holly thought it might be a good idea to get off the subject. 'Is this your house?'

'Do you take me for a fool?'

Holly shrugged. 'I'm not sure what I take you for. In fact, I'm not certain of anything any more. This is the second time in a week I've been kidnapped. All I'm trying to do is get through an assignment. A small enough ask in my opinion.'

'Your magazine should be more careful who they send you to cover.' Madame Liang sank gracefully into the chair opposite Holly and crossed her legs. 'Who else tried to kidnap you?'

'An acquaintance of yours. Justin Parker.'

Amusement gleamed in Liang Song's eyes. 'Raoul's little friend. Yes, he mentioned it. Not a serious attempt from what I gather.'

'Is this?'

'Oh you can be sure of it,' Madame Liang said softly. 'And, you'd better hope that Maguire shows himself.' She sipped her own glass of wine. 'There is just one more thing. Do not mention Raoul Dulac's name in the presence of my uncles. If you do it could be quite dangerous. Understood?'

'Why?'

'I think you know. We spoke of it during the interview. How did you find out?'

'Believe it or not, that question was a wild card. I threw it in to see what kind of an answer I'd get.'

Madame Liang's composure slipped slightly. 'I asked how you knew.'

'Everybody knows. When you appeared at the Dulacs' party last Sunday the whole room was talking about it. You can't keep that sort of thing secret in a place this size. I wouldn't be surprised if your uncles already know.'

'They don't mix with many Europeans. They would not understand.' She tossed her head, a look of displeasure on her face. 'That is beside the point. It is none of your business. You will not mention it again, is that clear?'

Holly smiled. It was not a friendly one. 'Perfectly. Just tell me one thing. How do you plan to fool your husband into thinking that you're a virgin?'

The speed with which the Chinese woman flew from her chair and slapped Holly's face was astonishing. Then she returned to her own chair and sat down, sipped her wine again and said calmly, 'I think we understand each other now, don't we?'

FOURTEEN

Holly would not have believed it possible, given the seriousness of her situation, but during the course of the next day she became desperately bored. Madame Liang Song was nowhere to be seen, although she left a note telling Holly to help herself to whatever she wanted. The refrigerator, pantry and bar proved to be well stocked, piles of magazines lay on various tables and two bookshelves displayed a wide cross-section of literature, in both French and English. Fresh clothes had been provided, all the toiletries she could ask for were at her disposal in an en suite bathroom. Unless there was one in the locked bed-rooms, there was no sign of a telephone. Holly had noticed last night that Liang Song had a mobile phone clipped to her belt. The outside world was inaccessible. Holly had the freedom of the house and garden, though whenever she went outside the two uncles, who never attempted any communica-tion, kept a close eye on her movements. She nicknamed them Chop and Sticks. It made them less menacing.

Television on a Sunday in Mauritius concentrated

on the spiritual and the radio covered sport, thus both religions were catered for. Culinary art not being one of Holly's specialties, she nonetheless amused herself for a while preparing an elaborate omelette with smoked salmon, cottage cheese and beansprouts as filling. The whole thing fell apart when she tried to fold it over so, taking a fork, Holly scrumfled – a family word, origin unknown, meaning salvaged, and usually bad-tempered scrambling – the whole lot together, before slopping it on a piece of toast. The end result was, predictably, abominable. She ate it anyway, having nothing better to do.

Picking up a couple of magazines, Holly strolled outside. She found a garden bench and, studiously ignoring Chop and Sticks who lurked in the background, tried to read. It was hopeless. She couldn't concentrate on anything and abandoned the idea in favour of a wander in the garden.

It was impossible to tell where the house was. It stood surrounded by a high stone wall, broken glass bottles set along the top. The heavy double gates were of solid wood and kept locked. She was guessing, but Holly assumed the place to be a Liang-owned holiday cottage. The house and garden had that look about them, adequately cared for but not cherished. There was traffic noise but it was some distance away. No landmarks were visible but she could smell seaweed and gulls reeled and screeched nearby. Waves breaking out on the reef were barely audible. Holly thought it strange that a holiday cottage, built presumably so that the occupants could enjoy the proximity of the lagoon, would have that very view screened from sight. She did a circuit of the garden, finding no way out. Defeated and feeling irritated by the silent scrutiny of the uncles, she went back inside, only to have one of them – Sticks, she thought it was – appear and carefully, with a faint air of disapproval, replace the magazines.

Sunday dragged by. Liang Song returned at six. Holly was almost pleased to see her.

'I trust you've had a pleasant day?'

'Look, I'm booked to fly to Réunion tomorrow.' It was a lie but worth trying.

'Sorry.' She wasn't. Her tone said she couldn't care less. 'You'll just have to be a no-show. I've had no word from Maguire.'

Holly shrugged but Connor's continued absence was of growing concern to her. She needed to know he was okay.

'How long do you intend to hold me here?'

'Until he shows up.'

'What if he doesn't?'

'He will.'

Holly wished she could be as sure.

At least Madame Liang was company of sorts. She was not willing to talk about herself and seemed to have an aristocratic, off-hand view of most things. Although conversation was consequently stilted, the two women found some common ground. The interminable boredom of the day was, to some extent, relieved. In response to being asked where the smoked salmon had gone, Holly took grim pleasure in informing Liang Song that she'd made an omelette with it.

The Chinese woman's eyebrows rose. 'An omelette! What was it like?'

'Delicious.'

'A pity. We were going to share it this evening.'

A little after ten, Madame Liang excused herself. For a second night, Holly was locked in her room. She showered, slid into bed, lay on her back and stared at the ceiling. Would anyone be worrying about her yet? The Merville? How about Detective Sham? He might have tried to reach her today. Holly lived in hope. She was under no illusions about her predicament. Whether Connor showed up or not, would the Chinese woman allow her to go free? That would depend on how confident she was in her own influence and invincibility. How about Quinn? She'd said she'd call him from Réunion but he probably wouldn't push any panic buttons until Friday at the earliest. Justin? Not likely. She'd told him of her plans to be away.

Monday went the same way as Sunday. Holly had never been particularly good at doing nothing. She tried reading various books but couldn't get into any of them. Desperation had her weed a flowerbed by the front door. She made a concentrated effort to endure a bad Hindu soap on television, at least Holly assumed it was a soap since it was about as riveting as the Australian ones. By substituting her own interpretation of the unfamiliar language, ham acting and melodramatic action on screen, she found herself mildly diverted for a time.

Around midafternoon, more to preserve her

sanity than anything else, she had a two-hour nap, waking groggy and irritable as a result. Once again, Liang Song returned at six in the evening. By then, Holly was ready to explode.

'You can't keep me here much longer. Maguire's not coming. Please, just let me go.'

Madame Liang was starting to show the strain too. 'You will stay as long as I choose.'

'I'm going mad doing nothing.'

The Chinese woman stared at Holly with hard eyes. 'Stop your whining. I can assure you, the alternative would be very much worse.'

It was no hollow threat. The implication was clear. Liang Song could so easily arrange for her to disappear permanently. It was on the tip of her tongue to issue the challenge 'You wouldn't dare', but Holly knew that, if needs be, Madame Liang could and would.

Locked in for the third night, Holly couldn't sleep. Tossing and turning, cursing her earlier nap, her thoughts churned. The more she dwelled on her predicament, the more certain it became that she was in extremely serious trouble. What could Connor do? Whichever way he acted, one mission or the other might be compromised. Perhaps he wouldn't show at all. He might consider that she would be safest if he didn't. But that had to make Liang Song even more suspicious. What if he couldn't? What if he were in some kind of danger on Rodrigues?

Round and round went her thoughts in a sickening maelstrom. Whichever way she looked at the situation there was no escaping the very real danger to Connor and herself. She was eventually dropping off to sleep when a commotion shattered the night's peace. A horn blared insistently at the front gates, long angry blasts that demanded immediate attention. It worked. Beyond her door, Holly heard Chop and Sticks shouting to each other in Chinese. Liang Song called sharply in the same language. Holly climbed out of bed and crossed to the window. Security lights flooded the garden. The horn didn't let up. One of the uncles ran to the gates, unlocking and opening them. Liang Song and the other stood together. As the horn finally stopped, an engine revved, tyres squealed, and a car roared through the gates, stopping only centimetres from the Chinese pair. Holly shouted his name from the window when Connor Maguire emerged into the floodlit garden, slamming the vehicle's door behind him. He gave no sign of hearing her.

'What the hell do you think you're playing at?'

Holly had never heard a man sound so furious. She listened very carefully. Her cry must have been audible to him because both uncles glanced towards the window. That meant he was trying to give her some kind of clue, or warn her of something.

Liang Song stood in silence, robe clutched tight to her throat. In the car's headlights, she appeared uncertain, frozen to the spot.

'Inside,' Connor snapped. 'If you've harmed her in any way . . . '

'No.' Madame Liang's hair swung as she shook her head nervously. 'She is not harmed. Please, see for yourself.' She turned and disappeared from Holly's view. After a quick look around, Connor followed.

Doors banged and the conversation became too muffled for Holly to hear what was being said until Connor's voice rose in anger. 'How *dare* you pull a stunt like this. You stupid bitch! She's a fucking journalist, for God's sake! She'll crucify me back home. What the hell were you thinking?'

Holly heard the extended low murmur of Liang Song's response. Then Connor's loud reaction. He wanted her to hear. What was he was trying to tell her?

'So what if I slept with her. That's not why I'm here. I don't know if she'll buy it, but now, thanks to you, I'm going to have to convince her to keep quiet. One bad report from that bloody woman and I'm dead. So is our deal. Christ! You bloody idiot. Get her out here.'

It didn't sound much like the Connor Maguire Holly knew.

'What do we do with her now? She knows too much.'

Don't overdo it, Maguire. Not on my account.

A key turned in Holly's door and one of the uncles beckoned her out. She quickly donned a red and white silk kimono she'd found in the en suite and moved towards the lounge. She could hear Liang Song pleading with Connor to calm down.

He looked at her briefly when she came into

the room. Holly relaxed slightly. She knew his facial expressions reasonably well. Connor was not as angry as he pretended. His show of outrage was to put the Chinese woman off balance and it seemed to be working. Taking his lead, Holly ran with it.

'What the hell is going on? Nice company you keep, Maguire. Thanks to you I've missed my flight to Réunion and stuffed up a perfectly good travel feature. You're more trouble than you're bloody-well worth. I'm sick of you and your schoolboy treasure. I wish I'd never heard of you.'

'Shut up,' he snarled at Holly before turning back to Liang Song. 'Satisfied? Here I am. What was so fucking urgent that you had to pick on this interfering journalist? Do you have a brain in your head? If this is the way you want to do things then we might as well forget our deal. I'm used to my associates showing a bit more professionalism.'

'Where were you?' Madame Liang's customary arrogance and composure had momentarily deserted her. She seemed unsure of herself.

'Where the hell did you think I was?'

'The hotel said you'd disappeared.'

He closed his eyes and rubbed fingers over them wearily. He looked very tired.

All Holly wanted to do was hold him in her arms. But the play had only just begun and there was a long way to the final curtain call. Everything rode on the success or failure of the next act. 'You've found out something new about the trea- sure, haven't you, Maguire? You waited until I left the island and then went after it. Jesus Christ, you sneaky bastard! I'm supposed to be covering the bloody story. What *is* it with you?' She paused for effect. 'Well? Did you find it?'

He removed his hand, shook his head and looked at her. 'No,' he said shortly. 'I didn't.'

'I keep on and on telling you, Maguire. It doesn't exist. This time the playboy adventurer has failed and you simply can't accept it, can you?' His eyes encouraged her to continue. 'All you're worried about is what your adoring Australian public will think. What a pathetically transparent creep you are. You're prepared to wear yourself out in an effort to find it. Look at you. What have you been doing, digging up the whole of Rodrigues?'

'I said, shut up. I'm fed up with your negative attitude. I'm not surprised that . . . what was his name? Dennis, that's it, had it in chunks and gave up on you. Why don't you just piss off back to Oz.'

Whoa, Maguire. That's a bit under the belt. But she played the game, rounding on him furiously. 'You may recall that I didn't exactly ask for this assignment. You're nothing but a bloody cowboy! I've a good mind to set the record straight about you.' *Pick up on this, Maguire, it's important.*

'How do I know you won't?'

Thank you. 'Who'd believe it? All you'd need is a counterpiece about women who can't take rejection. I'm no fool, Maguire. The oh-so-misguided public love you. They've never heard of me. I'd be the laughing stock of my profession.'

He nodded curtly. 'Freelance journalists like you

don't forgive and forget. What's the quid pro quo? What else do you want?'

Holly didn't hesitate. 'A completely frank interview about your two divorces. You've never given one. Australians will eat it up. You give me that and I'll make you sound like the jolly green giant if that's what you want. How about it?'

Liang Song cut through their bargaining. 'Do you trust her?'

'About as far as I can throw her.' Connor looked over at the Chinese woman. 'But on this score, she's right. The wrong publicity would make life a little hot for me but I could do more damage to her reputation. She'd battle to find work. I think we can work out a deal.'

Madame Liang, with an imperious wave of her hand, dismissed Chop and Sticks who, as usual, bowed and obliged. She folded herself into a chair, indicating that Holly and Connor should also sit. Holly chose the dragons and serpents. Connor perched on the other end. He was the first to speak.

'We have things to discuss.' His head jerked towards Holly. 'We can't talk with *her* here. Your uncles can take her back to the hotel.'

Madame Liang shook her head. 'Not so fast. You might have leverage to stop a bad report but what about me? Perhaps I was a little . . . hasty, but what's done is done. There's nothing to stop her going to the police. She has no proof but an inquiry would draw unwanted attention. That's the last thing I need.'

Connor jumped up and began to pace. 'Brilliant, just bloody brilliant.' He rubbed one hand through his hair. 'What in God's name made you do it?'

'I was worried. I didn't know where you were. There's so much at stake.' Madame Liang shot a glance at Holly. 'How much does she know?'

'Only that we're close to pulling off a deal together. Miss Jones is a hack journalist sniffing for a story, any story. She knows nothing about our venture.' He stopped pacing and, with his back to Holly, took a gamble. 'She is, however, aware that the shipping deal with Dulac fell over. The whole business sector in Australia knows about that.'

Holly backed him promptly. 'So that's it. I wondered . . . Look, Maguire, I appreciate your need for secrecy at this stage. How about an exclusive?'

He spun around and faced her, approval in his eyes. 'More to the point, how do I know I can trust you?'

Holly folded her arms and tried to look smug. 'A scoop. I'll write nothing until you give it to me.' She had never been good at acting but thought she was doing particularly well at the moment. 'Oh for God's sake, Maguire, you're too important a news item with *Out of Focus* for them to get you offside. You have my word. I'll write nothing until you're ready for it, provided I get a world exclusive. I'm prepared to trade. You give me this, I'll drop the personal story.'

He pretended to think about it.

'There's still a problem,' Madame Liang put in,

her self-confidence having returned with Holly's apparent acceptance.

'Yes,' Connor agreed. 'I'm way ahead of you. The last thing we need is for her to go to the police.'

Holly held her breath. *Please, Maguire. Make it good.*

'There's only one thing we can do,' Liang Song said matter-of-factly. She might have been speaking of putting down a stray kitten.

Satisfaction gleamed in Connor's eyes. He'd been leading the Chinese woman, hoping she would make such a threat. In a voice hard with anger, he gambled on Liang Song's reliance on his business connections. 'I didn't hear that. I don't operate that way. If this is how you do business, you'd better look for another partner.'

The Chinese woman shrugged as if it didn't matter. 'Do you have a better solution?'

Yes, Maguire. Do you?

'The deal's off,' he said flatly. 'You do what you must, I want no involvement. And I'll make damned sure no-one can point a finger in my direction. I'm looking for William Maguire's treasure and that's it. You're on your own and God help you if you get caught. Believe me, Madame, if the heat is turned up, the only one who'll burn will be you.'

Jesus, Maguire. This is a bit risky.

Connor went on. 'It's not only her, it's her father too. If he gets wind of this you'll feel the length of his arm even over here. There'll be nowhere to run. He'll do you through the media in ten seconds flat. I hope you're ready for that.' He stared Liang Song down. 'Not even your husband's family has enough influence to stop him. Everything will fall down around your ears.' He was getting through to her. 'Do it my way and I'll come on board. Do it yours and I'm gone.'

Madame Liang's milky white brow creased. 'What is your plan?'

'She comes with me. I'll make sure she says nothing.'

Nope. That won't do it.

Connor knew it too. He turned to face Holly then stood in front of her. 'You're in trouble, ducky. For that I'm sorry, but Madame Liang is right. We need some kind of assurance from you that you won't go to the police. Not here. Not in Australia.'

Holly could see he was desperate for help but couldn't come up with any way round the impasse. She stared at him, mind blank, frustration and fear strong in her face.

Madame Liang unexpectedly came to the rescue. 'You mention the girl's father. I have contacts here who know certain people in Australia. One word from me . . .' Long red nails scratched on the arm of her chair while she weighed up the option. Her eyes looked directly at Holly. 'If you value your father's life you'll say nothing about this. Is that understood?'

It crossed Holly's mind that for someone who was supposed to think that Maguire and the Chinese woman were working on a joint venture in the shipping industry, she was taking the melodrama too calmly. Outrage and derision were probably called for before Madame Liang had the same thought. 'Are you actually threatening my father?' She rose and pushed carelessly past Connor. 'Is that how you do business? My God! Anyone might think the two of you were talking state secrets. Have you any idea how few people would actually give a shit about your stupid partnership?' She spun and faced Connor. 'You have a reputation in Australia for fair play. You've blown it this time. Fact of the matter is you've teamed up with a gangster. How pathetic can you get?'

'How dare you!' Madame Liang jumped to her feet.

Holly turned back. 'You may be royalty in Mauritius, lady, but you sure as hell don't do it for me. I'll say nothing of this. Not because of your bloody threats, though God knows, I don't doubt you mean them.' She jerked her thumb over her shoulder at Connor. 'And not because I'm protecting his arse either. I'll keep quiet because I want the shipping story. I want exclusivity as well. Give me that and your gangland tactics will be buried. If the story is leaked to anyone else I'll blow both of you out of the water. Savvy?'

Is this working, Maguire? 'Now, may I please leave?'

'Go to your room. Get dressed. Wait there until I send for you.'

Madame Liang was going to make one hell of a matriarch when the time came.

Accompanied by an imperiously summoned Chop who went with her and waited outside the closed door, Holly dressed in her own clothes, then sat on the bed with her fingers crossed. She could hear the low murmur of voices in the lounge. At one stage she caught the words 'stupid' and 'high-handed' from Connor. Thirty-five minutes went by before Madame Liang called something and Holly was allowed back into the lounge.

Connor stood with his back to the room, staring out through a window. The stance gave Holly no indication as to whether she was off the hook or not.

'It has been decided that you will get an exclusive when the time comes.' Madame Liang's words brought Holly a wave of relief. They'd done it. Liang Song would hardly promise a scoop to someone she planned to kill. 'If, for any reason, our partnership fails to materialise, Maguire promises a personal interview. Either way, you'll have your story. If that is agreed, you may go. I do hope you enjoyed your stay with me.'

Holly bit back a sarcastic reply. 'Agreed.'

Connor turned and faced the room. 'Are you ready?'

She nodded. To get away from this house she was born ready.

'One last thing.' Madame Liang was back in control. 'Do not forget our earlier discussion. There are elements of my business with Mr Maguire that you may fail to appreciate. I will not take kindly to any adverse publicity. Take my words seriously.'

Holly very nearly told her where to shove her

words. What she did say came close. 'Lighten up, can't you. No-one cares, least of all me. You may look important in a mirror but out there you're nothing more than words on a page. I'm a journalist. That means I write what sells. And you, lady, are about as interesting as a stone.' She looked over at Connor. 'Can we go? I've about had as much of this as I can handle.'

He nodded and his mouth twitched slightly, but his words were addressed to Liang Song. 'I'll call you tomorrow.'

She inclined her head. 'Four o'clock would be suitable.'

Holly followed Connor to the car. He made a shushing sound through almost closed lips and squeezed out the words, 'Say nothing.' As they got in, Chop rushed to unlock the gates. For five minutes they drove in silence, Connor eyeing the mirror constantly to see if anyone was following. Certain they were not, he pulled over and took a torch from the glove compartment. He played its light over the interior of the vehicle, checking carefully that during his time in the house, the car had not been bugged.

'Okay, we can talk.' He reached for her. 'But not just yet.'

When they parted he let out a shaky breath. 'That was close back there. She wanted you out of the way.'

'Maguire?'

'You were brilliant. Just the right amount of outrage.'

'Maguire?'

'For a while there I didn't think we were going to get away with it.'

'Maguire!'

'What is it, baby?'

'If you ever call me ducky again you'd better brace yourself.' Holly grabbed a fistful of shirt and pulled him closer. When his face was just a few centimetres away she let go and put her arms around his neck. 'Thank you,' she whispered. 'I was kind of scared.' Then she thumped him none too gently on the shoulder. 'And as to that reference to Dennis, that was bloody low.'

He held her close. 'How about "pathetically transparent creep"? I mean, give a man some dignity.'

'Sorry. Something came over me.'

'Are you okay, baby? They didn't hurt you?'

'They were a bit generous with the ether. Otherwise I'm fine, barring a dose of terminal boredom. Where were you? When did you get back?'

'We'll talk about that later.'

'We will! You mean it, Maguire? You're actually going to tell me something? That'll make a pleasant change.'

She felt his silent chuckle. 'Can you knit?' he asked eventually.

'Of course not.' This was the Maguire she loved.

'Pity. Do you think you could learn?'

'Not in a million years.' Her face was buried in his shoulder and she was grinning. 'Not even for you.'

He eased back from her. In the darkness she sensed his eyes boring into hers. 'Then, my darling Holly, do you have any objection to being chained to a kennel all day so I don't have to worry about you?'

She pretended to think about it. 'You'll let me off for a run when you come home?'

'I promise.' His voice was warm and smiling.

'Forget it, Maguire.'

'I love you, baby.'

'I love you too.' She kissed him. 'No more duckies. Please, Maguire.'

'Not even a little one?'

'Not even an egg.'

They drove back to the Merville Beach Hotel. 'Your room should be safe enough for tonight,' Connor said. 'But I don't want to risk Madame Liang getting another rush of blood to the head. From now until Saturday, you don't leave my side.'

Holly figured that would be no hardship.

She ignored the message envelope that had been slid under her door. It was far too late to contact anyone. Whoever had been trying to get in touch would just have to wait. Besides, she had other things on her mind.

Holly pointed to the sofa and said, 'Sit.' She poured Connor a large scotch and matched its size with her own. 'Rodrigues first.' He took the drink and she sat down next to him.

'First?'

'Hang in there, Maguire. It's going to be a long night.'

'I'm tired,' he protested mildly.

'Speak.'

He took a deep breath. 'There are things you don't know.'

'Tell me about them. I spoke to Quinn. And before you decide he betrayed a confidence, I would remind you that I'm his only child. Given the choice between keeping a secret and my safety, guess which is going to lose every time.'

Connor sipped his scotch. 'Fair enough.'

'So I know about Scylla.'

He nodded.

'But I have also learned that Raoul Dulac keeps secret Scylla documents on his boat.'

'How on earth did you discover that? For God's sake, you haven't been snooping around there have you?'

'Give me some credit. Justin Parker saw Raoul reading one of them on their way back from Rodrigues. He told me.'

'You've spoken to Parker!' Connor sounded incredulous. 'Are you seriously insane?'

Holly grinned. 'Quinn said something along those lines as well. I had dinner with Justin on Saturday night. He's okay, just a bit mixed up.'

'Parker is a bit more than that. He's got a bee in his bonnet about the treasure and has become totally myopic. I agree that he's not exactly the criminal type but beware the one-eyed man.'

'If you insist. Now, could we get back to a few facts?'

'How much did Quinn tell you?'

'Your half-brother worked for Scylla. He was killed in the Seychelles. Raoul Dulac is involved. Oh yes, and a place called Larkswood in the Northern Territory has been monitoring communications between Raoul and Scylla. There's something going on in the Central African Republic that requires Scylla's expertise.'

'I will tell you the whole story, Holly, I promise. Just not tonight, okay? I really am bushed.'

'What was the real reason for Rodrigues? Give me that much at least.'

'It was mainly to do with Raoul. I've been sticking as close as I can to him. But after you left I spent one more day with Madame Liang's contact. I'm nearly done with that. The pieces are in place and the game's about to start. It's virtually out of my hands now. Australia has details of the volume, the ship's name, where the drugs will be hidden and when they'll be dropped off. Undercover bods will follow the delivery and, all being well, that's when the arrests will start. There are one or two loose ends to tie up with Liang Song but after that, I bow out and distance myself from the whole thing.' He rubbed fingers across his eyes. 'As far as I know, Scylla isn't doing anything illegal. Mercenaries are not socially acceptable, but as long as they have a contract and stick loosely to the Geneva Convention, the law can't touch them. That aside, Raoul has one or two little sidelines

450

that could get him into trouble. That's what I'm after. Enough evidence to put him away.'

'Did you come up with anything in Rodrigues?'

'Information is easily bought. I tailed Raoul all over the island. When he finally left, I went back to some of his so-called mates and found one who had a grudge. Raoul doesn't pay too well, nor does he necessarily come up with the money on time. Anyway, this chap confirmed that among other things, Monsieur Dulac is heavily into diamond smuggling, drug dealing and money laundering.'

'Can you prove any of this?'

'Not quite.'

'Tell me, how did you hear that I'd been kid-napped yet again?'

'Liang Song's contact in Rodrigues put the word out. It's a small place. I was found quickly enough.'

'Aren't you running a pretty big risk that Raoul will get to hear about your interest in his activities?'

'On my own, it's a risk I'm prepared to take. I'm gambling on his unpopularity. He double-crosses everyone.' Connor held up his now empty glass. 'Any chance of the other half?'

Holly rose to oblige.

'Are you satisfied now? I know I should explain about my brother but can it wait?'

'Yes.' She returned with his scotch. 'Thanks for telling me this much.'

'I didn't want you mixed up in any of it – not

Liang Song or Raoul Dulac. They're both bloody dangerous. Mmmm! This is good.'

She waited until he'd put the glass down. 'There are a couple of things you should know.'

'Sounds ominous.'

'Guy Dulac has become a positive nuisance. There's a detective tailing him who has warned me to be cautious. He seems to think I'm in some kind of danger.' Holly related the head–butting incident. 'I don't know what Sham wants Guy for but he's keeping tabs on him big time.'

'Another good reason for you and I to disappear.'

'Agreed. Guy Dulac gives me the creeps.' She paused. 'There's something else too.'

'Why am I not surprised?'

'I think I've found your treasure.'

Connor groaned and closed his eyes.

Holly watched him for a while. When it became obvious he wasn't going to comment she said, 'Don't you want to know where?'

'Not a lot.'

'Maguire!'

'Okay, where?'

She told him. 'We'll have to take the map and have another look but I'm fairly positive the escarpment is identical in shape. The waterfall flows down a series of terraces. They could be the steps.'

Connor's reaction was to sleepily open one eye. 'Anything else?'

'Why are you so tired?'

'I've been busy. Raoul Dulac seems to exist on no sleep at all.'

'Is that it then? No more hidden agendas? It's just that whenever I think I'm getting to know you, up pops yet another of your little breath-stopping gems. Have I got it all now?'

'In essence. A few gaps to fill in but that's about it.'

'Your gaps have a habit of assuming Rift Valley proportions. But I can wait. You'll have to tell me everything sooner or later.'

'Later is good.' He gave her a lopsided grin and picked up his glass. 'Have you finished the interrogation? Can I go to sleep now?'

Holly put her drink on the coffee table, took Connor's from his hand and placed it next to hers. 'You said it yourself, Maguire. Later is good.'

The message under her door had been from Justin Parker. It was to wish her luck in Réunion and say he hoped to see her again before she returned to Australia. Connor pulled a face when she showed him. He was less inclined to trust Justin than Holly. In the morning, a couple of telephone calls found them a self-catering studio apartment in Flic-en-Flac, which was on the coast just above Tamarin and conveniently close to the falls. Holly checked out of the hotel and waited in reception for Connor to bring the car. Three people observed her departure with mixed reactions.

Guy Dulac had been hanging around the hotel

on and off for two days. The hotel staff at reception assured him that Holly had not checked out. They obligingly rang her room several times and offered to take a message, something he refused. Guy was aware that his frequent presence was causing speculation. On the morning she finally appeared, he was in his car watching the entrance, his face hidden behind a newspaper. Elation turned quickly to frustration when he saw her suitcase, and then to annoyance when she slid into the passenger seat of a car driven by Connor Maguire.

Sham, in the hotel grounds to maintain his surveillance of the Dulac kid, was also surprised to see Holly. She should have been safely on Réunion. He surmised correctly that her companion must be the friend she mentioned who had been on Rodrigues. From the little Sham could see of him, the Australian appeared quite capable of looking after himself. Which was just as well if the interest shown by Dulac was anything to go by.

Justin Parker, returning from a swim, frowned with displeasure when he saw Holly following a porter who was carrying her suitcase to reception. Why had she lied about Réunion? Was that where she was going now? He hung back and waited, only to see her get into Connor Maguire's car. So, that bloody Maguire was back on the scene. Justin did not see Guy Dulac follow their car, nor did he notice Sham tailing Dulac.

Guy knew that Sham was behind him. There was nothing he could do about it. He had to see where Holly was going. Once he knew that, Sham could easily be taken care of. And then he'd show that snooty Australian girl a thing or two.

The dark blue Porsche 911 Carrera convertible driven by Guy Dulac – the cost of which made the car a highly noticeable rarity anywhere in the world and particularly so on Mauritius – raised no suspicions as it kept pace with Connor and Holly. The electrically operated roof was closed and heavily tinted windows made it impossible to identify the driver. Traffic between Grand Baie and Port Louis was heavy and the few glimpses Connor had of the vehicle aroused nothing more than admiration. He assumed, rightly, that the car belonged to one of the privileged class of sugar estate owners.

Once through the capital the traffic thinned out a little, although its volume was still substantial. With no reason to suspect that the Porsche was tailing them, it did cross Connor's mind that a vehicle with such power and handling excellence was wasted on the narrow, speed-restricted roads of Mauritius. Neither he nor Holly knew what kind of car Guy Dulac drove. When they turned right to Flic-en-Flac, the Porsche carried on past and was soon out of sight.

Guy Dulac knew that beyond Flic-en-Flac the road continued for perhaps a kilometre before, at the tiny settlement of Wolmar, it turned east and rejoined the main north-south motorway. If Maguire and Holly were planning to relocate, and the fact that she had her suitcase suggested they were, they'd be easy enough to find. First there was the little matter of Detective Sham to fix. Dulac accelerated away from the policeman. Five minutes later, he found a place to turn and sped north again.

Sham was surprised when Guy didn't follow Holly into Flic-en-Flac. That feeling was compounded when the dark blue Porsche raced past in the opposite direction. Although the tinted windows of the sports car made it difficult to see inside, Sham was able to tell that the arrogant little shit actually waved to him. He slammed on his brakes, turned at some risk to himself, and the oncoming traffic, and took off after him.

Sham was guessing. By the time he reached the turn-off to Flic-en-Flac, the Dulac boy was out of sight. Sham hung a left and drove fast towards the coast. Guy Dulac's tailing of Holly Jones had him very worried. If nothing else, he could at least warn the girl. Sugar cane grew almost to the edge of the road on both sides, deep storm drains the only thing holding it back. Sham's concentration was on his driving. When Guy Dulac's Porsche roared out in front of him over an access viaduct leading to a footpath into the field on his right, Sham instinctively took evasive action. He never even saw the ditch, or the telegraph pole. His last conscious thought was, this is going to hurt.

Guy had no trouble finding where Connor and Holly had taken accommodation. He hung around long enough to see Maguire emerge from one of the apartments, collect a suitcase from the boot of his car and go back inside. Satisfied, he turned his

Porsche for home, passing an excited crowd gathered around Sham's wrecked car. Perfect!

Far out in the Indian Ocean an unusual phenomenon had occurred. As Kathleen Maguire had observed a few days before, it was too soon in the year for trade winds. But the temperature of the sea was abnormally high for early September and unseasonal snows in Asia had kick-started a premature northern hemisphere winter. As cold winds blew south to meet warm air rising from the ocean, the two streams were on a collision course, one to fill the vacuum being left by the other.

Rain showers rode on low pressure from the north. Bands of cumulus cloud dumped their sodden load over the Southern Ocean with increasing velocity. The storms plunged earthwards, compression causing the air temperature to rise. Where an updraught from the sea met air that was descending, an inversion occurred. As the rain intensified to storm proportions, the descending mass broke through and atmospheric pressure at sea level dropped immediately. The earth's rotation did the rest, causing annual trade winds to spiral in a clockwise direction. A cyclone was born.

Weather boffins watched the unseasonal depression carefully. They gave it a number for identification purposes. Then, as the trough deepened and the storm's path became unstable and a serious danger to shipping, they gave it a name.

Cyclone Yvette was to blow itself out inside of

five days. It would not threaten any landmass. The cyclone was noteworthy only because of its unseasonal occurrence. But the accompanying storm surge, waves reaching fifteen metres with winds gusting up to 120 kilometres an hour, had their effect on the container ship *Lady Elise,* so named after the wife of an ex-Prime Minister of South Africa, to which country the vessel was returning. At some stage during the height of the cyclone, three, six metre long, two tonne steel containers, returning empty to their country of origin, broke adrift and plunged into the Southern Ocean.

They would float like icebergs, most of their mass under water. Against the blue-grey sea, what little protruded above the surface was almost impossible to detect. Until the containers floated ashore or sank, they would not obey the rules and give way to any vessel – sail or power.

After observing Holly checking out of the hotel, Justin Parker went to his room and made a phone call. It was to Raoul Dulac. When he replaced the receiver, he was frowning with annoyance. Raoul agreed. The journalist on her own was one thing. In the company of Maguire, quite another.

Justin hadn't been entirely honest with Holly. True, he genuinely regretted his actions on Rodrigues – that whole thing had been foolish. He was sorry he'd frightened her. As a matter of fact, Justin had become quite attracted to the bolshie Australian. But telling her he'd given up on

William Maguire's nest egg had been a complete fabrication. He was as keen now as he had been all along. Although he did not like Raoul Dulac and didn't trust him, he had no intention of breaking any ties until all attempts to find the treasure had been exhausted. Raoul had the contacts, local knowledge and influence that Justin did not. He had no doubt that a double-cross was Raoul's intention but reasoned that forewarned was fore-armed. If Raoul tried, he'd learn that Justin was not without his own little tricks.

His partner's reaction to the news that Holly and Maguire were a team again was typical and worried him. The Frenchman had replied, 'Sit tight. Make sure I can reach you. I'll find out where they've gone and get back to you. We must take Maguire's mind off the treasure one way or another.'

Justin didn't know what he meant but had the feeling that changing the man's thoughts would involve Holly, and he had no doubt that Raoul Dulac would be prepared to use any means at his disposal to bring about such a shift of emphasis. He could not shake off the premonition that Holly was in danger.

Raoul's parting words, 'Be prepared to keep them in sight until we can separate them,' had Justin thinking that, if necessary, the Frenchman would not hesitate to do something to separate them on a permanent basis. He didn't like it.

Justin fretted in his room. He'd grown up with the feud between William and Kavanagh Maguire – it was as much a part of his childhood as memories of games played, stories read, chickenpox and measles. The animosity between two branches of the family was one he never questioned. It was there, it was real and, on principle, he did not associate with any of William Maguire's descendants. The one exception was Anne-Marie. The treasure, if it existed, belonged to his mother. Of that, he had no doubt.

Connor Maguire had no claim to any of it. The fact that his ancestor was William's brother didn't come into it as far as Justin was concerned. There was no moral issue here – Justin was convinced he had right on his side.

On a more personal level, he intended to use his share of any monies generated by the treasure to further a passionate belief that the dodo could be brought back from extinction. The scientific glory of such a feat was something he craved. Justin, like many scientists, wanted recognition and resented the back-room image of biologists. This was to be his magnum opus, the reason he was alive, a contribution to science that guaranteed his name would live forever in the world's database of technical brilliance.

Then there was Holly. Justin had always been shy around women. To him, they represented a challenge he had no wish to face. They always seemed to expect more than he was willing to give, take more than he believed he had given, question more than they had the right to and draw up battle lines when he could see no need for a fight. Holly was different. He felt no sense of competition with her.

Waiting for Raoul's call, Justin was trying to juggle two loyalties. Like the cold winds from Asia meeting warm air rising from the Indian Ocean, Justin's emotions were on a collision course.

Holly and Connor were, for the moment, blissfully unaware of circumstances conspiring against them. They were alone together and loving it. Time-out time. A day snatched for themselves. At four in the afternoon Holly reminded him that Madame Liang Song would be expecting his call.

'Bugger her,' he said. 'She can wait.'

'Bad Connor.'

'So sue me.'

As she was discovering, the Peter Pan in him – the delightful characteristic that lit her entire soul – had a habit of revealing itself at the most unexpected times. Connor Maguire could be focused and serious if the necessity arose. He could be strong, stubborn, competent and calculating. The man could get angry, tough or sarcastic when it was needed. But when the boy surfaced and joined forces with the lover in him, he was an irresistible, sexy, hands-on, gentle, affectionate and wholly desirable creature who bore her away to some secret place where nothing and no-one else could enter, where the world backed off to hazy and the only thing that mattered, the only thing real, was being as one with each other. Yin and Yang. Call it what you will. Holly didn't care what it was called. It was happening. And that was all that mattered.

Everything else could wait.

FIFTEEN

Holly woke at first light and lay on her side, looking out at the serene beauty of the sea. Connor was curled into her back, one arm resting on her hip. She could feel his breath against her neck. If she moved he'd wake up, and she didn't want him to, not yet. She needed to savour this perfect moment. The lagoon looked like silvery grey satin. Soon a breeze would ruffle the surface, forming a canvas on which the rising sun could paint new colours of amber, then turquoise. But for now, the water appeared to be sleeping, breathing as gently as the man who held her.

Reality was the gull perched on a pirogue busily preening its feathers in preparation for another day. It was a restless Indian Ocean stretching to infinity beyond the coral reef. It was today and tomorrow and all the days after that. Cocooned between the tranquil scene outside and the man she had so recently given her heart to, Holly wanted this moment to be indelibly etched into her soul, there to draw on when reality was less than perfect, when life wounded and disappointed.

Something startled the bird and it flew off, screeching. Connor stirred, kissed her bare shoulder and snuggled closer. For one brief moment, Holly had captured perfection. Nothing, and no-one, could ever take it from her. She rolled over and burrowed her body into Connor's, the flawless few seconds a precious gift, handed out free of charge by fate for her to nurture and use or keep forever secret. As Connor's arms tightened around her and she responded to her need of him, Holly felt that an angel must have taken time out to truly bless her.

Later, he brought her coffee in bed. They sat together, him behind with arms and legs around her, and they watched in silence as the lagoon selected its colour for the new day.

'You know,' Connor finally said, his lips against her hair, 'I could stay like this forever.'

'Mmmm! Me too.'

'When this is over, when we're back home, let's make sure we give ourselves time for this. A lot of time.'

Holly put down her half-finished coffee and turned into him. 'Yes,' she whispered against his lips. Then remembered her manners. 'Please.'

Reality kicked in at eight thirty and dragged both of them back to its unsympathetic demands.

'One day. That's all we can give William's treasure.'

'Then we'd better get a wriggle on.'

Connor groaned. 'Yuh!' He took both of her hands in his. 'Come and have a shower with me.'

'Is that a good idea?'

'Probably not.' He pulled her up and folded his arms around her. 'Be strong. We can do this.'

Holly wound hers around his neck. 'We can? Are you sure?'

'Behave, Jones.'

She kissed a nipple, feeling him shiver. 'I will,' she promised.

'When?' His voice was low and urgent. 'Jesus, woman!'

Holly took a deep breath and moved back from him. 'Now?'

His dark eyes glowed with renewed desire. 'Now's good.' He moved reluctantly towards the bathroom. 'About that shower – I don't trust you.'

'That's nothing.' Holly followed him. 'I don't trust myself.'

Reality. They kicked it out again. But it proved doggedly persistent.

At nine fifteen, Connor put through a call to Liang Song. Judging by his expression and the one-sided conversation, she had to be giving an opinion on the virtues of time keeping. He arranged to meet with her the next morning and hung up, pulling a wry face. 'I'd like to be a fly on the wall when her number comes up. She'll go ballistic.'

'Serves her right.'

He grinned at Holly's lack of charity. 'Come on, Jonesy. Time to go.'

'Jonesy comes a close second to ducky.'

'Jones then.'

'Jones is good.'

'So it's the "y" you don't like. Does that mean I can call you duck?'

He did a pretty good impression of a different kind of duck himself when she threw a cushion at him.

They left the apartment still absorbed in each other and finding fun in every moment. Not even the telephone call to Liang Song had dampened their spirits. They didn't notice Justin Parker in a car parked further down the road.

The call had come in late the previous afternoon. 'They're in Flic-en-Flac,' Raoul said. 'You'll find them easily enough, they're renting a studio apartment overlooking the sea.'

'I've arranged a car. I'll get straight down there.'

'They're not going anywhere today. Be there first thing tomorrow.'

Justin didn't ask how he had found them. Raoul only had to make a telephone call or two and the Australians' every movement would be monitored. He experienced a rush of irritation that Holly was so cosily ensconced with Maguire. He'd have given her credit for better taste.

Parked in easy sight of their apartment by first light, Justin cared nothing for the new day's beauty. He tormented himself with visions of what might be happening on the other side of that closed door. Holly and Maguire eventually emerged, hand-in-hand, and climbed into Maguire's car. The bloody man was laughing at something she'd said. Justin followed them, waiting while they went into a bakery, then a grocer and finally a fruit shop. After that, they headed back towards the main road.

'That looks nasty,' Holly commented as they drove past the smashed wreck of Sham's unmarked police car. It was on its side, bent in a V-shape, windows shattered, roof and doors staved in, wheels buckled. A few enterprising scavengers had stripped it of anything they thought they might be able to sell, or put to good use.

The detective, who had hovered all night at death's door, was at last making a come-back. His vital signs were stronger and he had slipped from coma to sleep some time around dawn. That he survived at all was a miracle. For as long as he lived, Sham would never be able to recall anything about the accident, other than what caused it. Travelling too fast, close on eighty-five kilometres an hour, he'd swerved to avoid the Porsche and crashed into a storm drain. His car hit the far side of the ditch nose first, then became airborne, turning end over end until it met the immovable solidity of a telegraph pole, an impact that literally broke the vehicle's back. It was over in an instant. The crumpled wreck then slid back into the culvert. By then, Sham had lost interest.

Flying glass made superficial inroads to his appearance but the real damage was caused when his seatbelt sprang open on impact. His skull had been fractured, right arm and wrist broken, chest caved in by the steering wheel, ribs broken and a lung punctured. He had a jagged hole in his liver, both hips were broken and an ankle fractured so badly he would always walk with a limp. And just for good measure, the rear-view mirror eliminated the benefit of sight from his left eye.

Sham re-entered the land of the living with very little enthusiasm. Big-time, life-threatening events have a way of penetrating the consciousness ahead of anything else. He knew, even before registering pain, or the fact that his body seemed to be encased in swaddling, that he wasn't going to like it.

Both eyes had been bandaged. He heard his wife, quietly sobbing, somewhere in the room. An undamaged sense of smell told him he was in hospital.

'Wha . . . ?' Sham croaked.

His wife burst into tears. Closer to the bed, a matter-of-fact female voice told him that he'd had a car accident. Sham wondered where.

He drifted in and out of sleep with no idea what time it was, or even which day. Although heavily drugged to alleviate the pain, when his commanding officer paid a visit that afternoon the detective knew there was something he had to tell him. The only trouble was, he couldn't remember what. Without saying a word, Sham succumbed once again to the security of pain-killing medication and the opportunity was lost.

Connor agreed that the escarpment over which the waterfall began its downward plunge was identical to William's map. Although the whole area was overgrown and the terrain difficult, there was no mistaking the scalloped shape or terraced descent.

'My taxidriver told me that the hydro-electric scheme has virtually destroyed this river,' Holly said. 'When William drew his map it would have been much wider and fuller.'

'If his directions are accurate, the treasure should be somewhere over there.' Connor pointed down to the far side. From the top, the water dropped straight for perhaps ten metres then flowed over a steeply sloping rock shelf before plunging on between two cliffs and falling further into a large pool. After that was a series of smaller waterfalls, taking it to the bottom. Connor was pointing to where the lush forest grew right up to the edge of the stream. Before human intervention, the entire width of the escarpment would have formed part of the waterfall, rather like a miniature version of the horseshoe-shaped Niagara Falls. Now, with only a trickle, vegetation had taken root where it could and the walls of the precipice were virtually hidden. 'Might be a bit tricky getting down there. How's your head for heights?'

'Fair.' She was lying. Holly hated heights.

'Somewhere above that second pool would be my guess. We'll have to get around to the other side first.' Connor picked up a coil of rope he'd brought from the car and draped it over his shoulder. It was the only equipment he had with him.

The going was rough. There was no track and

the ground dipped and rose with little warning. The vegetation was so dense that at times it was not possible to see the waterfall. Connor proved reasonably sure-footed. All Holly could think was, what went down had to come back up. She was not looking forward to the climb. This stage of a relationship was not the time to discover that the object of your desires was out of condition!

Justin Parker, when he reached the place where Holly and Connor had compared their map with the scenery, made the same connection as Holly had done when she first looked at the Tamarin Falls. He had committed the map to memory, and he also came to the conclusion that the place to start looking was on the other side. No longer concerned with keeping up his pursuit, the only thing on Justin's mind was the treasure. He had to reach it before them. Instead of following Holly and Connor, Justin set off in the opposite direction.

Connor had two distinct advantages over Justin. The last five years of his schooling had been spent as a boarder at The Armidale School, a private Anglican establishment in the Northern Tablelands of New South Wales which, in addition to mundane classroom activities, gave emphasis to the hands-on teaching of bush survival skills. Conquering the outback came naturally to Connor, be it mountain or desert. Justin's rural experiences were confined to the occasional foray into university parklands around Oxford. Connor was also a natural sportsman who enjoyed excellent physical coordination. Justin was not. In the difficult terrain, he rather resembled a stork on ice.

The base of the falls could undoubtedly be reached by following the ridge until it fell away towards the coast and allowed an easy descent. That meant doubling back. Quicker by far would be to scale down the side somewhere close to the falls. This was what Connor intended, using the vegetation for footrests and handholds. Justin didn't think of this. All he knew was that Maguire had crossed the river at the head of the falls. If he hurried, Justin believed he could reach the bottom on this side, cross over and make it back way ahead of Holly and Maguire.

The rim of the escarpment was deceptive. Connor, who had taken his bearings from a constantly visible high point, could keep well back from the edge without losing orientation. Justin, on the other hand, had to stay close to avoid becoming lost. Stumbling over rocks, slipping on the uneven ground, sweat stinging his eyes, Justin suddenly lost his footing, landed awkwardly and started sliding towards the edge. He lunged out and grabbed a sapling to stop his fall. But the small tree had not yet established itself in the rocky earth. The taproot went down no more than three centimetres, the plant fed by a fine web of lateral roots, some of which spread above ground. With Justin's weight, the sapling pulled free. Fingers still scrabbling for an anchor, Justin gave a cry of horror when the land beneath him dropped away. There was nothing to hang onto, nothing to stop him. Arms flailing wildly, Justin disappeared over the edge.

He hit the sloping rock shelf ten metres below flat on his stomach, the impact snapping his head forward, nose and teeth taking the full force of the jarring collision. Before he had time to register shock or pain, momentum carried him forward and he plunged, cartwheeling into space, landing on rocks surrounding the first pool before bouncing over the rim to plummet, head-first, into the second. The water slowly changed colour. His head had been split open. Justin was dead before he stopped falling.

'What was that?' Holly asked.

'A bird perhaps.' Connor sounded doubtful. The call had been high and wild, cut off abruptly.

They waited but did not hear it again. They had crossed the river and were making slow progress around the far edge of the horseshoe. 'Just a bit further,' Connor said. 'Then we'll try to climb down.'

Holly could hardly wait!

It was impossible to see the bottom. Trees and shrubs obscured the view. Finally, Connor selected a spot. 'Here is as good a place as any.'

Holly looked over the edge. *I can do this*, she told herself. A sheer drop of no more than five metres, a ledge that might or might not hold their weight, a couple of boulders below that, then a sloping rock shelf which looked as slippery as it did hostile. After that, what little she could see because of the foliage, appeared to be a reasonably user-friendly, if a little shaly, incline. Holly translated that to mean a crumbling, bush-infested descent into hell. *Piece of cake! Oh shit, oh shit!* 'How long is that rope?' she asked.

'Long enough. It should get us to the bottom.' He glanced up as he knelt to secure one end of it around the thick trunk of a tree. 'Are you okay with this? I'll go down on my own if you like.'

Holly pulled a face. 'You have no idea, Maguire, how much I'd love to take you up on that.' She had butterflies in her stomach. 'But in the interests of intrepid journalism, I'm afraid you're stuck with me.'

'Have you done any climbing?'

'Heaps. In and out of bed every day.' She pointed to the rope. 'Just make sure that's tight. I'd hate it to come undone halfway down. It would ruin my day.'

'It won't. Trust me.'

'I do. It's the bloody rope I'm suspicious of.'

He tossed the other end over the cliff. It slithered down the slope, causing a cascade of small stones – a sinister sound it seemed to Holly. 'Wait here. I'll test that ledge first and give you a shout.' He picked up the rope in both hands, planted his feet on the edge of the escarpment, leaned out and stepped backwards.

Jones, you have to be insane! She heard him curse. 'Are you okay?'

'Fine.' His voice floated up to her. 'I'm on the ledge. It's safe enough, but be careful. There are sharp sticks everywhere.'

'Super,' she gritted. 'Just what I needed.'

'Want to stay up there?'

'No way.' She picked up the rope. *Don't look down.* She looked down. Connor's head was only a couple of metres below. 'This could take a while.'

'Take your time. Keep the weight on your feet. Lean out. That's my girl, you're doing fine. Now, slide one hand down. Not too far. That's it. Same with the other. Good. You okay?'

'Yuh.'

'Feel around with a foot, Holly. Keep your legs apart and find a new level that will support your weight. Got it? Now bring the other foot down.'

At this rate, Holly felt she might make the ledge by sundown. She kept getting her balance wrong, at one stage dangling helplessly until Connor could talk her back into position.

Holly's hands were so slippery with fear that she expected the rope would slide through her grasp. *Oh, thank God!* The feel of his hands on her legs, guiding and supporting, was reassuring. As she descended further, he was able to catch her around the waist and virtually lifted her down to the ledge. The look on his face was speculative. He was clearly having second thoughts about her ability to reach the bottom.

Never having done anything like this in her life, Holly used the rope as a lifeline rather than a safety precaution, gripping too hard and allowing it to rub the soft skin on her palms. By the time she joined Connor on the ledge – quite a substantial shelf as it turned out – both hands were smarting.

At this rate, she'd have blisters before she was a quarter of the way down. Connor noticed the damp sheen of nerves on her forehead. 'Baby, you don't have to do this.'

Holly leaned against him, mouth dry and heart pounding. 'I'll get the hang of it.'

'You're a plucky little –'

'If you say ducky you're over the side.'

She heard him chuckle. He put his arms around her. 'I love you, Holly Jones. You will marry me, won't you?'

Trust Maguire to propose at a time like this! 'Only if I survive.'

'You will. I'll make damned sure of it. Was that a yes?'

She looked up at him. His face was close. A lock of hair had fallen forward and a thin trickle of blood had dried near one eyebrow where he'd obviously run foul of one of the woody plants growing horizontally out of the rocks. Otherwise, he was unscathed and as cool as a cucumber. His eyes were tender and caring.

'That was a yes.'

He kissed her forehead. 'Good,' he said mildly, as though he'd merely been seeking confirmation of something he already knew. 'Let's do the next bit.'

'Is that it? I've just said I'll marry you. Can't you come up with something better than that?'

Connor smiled and shook his head. 'I don't trust you, Jones. You do that thing with your mouth and before I know it, I'm drowning in you. Can't it wait till we reach the bottom?'

Her foot dislodged a rock that went crashing to oblivion below. It reminded both of them that a crumbling ledge high on an escarpment was probably an inappropriate place for anything other than a brief rest.

Holly eyed the boulders. She didn't want to think about the sloping shelf, not yet. 'Let's go.'

'Hey,' he said softly, catching her to him again. 'It's not as bad as it looks. I'll be right there.'

She took a deep breath.

Half an hour later, nearly at the end of the rope and slipping and sliding down the last bit, Holly glanced towards the river. Through a gap in the foliage, she saw a body floating, face down, in a shallow pool of blood-red water.

Her spontaneous cry alerted Connor, who was braced against a sapling just below. 'What is it?'

'There.' She nodded past him. 'I think it's Justin.'

He looked. 'Oh Jesus! That must have been the sound we heard.'

'Can you get to him? I'll be okay. You'll be faster without me.'

Connor disappeared immediately, using only the vegetation to slow his descent. Holly realised just how much she must have slowed him down.

Only a minute or so later he came back into view, running across the rocks towards Justin. 'He's dead,' Connor called up to her. 'He must have fallen from the top.'

Holly looked upwards. It was a hell of a long way. Connor crossed back to the base of the escarpment. 'The last bit isn't too difficult.'

She eased her way towards him, hands on fire but ignoring the pain. The end of the rope seemed like losing a security blanket. She let go reluctantly. Shock over Justin helped her down the last part. She was thinking more about him than the descent. *Poor man. He must have been following us again.*

Connor caught her to him as she slithered out of control to the bottom. The feel of his hard, strong body was comforting. His arms went around her. 'I don't think you should go over there,' he advised. 'It's not very pretty.'

Holly cried a little against his chest. She hadn't trusted Justin Parker but, strangely, she'd liked him well enough. No-one should die without some-one's tears.

'What do we do now? We can't leave him here.'

'We'll have to. We can't move him. The police will have to be informed.'

'You go. I'll only slow you down. I don't mind waiting here.'

'Are you sure?'

She could see that he agreed, he just wanted to make certain she was okay about being left with Justin. 'I'm sure.'

'I'll come straight back as soon as I've reported it. May take a couple of hours, though. Don't, whatever you do, attempt to get back up on your own. Wait for me, okay?'

'I promise. You take care.'

He kissed her quickly and was gone. She could hear his progress for about ten minutes then there was nothing but the tinkling water. Holly sat beside the river and listened to the silence. It was as empty as Justin's soul and just as lonely.

Two hundred and fifty years earlier, give or take a decade, Mauritius was hit by the biggest cyclone in its history. With it came weeks of torrential rain. Rivers, swollen to capacity, burst their banks and fanned out, seeking new and previously unknown ways to the sea. All things being equal, William Maguire's treasure should still have been safe. Two-thirds of the way down the escarpment, it was well back from the normal volume of water coming over the falls. Even under flood conditions, the treasure remained unscathed. It was in a shallow cave, an overhang of rock protecting the entrance from rain and prying eyes. Only foraging geckos and ants knew it was there.

But William could never have anticipated the ferocity of that cyclone, nor the effects of unrelenting rain on an already sodden island. A landslide caused the Tamarin River to back up for several kilometres above the head of the falls. A wall of rock, mud and trees swelled the water level to ten times its highest known depth before giving up the struggle. Slow at first, then with terrifying momentum, it swept up and sucked in everything in its path until the surging, swirling river finally burst free over the escarpment to plunge earthwards in a mad scramble for the ocean.

Still, the treasure was safe, the overhanging rock

acting like a roof over the cave entrance. But as days turned into weeks, the build-up of debris at the base of the falls formed another dam wall and this time the valley below began to back-fill. Foaming, flotsam-filled water eventually reached the cave, flushing out the two small chests, all that was left of William's treasure. They slid forward and sank, dropping through the water to settle in what was normally the second pool under the waterfall, the same one where Justin now lay.

As the rain abated and the river fell back to its original course, the backed-up water drained away to expose the chests to the relentless pounding of the waterfall. It took time but, first one, then the other, burst open and surrendered its contents. William never knew. He had died of natural causes during the cyclone. Coins and precious stones were swept out of one pool and into the next, until they could fall no further and settled in the river bed. Silt quickly covered all evidence of the fabulous wealth. In time, it might have washed to the sea but that was not to be. The advent of hydro-electricity reduced the flow of the once mighty river to an ineffectual trickle. As the centuries rolled by and fluctuating weather conditions made subtle changes to the terrain, three gold coins worked their way back to the surface.

Holly's thoughts drifted. Her back was to Justin's body, she couldn't bear to look at him. The sun sat directly overhead, burning down and warming the quiet, isolated place that had claimed his life. Something glinted under the water. Holly moved, trying to see what it was. There was another, and another, all lying close together. When she realised what it must be, a great sense of calm descended over her. Kathleen Maguire had said, 'I have a strong feeling that the treasure and one other are destined to meet.' At the time, her words hadn't made sense. The treasure and one other, destined to meet. Justin? Holly left the coins where they were. It would be up to Connor of course, but she had a feeling he would decide that Justin, having paid the supreme sacrifice in his search for riches, should be allowed to keep the secret.

She had no doubt that the remainder of William's treasure would be in the river. Let it stay there. Let the violence of the past remain hidden and the violence of the present go, at last, in peace. Let the earth embrace that which man had once torn from her.

Holly sighed. She was becoming quite philosophical in her old age!

Connor returned nearly three hours later with the news that a police rescue team was on its way. 'We have to stay until they arrive.'

Holly pointed out the coins.

He stared at them for a long time. Then put an arm around her. 'You know, it's the finding that's satisfying.'

She nodded, waiting for him to continue.

'Of course, it might not be William's. But if it is, the money could do a lot of good.'

'True.'

'Could be cursed, though.'

'I'm not sure about that. Kathleen didn't seem to think so.'

'But she sensed evil. Perhaps it was a premonition about Justin.'

'Maybe.'

He gave her a hug. 'I'll write that cheque.'

Holly kissed him long and hard.

Two members of the police rescue team abseiled down the escarpment immediately next to the falls, as casual as you please, as if they were taking a Sunday stroll. Justin's body was photographed, gently removed from the pool, strapped onto a stretcher and winched up the cliff face. 'We'll be down here a while,' one of the rescuers said. 'There's a detective at the top who wants to ask you some questions. Can you make your own way up?'

'Not a problem,' Connor assured him.

Holly resigned herself to more pain than she felt she deserved. It was all very well for these bloody fit men. Would it be asking too much for at least one of them to stop and think that not everybody is thrilled at the prospect of scaling a fifty metre death trap?

The going up involved more physical effort than coming down. At least gravity helped on the descent and every step meant she had less distance to fall. Connor alternated between taking the lead and staying behind in case she fell. When they finally made it to the top, Holly felt her lungs were on fire. She had scratches on her face, arms and legs, the skin on both hands was blistered from the rope, and those that had burst were bleeding. Bright red from the exertion and covered in dirt, Holly lay on her back, gasping for breath. To her chagrin, Connor, who had made the climb twice and had worked doubly hard to get her up and down, appeared totally relaxed. It didn't help either when he said, with very little sympathy, 'Exercise program for you, Jones. As a matter of some priority.'

'But I hate all that stuff,' she complained.

'Sorry, baby.'

He wasn't sorry and that pissed her off too. But she was too damned tired to argue.

Detective Rafe Jolliffe, a big bluff man with suspicion in his eyes and scepticism in his voice, questioned them closely. He suggested that for such an isolated spot where tourists seldom managed to go, two people risking life and limb to climb down the escarpment and a third accidentally falling to his death, on the same day, seemed a bit of a coincidence. Especially since the deceased was known to both Holly and Connor.

'We didn't know he was following us,' Holly said.

'Why would he have been doing that?' Jolliffe asked.

Holly said the first thing that came into her head. 'He was jealous.'

'Of you, Monsieur?' Jolliffe looked at Connor.

'Yes.' Connor had a look on his face that said, *Where did that come from?*

'But why did you climb down?' the detective asked for the second time, having not accepted their first answer that it seemed like a good idea at the time. He nodded to Holly. 'You are inexperienced. It was extremely foolish.'

'Okay, okay.' Connor held up both hands in a gesture of surrender. 'It's my fault. I wanted to ask her to marry me. It had to be memorable, different. That's all.'

'Ah!' The man's intelligent eyes flicked from Connor to Holly. He saw a look pass between them. There was no doubt they were in love. But they were hiding something too. 'Mademoiselle?'

'She said yes,' Connor put in.

Holly actually blushed. As the colour in her face deepened she looked down, embarrassed by Connor's frank admission.

It crossed the detective's mind that these two were possibly only trying to conceal a private moment of passion. He was about to put that to them when Holly suggested he check her out with Detective Sham.

Jolliffe looked at her guardedly. 'You know Sham?'

'Yes.'

'How?'

'Have you heard of Guy Dulac?'

'Yes.'

'Sham is investigating him.'

'What has this got to do with you?'

'He has been making a nuisance of himself. Sham knows about it and made sure Dulac was aware that he was watching him.'

The detective nodded slowly. 'I see.' He thought for a minute, shrugged, and said, 'I'll speak to him later today.' He did not see any reason to let Holly know that Sham was lying in hospital, smashed up, semi-conscious and in no shape to verify anything. But he was encouraged. If this girl believed that Sham would vouch for her then she was probably telling the truth about the dead man. Sham rarely, if ever, misjudged people.

After providing details of where they could be reached, Holly and Connor were allowed to leave. 'I'll be in touch if I need any more information. Come to the station in Curepipe tomorrow. You'll have to sign statements.' With that, he left them to recover the rope.

'Jealous?' Connor was looping the rope around one shoulder.

Holly shrugged. 'It was the first thing I thought up.'

'Do me a favour.'

'What?'

'Next time you decide to spring a whopper with no warning, just clear your throat or something first so I know it's coming.' He put his free arm around her shoulders and they started walking. 'Better still, try not to do it.'

'I couldn't tell him about the treasure.'

'No,' Connor agreed. 'But you could have just said he'd dropped behind us.'

'Maguire.' Holly squinted up at him.

'Yes.' He knew her now. She was about to zap him with one of her special expressions.

'Sorry.'

Connor grinned. He didn't know her that well yet. But he sure as hell was having fun learning.

Back at the car, Holly suggested they have some of the food they'd bought earlier in the day. So far, she had managed to conceal the damage to her hands. Somehow they seemed to reflect her lack of fitness. Okay, so she hadn't been looking after herself, she knew that, but it was surprising just how taxing the climb had been. Holly would not admit, not even to Connor, just how out of condition she had become. It was a question of pride. The truth of it was she was soft and had been absolutely terrified.

They stood beside the car chewing crusty French bread with cheese. 'Fancy a little trip tonight?' Connor asked casually.

'Where?'

'Grand Baie.'

'Reason?'

'I thought a spot of break and enter would be diverting.'

Holly looked at him. 'On a certain person's boat? Haven't you had enough excitement for one day?'

'I'm running out of time.'

'What will you do if you find anything?'

'Depends on what it is.'

She was silent for a while. 'You want to tell me about it yet?'

Connor was staring straight ahead. 'Yuh, I guess I should.'

'You don't have to,' she said gently. 'Not if it hurts.'

'It always hurts.' His voice carried gratitude. 'But I don't want secrets between us.'

'I suppose I should explain about Dennis too.'

'When you're ready. I've guessed most of it.'

Connor collected his thoughts, then began to speak. 'Brian was sixteen years older than me. My mother married his father when she was very young. He died of cancer when my brother was eleven. A few years later she married my father and I came along. Brian was like a second dad. He was a sort of hero figure in my life. As early as I can remember we were close, though in fact we didn't actually see much of each other.' Connor stopped speaking for a moment, a small frown of recollection between his eyes. 'Brian was a bit wild, I suppose. He and my father never really hit it off. I think it was resentment that his mother had found someone new to love, though he was always protective of me.'

Holly made no comment, simply watched his face, giving him all the space he needed to assemble a story she was reasonably certain he'd never told in full to anyone else. His words seemed to come with difficulty, from some faraway place of pain. There was reluctance too, a hesitation to revisit memories which had clearly been shut away for so long. She wanted to tell him again that it was all right, that he didn't need to go on if he didn't want to, but she sensed he would anyway. The time was right for him.

'When I was three, Brian moved out. The situation at home had become very difficult. Dad can be pretty stubborn when it suits him. So could Brian. They were never going to get on. As I said, he was wild. No, not wild exactly. He was a loner. And like a lot of solitary people, it seemed as if he was constantly searching for something that would give meaning to his life. He couldn't settle for anything less than perfect but didn't seem to know what it was, or how to go about finding it. Brian couldn't hold down a regular job. He did all sorts of things. One minute working as a barman, the next on a construction site, or driving a taxi. Even applied to Qantas for training as a flight attendant, but they turned him down. That was when he took off to northern Queensland and found work as a jackaroo. My poor mother nearly went mad with worry.' A small smile of some remembered moment touched his lips. 'The thing about Brian was that he was utterly charming. My father used to say he could coax a concession out of Margaret Thatcher if he put his mind to it.'

Holly smiled. He'd have to be damned good!

'He came home for a visit one weekend when I was about twelve. Said he'd joined the army reserve. No-one in the family thought he'd stick with it.'

'Did he?'

'Yes. He'd finally found something he could do and liked doing. He enjoyed the physical side of it and the adventure. The only part he didn't particularly take to was the discipline, although even that didn't put him off. Brian loved it so much that after a couple of years he decided to enlist in the regular army.'

'There's a niche for everyone,' Holly said softly. 'It just takes some people a bit longer than others to find it.'

Connor shook his head. 'It's not that simple. The discipline ultimately got to him. Brian was a free spirit, not suited to the full-time rules of army life. It wasn't long before he was bucking the system at every opportunity. That meant trouble. The army kicked him out.'

'How long did he serve?'

'Three years.' Connor chose his next words carefully. 'Brian wasn't a bad person. It's just that he was . . . not so much easily led as . . . always looking for excitement. If he had seen active service it would probably have been different. He was a natural for Scylla. Army trained, not too bothered by moral ethics, permanently broke and always on the lookout for something exciting. They approached him and he joined up. It was the job he'd been seeking all his adult life. He was tailor-made for it.'

'Are most mercenaries ex-soldiers?'

'They tend to be. Scylla has scouts in the armed forces of many countries.'

'Is Scylla legal?'

'As far as I know. They keep a pretty low profile. Brian didn't say much but he did tell me that as far as he was concerned, the difference between Scylla and the regular army was that Scylla always had work. Didn't matter who it was for. Ethically, I have a problem with that. Brian didn't. He was entitled to his opinion.'

'I'm not sitting in judgment of him,' Holly responded to Connor's slightly defiant tone.

'Then that's something else which makes you unique.'

She laughed softly, lightening the moment. 'Look, I don't go along with the concept of guns for hire to the highest bidder but that's not a personal criticism of your brother.'

Connor glanced at her. 'Thanks.'

'I know Brian was killed in the Seychelles. Is that why you're after Raoul Dulac? Revenge?'

'No. Brian knew the risks. Whether we liked it or not, the rest of the family had to accept it.' Connor paused.

She waited.

'Brian had been with Scylla for several years when he met Emma. She was less than half his age – only seventeen. He fell deeply in love with her.' Connor broke off another piece of bread. 'I met her a couple of times. She was beautiful, a real gentle spirit. That was it as far as Brian was concerned. There was a choice to be made, Emma or Scylla.'

'Is that what she wanted?'

'Not at all. It came from Brian. His days of acting as if there were no tomorrow had to end. He decided to settle down and spend his life with Emma. I don't think she actually knew what he did for a living. He'd saved some money and planned to buy a pub in the Territory.'

'Quite a challenge for a young girl. The Northern Territory is not for the faint-hearted, especially running a pub.'

'Emma was from Darwin. Territory born and bred. She loved it up there.'

'And she loved Brian?'

'Very much. Despite the age difference, they were meant for each other. Emma accepted that Brian was never going to conform and responded to his complete devotion to her. She was a very shy girl. Brian brought her out of her shell. And in turn, she gave him stability, a purpose, and he loved her with everything he had. My brother would have died for her. In the end, he did.'

'What do you mean?'

Connor cut a chunk of cheese. 'He tried to resign from Scylla. By then he was quite valuable to them. The men respected and trusted him. His cool head under pressure and field experience made his team an example to the others.' Connor's voice went hard suddenly. 'Enter Raoul Dulac. He needed men to train raw recruits for a coup attempt in the Seychelles. Or so he said. The training would be done in South Africa. What he conveniently omitted to mention was an arrangement that a Scylla unit would also be available to fight. None of the men knew that until the mission was ready to go. My brother was exactly what

Dulac had been looking for and he saw to it that Brian's resignation was rejected.'

'Surely Brian could have walked away?'

Connor nodded. 'I suppose so. But don't forget that Brian still believed it was only a training exercise and must have thought that the money would come in handy. He put up token resistance, but in the end agreed to go.'

'And was killed because Raoul hid the truth?'

'I could have accepted that. The mercenary mind is a fairly muddy place where most of us never go. Brian chose his life and we had to respect the way things worked. No, it wasn't his death that got to me, though God knows the loss was hard enough to accept. That bastard, Dulac, had decided that a little insurance wouldn't go astray. Brian's resignation attempt was a worry. He needed him there when the fighting started. It was no secret why Brian intended to leave – men alone together out in the bush, there aren't many things they don't know about each other. Dulac found out about Emma and arranged that she be eliminated.' Connor broke off, a muscle working in his jaw. 'That's why I want him,' he said eventually.

Holly was stunned. She knew Raoul Dulac had very few morals but this was cold-blooded, premeditated murder. 'You have proof?'

'Not the kind that would stand up in court.'

'What makes you think –'

'I was told. After Brian's death a colleague, someone who had fought with him, said he'd heard that Emma's death was no accident.'

'Quinn mentioned a car crash.'

'Her vehicle ran off the road for no apparent reason.'

'Did this friend know any more?'

'The talk was that Brian's girlfriend had been taken out on Dulac's orders. That he had sent a message saying Brian was desperately ill. Emma, as Raoul had hoped, dropped everything to be with him. Brian was supposedly in the hospital at Katherine. It was late but she obviously didn't want to wait till morning. It's a four-hour drive from Darwin, nothing difficult. She never arrived.'

'But there's nothing to implicate Raoul? Scylla operates from somewhere in Western Australia. How could he have set up the accident from there?'

'Contacts. It wouldn't be hard. A telephone call would do it.'

'This is nothing but conjecture.'

'True. There are a couple of other things. Brian's colleague told me something else. A South African at the camp let something slip about Raoul Dulac's methods. Seems he has quite a reputation throughout Africa. In Angola he was known as *Kishi*, an evil spirit with two faces. His name in Zaire is *Mongo*, or the God of Death. Nigerians refer to him as a *Bori*, a spirit who spreads evil and possesses people, and in the Sudan he is believed to be an *Adandara*, a wild cat with witchcraft skills.'

'I still don't see how –'

'It's not just rumour, Holly. I know stories stick to someone like Dulac, and I accept that reputations can grow in this fashion, but exaggeration is usually based on fact. A number of things add up. Emma's parents confirmed that she received a telephone call from someone calling himself a friend of Brian's telling her he had been bitten by a snake and was in hospital in Katherine. Later we found out that the hospital in Katherine had never heard of Brian Anderson. Dulac took a call about two hours after Emma left Darwin. He sent for Brian and broke the news of her death in a car crash. At that stage, her car hadn't even been found. The next day, Raoul was overheard saying to someone, 'Don't worry about Anderson, he'll see it through now. I've made sure of it.' Connor took a deep breath. 'Other than that, I have no hard evidence.'

'You're not likely to find it either.'

'I know.'

'So what do you hope to achieve?'

'Raoul Dulac is a murderer. He might get away with that but he's also a crook. He must have records, somewhere. I plan to find them and come up with enough to interest the police so that they'll set up a full investigation. If I can get them to look into him they're likely to find that, financially, he's been holding out on Mauritius for years. He must have an offshore bank account, probably more than one, that he sure as hell hasn't declared. Internal revenue would find that extremely interesting. They'd take him to the cleaners. Dulac's got to be hurt. And the only way I can think of to do that is through his wallet with a complimentary decade or two in prison.'

'To pay him back for Emma?'

'If there's one reason it would be her. She had just turned eighteen, a kid. We never saw Brian again after Emma's funeral but he went a little crazy. He became deeply depressed apparently. Knowing my brother, with the one perfect thing in his life snatched away, he wouldn't have cared less whether he lived or died. He went to the Seychelles in that frame of mind. Raoul Dulac destroyed him.'

Holly remained silent.

'There's something else I blame him for. My mother's heart was broken when Brian died. She hasn't been the same since. Dulac didn't just kill Emma and Brian, he took away my mother's spirit. I hate the man's guts.'

'Surely you don't plan to take him on by yourself?'

'I'd rather not. I want to see him punished for something – as I said, anything will do. I don't see much point in stooping to his level to bring it about.'

'Is that the reason why you set up the shipping deal? Why you're risking retribution from the Triad?'

'The shipping partnership was so I could have a closer look at him. That's when I found out about his relationship with Liang Song. I also discovered that he had one or two illegal sidelines which, if I could get proof, would get him into serious trouble. The deal with Madame Liang was a bit of a coincidence really, but before I knew who I'd be dealing with I agreed to do it anyway. I'd seen first-hand what drugs can do. When I found out who was looking for an Australian connection I thought it highly likely that Raoul would be involved somehow. I jumped at the chance.'

'If he thinks you're on to him it could be dangerous.'

'That's another risk I'm prepared to take. I'm no mercenary, Holly, but if Dulac decides to come after me he won't find it easy. I can take care of myself.'

It was no idle boast. His condition wasn't in question. 'What's your intention if you find something on his boat?'

'Hand it over to the proper authorities.'

'And that's it?'

'Depends what it is.'

'Will that be the end of it for you?'

'Yes. If the punishment fits the crime. An arrogant bastard like that would find prison unbearable.'

'Even there he'll have the contacts to get even with you.'

'How will he know it's me? He has no idea Brian was my brother. And Liang Song confirmed when you were out of the room the other night that Raoul doesn't know of her expansion plans into Australia. It won't cross his mind to suspect me.'

'I hope you're right, Maguire. You'll already be dodging the Triads.'

Connor grinned at her sarcasm. 'I shouldn't be. The Liang Song sting has been set up in such a way that it won't occur to her that she's been double-crossed by me. In fact, I've made it look as if Raoul has had a hand in that.'

'That's all very well but don't you think she'll find it just a tad suspicious that she's locked up and you're not?'

'She'll assume I've covered my tracks.'

Holly wiped a crumb from her mouth, forgetting her hands.

Connor's eyes opened wide. 'My God!'

She tried to hide them but he'd have none of it. 'Show me.'

Holly did, reluctantly. 'Guess I'm not as tough as I like to make out, huh?'

He cradled her hands in his own. 'Why didn't you say? Jesus, Holly! They must hurt like hell.'

'It looks worse than it is. A soak in Dettol will help.'

Connor pulled her close.

'Maguire?' Her voice was muffled against him. 'Did you mean that proposal?'

He eased her away and kissed her lightly on the lips. 'Every word.'

'We haven't known each other very long.'

'Second thoughts?'

'Caution. Our combined track records aren't exactly impeccable.'

His eyes were locked with hers. 'I know what I want, Holly. I've never been more certain.'

Neither had Holly. 'When?'

'When do we get married? Whenever.'

'Next week? Next month? Next year? Next

century? No, on second thoughts, that's a hundred years away.'

'Whenever you want.'

'Are you always this amenable?'

'No.'

She lay the back of a hand against his cheek briefly. 'Good. That would be very boring.'

He opened the door of the car. 'Chemist, Jones. I can't take you home in this condition. Quinn would kill me.'

'Connor?'

'Yeah, baby?'

'Nothing. I just wanted to hear myself say it.'

SIXTEEN

Guy and Raoul Dulac were having one of their regular screaming matches. Like father, like son, neither would give any ground. Although the older man usually won these flaming encounters, he did so by foul means – with threats. Most of them bounced straight off Guy's not insignificant shoulders. Raoul had regularly relied on the sword of Damocles to get his own way. Intimidation was his tool for control and Guy learned from an early age that his father knew no other way. Giving as good as he got rarely brought retribution. It simply inspired Raoul to raise the stakes. No conscience, no filial loyalty. When Raoul Dulac felt thwarted by his offspring, he invariably resorted to threats which he would not hesitate to carry out if compliance were refused.

This time, it was all to do with the boat. Guy wanted to use it and his father had said no.

Their argument pushed into the personal insult stage, each tirade thrusting deeper in an effort to undermine the other and gain the upper hand.

'Watch your mouth, young man. I'm your father. I can cut you off without a penny.'

Guy had heard this many times. 'Feel free. You're broke anyway.' He knew the reference to the family's financial situation would infuriate his father.

It did. Raoul's eyes narrowed. 'You're on thin ice, you young fool. Last time you used the boat we had to lie to the police. We won't do it again.'

Guy felt a shiver of fear. That bloody detective's ongoing interest in him, despite the alibi provided by his parents, had been of considerable concern. Okay, he'd taken care of Sham, but that didn't mean the Corrine Vitry case would be closed. He didn't want the matter discussed in a loud argument. Servants hear things. Their loyalty was not to be relied on. His father had covered for him, certainly, and probably would again. But Guy was not positive of continued support if Raoul ever learned the truth. Better not provoke him any more. True to form, however, Guy backed down in his own inimitable style: 'The only time you use the boat is to fuck that bitchy little chink,' when Anne-Marie entered the room. Guy broke off, annoyed at the interruption. 'Can't you see we're busy?'

Anne-Marie's face was white, her eyes wide. 'Holly Jones just called. Justin Parker is dead.'

'What?' Raoul was genuinely shocked, not so much over the death itself as the inconvenience it would cause. 'What happened?'

'He fell off a cliff. I don't have any more details. She only rang so that I can tell his mother.'

Raoul snatched up the telephone. 'I'll make a few inquiries. Where and how he died could be important.'

Guy seized the opportunity and used his father's distraction to his own advantage. 'The boat?'

'For Christ's sake, son, take the bloody thing. But make sure it's back here by Friday.'

Thus it was that Justin Parker's death, indirectly, had one last terrifying consequence for Holly.

Guy's plans were hazy but one thing remained crystal clear in his mind. Holly Jones.

The boat was ready to go. Normally, he simply took the forty-six foot Chris Craft whenever he wanted it and his father seldom raised an objection. But yesterday afternoon he'd heard Raoul on the telephone saying, 'They're in Flic-en-Flac. You'll find them easily enough.' Having been there himself that very morning, Guy had pricked up his ears.

'Just find out where they go and let me know. If necessary, we can use the boat,' Raoul added.

Guy presumed that his father had been speaking to that ridiculous English friend of Anne-Marie's. The subject was obviously Holly Jones and Connor Maguire. He knew from the conversation that if Raoul learned he wanted to use the boat his answer would be no. If there was one thing Guy could be sure of, it was that life revolved around Raoul's needs and no-one else's. So he decided to pretend he knew nothing of his father's plans. The following morning, while Guy was out of the house, Raoul, quite by chance, had discovered the boat keys were missing from his desk drawer. He found them in Guy's bedroom, along with an overnight bag containing a change of clothes. When Guy returned, his father told him he couldn't use the boat. Hence the argument.

The timely intervention of Anne-Marie meant Guy's as yet unformed plans were back on track, after a fashion. That the Australian girl was in the company of Maguire was annoying. Alone, getting her on board would be easy. But Maguire looked like he intended to hang around, and for as long as he did, Guy's hands were more or less tied. All he could do was wait for an opportunity.

His intentions, once Holly was at his mercy, were rather more focused. Guy wasn't used to, nor did he take kindly to, rejection. The remark about him being a boy had been humiliating. Her continued coldness towards him a challenge. And, as Corrine Vitry had found out, you either went along with Guy Dulac's plans or you paid the price.

Corrine's only crime had been to say no to heroin. Guy wanted her to join him, assumed she would agree and became angry when she refused. So, while she was high on a joint, he'd given her a hit. The girl had surprised him by fighting wildly but the fix went in. Maybe it was bad shit, maybe he'd given her too much, but it became obvious very quickly that she was reacting badly. Guy panicked. He threw the rest of the drug overboard and, when Corrine stopped breathing, rolled her over the side too. It never crossed his mind to try and get help. He was too busy thinking of his own hide.

The story Guy told his parents, when it became obvious the police suspected him, was that Corrine had injected herself, that he had no idea she was into hard drugs or was carrying any that night. He admitted to dumping her out at sea. That was all. Solange and Raoul, while furious that he could have been so stupid, believed his story. To do otherwise would have meant confronting the idea that their son was less than perfect.

Guy had not used heroin since. He became convinced that Corrine's reaction was a result of some kind of lethal concoction and that he too might have suffered a similar fate had he injected himself first. He told himself he'd been lucky and vowed to stay away from the drug in future. But secreted away on the boat, he had a supply of amphetamines and barbiturates. He was looking forward to seeing their effect on Holly Jones. Having killed Corrine, and believing that Sham too was dead, Guy Dulac was beginning to feel that the law couldn't touch him. If the stuck-up Australian bitch didn't cooperate he could do it again. It would be up to her. They could have some fun and he'd bring her back. If not, this time he'd take the boat well out to sea before getting rid of her. Surely the sharks wouldn't miss two decent meals?

Raoul Dulac was not a happy man. As Guy had goaded, he was flat broke. The banks were threatening to call in his loans. He was in danger of losing the estate. Raoul needed to find William's treasure with some degree of urgency. It had never been his intention to share it with Justin. Now that was one problem less to deal with. Tamarin Falls. Raoul knew he would have to go there for himself but decided to give it a few days in case the police were still sniffing about in the area. He didn't want them wondering what he was doing.

Had Maguire and the journalist found anything? Perhaps he should wait until they left Mauritius. He wondered what kind of business deal Maguire was working on but quickly dismissed the thought. Even if he knew, he couldn't afford to buy in.

The boat, luxury cars, rebuilding of his home – which the fire insurance never came close to covering – depressed sugar prices and an extravagant lifestyle had all but cleaned him out. Raoul had plenty of money outside Mauritius – over the years Scylla, diamond dealing, drugs, and one or two other ventures had done exceptionally well, the profits supporting bank accounts in Switzerland and Hong Kong – but he needed money here.

Raoul had done the unforgivable and fallen in love with his mistress. He knew she didn't return his feelings. Their business relationship developed into something more intimate shortly after Song's arranged marriage. She was a passionate woman whose body could wait no longer. Married to an inexperienced boy, Song considered Raoul the perfect candidate to initiate her in delights of the flesh. He had not intended to fall in love. When it became apparent she did not love him in return,

Raoul told himself that the only way to keep his mistress was to cater to her expensive tastes. He had more than enough money outside Mauritius to keep Song happy.

It was Solange whom Raoul needed to satisfy. He wanted to be rid of her but if he left she would consider it her moral right to break him. And in the course of doing that, it was more than likely his offshore accounts would come to light. If he was able to leave her well provided for she'd be happy to see the back of him, that's if she brought her nose out of the cognac glass long enough to notice! So he fumed and fretted impatiently, hoping that Tamarin Falls held an answer to his problems and that he hadn't been beaten to the treasure.

Raoul had no doubt that William Maguire's treasure existed. When his parents told him that Kathleen had tried to swap a map for a chance to speak with Anne-Marie, Raoul had immediately become interested. He'd paid the nun a visit but she refused to deal with him. It hadn't been difficult for Raoul to gain access to Kathleen's safe deposit box. Although he only removed the map, he'd read a note that was with it. 'I have done as William Maguire seemed to desire and sent his journal back to Ireland. I have taken the precaution of removing the map.' That was it as far as Raoul was concerned. Untold riches had once existed. Chances were, they still did.

Then the burglary. The map had disappeared along with most of Solange's jewellery. Some stupid thief who probably had no idea what it was and no doubt threw it away. However, Raoul, ever cautious, had photocopied William's map.

Raoul realised that if he found the treasure he had no legal claim to it, which was why he brought in Anne-Marie. As a Maguire, she was entitled to a share, although Raoul had no actual intention of allowing her to keep it. The ungrateful bitch! Instead of being as excited as he over it, Anne-Marie deliberately went behind his back in a spiteful attempt to thwart him. That's when Justin appeared. And, if that wasn't enough, Connor Maguire turned up shortly after that. Raoul felt his plans were unravelling but, always the opportunist, saw a way of searching for the treasure without actually lifting a finger himself.

Justin had said Anne-Marie had given him a copy of the map, and Connor Maguire obviously had some kind of evidence of the treasure because he didn't do anything by half. Raoul began to worry. Too many people knew. If Justin's map, or whatever it was in Maguire's possession fell into the wrong hands, there'd be even more people after the treasure. Raoul didn't like long odds.

It was easy enough to arrange the burglaries. The African was a Scylla mercenary who asked no questions and carried out orders to the letter. He'd come back empty-handed from Maguire's room but at least his attack on Parker had yielded the Englishman's map. Parker would be less independent and easier to control if he had to rely on Raoul's copy. Which fitted in perfectly with the rest of Raoul's plan. If his association with Justin were kept quiet, the Englishman could be dealt with if anything was found. That only left Connor Maguire and whatever evidence he had of the treasure. Maguire wouldn't waste too much time on trying to find it, he was a busy man with many commitments. With a bit of luck he'd leave Mauritius empty-handed.

Then everything started to go wrong. If only that idiot Parker hadn't kidnapped the Australian journalist on Rodrigues and revealed that he and Raoul were partners, all would have been well. Now he was dead so that little problem was solved. Which still left Maguire and the journalist.

Raoul realised he was now back to square one. No treasure, no partner, no money. And unless he got lucky soon, no mistress. Of the four, it was Song he couldn't live without.

Around five thirty, Holly and Connor set off for Grand Baie. An ointment bought from the local chemist had relieved the pain in Holly's hands but she knew it would be some days before they stopped being sore to touch. When Connor suggested that he have a look at Raoul's boat on his own, she wouldn't hear of it.

'Are you usually this stubborn?'

'Only when the need arises.'

'An early night would be better for you.'

'No it wouldn't. I'd be too worried about you to take advantage of it.'

'What I've got to do is illegal.'

'Nice try, Maguire.'

He'd thrown up his hands, accepting defeat.

Holly could see how keyed up he was. She hoped that, tonight, Connor would find a way to put the deaths of Emma and his stepbrother behind him. His need for retribution was not in question and she understood that if he failed in this attempt he would simply carry on until he found whatever it took to do it. His determination would bring success sooner or later.

They found a quiet place to eat. A small taverna in a side street. Only two other tables were occupied. After giving their order, Connor, looking uncharacteristically nervous, broached the subject of their return to Australia.

'Have you . . . um . . . any more overseas assignments lined up?'

'Not as far as I know. Why?'

'Would you take one?'

'It's what I do.'

'When we're married, will you continue working?'

Crunch time! 'Yes.'

He nodded. 'Thought so.'

'Will you?' Holly countered, a hint of challenge in her voice.

His dark eyes were amused. 'Not much slips past you, does it?'

She ducked her head. When she looked up again, both of them were smiling. 'Force of habit.'

'I like it. Kind of keeps me on my toes. You have rather a catchy combination of feminist independence and feminine dependence.'

'Watch your mouth, Maguire.'

His laugh was a deep chuckle of shared pleasure. Holly joined him. She had never felt so relaxed with, or attracted to, any man, not even Dennis. But the business of her job had to be thrashed out. Holly sensed that Connor, because of the experience with his first wife, might prove a shade over-possessive of her time. And while that was flattering, she knew herself well enough to realise that it could easily become a cause of friction. There was only one way around the problem. Strong, solid relationships were based on compromise from both sides.

'Will my working bother you?'

'How much time do you spend away from home?'

'On average, about four months a year.'

He was wrestling with that – she could almost hear the wheels turning.

'Of course,' Holly continued, 'assignments closer to home would be worth considering.' *Compromise number one.*

He shook his head. 'I couldn't do that to you, Holly. You have to go where the job takes you. Anything else would be frustrating.'

Jones one, Maguire one. 'Are you sure you won't mind?'

Connor thought about it. 'I'll try not to. I'll miss you, though. It's the best I can do.'

'There is one other possibility.' *Not really a compromise. A closely held dream more like.*

He was waiting for her to continue.

'Well . . .' She'd never voiced this ambition to another living soul, not even Quinn. 'I've always wanted to try and write a book.' Holly half-expected him to laugh.

He didn't. 'What sort of book?'

'Fiction. Historical. An Australian-American theme. Adventure-romance.'

'That's a fairly crowded area.'

'I know. But I've got this idea.'

Before she could stop herself, she was telling him. For years, Holly had kept the storyline in her head. The book would be set in the late-eighteen, early-nineteen hundreds and be loosely based on a little known fact that Herbert Hoover, President of the United States from 1929 to 1933, had spent considerable time in Australia between 1897 and 1907 working in various managerial positions in the goldfields in Western Australia. That fact alone was interesting enough but what was not generally known was that Hoover's university qualifications as a mining engineer were questionable, that his job with the London-based firm of Bewick Moreing & Company as a mining surveyor had been secured with largely falsified credentials and that, once in Australia, Hoover proved to have a cavalier approach to shareholders' money – to the tune of eight hundred thousand pounds.

'He became a partner in Bewick Moreing,' Holly told Connor, 'by substituting his name on a deed of trust in a merger with a large Chinese mining company. If I use these facts and throw in a lot of fiction, the story should virtually write itself.'

'Would you make Hoover your central character?' Connor asked, showing a great deal of interest.

'No, but he could flit through the pages as one of the bad guys. He had a raging affair with a Kalgoorlie barmaid,' Holly added. 'I thought of writing the story from her perspective.'

'You'll have to do a hell of a lot of research.' Connor reached over the table and carefully picked up both her hands. 'Will it be enough for you?'

'More than enough. I'm not saying I'll be any good at it, and I confess to never thinking I'd have the chance. It would mean at least a couple of years without an income and with no guarantee of success once the book is written.'

'The money's not a problem, you know that.'

Holly looked uncomfortable.

'I'm rich, Holly. Get used to it.'

'It's just that . . .'

'You're used to being self-reliant?'

'Something like that,' she admitted.

'I'll take it out of your hide if it makes you feel any better.' He grinned. 'Forget the money. Convince me it's what you want to do.'

'Okay. I've always been fascinated by our history, and especially by some of the more colourful characters who danced through those times. Herbert Hoover was a con man with no qualifications and yet he went on to become President of the United States. Tie those facts in with the rollicking days of the Australian goldfields, a saucy barmaid, and God knows what my imagination can come up with and I believe I've got a story. And I love to write. It would solve the separation problem and I'd find it challenging.' She flashed a wicked grin. 'I might even consider a child or two between books.'

Connor's earlier tension seemed to have disappeared. His eyes lit up. 'More than one? Book, I mean.'

'Hell, no! I'm on a roll here. Both.'

His thumbs rubbed the backs of her hands and he turned them over to examine the palms. Soft red skin covered the burst blisters. He raised one hand, then the other, and gently kissed each in turn. 'If anyone can do it, you can.'

God how she loved him! 'Thank you. Um . . . Connor . . . this support of yours . . .'

He was way ahead of her. 'Guilty. I'd be behind you anyway but the thought of having you at home is rather appealing.'

'I hate to tell you this but I'm not exactly little woman material. The stove, kitchen sink and I have never hit it off terribly well.'

'How about computers?'

'Computers are good. I can do computers.'

'That'll do me. We can always eat out.' He was silent for a moment. 'Are you really sure of this, Holly? I don't want any thoughts of giving up your career just to please me. Am I harassing you?'

'Wrong word, Maguire.'

'What do you mean?'

'Harassment is making someone do something they don't *wish* to do.'

He grinned. 'I love you, Jones.'

'Good,' she said softly. 'I'd hate to think I was all alone in my new-found euphoria.'

It was nine thirty by the time they left the taverna. Grand Baie, at that hour on a Wednesday evening, was virtually deserted. Locals had, long ago, gone home to bed and most holiday-makers were ensconced in the luxury of their five-star hotels. The pounding beat of *sega* dance music carried clearly across the water. Tourist resorts were lit up like Christmas trees but few lights shone from residential areas on the far side. Out in the middle, where Raoul's boat rode on its mooring, was a black hole.

Leaving the commercial sector behind, Connor drove around the bay. Many Mauritians who owned private houses used them only as weekenders. Almost all had a boat of some kind. Connor was looking for a dinghy to borrow for an hour or so.

It was almost a case of 'take your pick', except that the prudent owners seemed to keep their oars under lock and key. Eventually they found a small pirogue that had a single paddle.

Dark cumulus clouds scudded across the night sky, breaking up the moonlight. There was a smell of rain in the air. The light breeze carried an uncomfortable chill. If it rained, they had no protection and would quickly become very cold. Having waded out to the boat, they were already wet to the waist.

'Ready?' Connor whispered.

'Yep.'

Connor held the boat while Holly climbed in then pushed it out a little further and jumped in himself. With only one paddle coordinating their movement, it was not easy. Connor sat at the back with the oar, paddling canoe style. The pirogue was bulky enough to make this method difficult but it was the best he could do. Holly, in an effort to help, leaned over the front and tried to paddle with her hands. She quickly found out that while the healing properties of sea water were not in question, the salt penetrating her blisters caused the wounds to sting painfully.

Nothing stirred, save for the incessant snapping of halyards in the light wind. Yachts of all shapes and sizes – cabin cruisers, commercial charter and game fishing boats – had the bay to themselves at night, with nothing better to do than swing lazily on their moorings. More than once, Connor had to quickly change course as yet another shape loomed up out of the darkness. And when clouds covered the moon, visibility was reduced to next to nothing. 'See the big spotlight over there?' he asked quietly.

'I see it.'

'Raoul's boat is about halfway across. We have

to keep a direct line between it and that red warning beacon behind us.'

Progress was slow. For a while, Holly thought they were getting nowhere. It was a constant battle to stay on course. The incoming tide wanted to push them sideways. After half-an-hour, Connor said, 'We must be nearly there by now.'

Holly had been thinking the same thing.

A break in the clouds allowed the half moon to shine freely for a moment. Connor stopped paddling and looked around. There were boats all round them but Raoul Dulac's had gone.

Holly heard Connor's intake of breath. 'Damn! It was here earlier, I saw it as we drove through Grand Baie.'

The night sky closed in again and, at that moment, the threatening rain made good its promise. Helpless to protect themselves, Holly and Connor were engulfed in a sudden squall. The rain hissed down, brief in duration but long on ferocity, soaking them within seconds. To make their predicament worse, the wind picked up.

Cyclone Yvette, far out in the Indian Ocean, had sent her first long-distance message. Short and sharp, it heralded the coming of rough seas. Their trip back did not take as long – the tide helped – but by the time they had secured the pirogue, both were shaking with cold.

Removing shoes, socks and jeans, they made the return journey to Flic-en-Flac semi-clothed with the car heater on full bore. It was better than freezing to death, though Holly did wonder what the police would make of them in the event of an accident.

Once her teeth had stopped chattering, Holly's thoughts turned to the whereabouts of Raoul's boat. 'He'd know about Justin by now, Anne-Marie would have told him. Perhaps he's been able to find out where it happened. If that's the case, he could well be anchored in the deep water off Flic-en-Flac tomorrow morning.'

It was the first thing they checked the next day. Sure enough, Raoul's boat was just where they thought it might be. Both Holly and Connor made the mistake of assuming that Raoul himself had brought it there. The sleek, game fishing Chris Craft appeared to be deserted. 'He'll be at the falls by now,' Connor guessed.

'Perhaps he won't be able to reach the bottom.'

'Raoul will find a way. He'll recognise the shape, just as you did. There'll be no stopping him now. I've got to put a spanner in that particular works.' Connor was dressing for his meeting with Liang Song. 'Are you coming up to Port Louis with me?'

'I've had about as much as I can stand of that woman. I'll stay here.'

He took her in his arms. 'Right here please. No wandering off. You have a tendency to get into trouble. Promise?'

'I promise.' She had her fingers crossed. With Raoul Dulac looking for treasure a good ten kilometres away there seemed to be no harm in taking a little swim.

'When I come back we'll go and sign those statements in Curepipe,' Connor said. 'I shouldn't be too long.'

Sham floated in and out of a drug-induced sleep. Over the past two days people had come and gone. Sometimes he woke alone in his room. At other times, the detective knew that someone sat quietly by his bedside. With both eyes still bandaged, his hearing and sense of smell had quickly compensated for the absence of vision. At around eleven o'clock, he became aware that a colleague from the Curepipe district – Rafe Jolliffe – was there and reading a newspaper. Sham recognised his aftershave. He was willing to bet that Rafe was studying the racing form section. 'What day is it?' he croaked.

'Thursday. You've been out of it since Tuesday.'

'What happened?' As yet, he had no memory of the accident.

'Could have been a puncture but from the looks of things, I'd say you were run off the road.'

The temptation to sink back into sleep was almost overwhelming but Sham realised he had to remember something important. Recollections came tantalisingly close, only to fade into the background. It was there, just out of reach. 'Where?'

'Near Flic-en-Flac. What were you doing down there?'

He had no idea. His last clear recollection was of having breakfast with his wife. 'I don't know. Mon dieu! If only I could think straight.'

'Take your time. You're lucky to be alive. The car's a write-off.'

Sham groaned as pain pushed through the intravenously administered analgesic. They had not told him how badly he'd been injured but he was under no illusions that the word *superficial* applied to him. He didn't wish to think about it. 'What's happening? Who's handling my case load?'

'It's being shared by a couple of stations. I've got one or two.'

'Who's doing the Vitry case?' At least his memory hadn't completely packed up.

'Me.'

A scrap of something dallied fleetingly in Sham's tired mind. It didn't leave a calling card and he was unable to capture it.

'I haven't had a chance to open the file. A tourist fell down the Tamarin Falls yesterday. I've been flat out with the paperwork on that one. That's why I'm here, actually. An Australian journalist who happened to be on the scene says you can vouch for her. Holly Jones. Mean anything to you? I'd like to eliminate the girl and her companion from the inquiry.'

And the thing Sham had been trying to remember with such little success came hammering back. Holly Jones. The Merville. Guy Dulac. Blue Porsche. Flic-en-Flac. Cane fields. 'Dulac,' he gasped, aware that the memory might fade again.

'Guy Dulac. He was following them. Deliberately ran me off the road.'

'Okay, calm down. We'll bring him in for questioning.'

'He killed the Vitry girl, I'm sure of it. No proof,' Sham was gabbling, desperate to make his point. 'Holly Jones could be next. You must –'

'Take it easy, old friend.'

But Sham would not rest until he was sure his concerns were being taken seriously. 'She's in danger. Dulac knows where she is. You must warn her.' He groaned. 'I don't know where she was going.'

'I do. We got an address when I interviewed her. I'll get straight over there. Miss Jones will be fine.'

Sham had become quite agitated. He reached out a shaking, searching hand, seeking contact with Jolliffe's arm, which he gripped tightly. 'She must be warned. Guy Dulac is an animal. He's extremely dangerous.'

'I'm on my way. You rest easy. I'll come back tomorrow.'

Sham's grip loosened and his hand dropped. The effort had cost what little energy he had. 'Arrest Dulac,' he mumbled. 'Don't let him get anywhere near the girl.' His eyes closed. Sham was once again in the warm embrace of medication.

Guy Dulac knew the waters round Mauritius like the back of his hand. Even at night and despite the unpredictable weather, negotiating the deep water channel from Grand Baie out through the reef to

517

the open sea presented no problem. Knowing how far out he needed to be for a clear run down the west coast, avoiding the bulge below Port Louis, not to mention the watchful eyes of the coast-guard, was child's play. Picking up the Flic-en-Flac repeater beacon on his radio, Guy easily manoeuvred the boat to a safe deep water mooring and dropped anchor. He grabbed a couple of hours' sleep and before first light, rowed ashore.

The owner of the holiday apartments where Holly and Connor were staying was a friend of his father. Not bothered by the early hour, Guy roused the man and booked a bed-sitter. Behind net curtains, he watched and waited. At nine, he saw Connor Maguire leaving on his own. There was no sign of Holly. At five to eleven, he caught sight of her heading for the beach. She dropped her towel and waded straight into the water. It took several minutes for Guy Dulac to realise that she was swimming towards his father's boat. He watched as she battled the rising swell, eventually reaching the vessel and clambering onto the aft duckboards. She immediately disappeared into the cabin.

'What the hell is she up to?' he muttered in absolute disbelief. He hadn't expected Holly to make it easy for him. Leaving the room, he quickly crossed to the beach and rowed out towards the boat.

Shivering slightly in the cool wind, Holly tried the cabin door and found it unlocked. She was not concerned about wet footprints. By the time Raoul returned, evidence of her presence should have dried. Holly allowed herself a few minutes to recover. Her swim had been more difficult than it looked. The sea ran a swell big enough to require all her energy and she was quite exhausted. Compared with yesterday's serenity, she might well have been in a different country.

Only one locker was padlocked. Holly located a skewer, knife and screwdriver. With a surprising lack of conscience, and in very little time, she had picked the lock. 'So sue me!' Connor's words seemed appropriate. Inside the varnished teak cupboard lay a single white plastic envelope. Holly didn't bother to open it. Embossed on it was the word *waterproof*. She checked it carefully. It looked airtight.

Under normal weather conditions she'd have been able to paddle back to the beach keeping the envelope reasonably dry. No such luck today. Hoping the manufacturers knew what they were talking about, she pushed it down the front of her one-piece swimsuit, making sure it was secure and its hard edges caused the least discomfort. With a quick peek into several other lockers, and a last look around the cabin, she went on deck.

Guy Dulac, stepping lightly over the transom, was the last person on earth she expected to see. She gave a little scream of fright.

'Stealing the cookies?' He smiled nastily. 'I wouldn't have expected that of you.'

Holly stood frozen to the spot, her heart hammering wildly. Caught stealing was nothing compared to the person who had discovered her doing it.

'Nothing to say in your defence?' He moved towards her. 'Now I wonder what you've got hidden down there. It might be fun to find out.'

The boat's deck was heaving in the rolling swell. Guy staggered back slightly to find his footing and Holly acted instinctively. She made a desperate dive over the side, catching her foot painfully on the railing. It was a clumsy action and she sank deeply before rising to break the surface. She struck out frantically, swimming for the beach. But Holly was out of condition and already weakened by the effort it took to reach the boat. Guy Dulac was as strong as an ox. He caught up with her easily, his strong hands on her shoulders forcing her under. Holly struggled wildly. Just as she thought her lungs would burst, the pressure eased. She broke the surface gasping for air, having just enough time to register Guy's grinning face close to hers before being pushed under again. Losing strength, head buzzing from lack of oxygen, Holly knew there would only be one more chance. Struggling for air, she brought a knee up, aiming for his crotch.

He sensed it coming, turning slightly, and Holly's last attempt to escape made contact with his leg. It was not a painful blow, though it would have been enough to get away had it reached her intended target. With no hesitation, Guy Dulac punched Holly square on the chin, knocking her unconscious.

At around eleven fifteen, just as Detective Sham finally remembered what it was that had been bothering him, Guy Dulac started the engines and headed out to sea.

Just after midday, Connor returned to Flic-en-Flac, found Holly's towel on the beach and registered the fact that Raoul's boat had gone.

At twelve twenty, Rafe Jolliffe, impressed by the urgency of Sham's concern, arrived to warn Holly about Guy. He encountered Connor returning from a search of the beach. Connor's concern over Raoul Dulac's missing boat was justifiable, but for reasons much more sinister than he had at first thought.

At twelve fifty, after a short telephone conversation with Raoul at his home, the detective instigated a land and sea search for Holly Jones. A police bulletin went out that Guy Dulac was wanted for the attempted murder of a police officer and the abduction of a tourist.

Not prepared to sit around and wait, and very afraid for Holly's safety, Connor Maguire took his own initiative and went into action a little after one in the afternoon. He made a mad dash across the island to Mahébourg, hoping to find Kathleen Maguire. Her ability to predict events was all he had – a desperate hope that Kathleen might, just might, be able to save the woman he loved.

SEVENTEEN

When Holly regained consciousness, her confused mind thought she must be having a nightmare. But that illusion was quickly shattered. The bunk on which she lay bucked and rolled crazily, throwing her from side to side. They were under power but the building seas seemed to be in charge, tossing them from one wave to the next. Each time the hull slapped hard into a trough, the boat would fight and shudder its way to the next crest before dropping, with a sickening lurch, down again. Waves crashed over the bow and the twin 200 hp Cummins diesel engines screamed in over-revved objection whenever the matched bronze propellers cleared water. The stern swung and sashayed over the sea like an ambling elephant's rump.

Holly raised trembling fingers to her face. They came away sticky with blood. The pain in her jaw was so intense she thought it might be broken. Her head throbbed, ribs ached and both blistered hands were bleeding again. She tried to sit up but the effort hurt too much. She was very frightened.

Cyclone Yvette, having gathered itself for a

furious five-day romp around the Indian Ocean, was in its third day. Larger than usual waves, which danced in support, would not unduly affect the sandy white beaches that were well protected by the coral reef. The shallower waters might churn and heave but that was to be expected. Cyclone-experienced Mauritians barely raised a ripple of interest over Yvette. Meteorologists had issued a Class 1 warning – one red flag raised on all government buildings. The cyclone's position and strength were reported on radio and television, but otherwise, aside from special nautical bulletins for those still at sea, it was business as usual. With very few exceptions, pleasure craft and fishing trawlers battened down their hatches and sought safety close in to shore. As cyclones went, the effect of Yvette was disruptive but not worrying. Nevertheless, no-one was prepared to compromise when it came to the safety of anything afloat. Cyclones were known to be notoriously unpredictable.

Guy Dulac was not thinking about the boat. In a kind of mad euphoric surge, he was pitting himself and the vessel against the seas. Having flung Holly onto a bunk, giving no thought to her condition, he popped a couple of amphetamines, pulled up anchor and headed due west away from land. By the time any sane person would have realised that the sea was getting dangerously rough, Guy had become drunk on its challenge. Fighting each wave, legs astride for balance, head flung back, he held an insane belief in his own invincibility. Nothing – not the sea, not the law – could touch him. Laughing, sexually aroused, strength flooding his limbs, Guy dared the elements to take him on.

The Australian girl could wait. She would be his reward, to be savoured at leisure, when his blood cooled from the adrenaline rush which he knew so well, this man-thing, this need to prove himself to himself.

Kathleen Maguire had woken that morning with a distinct feeling of disquiet, a sensation that she could best liken to a form of seasickness. She could see the red flags were up and had heard about Yvette on the radio. The air felt sluggish, almost heavy, the eastern sky dark, laden with moisture. Cyclonic, without doubt. Kathleen put the feeling of nausea down to inclement weather and went about her morning ablutions and prayers.

The fee-paying primary school where she taught was part of the convent. Kathleen was on playground duty and then had three consecutive periods of teaching. Engrossed in her work, by nine thirty, whatever malady was afflicting her had subsided. At eleven she was in the staffroom enjoying tea and a brief break. As Kathleen bit into a delicious, home-baked shortbread biscuit, she experienced a sudden shocking pain in her jaw. One hand flew up and pressed hard against it.

'Whatever is wrong, my dear?' one of the other nuns asked, concerned by the look of anguish on Kathleen's face.

'Tooth,' she mumbled into her hand. After the

first raw agony passed it was replaced by a numbing ache.

'You'd better see the dentist.'

There was certainly no way to teach in this condition. She could barely open her mouth. Kathleen had never known such discomfort. The nun's face lost all colour and beads of perspiration burst out on her forehead.

'Sister Kathleen, you look dreadful. Go and lie down. I'll see if Dr Kenny is available.'

The semi-retired dentist who took care of the nuns' dental requirements at a suitably reduced rate was not inclined to make house calls. 'Give her some aspirin. If she's no better in the morning, tell her to come and see me. Sounds like an abscess.'

Kathleen retired to bed with a hot-water bottle, two aspirin, and a growing suspicion that her so-called abscess was shaping up as one humdinger of a premonition. She couldn't hurry it. The best thing to do was lie quietly and see what else came to her.

Connor Maguire made it across the island in record time, arriving at the convent just before two o'clock. Permission to see Kathleen was denied on the grounds that she was unwell. With no time to waste pleading his case, Connor went walkabout within the convent grounds. It was not difficult to find the nuns' dormitory wing. The heavy wooden door stood open and he slipped inside praying no-one would notice. He assumed, rightly as it turned out, that the nuns' residential quarters would be deserted at this hour by all but the ailing. He found Kathleen's name halfway down the passage.

By now, Sister Maguire had developed several other symptoms. The feeling of nausea persisted and she was freezing. Every time Kathleen closed her eyes, the room turned into a roller-coaster. It hurt to breathe, her heart was pounding and her mouth was dry. She took one look at Connor's face in the doorway and knew, with sudden clarity, that he, or something connected with him, was linked to her mysterious malaise.

'It's Holly,' he told her tersely. 'She's missing. Guy Dulac's taken her.'

Kathleen's heart skipped a beat as Connor's fear communicated itself to her. 'Sit down.'

He did, and jumped straight up again. 'Can you help?'

'Yes, I think so. But you must calm down. You've brought a lot of nervous energy into the room.'

Connor returned to the single chair.

'I know it's difficult,' Kathleen said gently. 'I'll need a minute or two to put it together.'

He nodded, bit at a fingernail, then stared at her with hopeful eyes.

Kathleen closed her own. *The pain in her jaw? A blow of some kind?* 'Your friend has been hurt,' she said slowly. 'Here.' Kathleen tapped her jaw. 'It was sudden, unexpected. Perhaps a punch.'

Connor let out a low groan of despair.

Sick. Cold. Room spinning. The sea? It must be the sea. 'She's in a boat. It's out beyond the reef I think.' *Why did it hurt to breathe?* 'She might be tied up or injured. It hurts her to breathe.' Kathleen's eyes opened. 'I'm sorry. That's all I'm getting.'

Hurts to breathe. Holly's ribs. She'd have put up a fight. Connor knew Kathleen was on the right track. 'Is she alive?' he asked, fearing the answer.

'Oh yes. Most definitely. If she weren't I wouldn't be getting these signals. But she fears a great evil. She is in terrible danger.'

'I must get to a telephone.' Connor was on his feet. 'Speak to the police.'

The amphetamines wore off slowly. By the time they did, Guy had taken his father's boat further out to sea than he'd ever been before. Mauritius was well over the horizon. With the adrenaline-pumping drugs abating, Guy Dulac began to feel fear. He had never seen such big seas. They had to come around, get back to land. But how? Turning broadside to the weather would be suicide. Cutting back on the throttle was no good. He had to keep the boat's momentum, stay bow on to the waves. What if he increased the revs and turned under full power? It was worth a try.

Guy watched for a pattern in the chaos. Three big waves, one not so big, three big, one not so big, three big. *Now.* He spun the wheel and pushed forward on both throttles. The boat almost capsized as it shot forward along a climbing wall of water, slid over the crest and rolled in the opposite direction. *She's turning. Come on, you bitch! Bite. Three big ones coming. Come on, come on!*

The first wave caught the stern three-quarters on. They were still turning. It carried them forward, bow down, and threatened to tumble the boat in a terrifying pitch pole. Guy managed to bring the wheel amidships before both propellers cleared water. He eased off on power as the boat literally tipped backwards into the trough. He had only a few seconds. He nudged the throttles forward and they were fully about before the next wave hit.

Guy headed for home. He had no idea how far they'd travelled. Fuel was not a problem. The tanks had been filled in Grand Baie, 2500 litres of diesel, giving a cruising range of almost fifteen hundred kilometres. Under normal conditions Guy would expect to burn around 50 litres of fuel an hour.

It was of some surprise therefore when he noticed that the main tank was registering less than a quarter of its capacity. He switched briefly to the reserve and nodded as the gauge swung to full. At least now, going with the swell, they wouldn't be using as much.

What was he going to do with the girl? Originally, he'd planned to drop anchor somewhere on the leeward side of the half dozen or so uninhabited islands that lay just to the north of Mauritius itself. In this weather, that was out of the question. It might be best to dump the bitch overboard here and now. If he took her back she'd probably lay a charge of assault and abduction against him. The more he thought about it, the more sense it made.

'You awake yet?' he yelled down into the cabin.

Holly was more terrified than at any other time in her life. She didn't know which was worse, the dull ache in her head or the throbbing pain in both hands as she clung to the sides of the bunk in a cabin that smashed from side to side, rising and falling with each wave.

She knew the boat had turned. The crashing, thumping, jarring journey had changed, but only in so much as, at the crest of each wave there was a brief sensation of flying. In some ways, it was more frightening, less under control. There was a strong engine smell in the cabin. Holly had to get up on deck, breathe some fresh air, see what was happening. Ignoring Guy's shouted question, she rose unsteadily from the bunk. Water sloshed around her feet. About five centimetres of oily liquid covered the cabin floor. Through two small portholes her view was of a surging, plunging, wild world of dark grey sea. Holly was so busy trying to stay on her feet that she gave it only a passing glance.

She noticed something lying in a fold of the blanket and picked it up. It was a thin gold link bracelet with an engraved, heart-shaped locket attached to the fastening clip. The clasp was broken, its link pulled open. She didn't know what made her do it – some kind of instinct. Holly forced the gold ring closed and put the bracelet on her arm. She had no idea of its significance, but somehow sensed that it was important. Then she made her way unsteadily up to the main cabin.

'Nice of you to join me.' Guy did not look at her. His concentration was on the heaving ocean.

Holly paid him no attention. Hanging on to the table just to stay upright, she stared around them with horror. Walls of water in every direction. Her legs threatened to give way. As the boat slid sickeningly down another wave, she suddenly felt nausea rise and scrambled to reach the aft well deck. Outside, Holly grabbed the port rail and hung on as they plunged into the next trough.

At that precise moment, the bow slammed into something very solid.

The two tonne, six metre long container had been damaged when it tore free of its stacking on board the container ship *Lady Elise,* and it was taking water ever so slowly. For three days it had floated, sinking lower and lower into the water until only one corner protruded about a metre above the surface. Borne by the ocean, a slave to the forces of Yvette, it was headed for Mauritius. Guy Dulac had no warning. The container's solid steel twist-lock mounting sliced through the bow with ease. The sudden impact lifted Guy from his feet and flung him forward onto the wheel, his forehead smashing into the brass compass binnacle.

Holly was catapulted over the side and into the water.

Neither of them, therefore, had the slightest idea of the sequence of events that followed the collision.

If his senses had not been dulled in the wake of a drug-induced high, Guy would have investigated the low fuel reading for the main tank and found a ruptured line had flooded the bilges and caused a dangerous accumulation of diesel fumes in the engine compartment.

That was also where the boat's rack of heavy duty batteries was to be found.

When Guy last checked them, it had been necessary for him to remove a build-up of accumulated corrosion on the terminals. Typically, he had not replaced the wooden lid. An adjustable spanner, which was always used to work on the batteries, hung from a hook on the bulkhead beside them. On impact with the container it fell free, bounced once, and slid forward to form a bridge across two very clean connections of opposing polarity.

The resultant spark found favour with the airborne diesel fumes and a sheet of flame ripped through the bilges from one end of the boat to the other. Not surprisingly, this ignited the split fuel which floated there on a liquid bed of sea water.

Unconscious, Guy Dulac felt nothing when the spontaneous combustion lifted his father's boat out of the water. The Chris Craft, and its only occupant, were reduced to smithereens within five seconds of hitting the container.

Holly, who had just fought her way back to the surface, was struck by flying debris. She had enough presence of mind to duck dive and stay down for as long as she could before the need for air forced her up again. The sea close by seemed to be on fire. Of the boat, there was no sign. A couple of flaming planks of wood and some random flotsam was all that remained. The collision and explosion had not damaged the container. She could see it now, wallowing in the water. With a cut forehead adding to her already woeful condition, Holly knew her only chance was to reach it. The swell bore her to a dizzying height. Shutting her mind to everything but that one desperate hope, Holly swam as she had never done before. The container was only twenty metres away but, in the deep swell, it took almost half an hour to get there. By the time she did, Holly had reached the limit of her endurance.

Detective Rafe Jolliffe was dedicated, persistent, methodical and cautious. Taking spur-of-the-moment decisions was not his style. The girl's life was in danger, of that he had no doubt, but no-one, not even Guy Dulac, would be mad enough to put out to sea in these conditions. That the boat had disappeared was, in his opinion, an indication that the Dulac boy would be seeking shelter further along the coast. There were any number of places he could be. So when Connor Maguire made contact and said he believed the Jones girl was somewhere in the open sea, the detective did not take him seriously, especially since, when pushed, Maguire admitted that his information came from a psychic nun.

Frustrated, Connor telephoned the Royal Palm Hotel to try and book one of their helicopters.

They were grounded because of the weather. In desperation, he drove to the airport. After a considerable delay, an argument over safety and some outright bribery, one pilot agreed to take Connor up for an hour's sightseeing. By the time they were finally airborne only eighty minutes of daylight remained. *I'm coming, baby. Hold on.*

By straddling the corner and holding onto the lifting lug apertures, Holly had found a measure of safety. It wasn't much. The steel box rode the swell like a wallowing whale, sometimes plunging the exposed tip almost under water. At other times waves broke over it, blinding her with salty spray. Holly had no idea which way they were drifting – it would make no difference even if she did.

How long she floated, clinging to the container, was impossible to tell. Her arms and legs were numb, shoulders and thighs ached with cramp and twice she'd fought off the deepest desire to shut her eyes and simply let go. Whenever possible, as she rode high on a crest, Holly searched the horizon for any sight of land. She saw nothing but the grey surge of water in every direction. The stiff plastic envelope was still down the front of her swimsuit. Holly had forgotten about it until now. So much had happened because of its probable contents, but one sharp corner had pierced her skin and with each roll of the container, the stabbing pain became worse. Holly, somehow, had to get rid of the envelope. 'Dear God,' she prayed. 'Let someone find me.'

As soon as they were airborne, Connor dropped his bombshell.

'You want to go where?' The pilot was stunned by his apparent change of plans. 'No way. There's nothing out there but water.'

'I'll double the rate we agreed,' Connor snapped. 'Let's go.'

The pilot shrugged. It'd be a bit rough but not dangerous. Give the punters what they want. It was no skin off his nose. The man was obviously mad. 'It's a big ocean. Which way?'

Connor was operating on adrenaline, hope and an educated guess. 'North-west from Flic-en-Flac.'

They flew across the island and out over the ocean. As they went, Connor, who needed the pilot's full cooperation and experience, told him the relevant facts. It quickly became clear that his passenger was genuine, and at the mention of Guy Dulac's name, what started out as a bizarre joy-ride turned into an all-out race against time. But, from the sky, the sheer size of their search was daunting.

'We must work a pattern,' Connor told the pilot.

'What time did the boat leave Flic-en-Flac?'

'I'm not sure. Some time between nine and midday.'

The pilot did some calculations. 'Righto! We'll try a bit further west.'

Ten minutes later they had still seen nothing. 'We've only got another half-hour. After that, it'll be too dark to see.'

'Just keep looking.' Connor's voice was terse. He was staring down at the ocean, his eyes searching for anything at all.

They banked for a sweep further west and, at that moment, Connor caught sight of something white. 'There.' He pointed. 'See that? Let's take a closer look.'

The pilot hadn't seen it but obligingly changed course and took the helicopter lower.

'Good God, it's her,' Connor shouted. If Holly hadn't been holding the white plastic envelope he'd have missed her completely. Even knowing where she was it was almost impossible to make her out against the slate-grey sea. 'Take it down.'

'Are you crazy? Look at the size of those waves. We're too low as it is.'

'Radio for help.'

Before he could stop him, the pilot watched in amazement as Connor unstrapped his safety harness and rolled backwards through the open door.

Holly was exhausted, in pain and terrified. Twice she had nearly been washed off the slowly sinking container. She had neither seen nor heard the helicopter, but suddenly became aware that the sea, in addition to its heaving swell, was being churned up by some unseen force. Hanging on with one hand, Holly had removed the envelope only to find that, without it, her ribs had no buffer against the container. Though not much protection, it was better than none. The flash of white that caught Connor's attention was Holly's attempt to position the envelope where it would do most good. In doing so, she nearly lost her balance and flung out the hand gripping the envelope.

She was in dreadful shape. She had swallowed a lot of water. Numb with cold, the feeling in her fingers had largely gone. It was only a matter of time before the container slipped away from her. Nearly blinded by salt water, sick to her stomach, fear and pain had been replaced by a dream-like sense of the inevitable. Holly wasn't far from unconsciousness, knew it, and had lost the ability to care.

When Connor swam up and grabbed her ankle, her first thought was that a shark had attacked. He had to shout twice before she realised what was happening. His face, blurred though recognisable, seemed unreal. She wanted to believe but didn't dare.

He pointed upwards and she saw the hovering helicopter. Two yellow objects fell from the open door and landed in the sea. 'Life jackets,' Connor shouted. 'Hang on, baby. I'll get them.'

Buoyed by the inflated support, Holly relinquished her tenuous hold on the container, allowing Connor to take over while she clung to him. The helicopter above turned so that they could see the pilot. He held up ten fingers, closed his hands, then another ten. 'Twenty minutes,'

Connor waved his understanding. 'Twenty minutes, baby. Hold on.' He indicated the plastic envelope which she still clutched. 'What's this?'

'Scylla.' It was all she could manage.

If his face hadn't been wet from the sea she'd have seen tears of the deepest possible emotion.

Although the helicopter pilot also dropped a floating transmitter and light, he hadn't been strictly truthful with his indication of timing. Realising how exhausted the girl in the water must be, it was a ploy to give her hope. The coastguard took twice that long to reach them. By the time they did, it was pitch dark and Holly was unconscious. But Connor, holding her tightly, knew that nothing in this world could take her away from him.

Holly, if she had but known it, ended up in a hospital room just two doors from Sham. But like the policeman, she was warm and snug in the arms of pain-killing medication.

Surprisingly, after all she'd been through, her most serious condition was exhaustion. She was suffering from exposure but nothing too severe. Her jaw, though sore, had not been dislocated. Her ribs were merely cranky, and both hands, though tender, would recover fully. The cut in her forehead made by flying debris from the boat required no stitches, likewise the injury on her tummy. Both arms and legs were chafed and bruised but it was all superficial.

'A good night's sleep and some fluid replacement,' the doctor told Connor. 'Unless complications arise, she can go home tomorrow.'

Refusing to leave her side, Connor slept in a chair next to the bed. As dawn's first fingers of light crept into the room on Friday morning, Holly stirred, opened her eyes and saw him. He had a fierce five-o'clock shadow, his hair towel dried and not brushed, he was wearing a white hospital gown, and fatigue smudges coloured the skin around his eyes. She had never seen anything so beautiful in her life.

'Connor,' she croaked.

He was instantly awake. 'Baby?'

'Love you,' she mumbled.

He went to pick up one of her bandaged hands, thought better of it, tried to kiss her but stopped when he remembered her jaw and finally settled on a chaste brushing of lips in her hair. 'I love you too,' he whispered. 'More than I ever thought possible.'

She smiled weakly. 'So tired.'

'Go back to sleep, baby. I'll be here when you wake up.' He rose and went towards the door. 'I'll let the doctor know you're back with us.'

The hospital gown didn't quite meet at the back. She wanted to tell him but sleep engulfed her. As last sights went, however, at least this one guaranteed sweet dreams.

Later that day, Holly gave a statement to Rafe Jolliffe. Though still weak, she was anxious to leave hospital. Connor wanted her to stay another night but Holly had always had an aversion to hospital smells. Dressed and ready to leave, her impatience close to the surface, the policeman made it clear that nobody was going anywhere until he had every last detail.

Finally, Jolliffe closed his notepad.

'Can you let Sham know?' Holly asked.

'Come with me please.'

Holly and Connor followed, wondering what the detective was up to. He opened a door and ushered them inside. The man in the bed turned his bandaged head in their direction. 'Rafe?'

'How did you know?'

'Footsteps. Who else is there?'

Rafe Jolliffe drew Holly closer. 'I think you can tell him yourself.'

Holly stared at him. 'Hello Sham. What happened to you?' she finally managed.

'Miss Jones. Good to hear you. Had a little run-in with our mutual friend, Guy Dulac.'

'My God!'

'I'm pleased you're safe. I was worried he'd get to you.'

'He did. But not as much as he got to you.'

Sham flipped his good hand back and forth. 'I'll be okay. Then I'll go after him. What happened?'

Holly told him.

'Dead!' Regret was in Sham's voice. He shook his head slightly. 'The Vitry case, Rafe. What a way to close it.'

'Vitry?' Holly felt a surge of excitement.

'Corrine Vitry. It's more than likely that Guy Dulac murdered her.'

Holly held out her arm, realised the detective couldn't see it, and said, 'I found a bracelet on the boat. The initials CV are engraved on it.'

'Did you keep it?'

'Yes, it's here.'

Sham pulled impatiently at the bandages and raised one edge. 'Please.' He held out a hand and Holly passed the gold chain to him. The detective peered at it for a long time before handing it to Rafe and pulling the binding over his right eye back into place. He let out a shaky breath. 'Thank you.'

'Does it help?' Holly asked.

Jolliffe answered for Sham. 'It implicates him, that's all. Nothing can be proved now. But on Mauritius . . .' He shrugged. 'Let's just say this island thrives on gossip. You have done us a great service. Thank you. I hope, and I'm sure my friend here agrees, that it will help the girl's family.'

Sham nodded his bandaged head. 'I'd like to have seen Guy Dulac get life, not death. It would have been a greater punishment. Still,' he added with quiet satisfaction, 'the boy has paid dearly. We move on.'

'Wrong,' Jolliffe said. 'I move on. You stay right where you are.'

Sham grunted his annoyance. 'And you, Miss Jones? When do you leave?'

'Tomorrow.'

One shaking hand reached searchingly. Holly

took it in one of hers. Sham felt bandages and let it drop. 'Goodbye then. Please don't judge us by your experience.'

'I won't,' Holly promised warmly. 'I'll send you the article when it's published.'

Back at the apartment in Flic-en-Flac, Holly called her father. 'How was Réunion?' he asked.

'Um . . .'

'You know how much I hate that word.'

'I didn't get there.'

'Why not?'

'Um . . .' She threw a despairing look at Connor.

He gently took the receiver from her. 'Quinn? Connor Maguire. Holly's fine, just a little shaken. We'll be leaving here tomorrow. Arriving Sydney on Sunday. Our flight gets in from Melbourne at eleven fifty-five. I'll run Holly home. No, there's no need for that . . . You will? Okay, we'll see you at the airport.' He winked at Holly as Quinn's voice filled his ear. 'No, she's okay . . . well, pretty okay. I'll put her back on in a minute but first, ah . . . Quinn . . . sir. It's just that I'm going to marry her and I know I should have asked your permission but things got out of hand and . . . well, hell, Quinn, do you mind?' Connor listened for a while. 'Yes of course. Here she is.' He handed the receiver back to Holly.

Quinn was in full flight. She let him blow himself out.

'Finished yet?'

'Tell me everything.'

So she did. Well, nearly everything. Holly felt that her father could only take so much.

When she'd finished there was a long silence at the other end. 'Are you really okay, sweetheart?'

'I'm fine. Shaken but not stirred.'

'And the marriage thing?' This was the question he'd been dying to ask.

'Yep.'

'What's that supposed to mean?' Quinn's frustrated concern burst down the line. He yelled so loudly Holly had to jerk the phone from her ear.

'Do me a favour,' she said quietly, when it was safe to raise the receiver again, 'and don't shout. I've got a headache.'

'Put Maguire on.'

She did, and watched him listening for ages. Finally he spoke, 'I won't. I completely understand. I know, sir. They are. Okay, Quinn, sorry. Talk to you soon.' He hung up. 'Your father didn't want to talk to you again.'

'I don't believe he said that,' Holly had her arms folded, embarrassed and annoyed at the same time.

'Said what?' Connor's smile was slightly bemused. 'That he didn't want to speak to you?'

'Oh that.' She waved her hand dismissively. 'He was probably a bit emotional. No, the rest of it. You got the full fatherly thing, didn't you? If you hurt me he'd kill you. He said I was his little girl and he loved me very much. And then . . .' she choked back a laugh, 'and then he asked if your intentions were honourable.'

Connor nodded, grinning. 'You left something out.'

She thought for a moment. 'Sorry. Brain's not working properly.'

'He said rescuing you cut no ice with him since it was my fault his daughter was there in the first place.'

'That's not fair!'

Stepping forward, he kissed her very gently. 'It's okay, my baby. I'll take the flack for you on this occasion. Just don't make a habit of it.'

Holly leaned into him and kissed him back. 'I'm going to love you forever,' she whispered. 'Think you can handle it?'

'Yes,' he said huskily. 'I'm a big boy. I'll handle it just fine.'

If Holly thought the remainder of their time in Mauritius would be spent quietly, Connor soon put paid to that illusion. 'You know I'd do anything for you, don't you?'

She threw him a suspicious look.

'And you know I'm not letting you out of my sight again? Not ever.'

A distrustful frown appeared.

'And I wouldn't do anything in this world to hurt you?'

Hands on hips. 'Spit it out.'

He sighed. 'I really am going to have to work on some of your expressions.'

She waited.

'We have things to do.'

'We?'

'You can sleep in the car.'

Connor sported a kind of satisfied smile. It reminded Holly of a crocodile that had just spotted lunch. 'There are a few loose ends.'

'A few! From where I sit it looks more like a bowl of spaghetti.'

'I've made some calls, got things rolling. I know you probably don't feel up to it but we have to make tracks.'

'Where to?'

'Couple of places.'

He'd tell her when he was ready. 'Just one thing, Maguire, before you spring into action. You haven't explained how you found me.'

He looked slightly embarrassed. 'I don't think you're ready to hear it.'

'Try me.' Her eyes locked with his and he had nowhere to go.

'I went to Kathleen.'

Incredulity showed on her face.

'It was all I could think of,' he added. 'I was fielding one lot of bad news after another. You had disappeared. There'd been a warning that Guy Dulac knew where we were staying and then I hear that Raoul is still at home. Putting two and two together, I figured that you'd been taken by his son. When the police came up with nothing I was frantic enough to try anything.'

'She told you where I was?' Holly could hardly believe it possible.

'Kathleen said you'd been hurt and knew it was your jaw. She felt you were cold, frightened and in very rough sea. That's all I had to go on.'

Holly shuddered. It finally hit home just how lucky she'd been.

'If you hadn't been holding that white envelope we'd probably have missed you altogether. It was already getting dark. Even then it was hard to keep you in sight.'

'Did I say thank you?' she asked softly.

He pretended to think about it. 'Now you mention it, I don't believe you did.'

'Come here, Maguire.'

'Baby, everywhere on you hurts.'

One bandaged hand brushed his cheek. 'Find somewhere that doesn't.'

EIGHTEEN

'I'm sorry to do this to you,' Connor said as he helped her into the car. 'I know you'd be better off in bed. You look like hell.'

'Thanks, Maguire.' Holly knew how she looked. Her jaw was swollen and grazed, and bruising extending to one eye. The cut on her forehead was stained yellow with iodine. Both hands remained bandaged. And those were only the parts you could see. She walked awkwardly courtesy of the renewed pain in her ribs. The envelope cut, more itchy than sore, was a constant irritant. And, due to the difficulty of straddling the container in a sea from hell, Holly felt she'd spent a week on a very fat horse. 'I hope you're a patient man,' she said as they drove away from the apartment, 'because sex will be out of the question for a while.'

She heard him laugh quietly. 'Go for it, Jones! Straight to the heart.'

'Okay. If you insist.'

'Bad Holly.'

But her mind had gone off on a tangent. 'How did you get the car back?' As far as she knew, he'd left it at the airport.

'The pilot brought it to the hospital. He wanted to see how you were.'

'Nice man.'

'Very,' Connor agreed. 'When I tried to pay him he refused, said it was on the house.'

'Well, I don't suppose it's every day that his passenger throws himself into the sea. He'll dine out on that one for a while.'

'It's a bit more than that. Like the hospital staff and the police, he's embarrassed that a tourist could be treated so badly. Everyone is very anxious that your impression of Mauritius is not unduly tainted by Guy Dulac's behaviour.'

'They needn't worry.'

'It's not just because you're a journalist. Their concern is genuine.' He glanced at her. 'You've got a stubborn look on your face.'

'The article is already written.'

'What does that mean?'

'It means, I see no reason to change it.'

'Is that your polite way of telling me that you are the journalist around here and to mind my own bloody business and stop trying to tell you what to write?'

'Yes.'

'You've got it.'

Holly stifled a smile. Then she noticed that Connor was cutting across the island, well south of Port Louis. 'Where are we going?'

'Raoul Dulac's.'

'Are you crazy?'

'He probably won't be there. I told you I'd

made a few calls. There's some heavy-duty interest in dear Raoul. The stuff in that envelope
wasn't only about Scylla. He's been a busy man.'
Connor punched an imaginary hole in the air.
'Yesss! There *is* a God. The internal revenue boys
couldn't wait to have a word or two with our
friend. Don't worry about him, he's not the
reason we're going there. We're fetching
Anne-Marie.'

'Why?'

'She wants to meet her mother.'

The coldly arrogant French Mauritian and a
warm little Creole nun. Would it work? 'Is that a
good idea?'

'She's had a change of heart. Justin's death
affected her quite deeply. We spoke for a long time
earlier this morning. I felt I owed Kathleen something. There was no harm in trying. Anyway, after
a couple of false starts she listened. Seems that her
adopted parents only gave Anne-Marie half the
story. She'd always been told that Kathleen seduced
Raoul's father and then tried to blackmail the family when she fell pregnant. Anne-Marie grew up
believing that Kathleen deliberately produced a
Dulac child for nothing more than financial gain.'

'Did you tell her about Raoul?'

'I didn't need to. The truth came to light last
year. Anne-Marie overheard Raoul and his mother
discussing it. She went a little crazy for a while.'

Something in Connor's voice alerted Holly.
'The fire?'

'Yes. Arson was suspected, never proved.'

'That means she got away with murder. Are you *sure* meeting her mother is a good idea?'

'Anne-Marie never intended to kill anyone. She's genuinely sorry for that. She never got on with any of the family, in particular, Raoul. Learning the truth, that he was her father, and believing Kathleen had as good as sold her, tipped Anne-Marie over the edge. Technically it would be manslaughter rather than murder but, in my book, she's paid a high price for what she did. I'd like to help her find some peace of mind.'

'She's pretty set in her ways. Do you think that's possible?'

'With Kathleen's help.'

'And you can live with the knowledge that two people died because of her?'

'Yes.'

Holly thought in silence and concluded that she really wasn't qualified to judge. Her own upbringing had been so different from Anne-Marie's. She remembered vividly the day she found Dennis in bed with one of her so-called friends. If a suitable weapon had been handy at the time, she could not guarantee that either of them would still be breathing.

'Does that shock you?' Connor asked.

'No. But I had to think about it.'

'Good. I like having you on the same side.'

'Only because you don't have to work so hard.'

He ignored that. 'On my side, by my side. Which reminds me, I'm flying first class tomorrow. How about you?'

'You shit!'

'But I did take the liberty of upgrading your ticket. And watch your language.'

Holly grinned, then wished she hadn't. It hurt. 'Get used to it, Maguire.'

A dimple appeared.

She was watching his profile. Three weeks ago he was nothing more than a name, one she did not particularly like. Come to think of it, three weeks ago she had been little more than a shell – empty, aching, bitter and untrusting. Her work and his lifestyle had thrown them together. They had squabbled, traded insults and slowly learned to respect each other. They fought, made up, only to fight and make up all over again. They had faced danger together. He'd rescued her twice. In three short weeks she had come to love, trust and like the man.

Connor sensed her scrutiny. 'What?'

'Nothing. I was just wondering where Dennis went, that's all.'

He understood immediately. 'Sorry, can't help you there.'

She nodded, smiling slightly.

'I have a confession to make,' he said.

Holly waited.

'The treasure.'

'What about it?' She felt a rush of disappointment. Was he going to claim it after all?

'One way or another, Raoul will go after it. If he's in prison, and that's more than likely, he'll want some kind of insurance for the day he's released.

More than anything in this world, Holly, I don't want him to find it. Do you understand that?'

'Of course. But can we stop him?'

'It's already done. I've told Anne-Marie where to look. She's going to make sure Raoul doesn't get his hands on it.'

'How?'

'By uncovering it herself. Unless the authorities have some claim she'll donate half to Justin's mother and half to Kathleen's convent.'

Although Holly approved, she couldn't help thinking about Justin's mother and that damned feud. Half the value would only fuel the ancient family quarrel. On the other hand, the convent could do so much good with their share. 'I guess that balances it out,' she said finally.

'Win some, lose some,' Connor put to her. 'It's not a bad compromise.'

And Holly realised he was right. He'd done the decent thing. It was what she had come to expect of him. A lesser man would have been tempted to keep everything for himself. She leaned her head back, eyes closed. Tired and aching, Holly's strength was at a very low ebb. Yet, in her mind was a satisfying sense of peace, a feeling that all was right with the world.

'You okay, baby?'

She opened her eyes sleepily. 'Very much so.'

'You've had a pretty hectic three weeks. All because of me. Sorry.'

'You're forgiven.'

'I'll make it up to you. Promise.'

551

'And I'll hold you to that, Connor Maguire. Breakfast in bed, every Sunday.'

'My pleasure. What would you like?'

She smiled slowly.

'Behave, Jones!'

Holly decided she should, at least for now. She was in no shape to follow through. 'Have you laid your ghosts, Connor? The drug sting? Raoul?'

He nodded. 'All under control. Prison will nearly kill those two. They'll lose everything – money, possessions, position. I'm not a vengeful person, Holly, but Raoul and Liang Song deserve everything that comes their way.'

'Did Anne-Marie say anything about Guy?'

'She was okay but apparently Solange and Raoul took his death very badly. Surprising, isn't it? I never thought the Dulacs were that close.'

'They must have known what he was like.'

'I suppose so, considering his gene pool.'

Holly's exhausted mind had nearly shut down. 'There's no way Raoul can link any of this back to you, is there?'

'Not a chance. He'll be assuming the evidence went down with the boat. He's probably wondering who fingered him. The list of possibilities must be endless. Raoul's made a lot of enemies over the years.'

'How about the Triad?'

'It's amazing what you can do with a paper trail. Especially if it has the government's blessing. They'll find nothing to tie me in with the raid in Australia.'

Holly reached over and put a hand on his shoulder. 'Mission accomplished. What's next?'

'Haven't you had enough for one lifetime?'

She gave a lopsided grin. 'Come on, Maguire! You must have something up your sleeve.'

'Not a damned thing. Honest.'

She let her hand drop. Closing her eyes again, Holly murmured, 'How come I don't believe you?'

His fingers rested briefly on her leg. 'How does a month cruising the Mediterranean sound?'

'Bloody marvellous.'

She slept then, only waking when Connor cut the engine in front of the Dulacs' mansion. Anne-Marie must have been watching for them because she opened the front door almost immediately and ran down the steps. Connor leaned across and opened the back door for her.

'I'm so nervous,' she confessed. Then gave a gasp of horror as she took in Holly's face. 'Oh, my God. Did Guy do that? I'm so sorry.'

Holly couldn't help herself. First impressions of Anne-Marie had hardly been favourable. 'He was your half-brother.'

She was amazed to see tears spring from the Frenchwoman's eyes. 'I know. For most of my life I believed he was my nephew. Even so, I never liked him.'

'It's over,' Connor said. 'Put it behind you.'

He's right, Holly thought. It's hardly Anne-Marie's fault.

'Does Kathleen know we're coming?' Anne-Marie asked.

'She's expecting us.'

'How did . . . I mean, does she really want to see me?'

'Without doubt. She's waited a long time for this day.'

'You'll be fine,' Holly said gently. 'Just be yourself.'

'That's all right for you to say,' Anne-Marie replied with a touch of the old asperity, 'I've only just found out who I really am.'

Kathleen had chosen the derelict site of William Maguire's house to meet her daughter for the very first time. Holly waited in the car while Connor showed Anne-Marie where to go. When he returned there was a nice, soft smile on his face.

'It wasn't awkward at all,' he said. 'Kathleen held out her arms and Anne-Marie just fell into them.' He shook his head. 'What a hell of a long wait to hold your only child.'

'Come on.' Holly opened her door. 'I need a bit of time to absorb this place. We'll be gone tomorrow.'

Connor helped her out of the car. They stood together, shoulder to shoulder, leaning on the stone ramparts and saying nothing. Holly slipped an arm around Connor's waist. He placed one protectively across her shoulders. Out to sea, a grey expanse of mountainous waves boiled under an overcast sky for as far as the eye could see. Water pounded the reef, frothing, foaming white, shooting into the air before creaming over the coral. Wind plucked at their clothes, gusting so hard at times that Holly swayed with its force. The crystal-clear waters of Warwyck Bay had clouded with churning sand. Holly shivered and Connor's arm tightened around her.

Her thoughts were of William Maguire. No-one had forced him to become a pirate. His self-imposed exile couldn't have been easy but the wayward third son of Irish aristocracy who had plundered, raped and killed throughout the Sea of Zanj had undoubtedly left his mark. Not only his treasure. Also his seed. Holly wondered what the one-time corsair might have thought if he'd known that the reverberations of his life were still being felt 250 years after he departed this world.

Connor had been thinking of the pirate too. 'You know,' he said softly, turning Holly to face him, 'if it hadn't been for William I might never have met you.'

She lay a cheek against his chest. 'I don't know about that.' Connor breathed into her hair. 'I think Kathleen's fate theory would have seen to it that we'd have managed it somehow.'

Half-an-hour later, a quietly delighted Kathleen and an emotional Anne-Marie returned, arm-in-arm. 'I wonder if I could come with you?' Kathleen asked. 'Anne-Marie is going to pack her things and move to Mahébourg. We'll drive back in her car.'

'Where will you stay? Surely not at the convent?'

'No. My brother, Thomas, has quite a large house. I'm sure he won't mind. I'll be taking some time off to help Anne-Marie recover William's treasure.' She smiled at Connor and Holly. 'I could see this happening between you two. It was meant to be.'

'You said we'd meet one more time. Is this it?' Holly asked.

'Yes.' Kathleen's eyes roved carefully over Holly's injured face. 'It's finished. You have no more need of fear. There is nothing but happiness in your future.'

'To be perfectly honest, I never quite believed that sixth sense of yours. Now I owe my life to it. Thank you.'

'Tell your children about it one day.'

'Children! Will we have many?'

'As many as you would wish. I will not say more.'

Anne-Marie had her mother's arm tucked tightly through her own, as if she was afraid Kathleen would disappear. 'Did you know this moment would come, Mother?'

'I don't often see things about myself,' Kathleen said. 'It's too easy to mix up premonition with hope.'

Anne-Marie turned to Connor. 'Thank you for the things you told me this morning. For the first time in my life so much made sense.'

'What now?'

'Find William's treasure first. I've got some money of my own. Buy a house near my . . .' she stumbled over the word, '. . . mother. A lot of things I'm not proud of have to be undone. It's time to reinvent myself. That's the plan anyway.'

Connor nodded. 'Sounds good. How about Solange? What's she likely to do?'

'Drink herself to death,' Anne-Marie said sharply. Then sighed. 'See what I mean?'

Kathleen patted her daughter's arm. 'We can't rush these things, my dear.'

Connor reached into the glove compartment and passed William's journal to Kathleen. 'This belongs to you and Thomas.'

Kathleen ran her fingers across the old leather cover. 'If it hadn't been for this . . .' She smiled. 'How strange it is to think of all the coincidences that have led to this moment.' She looked up at Holly. 'See what I mean? Fate is fate. If just one person down through the years had done something even a little bit differently, perhaps none of us would be standing here now.'

A look of love passed between mother and daughter. Holly reflected that it wasn't only her life which had changed. And it was all down to one man.

That same individual's influence was also being felt by Raoul, though not with any degree of contentment. He was in a towering rage and trying to hide it behind a facade of overbearing arrogance. Two men from the internal revenue department studiously ignored his stinging sarcasm, as did two plain-clothed police officers. Raoul's study had been turned inside-out. Solange, her face a mask of indifference, looked on with an air of abject boredom. Only her eyes gave away the fact that she was enjoying the unfolding drama. The so-called devastation over their son's death was, for the moment at least, the last thing on either of their minds.

When Holly and Connor arrived with Anne-Marie and Kathleen, Raoul's anger and frustration reached new heights.

'What the hell are you doing here?' he demanded. No-one was sure exactly who he was addressing.

'I've come for my things,' Anne-Marie told him calmly. 'I'm going to stay with my mother.'

Raoul stared at Kathleen. 'Mother!' he said derisively. 'That's a joke. Common whore is more like it.'

That, as Connor later speculated to Holly, was the final straw for Anne-Marie. Raoul's thoughtless words did more damage to himself than he could ever have imagined. She turned to the men searching through a roll-top desk. 'I think you'll find what you're looking for in the master bedroom. There's a safe set into the floor. Under the carpet. The combination is 260949, my father's birthday.'

She stared Raoul down then smiled mockingly. 'Oh yes, and he has another supposedly secret safe in the conservatory. He thinks no-one knows. I came across it quite by accident. Even found the combination written on his desk blotter.' She crossed the room and pointed to a corner of the much scribbled-on pad. 'There – 007711. It's also the first six digits of a numbered account with Union Banque Suisse in Geneva.'

Raoul's face paled. 'You bitch!'

Anne-Marie looked him up and down. 'You bastard!' She smiled slightly at Kathleen. 'Sorry, Mother.'

'I couldn't agree with you more,' Kathleen murmured. 'Come, dear, let's get your things.' She cocked her head, listening. 'I could be wrong,' she said to Raoul, 'but someone seems to be knocking on your front door.'

An avalanche might start from a single stone but it soon catches up anything in its path. Something similar seemed to be happening to Raoul Dulac's life. The International Criminal Police Organisation, clearly not aware that Raoul was in trouble on other counts, had been investigating Scylla for some months. Any mercenary organisation attracts official attention and in the course of what started as routine observation, it had become known that the head of African operations was not too fussy about those he recruited. Wanted criminals and terrorists were numbered alongside thrill-seeking adventurers. The newly arrived Interpol agents were hoping for details. Thanks to Anne-Marie, they found more than they bargained for in the conservatory hideaway. Dossiers on some of the world's most notorious men and women were proof enough that Raoul had been flagrantly obstructing police enquiries in a dozen different countries. Those who still managed to avoid capture, despite the damning evidence of Raoul's files, would not take kindly to their betrayal. And like many clandestine individuals, their arms were long. Raoul Dulac's chances of surviving a healthy spell in prison seemed very unhealthy.

All in all, the prognosis for having two cents to rub together if Raoul survived long enough to serve what was likely to be a considerable prison sentence, didn't look very rosy either.

He knew it too. As document after document revealed the full extent of his illegal activities, he was grey, sweating and shaking.

Solange, already inebriated, celebrated her husband's financial and personal destruction by opening a bottle of Dom Pérignon. She was not in the least put out when no-one accepted a glass. The ramifications of Raoul's arrest on her precarious financial position had not, as yet, made their way through her alcohol befuddled mind. She subsided into a maudlin state, to contemplate the bubbles.

Holly and Connor stood outside waiting to say goodbye to Anne-Marie and Kathleen. 'Does this make up for what Raoul did to your brother and Emma?'

'It comes close.'

'You've done what you set out to do. He's a broken man.'

Connor sighed. 'Human emotion is a peculiar thing. It doesn't feel half as good as I thought it would. I almost feel sorry for him.'

They saw a car turn into the long drive. It slid to a stop in front of them and the driver's tinted window was lowered. Madame Liang Song was behind the wheel. 'Is it true?' she asked. 'Has Raoul been arrested?'

'So it would seem,' Connor replied.

'What are you doing here?' Her eyes narrowed. 'What has this to do with you?'

'Not a thing,' Connor lied. 'I'm here with Anne-Marie and her mother.'

'Her mother! She died in the fire last year.'

'Her natural mother,' Connor explained. 'Or perhaps you didn't know that Anne-Marie is Raoul's daughter, not his sister?'

Liang Song's beautiful mask of a face showed no expression. 'I repeat, what has this to do with you?'

'Anne-Marie's mother is a Maguire.'

Madame Liang's eyes flicked to Holly's face, then back to Connor. 'I don't like surprises.'

'And neither do I.' Connor's voice was steel hard. The implication clear.

Liang Song looked back at Holly. 'I did what I thought best.'

As apologies went, it was probably about as stylish as the Chinese woman could concede. 'Well,' Holly said with a tight smile, 'I think that says rather a lot about you.'

The insult went straight over Liang Song's head.

Just then, handcuffed, dishevelled and wild-eyed, Raoul was almost carried down the steps towards a police car. He looked across at Liang Song. Tears welled and burst free to run unchecked down his cheeks. 'Song,' he cried out, brokenly.

The Chinese woman's eyes passed coldly over

him. She pulled the gear lever into drive, staring straight ahead. Her words were meant for Connor. 'I'll contact you next week. The final arrangements should be in place by then.' The automatic window slid upwards, stopping ten centimetres from the top. 'Goodbye.'

'Song! Ma chéri!' Raoul stumbled and would have fallen but for the police officer at his side.

The window closed completely and Liang Song drove away. Raoul left in a police car a few seconds later.

'Not exactly grief-stricken about her lover, was she?' Holly commented.

'Hard as nails,' Connor agreed. 'Congratulations by the way.'

'What for?'

'Restraint. I was expecting one of your little gems.'

'What are you talking about?'

'Your parting shot to Liang Song. If she ever figures out what it means she'll probably set her uncles onto you.'

'Maguire, I'm tired. I'd very much like to sleep until we leave to catch that plane tomorrow. Is there anything else we need to do or can I count on your company? Preferably curled up with me. If it's little gems you're after, would you take a rain check? My mind is one second from sleep mode.'

He kissed her gently on the lips. 'Some women would go to any lengths to get me into their bed.'

Holly's mouth twitched. 'Piss off, Maguire.'

'That's my baby.'

EPILOGUE

Quinn was waiting for them at Sydney Airport. He took one look at Holly and, before they even reached him, let everyone within ten metres know of his displeasure. 'Good God, man! What the hell have you done to my daughter? What went on over there?'

They took him for a drink, or three. Because as Holly had mentioned, before the plane touched down, calming her father's ruffled feathers could take a while.

It did. Quinn was halfway through his second gin and tonic before he stopped huffing. 'You lied to me,' he accused Holly.

'No I didn't.'

'You left stuff out. Same thing.'

'Sorry, Dad.'

Quinn's eyebrows quivered. The unexpected apology had momentarily distracted him.

Holly seized on the advantage. 'I didn't want to worry you.'

'You're forgetting how well I know you. I was worried. Anyway, you took some insane risks. In

God's name, girl, what made you go on board that boat?'

'Um.'

'Don't say that word. You know I hate that word.'

Connor intervened. 'She wasn't to know it was Guy, not Raoul, who'd brought it there.'

Quinn fixed him with a challenging glare. 'You lied to me too. All that stuff about Scylla and pirate treasure. You conveniently forgot the whole drug issue. Triad indeed. My daughter could have died.'

'I'm sorry, Quinn. I had no idea you'd send Holly.'

Quinn took a disgruntled pull at his drink. 'Seems like I was wrong about a few things,' he admitted reluctantly. 'Apart from her hands, my darling daughter seems to have brought the rest on herself.'

'Thanks, Quinn,' Holly said dryly.

'You're taking a break, Big Shot. No more assignments for a while.' He waited for her to react. She didn't, so he repeated himself. 'Did you hear me? I said no work from me.'

Holly and Connor exchanged glances.

'What is it?' Quinn demanded.

Holly nodded her permission and Connor told him. 'Seems like your daughter is an aspiring author.'

'She is?' It was news to Quinn.

'Even has an idea for a novel in her head.'

'There is?' Definitely doubtful.

'After we're married she's going to start work on it.'

'Really?' Relief. 'And when will that be?'

'Soon. She needs looking after.'

'You can say that again.'

Both men kept glancing at Holly, who allowed their conversation to flow around her. She was perfectly content to sit and listen.

Quinn pushed his luck. 'Do you intend to have children? It's just that Delia and I would like grandchildren before we get too old.'

Connor rose to the occasion. 'Absolutely.'

'Excellent.' Again, Quinn's eyes took in Holly, who simply sat gazing into space. 'She's twenty-nine next week, did you know that?'

'No, I didn't.'

'Getting a bit long in the tooth for children.' Pure enjoyment shone in Quinn's eyes. He was getting away with it – a first. 'You'll have to get a move on.'

Connor looked surprised as well. It was not like Holly to let such comments pass. 'Just as soon as we're married.'

'A big wedding?'

'I don't think so. Something private. Between us we've had three practice runs.'

Two sets of eyes bored into Holly's. She realised suddenly that both men had concern written all over their faces. 'What? What have I done?'

'We're waiting,' Quinn said.

Holly looked helplessly from her father to Connor. 'For what?'

'Son,' Quinn turned back to Connor, 'I don't know how you did it.'

Connor smothered a smile. 'I think she's just tired.'

'What the hell are you talking about?' Holly had had enough of these two who appeared to have ganged up against her. 'What do you want from me? Stop speaking in riddles, for God's sake. I'm not up to playing silly bloody games.'

'Ah, sweetheart,' said her father. 'Welcome back.'